CUNARD

Library

Out of respect for your fellow guests, please return all books as soon as possible. We would also request that books are not taken off the ship as they can easily be damaged by the sun, sea and sand.

Please ensure that books are returned the day before you disembark, failure to do so will incur a charge to your on board account, the same will happen to any damaged books.

www.oceanbooks.com

The Romantic

The Romantic

The Real Life of Cashel Greville Ross

A Novel

WILLIAM BOYD

VIKING

an imprint of

PENGUIN BOOKS

VIKING

UK | USA | Canada | Ireland | Australia
India | New Zealand | South Africa

Viking is part of the Penguin Random House group of companies
whose addresses can be found at global.penguinrandomhouse.com

First published 2022
005

Copyright © William Boyd, 2022

The moral right of the author has been asserted

Set in 12/14.75pt Dante MT Std
Typeset by Jouve (UK), Milton Keynes
Printed and bound in Great Britain by Clays Ltd, Elcograf S.p.A.

The authorized representative in the EEA is Penguin Random House Ireland,
Morrison Chambers, 32 Nassau Street, Dublin D02 YH68

A CIP catalogue record for this book is available from the British Library

HARDBACK ISBN: 978–0–241–54202–6
TRADE PAPERBACK ISBN: 978-0-241-54203-3

www.greenpenguin.co.uk

Penguin Random House is committed to a
sustainable future for our business, our readers
and our planet. This book is made from Forest
Stewardship Council® certified paper.

For Susan

A man's life of any worth is a continual allegory – and very few eyes can see the mystery.

John Keats

A novel is a mirror, taking a walk down a big road.

Stendhal

Author's Note

'I was born somewhere in Scotland, in the early morning of 14th December 1799. Later that day, the former President of the United States of America, George Washington, died at his home in Mount Vernon, Virginia. I believe there was no connection between the two events. It is my birthday tomorrow and I will be eighty-two years old.'

And so begins the unfinished, disordered, somewhat baffling autobiography of Cashel Greville Ross (1799–1882), an autobiography – plus related material – that came into my possession some years ago. It consists of around a hundred pages of handwritten reminiscences, dated December 1881, along with tied bundles of letters received, drafts of letters sent, some little sketches, maps and plans, some photographs, some published books filled with notes and marginalia, some small paintings, etchings and silhouettes and a few objects – a tinder box, a musket ball, a belt buckle, a tiny brittle lock of hair tied with a faded silk ribbon, a few silver dollars, a fragment of Greek amphora, and so on.

This small but intriguing trove was all that had eventually amounted from the life of this individual. It was, in a real way, everything that remained of him and was a fragmentary history of the time he had spent on this small planet. He had tried to write the story of his life, but failed.

However fascinating, these scribbled pages and these few artefacts are not much upon which to construct a portrait of the man – not much for a lifespan of eighty-odd years. What do we leave behind us when we die? At first it seems prodigious: all that mountain of 'stuff' we acquire, all the possessions, the bric-a-brac and copious documentation accumulated over the average life. But inexorably, and surprisingly swiftly, it begins to diminish and after a few decades, a half-century, a century, it can amount to virtually nothing.

It depends on who you are, of course – but most people don't leave much of a trace or record behind them once their goods and chattels are dispersed; once the memories of this or that individual quickly blur and fade as the younger familiars die out themselves. Diaries and letters moulder and become either bland or incomprehensible; legal documents lurk unsought-for in filing cabinets and bank vaults; photographs of family and friends become unidentifiable – become photographs of anonymous people – and while anecdote and legend may survive a little longer, assuming that the person did anything of note or achieved any sort of fame, modest or otherwise, the fact is that for the huge majority of people in human history their fate, after a couple of generations or three, is to become effectively unknown, forgotten, a ghost. All that remains is a name on a headstone, a notation in a census-count, an online obituary, a mention in a newspaper and – if they're lucky – a date of birth and a date of death.

So, who was this Cashel Greville Ross? What was the nature of his real life? How can its unique ontology be reconstructed? At least there is some evidence to hand, to begin with, but how far can it be trusted? There are many large, conspicuous gaps. To attempt to embark on writing a biography of this person – a total stranger – a man born well over two hundred years ago, seemed to me to be, if not entirely impossible, then an enterprise that would consist of meagre, unsatisfying supposition, in the end – all 'perhaps', 'conceivably', 'might have', 'possibly'. It would be half a life.

Maybe that is true of biography in general. A wise man once said, 'All biography is fiction, but fiction that has to fit the documented facts.'* If this first part is correct, then perhaps it's a more interesting proposition to extend that licence. The objective should be to go further than the documented facts, to go beyond

* Donald Rayfield, *Anton Chekhov: A Life* (new edition 2021), p. vi.

that boundary of the factual palisade. And, intriguingly, it is only fiction that allows us to do this. Instead of trying to write a biography of Cashel Greville Ross, I thought there was a very good case to be made that the story of his life, his *real* life, would, paradoxically, be much better served if it were written instead – openly, knowingly, candidly – as a novel.

W.B.
Trieste
February 2022

I

Cashel always claimed that his first memory was of a man in black, leading a black horse. A man who – he then suspected – wanted to kill him, for some reason. This occurred when he was about four or five or six years old (he would vaguely recall) and the encounter took place when he was mooching around late one wintry afternoon in the big copse behind the cottage where he lived in County Cork, Ireland. He heard distant hunting horns and snatched halloos from the fields beyond and then, closer to hand at the fringes of the copse, out of sight, came a thrashing and snapping of vegetation, of something sizeable pushing and forcing its way through the undergrowth.

For some reason Cashel felt fear grow in him and chill his body. And then, wheeling round a substantial stand of holly, came a man leading a horse, a big, muscled, ebony stallion, huffing and blowing, its neck and shoulders clotted with a beige lather. Cashel could smell the tack and the musky, salty whiff of the horse's sweat thickening the air beneath the trees. The tall man holding the reins was in a black, knee-length coat, silver-buttoned, wearing a black top hat that made him seem even taller. His black riding boots were polished to a bright glossiness, with small blunt silver spurs, Cashel noticed.

This was Death, Cashel thought – so he claimed – come to seek him out. Or the man in black was the Devil himself.

But it wasn't Death and it wasn't the Devil – it was a man leading an exhausted horse through a wood. A square-jawed man with a wide moustache, tobacco brown.

'What's your name, little boy?' he asked.

'I'm Cashel, sir.'

'Where do you live, Cashel?'

'In the cottage on Glanmire Lane.'

'Ah. Do you, now . . .'

The man stared intently at him from his great height and reached out his free hand as if to touch his face – or catch me by the throat, Cashel thought, and strangle me dead. But then the stallion stamped its feet and whinnied, tugging at the reins the horseman held in his gloved left hand.

'He's lost a shoe so I can't hunt,' the man said reasonably, as if he owed Cashel an explanation. 'I'll give that bastard farrier a kick up the arse, all right.'

He pronounced the word 'ahse'. His accent was strange, Cashel noted, the same as the girls who lived in Stillwell Court. English voices. They didn't speak in the same way as he did or the other people he knew.

'Yes, sir.'

'You'd better cut along home, Cashel, old chap,' the man went on. 'The hunt's coming through and they might take you for a fox.'

'Yes, sir.'

Cashel turned and pelted breathlessly home to the cottage where he lived with his Aunt Elspeth.

He found her in the scullery, peeling potatoes.

'I've just seen the Devil,' he said, trying to control his panting, and described the man in black with the wide moustache, leading the giant horse, and the strange accent he had.

'Don't be so silly,' his aunt said, drying her hands briskly on her apron. 'That'd be one of Sir Guy's friends, over from England for the hunting. Don't be a gomeral. The Devil's not coming for you yet, no, no.' She laughed quickly to herself. 'He's got plenty more work to do before he comes looking for you, Cashel Greville.'

She heaved him up into her arms – she was a tall, strong young woman – kissed his cheek and took him into the parlour to look out of the window onto the lane. Half a dozen hunters were cantering heedlessly down it, great clods of mud thrown up, spattering, from the horses' hooves.

'Was he nice to you, this man in the top hat? Was he a nice man?'

'I don't know.'

'Did he ask you your name?'

'He did.'

'Did you tell him?'

'Yes.'

'Right. Good.'

'And he asked me where I lived.'

'And did you tell him that?'

'I did.'

She set him down on the tiled floor.

'Was that wrong to tell him, Auntie?'

'Come along and have your tea.'*

Elspeth Soutar, Cashel's aunt, a Scot from the Dumfries region, was unmarried and in her early thirties. She was an educated woman and governess to the two daughters of Sir Guy and Lady Evangeline Stillwell, of Stillwell Court, County Cork, Ireland. The girls were Rosamond (sixteen) and Hester (fourteen) and Elspeth had been responsible for their education for almost ten years, now. It was tacitly apparent to everyone that her tenure as governess was coming to its inevitable conclusion as the girls' entry into society approached. Thereafter, there would be no necessity for any more pedagogical refinement.

Cashel knew Rosamond and Hester well. They would play with him when he was a toddler, almost as if he were a household pet. Sometimes they would dress him up as a doll, in a frilly skirt and bonnet, or a toy soldier, or a savage Aborigine. They

* What is to be made of this story, a story Cashel Greville Ross retold throughout his life? Whatever the truth about it – a frightened little boy in a darkening wood; a tall man in black leading a nervy, shying black horse – its repetition has embellished all possibility of verification out of existence. But in a sense, as it applies to Cashel Ross, it doesn't matter. This is the biographical arena where the anecdote becomes the legend that sanctions its own truth – a personal narrative that creates its own 'reality'. More to the point, the encounter, as he described it, established a tone, an atmosphere and import that would prove very apt to his life's story as it unfolded. This is exactly what his first memory *should* have been like: it suited the man he became. Therefore, it was true.

were fond of him and kissed and carried him and hugged him a great deal until he grew too rough and ungainly. But the familiarity remained. They had a host of nicknames for him: the Cashelmite, Cash-Cash-Coo, Cashelnius the Great. They could almost have been older sisters but for the social distance. Elspeth Soutar was staff, after all, and, therefore, so was her little nephew.

Cashel never saw Sir Guy. A remote, almost mythic figure, he seemed always away – in Dublin, in London, on the Continent – and Cashel never really ventured into the grand salons of the house. He tended to stay in the nursery with the girls. Consequently, he very rarely met Lady Evangeline either, who, it seemed, was always ill and stayed for months at a time in her suite of rooms on the second floor, attended by a nurse and receiving weekly visits, all year round, from old Dr Killigrew with his patent medications from the nearby town of Castlemountallen. The few glimpses and encounters he managed left him with the impression of someone very stiff and upright, but at the same time very pale and fragile. As thin as paper, he thought – as thin as crumpled waxed paper.

Once, when Rosamond and Hester were wheeling him around the corridors in a small toy cart, they bumped into Lady Evangeline, fully dressed in a lace headcap and a gown of shimmering ultramarine silk, being helped down the stairs to some social engagement.

'Who is this little boy?' she asked Rosamond.

'He's Elspeth's charge, Mama,' Rosamond said. 'Her little nephew. The orphan, remember?'

'I don't recall,' Lady Evangeline said vaguely. 'Or perhaps I do, now you mention it. The orphan. Yes. Is he a well-behaved little boy?'

'Oh, yes. He knows that if he misbehaves we'll give him a good thrashing,' Hester said.

Lady Evangeline smiled thinly and the nurse led her carefully down the stairs to the drawing room.

When he was old enough to understand – when he was five – Aunt Elspeth sat him down and told him the sad story of the deaths of his mother and father, Moira and Findlay Greville, both drowned in 1800 when the packet to Belfast had sunk in a storm in the Irish Sea. There was a small amateur double portrait of a wooden-faced couple set on the mantel of the sitting room, the only visual record of his parents.

'They left on a boat for Belfast before you,' Elspeth explained. 'You were meant to go with them but you were sick with the croup so I was told to follow with you a week later. Thank the Lord you didn't go with them.'

'Was it a shipwreck?' Cashel asked.

'Yes. The ship went down with all hands.'

'What does that mean?'

'There were no survivors. Everyone was drowned.' Elspeth smiled sadly. 'That's how come you're living with me, my darling.' She stroked his thick fair hair, ploughing it with her stiff fingers. 'I'll never be your true mother but in every other shape or form I'm just as much a mother to you, wee lad, don't you worry.'

Elspeth had placed the double portrait in his lap as she gently related the story to him. Cashel looked at the ashen-faced puppets that were meant to be depictions of his mother and father. The man had a dense, spade-like beard. The woman wore a tight bonnet and seemed to stare out of the picture with sightless eyes.

'That's Findlay Greville,' Elspeth pointed. 'And that's my dear wee sister, Moira, bless her soul.'

'So, if I was on that ship I'd have drownded as well,' Cashel said, the reality of his situation slowly beginning to solidify itself in his young mind. He didn't know the words then, but he was beginning to understand the concept of his being parentless, of being an orphan.

'I'm very glad I didn't go on that ship, Auntie,' he said. 'And I'm very glad I came to live with you.'

He was surprised at the ardour of the hug she gave him and by the shine of tears in her eyes.

'You're a good boy, Cashel Greville. The best.'

*

Of course, Elspeth Soutar, being a very proficient governess, made sure that Cashel was as well educated as the Stillwell girls had been. He was writing and reading at the age of five. When, aged seven, he was sent to the dame-school in Castlemountallen he was immediately moved up two classes to study with the nine- and ten-year-olds. He still found the lessons – Latin, Greek, composition, mathematics, divinity – very easy and straight-forward, he said.*

Life at Stillwell Court in the early nineteenth century was as ordered and seemingly unchanging as it had been throughout the eighteenth. The extensive demesne had been gifted to one Colonel Gervase Stillwell, an officer in Oliver Cromwell's army of 1649. The grant consisted of some five thousand acres in total, spread largely along the north bank of the valley of the Baillybeg river between Castlemountallen and Fermoy, with other plantations and farmlands added elsewhere in County Kerry and County Waterford. Gervase Stillwell, in addition, became the 1st Baronet Stillwell in 1659. In 1782 when Sir Guy Stillwell, 5th Baronet, inher-ited the property on the death of his father, Fielding, he sold off the distant Kerry and Waterford farms and woodlands and used the capital to build Stillwell Court, a project that took the best part of a decade, cost many thousands of pounds and resulted in the Stillwell family incurring serious and lasting debt. Mortgages were taken out with banks in Dublin, London and Amsterdam – and then the mortgages were re-mortgaged, the debt underwritten

---

* There is a poem on a fragment of yellowed paper stuck in a scrapbook that is written in an obvious child's hand. This may be the only record of Cashel's intellectual precocity.

> *The sun it rises every day*
> *To spread its bounty, ray by ray.*
> *At night it sets to take its rest*
> *And then at dawn we are newly blessed.*

And beneath it the beginnings of a Latin translation:

> *Sol oritur cotidie*
> *Ad suam largitatem . . .*

by the ceaseless flow of rents from the Stillwell estate's farmer-tenants. Yet, as far as the Stillwells were concerned, nothing in the quality and style of their lives ever changed at all. The funds required to live exactly as they wished seemed always to be available – in Ireland, as elsewhere, there were many ways and means for the privileged aristocratic minority to thrive.

And, as the house was slowly built over the years, so were the gardens laid out, a wide parterre constructed, hundreds of trees planted, a small river dammed to create a substantial lake with cascades, and a long 'ride' carved through dense beech woods. Sir Guy was determined not to compromise or sacrifice the vision he had of the Stillwell family seat. They were finally able to move in shortly after Rosamond was born and, fifteen years later, by the time Cashel had begun to take some kind of stock of the place he was growing up in, it had already achieved a patina of permanence, of longevity. The limestone of the big house's facade had weathered; dense ivy covered an entire gable end of the east wing; the stable block had seen two generations of hunters; the trees in the landscaped park were substantial; thick rushes and alder grew on the banks of the artificial lake; the crested, ornate gates – portals to the east and west drives – with their twinned lodges on either side, seemed to declare that Stillwell Court had been here for many ages and would remain for many more to come.*

*

* This description of Stillwell Court comes from *Eminent Demesnes in the County of Cork, Vol. II* (Dublin 1845):

> *Stillwell Court is a substantial manor house built in the Georgian style towards the end of the last century. At its core is a three-storey eight-bay block with astylar three-bay wings. The façade is silver-grey limestone and the hipped roof sits nicely behind a low blocking course. The baseless Doric columns of the porch support a weighty entablature. The two-storey servants' quarters are well screened by shrubberies. The stable block and kennels have a small triumphal arch as an entrance (a whimsical touch) and by the demesne wall is a single-storey keeper's house in brick laid in Flemish bond with an octagonal wet larder or game store.*

Elspeth Soutar's relations with Cashel were warm and close. When he was too big to pick up and cuddle, she would ask him to sit on her knee in front of the turf fire and tell him stories about her childhood in Dumfries. She had a Scottish accent that Cashel unreflectingly acquired though once he began attending at the dame-school his Irish brogue inevitably thickened and covered over what Scottishness remained.

It was a linguistic journey inadvertently encouraged by the cottier children he played with further down Glanmire Lane, outside the high walls that surrounded Stillwell Court and its park. Along both sides of the lane Sir Guy Stillwell had paid for the construction of ten cabins for his cottiers, so-called, indentured tenants and reliable casual labourers. Cashel was friendly with two of the older boys of the Doolin family. Pádraig Doolin was a herdsman and a woodcutter. He and his wife, Aoife, had six children aged from eight years old to newborn, and Cashel was friendly with the two eldest boys, Callum and Lorcan. Callum was raw-boned and excitable; Lorcan sly and obviously clever. Sir Guy paid for him to attend the dame-school in Castlemountallen in the hope that a little education – literacy, even – might allow him a chance to move out of the never-ending poverty that the cottiers seemed destined to live in for ever.

From time to time, once a month or so, sometimes twice, Elspeth would instruct Cashel to 'go and play with the Doolin boys'. It was, Cashel realized, an injunction, not a suggestion; and even if he didn't particularly want to go he sensed from the tone of her voice that it was not worth objecting. On these occasions she would give him a present for Mrs Doolin – a pie, a jar of jam, an old shawl – as if to justify the visit. It was always in the afternoon and she would add, 'Don't come back until suppertime, mind.' And so Cashel would trudge off down the lane to the cabins, offering in hand, to spend two or three hours with the Doolin family.

On this particular spring day – it was cloudy and drizzly and the lane gleamed with thin tainted puddles in its rutted surface, scarred by the traffic of carts and drays – Cashel set off with a bundle of flax yarn and walked the half-mile to the cabins. He was somewhat disgruntled as he had been quite happily caught up in an elaborate drawing of a huge fortified castle (inspired by a visit to Charles Fort in Kinsale) and when he had protested Elspeth had snapped at him: 'I want you on your way, boy.' She said she had to prepare a course of French lessons for the Stillwell girls as they were about to make their first venture into the continent of Europe and she needed absolute peace and quiet.

The Glanmire cabins were all uniform. Built of mud-and-straw walls, eighteen inches thick, and thatched with potato stems, they looked more like growths than structures. Each cabin had an acre and a half of land to grow potatoes, every one had at least one cow, some two, and there were hen runs and pigsties. These simple dwellings had no chimneys, however, and the smoke from the turf fire inside had to leave the main room – the only room – through a door or a window.

Cashel approached the Doolin cabin and saw two of the little girls, quite naked, chasing the hens in their run, screaming with pleasure. He called out his name and Mrs Doolin invited him in. She was sitting on a stool by the fire suckling her newborn, another girl. She had no name, yet.

'Come away in, Cashel, my bonny boy.'

Cashel's eyes were already stinging from the peat smoke, hanging like a grey cloud beneath the rafters; the smell of something sour was in the air, incubating. He handed Mrs Doolin the flax he was carrying, unable to stop staring at the baby guzzling at her pale, dark-nippled breast.

'I've had you at my titties too, Cashel, dear. I was your wet-nurse when your auntie brought you home from Scotland, poor wee orphan fella that you were.'

'Yes, I know,' Cashel said patiently. He knew what a wet-nurse was. Mrs Doolin told him this fact almost every time he came to the cabin, as if somehow there was a deeper, almost familial, connection between them because he had drunk her sweet milk – that he was more to her than the orphaned nephew of the Stillwell governess. Mrs Doolin, always pregnant, always giving birth (three of her children had died), was famous for her copious supply of milk.

9

She stood up, the baby still suckling, and went to the door to call for Callum and Lorcan.

Cashel looked around. There was the simple wooden bed with its horsehair mattress and blanket and thick straw laid against the wall for the children to sleep on. They had a painted chest, chipped black, a table and three stools. By the fire stood the big pot for cooking potatoes and, beside it, the spinning wheel for making linen cloth. Callum thought, as he always did, of his bedroom in the cottage – the bright gingham curtains at the window, the knitted rug, the warm eiderdown, the commode with the chamber pot. Here the family all relieved themselves on the midden outside where the pigs rooted freely. How he wished, suddenly, that his aunt hadn't sent him here to play with the Doolin boys. He hadn't been disturbing her, sitting at the kitchen table with his pencils and sheets of paper.

Still, he smiled politely as Mrs Doolin regained her seat by the fire and shifted the babby to her other breast. Her feet were bare and black with grime, her toes like tortoiseshell claws, he saw, and looked down guiltily at his buckled shoes, poking out from his breeches. He undid the buttons on his jerkin, as if that made him more at home here in this room, more informal, more at ease.

Then Callum and Lorcan sauntered in, grinning, hurling sticks loose in their hands.

'Well, hello, hello, Cashel,' Lorcan said, adding mysteriously, 'talk of the Devil.'

'Fancy a knock-about, Cashel?' Callum said, holding up his hurley.

'I don't have a stick.'

'Sure, we've got a spare,' Callum said. 'We can get Diarmuid over from next door and we'll have a bit of a game. You can keep goal.'

An hour later, Cashel limped homeward, his shoes in his hand. He hated hurling, and Callum Doolin, he was convinced, had deliberately hit him on the ankle, swinging his stick hard at the ball long gone. Blood flowed and Cashel yelled that his ankle bone was chipped.

'Don't play hurling, then, you babby!' Callum jeered. 'We don't play with girls.'

As Cashel neared the cottage the lane rose over a small bridge, allowing him to look down on his home and the neat walled garden at the rear. He stopped abruptly. A dark figure was down at the far end. A man in a black greatcoat, tall-hatted. This man opened the door in the rear garden wall and disappeared, closing it behind him, heading into the dense woodland beyond.

That garden door in the rear wall was permanently locked, Cashel knew. The wood beyond was out of bounds: 'Private property,' Elspeth said. 'They rear pheasants there and shoot them. It's dangerous.' And, as a result, Cashel had never ventured there. It was closely planted, full of coppiced oak and elm, a damp, gloomy wood anyway, choked with brambles and nettles.

But now this man? Was this a burglar? A murderer . . .?

He ran into the garden and up to the door. Locked. Locked from the other side, obviously. Baffled, he sped to the back door. Inside, there was no sign of his aunt in the kitchen, the scullery or the front parlour. He felt fearful and didn't want to go upstairs to the bedrooms, suddenly terrified at what he might find there.

'Auntie!' he yelled out, desperately, plaintively.

'Cashel?' came the immediate reply.

He ran to the staircase. His aunt was on the landing at the stair's turn, in her dressing gown. A second glance registered that her long dark hair was down, hanging loose over her shoulders. He very rarely saw her with her hair down and, even in this fraught moment, acknowledged how different she suddenly looked – how beautiful, how young . . .

But she was angered, her eyes thinned.

'What're ye doing back? I said suppertime!'

'That Callum Doolin broke me ankle!'

'My ankle.'

'He broke my ankle playing hurling. It hurts, Auntie. Look – there's blood.'

And she set to – boiling a kettle on the range, folding a soft cloth, wetting it in the hot water and gently dabbing away the dried blood. She even wrapped a gauze bandage round his ankle that made him feel somehow noble and brave.

Elspeth kissed his forehead. Cashel noticed that her eyes were red, as if she'd been crying.

'They may be rough boys, but they mean well.'

'No. He did it on purpose. Lorcan's my friend and Callum's jealous.'

She soothed him, made him a cup of sweet tea and, calmed, he went back to the drawing of his marvellous fortifications. Half an hour later she was downstairs in her blue dress, her long hair pinned up, secured by combs, preparing their supper of new-baked bread and a mutton broth. Only then, tranquillity re-established, did Cashel begin to wonder again about the man he had seen at the garden door and his aunt's strange state of undress. Had she been sleeping? Had she felt unwell? Was he a doctor? It was a mystery that he should try to solve, he told himself, and he knew the answer lay beyond the cottage garden – in the dark coppiced wood with its briars and stinging nettles.

The next day was Sunday and, after the service for the Protestants in the servants' dining hall in Stillwell Court (a prayer, a hymn, a reading), Cashel told his aunt that he was going back to the Doolin cabin to show Callum his bandaged ankle and make him confront the damage he had done. But, once up the lane and out of sight of the cottage, he hopped over the drystone wall and made his way through the wood. It was difficult going – the undergrowth was thick and the long, barbed shoots of the brambles were everywhere, tugging at his clothes. Eventually, he arrived at the cottage garden wall. There was the door and he tried it. Locked.

That the man had gone out from the garden and now the door was locked behind him meant that he must have had a key . . .

And there was a path cut from the door that led into the wood – nettles scythed away, overhanging branches pruned. It was not well worn but it was indisputably a path. Cashel set off, following it, his heart-thump suddenly audible, he thought, aware of the dangers lurking in the wood. The path turned this way and that. Once he paused, seeing a cigar butt, two inches long, on the ground before him – damp, unfurling. He picked it up and sniffed it – that sour, sweaty, faecal smell still lingered. He threw it away. The path curled round the bole of a large ash tree and there, in front of him, was another wall, the demesne wall, ten feet high, and a tall iron-barred gate set in it.

Cashel pulled down on the handle to open the gate but it too was locked. Through the bars he could see the keeper's cottage on the Stillwell estate with its octagonal game larder, and beyond it the rear aspect of the big house with its pall-mall court and the deep ha-ha. He thought he could make out Hester in a cream dress, trying vainly to fly a kite in the fresh breeze.

So, Cashel thought, the man in the cottage garden had come from Stillwell Court, that much was clear. But who might he be?

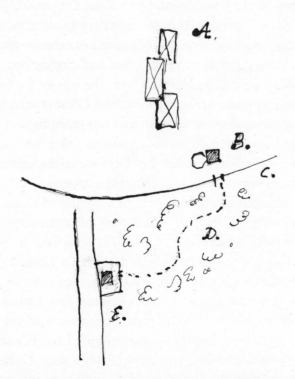

The route from Glanmire Cottage to Stillwell Court. A. Stillwell Court.
B. The keeper's cottage. C. The demesne wall. D. The path through Glanmire
Wood. E. Glanmire Cottage on Glanmire Lane.

The gamekeeper? And what business did he have with his Aunt Elspeth . . .?

Cashel made his way back along the path, retracing his steps to the cottage. He was pleased by the result of his investigations but the answers to his questions were beyond him. He skipped over the wall and entered the cottage through the front door.

'I'm home, Auntie,' he called.

Elspeth was in the sitting room, drinking tea.

'How were the Doolin boys?' she asked. 'Did Callum say sorry?'

'They were out,' Cashel lied quickly. 'So I spoke for a minute or so with Mrs Doolin. She thanks you very much for the flax.'

'Poor woman,' Elspeth said. 'Still, she's luckier than some, I suppose.' She beckoned Cashel over. 'Come and sit down. I have some news. Momentous news.'

Cashel didn't particularly want to hear any momentous news but he sat himself down on the slipper chair opposite her.

'We're leaving Stillwell Court,' Elspeth said brightly.

'What?'

'My job here is done. Those girls are as educated as they'll ever be and they're both going to France next year, withal.'

'We can't leave here. What about me?'

'I'm no longer required. The family has been very generous.'

'But surely we can stay on here in the cottage?'

'No. We're going away.'

'Where?' Cashel felt salt tears sting his eyes. He couldn't imagine a life elsewhere.

'Not far away. Not to the ends of the earth, darling.'

'Where are we going?' he repeated dolefully.

'We're going to England,' Elspeth said. 'To a place called Oxford.'

2

It was an unusually hot day for early June and Cashel felt the sun warming his shoulders even though it was just past seven o'clock in the morning. School started promptly at eight and he had to tramp over a mile to reach it. He always gave himself plenty of time – if you were late, even by one minute, Dean Smythe would leather you. 'Punctuality is not a habit,' the dean would say, as he reached for the belt, 'it's a virtue.'

Cashel shifted the burlap sack he was carrying from his left shoulder to his right. The sack contained his lunch – a hunk of Aunt Elspeth's new-baked bread, a lump of cheese wrapped in a cabbage leaf, an apple and a stoppered flask of watered-down cider – as well as a bottle of ink, a box of quills, his penknife, and a bible. Every boy had to have his own bible at Dean Smythe's Academy.

He was striding briskly down the Botley Road, heading through the countryside for the centre of Oxford where the school was to be found. To his right he saw the church of St Thomas the Martyr amongst its venerable lime trees, and soon enough he was crossing the Isis Bridge and found himself in the town proper. 'A small town with many beautiful buildings,' was how Elspeth had described Oxford to him – though it should be called a city, he corrected himself, seeing as the place possessed a proper cathedral.

There was a dust haze hanging over the turnpike, raised by the wheels of the considerable morning traffic. The coach from Cheltenham had passed, rattling along at heedless speed into the town. Drays with kegs of beer headed for Oxford's inns and taverns, and dog carts and barouches all added to the clatter of the endless coming and going – even the noise was different here in England, he thought, everyone so busy – a far cry from the rural peace of Stillwell Court and Glanmire Lane.

As he crossed the bridge over the Isis he smelt the stink coming off the Oxford canal wharf and ducked down the alleyway that led him to Penny Farthing Street where the school was. He entered the cobbled lane and saw that the old soldier was still there with his pewter begging bowl set before him by his wooden peg-leg. His other leg had gone, also, but he allowed his canvas trouser to flap emptily, the better to provoke sympathy, Cashel supposed. His crutches leant against the stucco wall behind him. He wore his filthy scarlet jacket with its one tattered, fringed epaulette, and Cashel saw that he had added some kind of shiny medal to his breast.

'Hello, schoolboy!' he shouted at Cashel. 'Spare a farthing in Penny Farthing Street for an old soldier.'

'Haven't got a farthing, sir,' Cashel said, which was true, though he had three pennies in his jerkin pocket.

'What's in that sack you're carrying?'

'My luncheon, sir.'

'Anything to drink? I'm fair parched standing in this here hot sun. Not as hot as Portugal, mind you, where my two good legs got blown away by the Frenchies.'

'I've only got cold tea,' Cashel lied, immediately regretting the admission.

'A sip of tea would wet the whistle nicely, thank-ee kindly.'

Cashel sighed and rummaged in his sack for the bottle.

'See? It's only weak tea, sir.' He held the bottle up for verification.

The soldier snatched it from him, drew out the cork and had a swig.

'That's fucking cider, you devil!'

He took some more swigs and handed the bottle back half-empty, grinning, showing his few brown stumps of teeth.

'Tried to fool me, eh?'

'You can finish it off,' Cashel said, handing it back. He would not be drinking from that bottle now those lips had touched it.

The soldier glugged the rest of the cider down.

'You're a good lad,' he said. 'And make sure you finish your schooling, boy. Don't end up like me, God preserve you.'

Cashel put the empty bottle in his sack and headed off down Penny Farthing Street towards the school.

Dean Archibald Smythe's Scholarly Academy (For Boys) was situated on the ground floor of a four-storey, pocked and flaking, somewhat dilapidated town house. The dean's living quarters were on the floors above. At the rear of the house, as a kind of annexe, was a very large room, almost like a barn, which was the schoolroom. High-ceilinged, it was lit during the day by a row of plain windows close beneath the ceiling, side by side, like a clerestory. It must have been some kind of meeting room or warehouse, Cashel thought, before it was turned into a school.

On both sides of the room were two long refectory tables – enough to take twenty chairs each. And on the wall above one was the painted sign 'Scholars' and, above the other, 'Simpletons'. Dean Smythe's educational ethic was straightforward: this was the divide his pupils must cross. Simpletons had to strive to become Scholars. Scholars must endeavour not to descend to Simpleton level. Promotion and demotion were regular occurrences. At the head of each table was a kind of elevated pulpit with a seat and a lectern, designed for the pedagogues: Dean Smythe took care of the Scholars; his assistant, Marmaduke Seele, was responsible for the Simpletons.

Cashel entered the big room and saw he was the first to arrive this morning. He took his allotted seat at the Scholars' table – he had never sat at the Simpletons' – and set out his quills and ink. Just as the Academy did not provide lunch for its pupils, it did not provide writing materials, either.

'Morning, Ross,' came a reedy voice. 'My, you're keen.'

Cashel didn't respond immediately. Even after two years gone by, he kept forgetting that his surname was now Ross, not Greville.

He turned to see Marmaduke Seele crossing the room, a ledger under his arm, and then climbing into his pulpit. He wore a greasy topcoat and the white stockings below his knee breeches were grey and darned and patched. His shoes creaked as he climbed the steps and sat down.

'Oh. Yes. Morning, sir.'

Seele was a skinny man in his thirties with a poor, patchy

moustache. Dean Smythe treated him with undisguised disdain and contempt and, thus encouraged, the bigger, bolder boys mocked him mercilessly. Cashel quite liked Seele, in fact. He himself was always being mocked for his Irish accent –'Oirish' was his nickname – so he felt a strange bond with Seele.

'Soon be the summer holidays,' Seele said. 'Looking forward to the summer, Ross?'

'Yes, sir,' Cashel said, unreflectingly, but he wasn't sure he much looked forward to anything these days – life was so strange.

Dean Smythe bustled in, looking at his pocket watch. He was a small, portly man, in his fifties, with a smiling, roseate, chubby face. He still wore an old-fashioned short wig – somewhat askew, this morning. His fussy, busy manner disguised the brutal temper of a fierce disciplinarian. Boys were routinely leathered several times a day at the Academy.

And now, behind the dean, the Academy's pupils began to file in, shiftily, in ones or twos, whispering, most going to their designated places on the Simpletons' table. This morning Cashel only had two Scholar companions – little Benjamin Smart ('Smart by name, smart by nature,' the dean would observe, regularly) and burly Ned Masterson, who was seventeen and growing a beard. At the luncheon break he would pointedly smoke a pipe, as if to confirm his maturity. He looked stupid, as he coughingly puffed away, with his wet lips and his big, round, heavy-featured face, but he was almost as clever as Cashel. He wanted to become a priest and so was a favourite of the dean.

The three scholars were set their morning's work – to translate a page of Ovid from *Epistulae ex Ponto*. The dozen Simpletons were taken through their nine-times table by Mr Seele.

Cashel stared at the text in front of him – *Quod legis, o uates magnorum maxime regum*, he read – but his mind felt strangely inert. He knew why. It was because Elspeth had told him at breakfast that Mr Ross was coming to stay for a whole week.

Cashel knew that he was deliberately not confronting the reality of the 'Oxford Situation', as he termed it. He had a piecemeal understanding of what had happened since they had left Stillwell Court but there were gaps and he found himself quite happy not to try and fill them in, for some reason. Not knowing everything can be quite a tolerable state of existence, he had come to realize.

When they finally left he wept, unashamedly. In an entirely illogical way he felt that his life was ending – certainly the life he knew – and nothing in the future, his future, enticed him remotely. Elspeth patiently let his tears flow and it seemed to him he sobbed all the way to Dublin, where they caught the packet to Bristol. At Bristol docks there was a brougham waiting for them and a cart to carry their trunks on to Oxford. It was on the journey there – it took them a whole day as the roads were muddy – that Elspeth, calmly, authoritatively, told him of the circumstances of their new English life.

'You have to do what I tell you, Cashel, my dear. No ifs, no buts. Do it for me. It's not complicated but it's very important. If you let me down there will be serious consequences for me – and for you. I could go to prison.'

This prospect was what chilled and frightened him – there could be no more potent threat, however vague. What crime had she committed that would send her to prison? He gladly promised her, on his soul, that he would do as she asked. He listened hard.

The first new fact to take in, she told him, was that their names were going to change. Elspeth Soutar was to become Mrs Pelham Ross. Cashel would no longer be Cashel Greville but instead would become Cashel Ross. He could keep Greville as a middle name, if he wanted, but to Oxford and the world he was to be Cashel Ross. Moreover, he was to be her son, henceforth, not her nephew. 'Auntie' was gone – if he wanted to address her it should be 'Mama'. Understood? Try it.

'Yes . . . Mama. But why are we doing all this?'

'So that we can live in a new way, with new freedoms and new comforts. I'll never have to be a governess again. I don't have to work. We'll have a nice home. We'll have enough money for everything.'

'Right.'

She kissed him on the cheek.

'And there's one other thing you should know.'

'What is it?'

'I'm pregnant. You know what "pregnant" means?'

'Yes.' Then he added, 'Mama.'

'Good boy. In a few months you'll have a new baby brother or sister. You'd like that, wouldn't you?'

'Yes. That would be nice,' he said dutifully, not really taking the information in. What was the opposite of 'nice'? It was all too much.

Elspeth took his hand and squeezed it.

'So, you understand why we had to make a new life for ourselves – for our new little family.'

'I do. I can see that . . .'

'Can you remember all this? Can you do it for me? No one must ever know about our lives before, in Ireland, at Stillwell Court.'

'Of course. I can do it.'

She hugged him close.

'I know it all seems very strange to you now,' she said softly. 'But you'll get used to it quickly – and it's for the best, my dearest. You and I are going to be very happy. Very.'

The house they came to occupy on the Botley Road, a mile outside Oxford, was called the Glebe. It was a substantial, square, white-stuccoed house – new, built some twenty years previously – set back from the road behind a gated driveway. There was a gravelled sweep around an ornamental fountain and a small porte cochère. Behind the house there was a wide sheep-cropped lawn with a walnut tree and a big revolving summer house. With a little effort the wooden structure could be turned to face whatever sun was available in whatever season.

To one side was a neat walled vegetable and fruit garden, an orchard, and a barn that contained their barouche and wooden loose boxes for the nag that pulled it. They had an elderly man-servant called Doncaster, a young housemaid (Daisy), a cook (Mrs Pillard) and a young stable-boy and gardener called Albert who lived out, in Botley village, but who was always present, it seemed, dawn to dusk.

The staff had their quarters in the attic. Cashel had his own bedroom on the floor below, and below him, on the first floor, Elspeth had her suite of rooms. The house was well and tastefully furnished. There was a drawing room, a parlour, a dining room, and a music room with a square Broadwood piano. The kitchen, scullery, larder and laundry room were in a wing of outbuildings attached to the east corner of the main house.

It took Cashel almost three days to explore and comprehend the new geography of their lives – to see what potential the Glebe might offer him. After the little cottage in Glanmire Lane it was almost as if they had moved to a palace. He couldn't really understand how or why but, somewhere in the back of his mind, the realization slowly established itself that Aunt Elspeth – 'Mama' – had suddenly, obviously, become rich.

Mr Pelham Ross himself arrived some three weeks after they had moved in. Routines had by then been well established and the staff seemed to know and carry out their duties capably. Cashel had been enrolled in Dean Smythe's Academy (ten guineas a term) and he and Elspeth had explored Oxford and its environs in the barouche, efficiently driven by young Albert.

Elspeth gave Cashel a day's notice.

'If you address him, you're to call him "Father",' she said.

'But he's not my father. Findlay Greville was my father.'

She shook his shoulders vigorously, as if she could shake sense into him.

'You promised me, Cashel! You swore on your soul. You can't let me down.'

He began to sniffle and she hugged him.

'Maybe this'll help. Think of it as a game we're playing,' she said, more consolingly. 'You and me against the world, fooling everyone. Now, wouldn't that be a grand thing? Let's play our game together. Let's pretend.'

At least this was a concept he could grasp. Let's make-believe. He could do that.

Pelham Ross turned out to be a tall lean man, clean-shaven, his greying hair beginning to recede at the front, Cashel noticed, when the man removed his top hat. He wore well-tailored expensive clothes – a double-breasted Nankeen jacket and tapered pantaloons. The high-standing collar of his shirt reached the corners of his mouth. His black cravat was silk. Elspeth brought Cashel into the drawing room to meet him and they shook hands.

'Good day to you, Cashel.' He had a deep, rather serious voice.

'Good day to you, sir . . . Father.'

There, Cashel thought. I've said it. The man's face was unmoved. Immobile. Then he gave a little smile.

'How do you like your new home?'

'It's very nice, sir.'

'And your school? Are you doing well there?'

'I'm a Scholar, sir. It's not too hard.'

Ross chuckled at this, glancing at Elspeth who seemed noticeably to relax.

'Clever lad,' Ross said. 'I hope to see more of you but I've got to go away regularly to South Africa. I have businesses there.'

Cashel wondered if South Africa explained their new prosperity.

'That sounds exciting,' he said. 'I'd like to go to Africa one day.'

'It is exciting – and boring. Takes so long to get there. I'll miss you two. But I'll be back.'

Elspeth poured them both a glass of Madeira and Cashel noticed that Ross's hands were very clean, his nails shiny and short, as he cut the tip off a thin cigar and lit it carefully with a taper, puffing smoke, blowing on the burning end and piercing the other with some kind of needle device, as if he were engaged in some miniature engineering experiment. He was a calm and dignified presence and Cashel sensed his anxieties and his reservations beginning to recede. Pelham Ross seemed to offer no threat. Maybe everything would be all right. He could see – now the man was here – how happy Elspeth was in her new incarnation as his wife.

Daisy, the maid, came in at this juncture, smart in a new blue dress with a lace pinny, carrying a tray of vol-au-vents and sweetmeats which she set down on a lacquered table to one side.

'You can go up to your room, now, Cashel. We're expecting some neighbours – we want to introduce ourselves,' Elspeth said, putting her hands on his shoulders and steering him to the door.

'Yes, you cut along, Cashel,' Ross said. 'This will be boring, I guarantee.'

'Goodbye, sir.'

'And I'll bring you a present back from Africa,' Ross said vaguely, relighting his cigar.

Elspeth leant down and whispered in his ear as he left the room.

'Well done, darling, clever boy.'

That night, Cashel lay in his bed unable to sleep, something nagging at him, some distant memory half-triggered, and trying to come to terms with this 'game' they were all playing. Elspeth pretending to be married; Cashel pretending to be her son; Mr Ross pretending to be her husband and Cashel pretending he was his father. He heard Ross's deep voice murmuring as he climbed the stairs and Cashel slipped out of bed and crept onto the landing, peering through the banisters to see Elspeth and Ross, lit by the candle Elspeth was carrying, as they climbed the curving stairway to the first floor. Just before they entered her bedroom he saw Ross run his hand up her back and squeeze the curl-shadowed hollow at the nape of her neck.

Ross stayed two days and then left on his African adventure. Cashel asked what he did in South Africa and Elspeth gave unsatisfactory replies, saying only that he had many business interests there, trading, mining, banking. In fact, he was absent for months as Elspeth's pregnancy advanced and Cashel's curiosity diminished. She became big-bellied and very fatigued, spending most of the day in bed. A doctor came to visit from time to time – a young man with bushy whiskers and small rimless spectacles, called Dr Jolly. It was he who informed her one day that she was in fact pregnant with twins. Some sort of trumpet-like listening advice that he pressed to her belly indicated two hearts beating within.

In February 1809, the twins were born. Two boys, who were named Hogan and Buckley. Cashel now had two 'brothers', a fact he found rather pleasing, even though he was a decade older than them. An elderly nanny – Miss Creevy – was hired to look after them. She had a room next to the nursery but seemed to pay the twins cursory attention. Most nights as he lay in his bed Cashel could hear one of the babies whimpering endlessly – Buckley, apparently, who was the smaller and sicklier of the two.

Pelham Ross returned eventually to meet his two new sons and Elspeth regained her verve and vigour. Cashel was growing taller fast, Ross remarked, tall for a boy of his age. At school he continued to dominate the Scholars' table, though Masterson left to go up to the university. To everyone's surprise the dean announced a long-weekend holiday in celebration of Ned Masterson's success and the honour he brought to the Academy.

Everything is normal, Cashel repeated to himself as he trudged home to Botley to enjoy the free day. Everything *seems* 'normal', anyway, he corrected himself, but he knew deep inside that in fact this was very much not the case.

When Cashel was thirteen he experienced his first nocturnal emission. He knew what had happened and it caused him no consternation. He had been vainly frigging himself for over a year and he was pleased that there would now be palpable results along with the pleasure, henceforth.

In their lunch breaks at the Academy the boys would sit in a row on a low wall that bounded a paved courtyard area outside the schoolroom. The talk amongst them was almost always to do with 'smut' and mainly to do with masturbation and its techniques – tugging, pulling, flogging, frigging, fetching mettle, nubbing and strumming were the favoured euphemisms.

But they weren't sufficient protection. The dean overheard two of the boys – Rhodes and Bramerton – talking 'filth'. He not only leathered them but sent them home for a week to confess their transgression to their parents. He then delivered a lecture to the assembled school – there were twenty-two pupils this particular year – on the Sin of Onan.

Dean Smythe stood in his pulpit and berated the ranked boys standing nervously in front of him. He spoke of the terrible dangers of 'self-pollution', this 'melancholy and repulsive, solitary act'. He warned them that they would destroy their health, go blind, be unable to father children themselves and eventually slip into dementia and agonizing, shameful death. He read from the large bible set before him on the lectern.

'Genesis, chapter thirty-eight, verse nine: "And Onan" – there is the degenerate's name, Onan – "when it came to pass went in unto his brother's wife, that he spilt it" – it, his seed – "upon the ground. And the thing he did displeased the Lord; wherefore he slew him."' Dean Smythe paused here for better dramatic effect and allowed his eyes to range over the cowed boys in front of him. 'He spilt his seed upon the ground – he committed the Sin of Onan – and the Lord slew him. Can anything be more clear? Commit this sin and you will DIE!'

The shock and terror engendered by the sermon wore off remarkably quickly and instead provoked untypical biblical exegesis as the Scholars and the simpletons, for once united, consulted their bibles and read Genesis, chapter thirty-eight, with forensic attention. There was incomprehension, misunderstanding and dispute. Nowhere, everyone remarked, in the key verses, was there any mention of frigging. Benjamin Smart suggested that the injunction was general – spilling seed on the ground was bad but straightforward fornication was allowed. Cashel wasn't sure, but he was disturbed – as if the dean's dire warnings were directed specifically at him alone – and for a week he managed to keep himself pure, until he started masturbating again.

The twins, Hogan and Buckley, were not identical. By the time they were two, Hogan already looked significantly bigger and brawnier. Buckley was a slimmer, weaker variant of his sibling. They both had dark hair and brown eyes but where Hogan had limitless reserves of energy, Buckley often sat quietly by himself for an hour or more, even without toys to preoccupy him, quite happy in his inertia. Cashel wondered if he were a bit simple. They both idolized him, their big brother, and followed him around like dogs. Cashel also noticed how fond Pelham Ross was of his twin boys. In their presence his sophisticated, watchful reserve disappeared and he would pick them up and fling them screaming into the air, catching them as they fell, or lie them on their backs and tickle their bellies until hysteria set in, or clamber round the nursery on all fours with one or the other twin on his back as if riding a horse. He was a different man with the twins.

After they were born he was far more often at the Glebe, visiting at least once a month, staying only for a couple of days or so, but all the same a regular paterfamilial presence. He paid attention to Cashel but there was no rough and tumble, no physical contact beyond a handshake. He was polite, he seemed interested in Cashel's welfare, but they did nothing together. Cashel found it easy to avoid addressing him as 'Father' although Elspeth still encouraged him to do so. Whenever Pelham Ross stayed at the Glebe Cashel was always reminded of the 'game', the secrets they were keeping and the pretence that had to be maintained, and he found that it made him uneasy. When Ross was absent he almost forgot about it entirely.

Cashel's voice broke, pustules appeared on his chin and around his mouth and a small furze of pubic hair seemed to grow above his cock almost overnight. One day he realized he was taller than tall Elspeth. Marmaduke Seele took him aside and asked him his plans regarding going up to the university and speculated which of the Oxford colleges would be best suited to his particular talents. Seele had briefly been a Balliol man himself (before being rusticated for debt) and thought the college might be ideal for Cashel. For the first time Cashel began to think about the future, of what it might hold for him, of what might he become. It was 1814, he told himself, Boney was in exile,* there was peace at last after endless war, everybody was celebrating, and interesting changes were definitely in the air.

The twins were now five years old and loudly boisterous, Mrs

* After his abdication, Napoleon Bonaparte was exiled to Elba and arrived there on 30 May 1814. He was allowed to retain his title of 'Emperor' and so, for ten months, became the Emperor of Elba.

Creevy was long gone, worn out by her charges – even Buckley seemed more animated – and Cashel found the only way he could escape their constant attention and the household hulla-balloo was by sneaking off to the summer house at the end of the back lawn. He made it his own place, bringing in some furniture – an old rug, a desk, a chair, a bookcase – and rigged up a kind of divan bed covered with a Kashmir shawl and some pillows where he could stretch out and read, undisturbed. It became his domain.

However, he was always careful to disguise his journey there, choosing a simple subterfuge of leaving through the front door, as if he were walking into town, then veering off unobserved to the stables to have a word with Albert, if he was there, and then, casually, he could skirt by the walled garden and dart unseen into the summer house. Hogan and Buckley searched for him in vain.

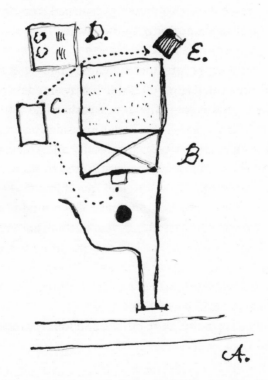

The route to the summer house. A. The Botley–Oxford Road. B. The Glebe. C. The stables. D. The walled garden. E. The summer house.

One summer afternoon while he was making his circuitous way to the summer house, he bumped into Daisy, the housemaid, as she emerged from the walled garden with a heavy basket of plums and greengages in her hand.

'Oh, Daisy, hello, it's you.'

'So it is, Master Cashel,' she said, smiling at him in her sly way.

'Can I pinch some of those plums?'

She held out the basket for him, still smiling in a rather knowing manner, Cashel thought, as he filled his pockets. It had not escaped his notice that, since his voice had deepened and he'd grown six inches, Daisy had taken more interest in him. She was in her early twenties, now, a short, strapping young woman, with a mass of thick brown hair stuffed carelessly under her bonnet. She had a broad face with a snub nose that was too snub, Cashel thought, making her upper lip seem unnaturally long. But she was a lively, efficient, self-confident person and Elspeth relied on her a great deal for the running of the Glebe.

'And where are you off to, Master Cashel? The summer house?'

'Yes, as it happens. I have to finish reading a book by tomorrow and I need some peace and quiet away from the two monsters.'

'Peace and quiet, mmm? I knows what you get up to in that summer house . . .'

She had a marked Oxfordshire accent. Her family lived in Charlbury in the Evenlode Valley, some fifteen miles away from Oxford. Her father had died and her mother swiftly remarried. 'But I didn't like my stepdad,' she had once confided in Cashel. 'He were a bit too fond of me, if you know what I mean, so I took myself off to Oxford to look for work and lodgings. And here I am.'

Now, Cashel felt his mouth going dry.

'What do you mean by that? "Get up to"?'

'I saw you going in there the other day and I crept up and spied on you. And I saw what I saw.'

'What?' Cashel's face was hot.

'I saw you pulling on your po-go, Master Cashel, that's what I saw through the window.'

He said nothing. Swallowed hard. It was true, worse luck. No denial could save him.

'If you ever want a helping hand, you be sure to let me know.' She turned and sauntered off, hips swaying under her skirts.

Cashel didn't let her know – and when they encountered each other in the house nothing seemed to have altered since their charged conversation. But he kept on going to the summer house as usual and, one warm afternoon, with Elspeth out for a ride in the barouche with the twins, there was a light rap on the door frame and Daisy stepped into view.

Two weeks later, Cashel was fishing in the Cherwell, down by Merton Fields, with Ben Smart. The day was sultry, and the thin clouds that screened the sun gave a strange opaque bony glow to the flowing river water, as if it were ashy, somehow.

Cashel watched Ben cast his line skilfully under overhanging willows. For an uncoordinated lad he fished well, he thought. In an unforced, natural, almost inevitable way, the two had become good friends over the years they had spent at the Scholars' table in Dean Smythe's Academy. Ben had tried to grow a downy dark moustache to make himself look older but wasn't really succeeding in that regard.

'You remember that sermon that Dean Smythe gave us?' Ben said, casting again into the stream. 'About the Sin of Onan?'

'Of course. Never to be forgotten.'

'It's been on my mind and I think I've finally understood it.'

'Oh, yes. And I feel you're about to inform me of your exegetical conclusions.'

'It's not about frigging, you see. That's a wanton distortion. It's about not doing it with your brother's wife – even if he's dead.'

'No, no, you must be wrong. The Lord instructed Onan to do it with his brother's wife.' Cashel paused, realizing this was the moment – he needed to confess.

'The Sin of Onan,' he went on, as casually as he could manage, 'is actually about *coitus interruptus*.'

Ben silently wound in his line and laid his rod on the riverbank. He turned and faced Cashel, hands on hips, staring at him.

'And what do you know about *coitus interruptus*, Ross, you blackguard?'

'I've done it.'

'You've kept this from me. Tell all, or I'll never forgive you.'

And it came tumbling forth as Cashel related to him, in considerable detail, everything that had happened between him and Daisy that day and what she had instructed him to do.

This isn't going to take place, Master Cashel, Daisy had said, unless you follow my strictest rules. She walked into the summer house and stood before him. I will, Cashel said instantly, I'll do everything you say. Then Daisy lifted her skirt briefly and showed Cashel the dark triangle of hair where her strong thighs met, then dropped her skirt. You can have the real thing, she said, but – but – you have to get off the coach before it reaches the inn, if you catch my drift. Cashel thought for a second. When you think you're about to explode, Daisy added, you retreat. Yes, I understand, Cashel said, realizing what she meant now.

Daisy sat down on the divan opposite him and lay back. Get them breeches off and keep your kerchief in your hand to catch yourself. Cashel shucked down his breeches and reached for his kerchief as Daisy spread her legs and hauled up her skirt. Cashel moved forward, cock already rigid. Daisy put her hand on his chest. One last thing, she said. I don't want to get knapped, see, like every other housemaid and chambermaid in Oxford in pod with a bairn on the way. If you don't perform as I say I'll tell your mother you forced yourself on me. That clear, Master Cashel?

Clear. Very clear, Daisy. Even though he was in a swoon of lust, Cashel did everything he was told.

On the riverbank Ben looked at him, disgustedly, jealously.

'So you withdrew your *arbor vitae* from her cloven inlet?'

'Exactly that. I committed the Sin of Onan. Q.E.D.'

'I assume you're going to enlighten the dean on his misreading.'

'Hardly.'

'How many times?'

'Five, so far.'

'Liar. Foul liar.'

'Honour bright, Ben. I can't quite believe it myself.'

Strangely, the next day, there was no sign of Daisy about the Glebe. He asked Mrs Pillard where she was and Mrs Pillard said, darkly, that he had better ask Mrs Ross. Cashel sought out Elspeth and, as unconcernedly as he could manage, wondered if Daisy was having a day off.

'No. She's been dismissed, I'm afraid,' Elspeth said firmly.

'Dismissed?'

'She is no longer in our employ.'

'Why? What happened?'

'Pilfering. It seems she's been pilfering for months – for years, for all I know.'

'Daisy? Surely not? She loves working here. She told—' He stopped himself.

'What's it to you, Cashel?'

'Nothing. I just thought you liked her.'

'I do. I did. Until I found out she was a thieving minx.'

'There's nothing more to be said, then,' he added, carelessly, he hoped.

'I'm interviewing another maid this afternoon. Domestics come, domestics go. It's the way of the world.'

'How did you discover her?'

'Hogan did.'

'*Hogan?*'

'He went up to her room – he shouldn't have been there, I know – and turned out a chest he found under her bed. It was full of our stuff – silver, china, gewgaws.'

'Hogan? But how—'

'He brought down a sauce-boat that I thought had been lost. I asked him where he found it and he showed me. She was very clever. She only took things that were rarely used, small things easily not missed. An ivory thimble, a christening spoon, a Toby jug in the back of a cupboard. I had no option.' She looked closely at Cashel. 'She wasn't to be trusted. You can't have a servant in your house who can't be trusted.'

'Yes, I can see that,' Cashel said, nodding sagely. 'You had no choice.'

The next time Cashel saw Hogan he gave him a heavy thwack with the flat of his hand on the back of his head which made the boy cry.

Daisy's malfeasance troubled Cashel. He felt guilty about her sudden dismissal – illogically, as if his own sexual transgression with her had somehow brought about her unmasking as a petty thief. Damn that boy, Hogan! Yet, as he thought on, he wondered if her overt advances to him had been part of another, larger plan in her mind. What would she have asked him to furnish or provide once he was fully in her sway? He would have done anything, he knew, out of pure, hot desire and with the further threat and fear of exposure always lurking – the most potent lever against him. He found himself thinking again, reluctantly, of Dean Smythe's sermon and its dire warnings and repercussions. Had he escaped some awful fate? Had he sinned? Was this the price for committing the real Sin of Onan? He vowed never to be so tempted again.

The new housemaid was duly appointed – Mrs Rosebury, a sour-faced, humourless woman in her thirties, widowed with three children. Cashel felt himself ill, troubled by the whole affair, and Dr Jolly was summoned. He diagnosed a fit of the ague and prescribed some of his potions – a tincture of Turkey Rhubarb and his own patent Restorative Nervous Cordial – that made Cashel feel marginally worse.

Pelham Ross returned for a stay of three weeks, much to Elspeth's and the twins' joy. Cashel rose from his sickbed and, given the distraction Ross's presence provided, began to feel better. Ross seemed in genial mood – all was well with his world – and for the first time Cashel felt the new force of his interest. There was talk of university, a career in the law perhaps, or even of joining Ross in his various business ventures.

One morning at breakfast – Cashel and Ross were the first downstairs – the discussion was renewed. Ross quizzed him about his strongest subjects; Latin and Greek, Cashel replied. Then it must be the law, Ross said and as a qualified lawyer you'd be well suited for the world of commerce, of buying and selling, with some advantage.

'I'd still like to travel the world,' Cashel said. 'Perhaps I could be of use in your South African affairs.'

'South Africa? What about it?'

'Your mines, your entrepots.'

'Ah, yes. South Africa is over, alas. Everything wound up. Pass me those kidneys, will you? I've the hunger of a wolf this morning.'

There was something about the glibness of this answer that gave Cashel pause. South Africa was routinely cited as the reason for his long absences from the family. Elspeth would remark, 'If only Pelham worked in Europe and not so far away. Still – needs must.' And that was the end of the matter. And now, suddenly it seemed, it was no more.

Ross acquired two horses, a big bay hunter and a smaller sorrel mare, and he and Cashel started to go on rides together through the great expanse of meadows south of the city. Cashel, never wholly comfortable on the back of a horse, had to admire how at ease Ross was in the saddle as he cantered along a loop of the Isis, leaping effortlessly over hedges and wooden gates. Cashel would dismount and lead his horse rather than risk a tumble, for which he was subject to Ross's gentle mockery. 'We'll make a horseman of you yet, lad, don't you worry.' He was pleased to be sharing time with Ross – unknown almost, hitherto – and he sensed the polite reserve that had existed between the two of them begin to dissolve.

Ross was sophisticated and well travelled; he talked to Cashel of his stays in Brussels, Paris and Vienna. He advised him – after he had taken his degree, of course – to spend a year or more travelling at his leisure through Europe, volunteering to subsidize such a trip as well. See something of the world, Cashel, while you're young and without responsibilities, he advised. Then you can find yourself a wife and a profession without dreaming of opportunities never experienced. Such a voyage pre-empted all kinds of regrets, he said, speaking from personal experience.

One evening before supper, a fortnight into his stay, the family was gathered in the small drawing room. Mrs Rosebury had brought Hogan and Buckley down from the nursery to spend half an hour with their parents before their bedtime. Hogan was sitting on Ross's knee, laughing and chuckling as Ross bounced him up and down as if he were riding a horse. Buckley was foraging for something under a table while Cashel sat with a glass of sherry in his hand. Elspeth topped his drink up from the decanter.

'Cashel, old fellow,' Ross called from across the room, 'Would you fetch me a cigar from the humidor in my study? This young horseman, here, refuses to dismount.'

Cashel picked up a candelabrum and stepped upstairs to the small room off the landing where Ross had established his study. A big partner's desk filled most of the space but there was also a low glass-fronted bookcase on top of which stood the walnut humidor with a brass handle. Cashel lifted the lid and some sort of mechanical device within made the front drop down and three staggered, grooved drawers present themselves. Ross smoked three or four cigars a day, Cashel had noticed, and he had a good supply here, some three dozen or so thin knobbled cheroots, darkly brown, almost black. Cashel selected one for Ross and then took one for himself. He fancied himself as a cigar-smoker, not a pipe-smoker like the older fellows at school. Altogether too fussy, he thought: all that tamping down, the effortful lighting and relighting, puffing away, not to mention the messy and tiresome business of cleaning the thing. He slipped the stolen cigar in his jacket pocket and held the other one to his nose, rolling it in his fingers to release the raw tobacco smell.

Something clicked in his brain then – some image, some lost memory signalling – but whatever he was unconsciously trying to remember was elusive. He could hear Buckley downstairs, wailing, and lingered a while in the study, aimlessly trying the drawers in the desk to see what they contained. The lower drawers opened, and were empty, but the top two drawers were locked tight. Why? he wondered, idly, and set off downstairs with Ross's cigar.

The mystery of the locked drawers nagged at him, however, along with the broken and teasing association of memories that the cigar had triggered. What was he half-remembering? Perhaps it was something in a dream, he told himself, and so there would be no logical connection – it would be for ever irretrievable. But the locked drawers . . . What was Ross hiding there that demanded such security in his family home?

The next week Ross went up by coach to London to see his lawyer and his banker, he said, adding that he would be away two or three days. Cashel went to the stable and retrieved a long thin nail from the tool box that Albert kept there and, with the aid of a pair of pincers, bent the sharp end of the nail down by ninety degrees to form a crude key. He waited until Elspeth had left the house, crept into Ross's study and closed the door.

The simple key, after a certain amount of jiggling around, proved sufficient to manipulate the small lock on the right-hand drawer and Cashel pulled it open to reveal a mass of papers. Nothing seemed particularly interesting: letters, receipts, bills to be paid. Why lock a drawer full of such mundane, uninteresting stuff? he wondered. He had been half-hoping for some cash, a sovereign or two. Then his attention was caught by a letter. He took it out of the drawer and went to the window so the light would fall on the tiny copperplate handwriting. The seal was broken so he unfolded it.

'Dear Sir Guy,' he read.

He read it again, his throat constricted, his breathing suddenly short.

He went back to the drawer and took out an account of goods delivered from a timber merchant in Castlemountallen, County Cork, addressed to 'Sir Guy Stillwell, Stillwell Court'.

He felt an alarming thudding in his chest and his hands began to shake. He closed his eyes, trying to calm himself.

In his mind's eye he saw the stub of a cigar on the path through the wood from Glanmire Cottage to Stillwell Court. Saw the man in the tall hat at the garden door. Everything at once became clear – and yet everything was a mystery.

Trembling, almost tearful, he put the account back in the drawer and closed it. He had to go and sit somewhere quiet and undisturbed so he could fathom exactly what this devastating information implied and what conclusions were to be drawn. He was going to take his time, do nothing impetuously. He stepped out of the study – and stepped back in again. With his bent nail he carefully re-locked the drawer and then went out to the summer house to think and ponder what he might do next.

Cashel was pleased at his due caution, his prudent restraint. He deliberately didn't think of the future, but concentrated on this one fact that had now been revealed to him – this one shocking fact – namely that Mr Pelham Ross, 'husband' of Mrs Elspeth Ross, and genuine father of the twins, was in fact Sir Guy Stillwell, of Stillwell Court, County Cork. What did that imply? How did that change everything? What was the complex subterfuge that had led to the existence of this pseudonymous family in the Glebe, Oxford? Only his Aunt Elspeth could tell him what the truth was.

He waited until after dinner, when Mrs Pillard had cleared away the remains of their boiled chicken and ragout of carrots. Cashel found he could hardly eat but forced himself and tried to make conversation as he normally would though Elspeth, he could sense, was aware that something was amiss and as soon as Mrs Pillard disappeared to the kitchen she asked him if everything was all right.

'Well . . . No,' Cashel said. 'Could I have a private word with you?'

They took the candles from the dining room and went into her small parlour, her sewing room, and sat down.

'You're making me nervous, Cashel,' Elspeth said. 'What is it?'

'I'm going to ask a question of you and you must swear to answer me truthfully.'

'Of course, my dear. I would never lie to you.'

'Swear on your soul.'

'I swear on my soul. This is silly. What on earth can—'

'Why is Sir Guy Stillwell disguising himself as Mr Pelham Ross?'

The shock on her face was like a caricature, Cashel thought, watching her first cover her mouth with a hand and then press her fingers hard into her temples, her eyes tight shut. She gave a kind of shudder and swayed in her chair to such an extent that Cashel thought she might fall out of it in a faint.

'How did you find out?' she asked in a small voice.

'It doesn't matter. Just tell me what's going on here. Please.'

She closed her eyes again and spoke quickly in a monotone.

'He cannot live with me as Sir Guy Stillwell because he is married to that vile woman and she will not release him. And so we came up with this solution, here in Oxford, where nobody knew us . . .' She opened her eyes. 'We changed our name. Nobody suspects anything at Stillwell Court. They're used to his long absences. It was the only solution.'

'To live a double life.'

'Yes. It's not so unusual, you'd be surprised to learn. In fact, don't we all in some way or other, live a double—'

'It's not the same, Aunt,' Cashel interrupted.

'It was forced upon us when I became pregnant with the twins. That was when we realized that the . . . the "arrangement" we had at Stillwell Court was unworkable – it was over.'

'How long had you and Sir Guy been . . .' He searched for a bland word. 'Involved?'

'For many years.'

'Please tell me the whole story.'

'Will you pour me a small brandy, please?'

Cashel fetched the brandy decanter and two glasses from the drawing room. He poured them each a measure and Elspeth took a sip, then began.

She told him she had been employed by the Stillwells as a governess to Rosamond and Hester when she was in her mid-twenties. The girls were then six and four. Lady Evangeline was already a semi-invalid, 'trapped in her fantasies of illness'.

'Of course, at the beginning I lived in the Court,' she said. 'Sir Guy was a handsome and imposing man and –' she paused – 'he began to pay me attention.'

'And one thing led to another.'

'Yes. That's a way of putting it.' She straightened her back and took another sip. 'I'm not ashamed, Cashel. He and I became very close. We remain so. These are true feelings for each other that we share. We understand one another. There was nothing opportunist about our connection, as you can tell. Why would we be here in Oxford if it were so?'

She went on. After their liaison started they were very careful. Nobody suspected. She moved out of the Court to Glanmire Cottage, outside the walls of the estate, the better to maintain a seemly distance. Sir Guy made a path through the wood from the keeper's cottage. He often went to the keeper's cottage, from where he could visit her unobserved.

'And those visits would coincide with you sending me off to the Doolins for a couple of hours.'

'Yes, as I said, we were very careful. But then—' She stopped and closed her eyes and again began to sway in her chair. 'Not careful enough. I became pregnant . . .'

Cashel heard the blood start to rage and boil in his ears.

'Pregnant?'

'With you.'

He could say nothing as he took this in. He tasted sour vomit at the back of his throat.

'He's my father?'

'Yes.'

He screamed at her: 'Didn't you just say you never lied to me? You whore! You whore from hell!'

Cashel lay still on his divan in the summer house, his arms folded across his chest as if he were entombed in some coffin for all eternity. He could still hear the echo of his rage reverberating in his head and the smash of the crystal decanter as he threw it against the parlour wall. 'You've lied to me all my life!' he had shrieked at her, tears flowing. 'You've lied to me all my sad bastard life!'

She clutched at him but he threw her off and ran from the room and out of the house. He paced up and down the Botley Road for an hour or two, he supposed, sobbing in disgust and shame at the horrible revelation. Then a kind of cold calm descended on him, suddenly. He blew his nose, wiped his wet cheeks dry and crept back to the summer house. The Glebe was dark, the night a black net over everything, with no moon. Owls hooted in the garden. He lay down on his divan, quite still, with folded arms, and formulated his plan.

He was up before dawn and made his way silently into the house. In his room, on his pillow, was a letter from her, sealed, with his name written on it. He put it in his pocket. He gathered together the few shillings he had saved, stuffed a shirt and a canvas jacket in his burlap bag, along with a few other oddments he thought might be useful to him, and changed into his stoutest boots. He lifted his greatcoat off its peg behind the door, placed his John Bull topper on his head, tiptoed out of the house and then walked into central Oxford. He would never return to the Glebe, he resolved. Never return to the 'House of Betrayal', or 'Mendacity Hall', as he now thought of it. He was going to make a new life for himself, somehow, somewhere, anywhere.

But first there was breakfast to be had. He spent a shilling in a chop house in Cornmarket Street. He was starving, having barely eaten the night before. He ordered a pork chop and a leek pie and gravy with two fried eggs. Replete, he wandered over to the Roebuck Inn to see when the next coach to London left. Over breakfast he had settled on London as the place to go – somewhere he could disappear and make his fortune – or, once in London, maybe catch a ship to somewhere, to Africa or the Orient, thinking that the further away he travelled the more his compromised past would recede behind him, like a hot red sun dipping below the horizon. He could start his life afresh, on a new day.

In the yard of the Roebuck he saw the Gloucester to London

coach canted over on its side with one wheel missing and the passengers and their unloaded luggage standing around aimlessly. The team of horses had already been led away. He asked an ostler what had happened and was informed that 'an axle had done broke' and it would be at least three hours before the coach was ready for the London road again.

The salty pie had made him thirsty so he wandered off again looking for a tavern. He could hear the thump of drums coming from Broad Street so he headed in that direction, curious. He passed the black sooty facade of Balliol College on his right and mentally cancelled that dream. Becoming a Balliol man was now impossible, he realized, and he looked ruefully away from the porter's lodge and concentrated on what was taking place up ahead.

There was a market of sorts down the middle of the Broad – farmers selling cheese, fruit and vegetables, and rabbits and hens in wooden cages – and also a small crowd gathered round some soldiers in their red jackets, white breeches and long black gaiters. They had raised a golden flag with the numbers '99' embroidered on it in blue. A drummer was beating a steady rhythm on a bass drum and four soldiers with shouldered muskets were marching smartly to its beat, following the drills shouted at them by a stout sergeant with a chestful of medals.

'Join the Ninety-ninth Hampshire Regiment of Foot!' the sergeant broke off to yell at the young men in the crowd. 'You, you and you! Take the King's shilling, lads, and make a fine future for yourself in the English army!'

He was a stout, full-whiskered, broad-shouldered fellow. The tall man on the bass drum was a corporal. 'Join the Fighting Hampshires, boys! There's no better regiment in the kingdom!'

Cashel, smiling to himself at their ludicrous hyperbole, watched the marching soldiers for a moment or two and then ducked into a basement tavern.

It was dark inside. Lanterns and candles were burning even though it was only mid-morning – the small grimy windows let in a meagre, greasy light. Farmers from the stalls outside, in their smocks and wooden clogs, sat on benches by the long tables with their pots of porter. Cashel approached the bar, put down his six-pence and asked for a gin and water.

He gathered up his change and took his glass to a window seat from where he stared at the legs and skirts of passers-by moving to and fro, almost unconsciously adjusting their pace to the hyp-notic beat of the bass drum. *Thump, thump, thump.* He wasn't used to gin and he soon felt his head begin to swim a bit with the alcohol, despite his big breakfast. Good, he thought, I can do what I want with my life now, with no one to gainsay me – eat breakfast, drink gin, eat breakfast again. He was free, a free man. Then the bass drum stopped and was replaced by the martial *rat-a-tat-tat* of the side drum. Someone started playing a march on a fife and suddenly he heard a round of applause.

Curiosity overcame him and he drained his glass and stepped outside again. The drummer was showing off – drumming and throwing his drumsticks in the air and catching them as they fell, almost without breaking rhythm, it seemed. Cashel pushed his way to the front of the gawping crowd and was spotted by the sergeant.

'You're a likely lad, my son. Come and join the army.'

'I'm going to London,' Cashel said.

'Don't go there, my boy, it's a sink.'

The crowd laughed their agreement and the drummer began a roll that drew Cashel's eyes, watching the man's hands – they seemed perfectly still, yet the individual beats crescendoed to a ceaseless flow of noise.

BANG! The drumming stopped and the crowd applauded again.

'How old are you, boy?' the sergeant asked.

'Sixteen, sir,' Cashel lied.

'Here, give him a couple of sticks, Silas,' the sergeant said to the corporal. He took a couple of spares from his belt and handed them over. Cashel put his sack on the ground and took them.

'You're a big lad, you could carry a drum, easy. Now, copy what this fella does.'

The drummer beat out a rhythm. *Rat, tat-tat-tat, rat-RAT*. Cashel copied him.

The drummer tried another combination. *Rat, ratty-tat, ratty-tat, rat-RAT*. And Cashel matched him.

'Strewth, he's a natural, ain't he, Silas?'

'As natural a drummer as I've seen in many a long year, Sarge.'

'Join the Hampshire Foot, son. Become a drummer-boy.'

Cashel felt the weight of the heavy drumsticks in his hand. The gin gave him confidence and he beat out an impromptu rhythm on the skin – *rat-rat-rattata-ratatta, rat rat-a-tatta-rat-TAT-TAT* – and the crowd whooped and applauded. Here was his future, he thought – in the English army – and on his doorstep, moreover. He didn't need to go all the way to London.

'What do you say, laddie? Is it the Fighting Hampshires for you?'

'Yes, sir, Sergeant. Sign me up!'

3

99th *(Hampshire) Regt. of Foot*
Alcantaz* Barracks
Portsmouth

14th December 1814

My dear Ben,

   It is my birthday. I have reached the grand old age of fifteen
(tho' everyone here assumes I am seventeen). I'm now a fully trained
drummer and private soldier in one of His Majesty's Line Regiments.
Who could ever have divined such a fate for me? I trust I am much
missed at the Scholars' Table at the Academy. The dean won't mind my
absence as long as my fees for the term have been paid. Money for jam.

   Thank you for forwarding on Mrs Ross's anguished letter. I shall not
be replying. Be so good as to let her know that, as far as you are aware,
I'm in Scotland searching for members of my family – she will guess at
once what you are talking about. I'm known here in the regiment as
Cashel Greville as I don't wish for anyone to find me. You are very
patient tho' I can imagine you are about to expire with curiosity over
what has come to pass. I will explain everything – my flight, my
disappearance, my new profession – when we are once again face to face.

   Life here in barracks is dull and routine but I am in good spirits.
I am, I have discovered, a more than proficient drummer and a passable
soldier. We drill and drill on the heath, turning marching columns into
neat static squares, learning to shoot our muskets in disciplined
volleys – yes, I can master Miss Brown Bess, also. We eat simply but

---

* Alcantaz is a village north of Lisbon where, in 1761, during the Seven Years'
War, the newly raised 99th Foot took part in a bloody skirmish where the regiment drove out a superior force of French troops from the fortified village,
with many casualties on both sides. It was the regiment's first battle honour.

copiously. I am tolerably happy (who dares ask for more?) and I save most of my shilling a week. There is talk that the regiment may be despatched to Jamaica again. Now that would be good fortune – what stories could I relate therefrom?

I will write again soon. Give my respects to Mr Seele (discreetly). I am, my dear Ben,

Your affectionate friend,
Cashel Greville

Cashel had settled fairly easily into peacetime soldiering. The 99th (Hampshire) Regiment of Foot had been raised by Colonel Sir Wilfred Walcott in 1760 towards the end of the Seven Years' War and had seen service in Portugal, the Revolutionary War in the Americas and also in Jamaica during the Second Maroon War of 1795. The current colonel was Sir Wilfred's elderly son, Colonel Sir Marston Walcott, a man in his sixties, who tried to preserve everything that his father had achieved: the purpose-built barracks on the outskirts of Portsmouth, the precise details and style of the regiment's uniform and strict discipline. Only in weaponry would he admit to any innovation – every man was issued with the new 1810 India Pattern musket – and otherwise to all intents and purposes the 99th remained an eighteenth-century regiment.

Cashel inadvertently benefited from this reactionary fervour. Colonel Walcott refused to allow bugle calls to supersede the roll of drums as a means of transmitting orders and instructions to the troops. Each company – there were currently six in the regiment – had two drummers and one fifer. 'If I see any man with a bugle-horn I will have him flogged,' Colonel Walcott had been known to declaim. Consequently, Cashel had to learn the sixteen or so distinct drumbeats that signalled such manoeuvres as Quick March, Halt, Make Ready, Present, Fire, Seek Parley, Charge, Retreat, Enemy Cavalry Approaching, The Colours are Safe, and so forth. Drummers also beat time for Camp Calls – such as Reveille, Alarm, Stand To, Dinner is Served and Prepare to March – as well as participating in route marches, ceremonial parades, floggings and burials.

Cashel's fellow drummer in his company was a tall young man from Lyme Regis called John-Henry Croker. He had a loose mouth – his fat lips set slightly askew – that had the effect of giving him the permanent beginnings of a laconic smile. It could be disconcerting on occasion. When he spoke, his lips pouted and moved from side to side as if he had some kind of speech impediment. Cashel soon grew used to the affliction. Croker was a burly fellow, tall as Cashel. Drummers were often selected for their height as the side drum was cumbersome (and heavy) and hung to the knee. Short men found it an awkward burden. In any event, the drummers, because they were so few in number, considered themselves a form of elite within the regiment. When the regiment formed a square on the battlefield all the drummers gathered round the colours in the centre. Twelve side drums beating out an order carried easily to every corner of the infantry square, even taking into account the considerable noise of a nineteenth-century battle – muskets and artillery firing, horses neighing, orders and encouragement shouted, casualties screaming. Drummers also were responsible for tending wounded men, hauling them from where they had fallen in the firing line and bringing them to safety at the square's centre and administering what first aid they could.

But, as far as Cashel was concerned, after two months of rigorous training, this was all still theory. The big war in Europe was over; and the war in America seemed to be fizzling out, now that Washington had been burned to the ground along with the White House,* so overseas postings were now the allure. Lieutenant Rollo Abercorn, Cashel's company commander, followed news of distant conflicts avidly. Insurrection in Majorca, a punitive expedition against the Ashanti in West Africa or garrison duty in Jamaica – anything to quit the tedium of barrack life in Portsmouth was his dream, so he confided in Cashel. They had struck up an unusual, almost semi-informal relationship since Abercorn had discovered, during an inspection of the company's barrack room, Cashel's small collection of books (Robert Burns's *Poems*,

---

* The so-called War of 1812 – that in fact ended in 1815.

Chiefly in the Scottish Dialect and *Caleb Williams*, Horace's *Odes*) that included a copy of General Ivo Bovington's celebrated treatise, *The Operations of War* (1795). Surprised, Abercorn had quizzed Cashel on this choice of volume and Cashel had replied that, seeing as he had now become a soldier, it behoved him to study his profession, surely – just as if he had become a butcher or a mason or a carpenter.

'Fair point, Greville,' Abercorn had said, flicking through the book and noting Cashel's marginalia, visibly intrigued. 'I can see you've read it closely. You must tell me what you've learned.'

'To my mind, it seems unduly complicated, sir. The theory of warfare, I mean.'

'Well, of course all theory goes out the window when the first shot is fired.'

'Not according to General Bovington,' Cashel said. 'Consider his epigraph: *Gladiator in arena consilium capit.*'

'What?' Abercorn looked vague.

'Seneca, sir. "The gladiator in the arena makes his plan."'

'Be that as it may . . .' Abercorn looked sharply at Cashel. 'Your boots need a good polish, Greville.'

'Yes, sir.'

Once a fortnight, the men in Lieutenant Abercorn's company were allowed a day off in Portsmouth, though they were ordered to wear their uniforms into town. John-Henry Croker and Cashel wandered the mile and a half from the barracks into Portsmouth's outer precincts, smart in their black stovepipe shakos with the gleaming big brass plate, the red long-coated jackets with their nine laced buttons and pale cream breeches. As drummers, they were distinguished further by their jackets being stitched with stripes of lace in pattern repeats on the sleeves. It was hard not to walk with a bit of a swagger to their stride. Little children followed them, marvelling. Croker was heading for a bawdyhouse he frequented in Portsea, Cashel to his favourite tavern to get drunk on ale, so they parted company.

At the Three Jolly Bakers on Wish Street, Cashel settled himself in a corner booth with a pewter mug of beer. As he always did when he had some unobserved time alone, he took out the letter from his Aunt Elspeth – no, his mother, Elspeth – that she had placed on his pillow the night of the terrible revelation, as he thought of it. It was now somewhat creased and grubby from so much handling and rereading but its force had not diminished. He spread it flat on the tabletop in front of him and perused it again.

He must have read it thirty or forty times, he supposed, but even that familiarity didn't prevent the upsurge of complicated emotions the letter provoked. Love for his aunt – now his mother – mingled with fury at her years of duplicity, mollified moments later by an acknowledgement of the powerful reasons why she needed to maintain such a pretence. He understood, then he was angry, then bitter, then sorry for her. These feelings grew and rose and fell and slowly turned into a sadness and weariness of spirit at the loss of his family, his brothers, his home – and then that mood was replaced in turn by a stalwart self-possession and a certain pride in his audacity at refusing to accept this shameful status quo.

How could he have stayed on in that house? How could he have faced Sir Guy – his father! – now that he knew everything? Sometimes he rebuked himself for his curiosity – why had he unlocked the locked drawer in the study and thereby changed his life for ever? Forbidden fruit, he thought: like Adam he had transgressed and as a result had been driven out of his modest paradise, the Glebe and his life in Oxford, into the fallen world, the world of sinners and Alcantaz barracks.

But better to know the truth than live on, ignorant, in a lie, he told himself.

He read the letter again. Elspeth had started by apologizing and begging abjectly for his forgiveness:

Think about my position as a young governess in a grand house. When I discovered that I was with child what could I do? Everything that happened next was done with Sir Guy's help and heartfelt collusion. So many men in his position, finding himself in such a situation, would have packed me away to Dublin or Belfast with a few sovereigns to fend for myself. And that would have been the end of me – a fallen woman with a fatherless child.

And so she and Sir Guy had concocted a story. As her pregnancy advanced – she concealed it artfully for as long as possible – she requested a leave of absence to go and tend her sister in Scotland who was sick, confined to bed and expecting a child, she said. A house was rented for her in a suburb of Glasgow where she posed as a widow (husband a sailor killed in a naval battle) and, at term, Cashel was born. She did indeed have a sister, Moira, in Dumfries, a schoolteacher, who was not made privy to her secret. Their parents were long dead and there was no family, close or distant, who could expose the subterfuge, as long as she kept herself to herself. Cashel's birth then demanded the second fabulation. Moira and Findlay Greville 'perished' in the Irish Sea, in early 1800, leaving their infant son in Elspeth's care. Sir Guy generously consented to her return with her orphaned nephew and life at Stillwell Court was renewed with nobody any the wiser. Everything had worked to perfection. Lady Evangeline had barely noticed her few months' absence and the girls were thrilled to have her back. And with a little baby boy to play with and spoil.

She must have acted her part well, and of course, Sir Guy kept his distance, feigning indifference. No wonder I never saw him as I grew up, Cashel thought. Did he, while I was a baby, pick me up and dandle me on his knee during his clandestine visits to the cottage? What must it have been like for him, he wondered, to have your unacknowledged son living a few hundred yards away beyond the demesne walls? It was like something from a fable or a fairy story, he thought – except it was all true and had happened to him. And now he had a real aunt in Dumfries, Moira Soutar. Would Elspeth finally have told her the secret, warned her . . .?

Cashel closed his eyes, as he always did when his thoughts led him in these various hypothetical directions, and wondered what would become of him now. What would the rest of his life be like? It was as if his existence, his very being, had been turned upside down and inside out. He felt – anger flaring again – that he

48

had had this exile forced upon him, been cast out from everything he knew and took for granted. A boat tossed about on
stormy seas; a leaf torn from its tree and sent spinning by the
wind; a piece of driftwood cast ashore on some foreign strand . . .
The familiar metaphors beguiled him for a while. He went up to
the bar and ordered another tankard of ale – and a glass of gin
and water. Inebriation was as good a short-term way of coping as
any, he felt. He didn't want to think about the truth any more.

Cashel and Croker were beating 'Reveille' on the parade ground
early one morning in March. It was bitter cold and their breath con-
densed in front of them, hanging still in the air for a few seconds
before dispersing. They beat hard, the better to warm themselves.

'Freeze your bollocks off,' Croker said.

Cashel noticed he was wearing fingerless gloves, made of grey
wool.

'Where did you get those gloves?'

'Mother dear knit them for I.'

'Could she knit me a pair?'

'For a shilling, I reckon she would, Irish.' He looked up. 'Hang
on. Here comes Mr Bright-and-Early.'

They saw Lieutenant Abercorn striding across the parade
ground, his sword banging against his legs. As he passed he
shouted something at them.

'What's that, sir?'

Abercorn paused and came back to them. They could see how
excited he was and so stopped drumming.

'Boney's escaped from Elba.* Stand by, lads – this war's not
over yet.' He hastened away.

'Why's he so hungry to go to war?' Croker asked. 'Pillock.'

'Why be a soldier, otherwise? You want to fight an enemy. It's
your calling.'

* On 26 February 1815 Napoleon Bonaparte managed to escape his enforced
exile on Elba, arriving in Cannes on 1 March on a brigantine disguised as a
British frigate.

'I don't want a fucking enemy.'

'So, you just want to do drills and stay in barracks all your soldiering life?'

'It would suit me fine.'

Cashel shook his head.

'Something tells me you're not going to get your wish, Johnny-boy.'

Croker poked him in the ribs with his drumstick.

'Ouch!'

True enough, there was a real stir about the regiment as this news was broadcast. Colonel Walcott had them all out on the heath, day after day, forming squares and firing volleys as if Bonaparte was about to invade any moment. There was a great increase in supplies also, wagons arriving at the barracks with victuals and forage, tents and ammunition. Horses deemed unfit were sent to the knacker's and new ones stabled. But March slipped into April and the regiment received no movement orders. Lieutenant Abercorn told Cashel, during one of their chats, that he had heard that the Duke of Wellington was already in France making his plans. Cashel said nothing, trying to ignore the unease that was building in him. When he'd signed up as a drummer-boy it had been a simple act of escape – an act of renewal – and he'd given no thought to any martial activity. Still, one good consequence of his decision was that, as a drummer, his day was filled. The other soldiers, when the drills were over, mingled with their families, if they had them, and waited, idle. But the dull life of a peacetime regiment already seemed over as they moved inexorably on to their wartime footing. Cashel felt his foreboding cancel out any slight excitement. True, he now knew how to load and fire his musket – but could he fire it at another human being?

Finally, the move came about in May. Suddenly everyone was told to have their packs filled and ready and be prepared for embarkation to France in forty-eight hours. This time passed, and then another forty-eight hours. A week later, the regiment, led by the drummers and the fifers, marched from the barracks through Portsmouth to the harbour – cheered on by the local populace – and embarked on three merchant vessels, the *Princess Louise*, the *Martlett* and the *Bodium Castle*, and sailed across the Channel to the port of Ostend where they disembarked and waited to see what Napoleon Bonaparte would do next.

It was an unseasonal, wet early June, Cashel thought, looking up at the low grey clouds as the drizzle fell. He was in Belgium, part of a mighty army, and it was the first time he had left the shores of Great Britain, the Kingdom. He looked out over a few acres of yellowing corn with a line of poplars at the field's edge beyond. Through the trees he could spot a flint-harled church and the air was full of birdsong; and though he was 'abroad' it looked very much like Hampshire to his eyes. He wandered back into the empty grain warehouse where the company was billeted. They slept on straw palliasses and to pass the time killed the mice that infested the barn – hundreds of little rodents that they heaped outside for the crows and jays to feast on.

Neither he nor anyone else, it seemed, had any idea how the campaign against Bonaparte was going, since he'd made his daring escape. Even Lieutenant Abercorn was vague. 'He's heading north,' was as detailed a comment as he'd make. 'We stand by, Greville,' he said. 'That is our duty.'

Corporal Silas Mill wandered past the barn accompanied by his wife. Mill had been the drummer who'd recruited him at Oxford and he was in charge of the regiment's drummers when they functioned as a unit. His wife, Mildred, who along with the many other wives was part of the regiment's travelling commissariat, knew Cashel. She was Irish, from County Wexford, and felt there was a bond between them. She did him little favours from time to time.

'Cashel, me darling, how are ye?'

'Fit and well, Mistress Mill, if a little damp.'

'Anything for the wash-house?' Amongst other duties she was in charge of the regiment's laundry.

'I've a couple of shirts. I'll bring them round.' He turned to Mill. 'Any news, Corporal, sir?'

'We'll be heading out before too long,' he said cryptically. 'Don't you worry, Greville, we'll not leave you behind.' Yes, Cashel thought, that much is true, at least.

But Mill was right. They did head out two days later. It took them a week to march from Ostend to a small town called Hal where they met up with a large section of Wellington's army, over ten thousand men, he was told. But in Hal there was no dry barn to sleep in, mice or no mice. The regiment was billeted in open fields under makeshift tents made from greatcoats and ram-rods. As ever, the drummers were busy beating out instructions. Cashel began to feel hungry, and tiring of the broth and biscuits they were served for breakfast, lunch and dinner, he managed to buy a couple of chickens from a farmer. Croker and he built a fire and they roasted the birds, one each.

'How come you've got money on you, Irish?' Croker asked, tearing a leg off his bird.

'Because I don't waste my wages a-whoring, like you.'

'The Virgin Drummer,' Croker mocked him. 'A shy bairn gets nowt.'

'I'm no virgin,' Cashel said, thinking suddenly of Daisy. 'Your pizzle will fall off one of these days, mark my words. The Poxy Drummer.'

Croker laughed, genuinely. Cashel amused him, he said.

On Saturday 17th June the regiment was ordered to prepare to march and, to the men's consternation, they discovered that they were the only regiment in the force at Hal being sent eastwards. Thousands of men were being kept back, for some reason, and it was not clear why the 99th was being singled out or where they were going.

They marched on muddy country roads under steady rain. When they stopped, well into the night, they were all soaked and sat on their packs on the roadside, waiting for dawn, smoking pipes or trying to sleep sitting up. Early the next morning, at first light, Colonel Walcott addressed the entire regiment and shouted information at them. Bonaparte's army was a few hours away, heading for Brussels.

'And we're going to stop him, men, stop him in his tracks and make him wish he'd never left Elba!'

There was a half-hearted cheer at this and Cashel felt his guts slip and churn inside him. It looked as if the 99th was going into battle.

They marched through tall fields of rye, barley and corn, the drummers beating out a steady thumping rhythm to encourage the drenched and tired men. As the morning progressed the rain began to ease. The sun made an appearance but the earth beneath their feet was dank. The wagon train was halted at a crossroads and the companies formed queues to be served their ration of rum. It was thick and a little on the sour side, Cashel thought, but it was plentiful – tin cups filled to the brim. The colonel was revered for his generosity when it came to grog. Everyone began to feel significantly better. They formed up again in columns and marched off towards a long ridge line in the distance.

Cashel had noticed a finger post at the crossroads and remembered the names on it: Hal, Nivelles, Waterloo and Genappe. They had come from Hal and the road they had taken was in the direction of Nivelles. Would this impending battle – for they were surely marching into battle – be remembered as the Battle of Nivelles? he wondered.

They began to climb up towards the ridge line and now found themselves passing other regiments, sitting on the ground, waiting – Germans and Dutch in the main, though an Irish regiment raised a cheer of sorts as they passed by. Soon they came upon a field of corn, completely flattened like a woven rug – evidence of the resting place of a large body of men now moved on – and the regiment was halted and they were ordered to sit down. Packs were slipped off shoulders, muskets stacked, pipes lit. This was to be their starting point, clearly. But what lay over the ridge line?

Cashel unhooked his drum from its webbing and sat down carefully on it. Croker flung himself full length on the flattened corn and gripped his belly with both hands. He groaned quietly.

'What's the matter?' Cashel asked.

'It's as if . . . It's as if I've got a small bird trapped in my guts and it's trying to find a way out.'

The night before, when they had stopped by the road, Croker had gone foraging in the fields and returned with his shako full of small new potatoes. He'd cut one open and offered it to Cashel.

'It's green,' Cashel said. 'Never eat a green potato.'

'Rubbish, that's not green,' Croker said. 'This is meat and drink to you, surely, Irish boy.'

Cashel declined. Croker cut the potatoes into dice-sized pieces and added them to the lukewarm broth he'd been served.

'Damned delicious,' was his verdict, as he chomped away. 'Don't know what you're missing.'

And now he was suffering. He stood up and headed for the area demarcated for urination and defecation – Colonel Walcott was adamant about such hygienic arrangements whenever the regiment was in the field or halted on the march – and Cashel saw him drop his breeches and squat down. Serve the silly bugger right, he thought.

He asked Silas Mill if he could go to the ridge line and have a look, but Mill refused permission. You'll have plenty of opportunity to see the battlefield, later, he said. As close a view as you like, Greville. So Cashel sat on, chewing on a hard biscuit, waiting for Croker to return from his shit.

A weak sun appeared fleetingly as the rain clouds thinned, and rose higher in the sky. It was strange to think of two huge armies, thousands and thousands of men, just out of sight over the hill, laboriously manoeuvring for territorial advantage, he supposed. It was surprisingly quiet. Occasionally he heard the odd distant shout and the distinctive sound of rattling gun carriages moving on some lane out of view, but otherwise it was just the noises of the countryside. A breeze blew, stirring the heavy heads of the rye field to their right, a cow lowed in some far-off pasture, he heard a lazy cock crow. He looked out over the resting regiment – five hundred or so men, sitting and lying. Some of them amused themselves as they waited by trying to trap the birds, thrushes and starlings, that flocked to feed on the trampled corn.

Cashel rummaged in his pack and drew out his volume of *The Operations of War*. Opening it at random he read:

The march of a column may be retarded by a very inferior force. The uses to be made of this circumstance are manifold.

He found a pencil stub in a pocket and made a small tick in the margin.

Croker returned, pale-faced, and sat down very carefully.

'Whor. It's like I'm pishing out of my arse.'

'Thank you, kind sir. Most interesting.'

'Oh, no. Hang on!' He jumped up and ran off to the makeshift latrine again.

It was before noon – Cashel had no pocket watch – when he heard the first explosion of cannon. And then, as if it were a signal, there began a general incredible din of firing that, though it ebbed and flowed somewhat, continued without ceasing, hour after hour.

The battle had begun but they had no idea at all what was happening or which side might be winning. Sometimes they could see white smoke drift across the ridge line, like thick mist. A rogue cannonball came bouncing over the ridge and smashed into a group of men, taking the arm of one clear off, he was told. And then, carried on the breeze, Cashel heard the steady beat of the French drums – *PLAN rat-plan, PLAN rat-plan* – and he smiled to himself. He had heard veterans in the regiment talk about this, the particular French beat. They called it *OLD-trousers, OLD-trousers, OLD-trousers*. It wasn't an instruction or an order – it was beaten solely to encourage, the relentless rhythm stirring the morale of the advancing men. We should use it in our army, Cashel thought – nothing like a beating drum to make you feel bold.

Croker returned from emptying his bowels for the fifth time.

'Fucking agony,' he said. 'It's like I'm on fire down below. Shitting broken glass.'

'Well, I did warn you. Green potatoes—'

'Yes, I know, thank you, Irish. They're all mocking me down there. Taking bets on how many times I'll go.'

At about two o'clock, Cashel guessed, early in the afternoon, they all saw a larger column of smoke rising up above the ridge line and the noise of discharge – musket and artillery – increased. Lieutenant Abercorn passed by and Cashel asked him what the smoke betokened.

'A chateau on fire,' Abercorn said. 'At the very right of our line. We hold it, but there's a devil of a fight going on down there.'

'Might we be sent to support the men in the chateau?' Cashel asked.

'Who knows? We await our orders, Greville,' he said vaguely, and wandered off.

Croker pointed to the rye field to their right, two hundred yards or so away, on the other side of a farm track.

'I'm going down there,' Croker said. 'Make myself throw everything up. I won't let those bastards laugh at me no more.'

He stood up, fingers plugged into his arsehole, and scurried off. Cashel watched him slide down a small incline, cross the track and wade into the tall rye, before squatting down and disappearing entirely from view. Then he heard the thud of a horse's hooves and saw a rider canter up to Colonel Walcott's headquarters – he was further down the slope with the colours – and hand him some written orders. He saw the captains and the lieutenants summoned and given their instructions and they strode off to their companies.

Moments later Corporal Mill appeared.

'Get down to colours and beat "Form into Columns" on my order.'

'Yes, Corporal.' Cashel stood and hoicked up his drum, fitting it onto the webbing hook.

Mill was looking at Croker's drum, standing there.

'Where's fucking Croker?'

'He's in that field there, sir, being sick.' Cashel pointed to the rye.

'He'll be sicker than a sick fucking dog if I lay my hands on him. Get him back here. Now!'

Cashel unhooked his drum and trotted off in the direction of the rye field. He could see the little defile Croker had made as he had stumbled into the crop. He climbed up a gentle rise and, suddenly, was confronted by a sight that made him gasp audibly. There was the battlefield laid out before him like a model panorama in a museum.

In front of him, a mile or so off, was a small solid chateau with outbuildings all ablaze, it seemed, thick smoke rising in the air. The ground in front of it and on all sides was paved with dark dead bodies, like stacked timber, hither and thither. In some shock, he switched his gaze away and looked to his left to see square upon square of Wellington's army – fifty yards apart – with thousands, it seemed, of French cavalry flowing between them as water flows around boulders in a shallow stream. The noise of the volleys was constant, like stones shaken in a gourd, and he could see how the French horses staggered with the blows from the fusillade of unceasing musket balls, the riders falling as they toppled. Dense shreds of white smoke blowing thickly, almost like huge linen sheets, obscured the view from time to time.

In shock he snatched his gaze away from the battle, slid down a steepish muddy slope, crossed the farm track and waded a few feet into the field of rye.

'Croker! Where are you?' he shouted through cupped hands, over the din of the muskets and artillery.

Croker reared up a few yards in front of him, wiping vomit from his chin.

'I'm empty, thank God,' he yelled back. 'Top and bottom. There's nothing left in me, man.'

'We're moving out! Mill is in a fearful wax with you.'

'Fucking Mill. Whoreson Mill.'

Croker pushed his way through the chest-high grasses, belting his breeches tight.

'Pints came out,' he said. 'Gallons. Who knew we carried so much liquid inside us?'

He paused, put his hands on his knees, coughed and spat.

'Let's cut along, Croker. For Pete's sake.'

They turned and ran across the track, then stopped abruptly as they heard a horse whinny and looked round.

Fifty yards away were four horsemen, three with long lances, their giant horses wheeling, spooked, stamping and rearing. They were French, he saw instantly, with the red cockades on their helmets curved forward, their silver helmets flashing in the weary, smoky sunlight, their smart blue-and-gold uniforms looking crisp and new, somehow.

Astonishingly, Cashel found his brain quickly analysing the precarious situation. These lancers had charged a British square, swung around it, lost their bearings, picked up a cavalryman on the way and galloped over the ridge line looking for more of the enemy.

And now the enemy had been found.

Cashel heard a shout of 'Voilà!' as he and Croker turned and bolted down the track. But already he could hear the heavy thud and beat of the horses' hooves behind them as the lancers quickly gained on their quarry.

Croker had a head start and was ten paces ahead of Cashel. Cashel veered to one side as the first lancer passed him and he watched in horror as the man's lance entered Croker's back – deep – and was withdrawn, as smoothly as a knitting needle going into a lump of lard. Croker went down.

Then Cashel felt a lance go through his left thigh – felt his flesh parting, painlessly – as another horse and rider pounded by. For a split second he saw the lance point – like a snake strike – flash through the front of his canvas breeches and then disappear. He still felt no pain though he sensed the hot wash of blood soak his leg and groin. He fell over.

The four horsemen had stopped and wheeled round by Croker's body. One of the lancers jabbed and dug the point of his lance deep into Croker's side to make sure he was dead. They looked up and saw Cashel as he slowly stumbled to his feet. He heard their shouts of gleeful laughter and one of them was pushed forward for the kill. Après vous. Cashel rested all his weight on his good right leg. His left trouser leg was dripping blood, now.

The chosen lancer grinned, lowered his weapon and kicked his spurs into his horse's side and then – *BOOM!* – the cannonade erupted. And, to Cashel's dumb astonishment, the lancers were shredded, as if they were carrots in a grater or turnips in a cutter. Four men on four horses became small bits of four men and four horses. A helmet flew fifty feet up into the air, a shiny breastplate became a confetti of silver coins as the pulverized parts of horse and man were blown into the rye field as if smitten or cuffed by God's hand – a heavy chaff, like wet leaves – leaving a congealed puddle of bloodied bone and meat and mangled uniform steaming on the cart track.

Cashel now felt the pain burn through his left leg and he fell over again. The last thing he remembered was Lieutenant

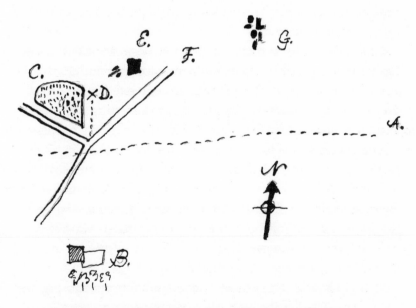

The French Lancers' attack. Waterloo, 18th June 1815. A. The ridge line.
B. Chateau de Hougoumont. C. Field of rye. D. The location of the attack.
E. The 99th (Hampshire) Regiment of Foot, at rest. F. The Nivelles–Waterloo road.
G. The village of Mont Saint-Jean.

Abercorn's face as it loomed over him. He tried to speak but no words came and everything went dark.

'It's very good of you to visit, sir,' Cashel said to Lieutenant Abercorn. 'I'm feeling pretty well, all things considered.' Which was not true.

The lieutenant had his left arm in a sling and there was another officer with him, smiling kindly down at Cashel as he lay in his low bed – an artilleryman, Cashel saw from his uniform.

'They saved your leg,' Abercorn said. 'Lucky chap.'

'Yes, sir. I know.'

'They whip them off, normally, no questions asked, don't they, Openshaw?' He turned to the artillery officer.

'Quick as a flash,' he said.

'I'm more than grateful to have been spared that ordeal,' Cashel said. 'They tell me I'll walk with a limp for a good few years, however.'

Cashel was lying in a low truckle bed in a large, high-ceilinged, beamed room – a former chapel in a nunnery in central Brussels. There were about forty wounded men occupying similar beds in the room – many minus limbs – while nuns moved quietly about, here and there, in strange white bat-winged cornettes.

Lieutenant Abercorn went on to relate what had happened that afternoon of the battle. The four horsemen – the cuirassier and the three lancers – had been spotted by men in the regiment but Cashel had not heard their shouts of warning, such was the general noise from the battle over the ridge. Luckily, a troop of artillery was passing through the lines of Germans nearby and a gun was swiftly unlimbered, loaded with two canisters of shot and brought to bear on the French horsemen.

'This is Captain Openshaw,' Abercorn said, introducing his companion. 'He was the man who gave the order to fire.'

'What can I say, sir. You saved my life with your quick thinking.'

'It's the canister shot, you see,' Openshaw said. 'At close range it's devastating. We were only a hundred yards away. Two canisters, four hundred balls.'

'The effect was impressive, sir. Mighty impressive.'

Abercorn went on to relate what happened next. Cashel, now unconscious through loss of blood, was put on a cart with other wounded from the battlefield and carried off to Brussels. Every hospital was full – which was how come he ended up in this nunnery. There was no surgeon available, Abercorn went on, luckily for you – otherwise you'd be a one-legged man. By the time a surgeon arrived the nuns had dressed your wounds and there seemed no need to amputate.

'He did cut away a lot of flesh, however, I was told,' Abercorn added jauntily. 'He had come all this way, after all, and wanted to be on the safe side. Any road, you'll have two lively scars to show to your grandchildren.'

'Croker was dead, I assume,' Cashel said.

'Yes. And, as the regiment had to move off, we were obliged to leave him lying there, alas.'

Abercorn explained. By the end of the afternoon the impetus of the battle had shifted to the British and the Allies – the Prussians were now pressing on Bonaparte's right flank and the French army was looking at a devastating defeat. All regiments – British, German, Dutch – were summoned to the line.

'So, the Ninety-ninth found itself in the final charge. We had a merry old time cutting down the fleeing Frenchies, oh, yes.' He pointed at his arm in its sling. 'One fellow was feigning dead. He jumped up, all of a sudden, and stabbed me in the shoulder with a bayonet. I took him down with my sword, swiftly – but the damage was done, hence the sling.'

'Bravo, sir.'

'However, later that evening, when Corporal Mill went to retrieve Croker's body, the local scavengers had been at him, unfortunately. He was stripped naked and all his teeth were knocked out and gone.'

'Why? For pity's sake.'

'For dentures. A full set of a young man's teeth, top and bottom, will fetch you thirty guineas in London.'

Cashel could imagine how this fate would have upset Croker.

'I see. So he was disfigured.'

'I'm afraid that was the case. Anyway, the battlefield was a general charnel house, wasn't it, Openshaw?'

'A bloody, hellish abattoir,' Openshaw confirmed. 'Thousands dead, lying in the field. Thousands, piled up like breastworks, here and there, five, eight deep. Extraordinary. Thousands of horses, as well, don't forget. Poor bloody horses – that shook me up, I don't mind telling you, Greville, seeing the horses – legs shot off, guts spilt out, still alive, still eating grass, can you believe it?' Openshaw looked serious for a moment and they were all quiet, thinking back.

'Anyway, we won, sir,' Cashel said, trying to change the mood.

'Oh, we certainly did, didn't we, Openshaw?'

'A great day. Marvellous day.'

'And what is the battle to be called, sir? The Battle of Nivelles?' Cashel asked.

'No. The Battle of "Waterloo", apparently. I must say I prefer Nivelles, don't you, Openshaw? The Battle of Nivelles . . . has more of a ring to it.'

4

'How're you feeling, my dear?' his mother asked him.

'Very well, in fact,' Cashel said. 'I might have a short walk in the garden later. Get some fresh air.'

'Take Buckley with you and use him as a support.'

Elspeth bent her head and kissed his brow.

'I'm so pleased you're back, my darling,' she whispered. 'I can't tell you how pleased I am.'

Cashel smiled and said nothing, though he thrilled to the endearment. A mother's requited love, he thought: the most intense of feelings.

He dressed and limped downstairs to find his brother Buckley, who was now more grown, a proper boy, but still a small and slight seven-year-old. He wasn't ill or unformed – he just hadn't grown in the way his twin brother, Hogan, had.

'Take me round the garden, Buck, old chap,' Cashel said.

He and Buckley made a few circular tours of the back lawn. Buckley prattled on about school – both he and Hogan were at the dean's Academy – and what some fellow had done with a dead mouse that had caused him to be leathered by the dean and then expelled. Cashel was half-listening, thinking about the summer house as they passed it in their circuits and the unexpected role it had played in his life. For some reason he still found it hard to consider Buckley and Hogan as his full brothers, even though they manifestly and genetically were, as if he still couldn't slough off his old identity. Still clinging to the old lie, he thought, of being the orphaned son of those chimaeras Moira and Findlay Greville. They were all Rosses now, he supposed, now he had come home and all was forgiven.

On their last turn, Hogan appeared, to announce that supper was ready. He was a taller, dark boy with a sly and knowing demeanour, Cashel thought. He tripped Buckley up for no reason and pushed him down as he tried to rise a couple of times until Cashel stopped him. A natural-born bully, he thought. Cashel gave him a clip about the ear and Hogan spat at him, the thick gob of spit landing on his coat front and hanging there like a viscid brooch. Cashel gave him a harder clip which made him yelp with pain. Buckley laughed heartily, mocking. The three Ross brothers at play, Cashel thought uncomfortably, as they trailed back inside for their supper.

He had spent months in the nunnery at Brussels. At one stage there were only five wounded men left from the battle at Waterloo, the others having died or recovered sufficiently to be reunited with their loved ones or their regiment. For some reason the wound at the back of Cashel's thigh refused to heal. It would scab over and then become inflamed and infected again. Pus would form and provoke a fever in him. The nuns thought some piece of foreign matter had entered the muscle with the penetration of the lance and was still there, causing the repeated inflammation. They cleaned and re-cleaned the wound and applied poultices – of various recipes – and the infection would retreat, before it returned again.

At one very serious juncture of the inflammation's recurrence, towards the end of 1815, a new surgeon had been summoned to give a diagnosis and, through his fever, Cashel heard talk of amputation as the only sure means of effecting a cure. He was conscious enough to utter an adamantine cry of 'No! Never!' and the surgeon, a Belgian, satisfied himself with cutting away more of the inflamed flesh around the wound where the lance had entered. His scar there was like a puckered rosette the size of a saucer.

As time passed, and with the application of more poultices, the infection left, seemingly for good, and Cashel began to regain his strength and walk tentatively about, albeit with a limp. The thigh muscles on his left leg had atrophied and for many weeks during his recovery he needed a crutch, and then a cane, to ensure his stability.

In the New Year he was shipped back to England with the last few men of the 99th's wounded and billeted in a room in an almshouse in Greenwich. Colonel Walcott's wife, Lady Gertrude, had founded and built this hospice at the beginning of the century as a charitable institution for the badly injured and crippled casualties of the 99th (Hampshire) Regiment of Foot. Cashel was granted a place there as the very last 99th man from Waterloo to leave Brussels, almost seven months after the battle itself.

The almshouses formed a simple courtyard around a lawn divided by paved paths. The invalids and severely wounded men – around sixty or so – lived in small single-roomed dwellings, one up, one down, around this quadrangle. There was a simple chapel for worship and a hall and kitchens for dining. Almost all the men there were amputees, some missing two or even three limbs, or else had other unsightly disfigurements – blindness, burned and shockingly scarred faces, missing jawbones and other terrible deformities caused by the ordnance of modern battlefields. The inmates wore a kind of olive-green dungaree with brass buttons and peaked foraging caps. Everything was free, paid for by Lady Gertrude's endowment: accommodation, clothing and three meals a day. There was an obligatory chapel service on a Sunday – morning prayers were voluntary.

Cashel, marked out only by his diminishing limp, was regarded by the other amputees as something of an imposter. His upstairs neighbour, a man called Hector Blow, had lost both legs and an eye in Portugal during the regiment's brief participation in the Peninsular War. What seemed to incense him most was that Cashel had a room on the ground floor yet he had been given the upstairs room and had to bump himself down the stairs, 'on his skinny arse', in order to reach his bath chair.

Cashel offered to swap but, once allocated a room, that was that, it seemed. He didn't care. Blow was an irritant but he,

Cashel, felt himself healing, daily growing physically stronger in the peace of the almshouse with its regular, copious meals. He was glad to be able to avail himself of this strange limbo in Greenwich as he pondered what direction his life would take next. He acknowledged that he had no real idea – but he was quite happy to let time crawl by, assuming some indication would make itself known to him in due course.

But Blow's antagonism was strengthened when Colonel Walcott came to the almshouse to present Cashel with his Waterloo Medal. This came with the award of a two-year pension of ten pence a day, as Cashel had now been officially deemed 'unfit for service'.

One morning, shortly after the little medal ceremony, Blow confronted him with three other amputee cronies, leaning on their crutches.

'You disgust me,' Blow said aggressively. 'There you are standing fair and square on your two pins. Look what we've all lost.'

The others held up their stumps or pointed to their peg-legs, muttering aggrieved concurrence.

'We were at battles too,' Blow went on. 'We paid a price for the regiment. So where's our fucking medal? Where's our two-year pension?'

'It's got nothing to do with me,' Cashel protested. 'I didn't ask for anything. I'm just glad to be alive. Go and complain to Colonel Walcott.'

Another man, named Bakewell, prodded at Cashel's left leg with his crutch.

'That isn't even a proper limp,' Bakewell said. 'Like you've got some little pebble in your shoe, God damn your eyes, fucking Waterloo man.'

'I didn't ask for anything,' Cashel repeated, growing angry himself. 'I didn't ask to be skewered by a French lancer. I didn't ask to see my best friend die in front of me.'

'Poor little you,' Blow mocked him. 'You've seen nothing, you milksop. Pass me your kerchief, Bakewell, I want to wipe the tears from my eye.'

It was the building animus against him from the amputees, and the realization that he was in fact the only four-limbed, undisfigured man in the almshouse, that made Cashel pick up his quill and write to his mother at the Glebe and ask if he might come home to finish his convalescence.

As he began to write he felt strong emotions grow inside him and he realized how much he had missed, and was continuing to miss, his mother. They had lived alone together as a couple for the first eight years of his life, after all, and the bond between them was powerful. More powerful, paradoxically, because he hadn't known she was his mother. During his months in the nunnery and then at the almshouse he had had all the time he needed to think about Elspeth Soutar – what she had done and what she meant to him. And as he formed the words on the page – 'Dearest Mother' – the thought came to him that it wasn't too late to re-establish that bond. He was still very young, despite his adventures; he was still her 'boy', her Cashel.

It turned out to be a long letter as he told her his circumstances, where he was and everything that had happened to him in the two years since he'd stolen away from the family. She wrote back immediately, full of heartfelt joy and warmth, and so, a week later, Cashel stepped carefully down from the London coach at the Roebuck Inn, wearing his faded and patched uniform, and saw his mother standing there weeping openly, with two nervous boys beside her – his young brothers, Hogan and Buckley. The family was finally reunited.

Mr Pelham Ross – Sir Guy Stillwell – was not present, however. He was actually away in India – Elspeth swore this was true – on a new business venture, trying to revive the Stillwell fortunes. In fact, Cashel was quite pleased by his absence. He had no idea how his next meeting with Sir Guy would progress, or, indeed, how he would feel face to face with him for the first time in the full knowledge that he was his natural father. Sir Guy would be gone a year or more at least, Elspeth said, and they had high hopes for his Indian venture.

Cashel grew stronger and he reacquainted himself with Oxford. Ben Smart was now an undergraduate at Jesus College. He and Cashel had corresponded intermittently over the two years of Cashel's regimental life so there was not much to add apart from his limited account of the Battle of Waterloo. Ben was studying Divinity with the objective of becoming a parson but, he confessed, he had something more worldly in mind – journalism. He had started a single-sheet weekly newsletter in Jesus College that he sold for a farthing. 'So cheap almost every-one bought it,' he said. 'But what does one farthing times a hundred, times ten, add up to? Nice little income, I'd say.'

'Very nice, indeed,' Cashel said, doing the sum.

They were walking down Ship Lane on the way to a tavern in Cornmarket called the Seven Goats.

'Makes me think,' Cashel said. 'Maybe the university is for me, after all. I was educated a bit but I could do with finishing off.'

'After what you've experienced? The life you've led?' Ben scoffed. 'It would be like going back to school. Worse. You wouldn't believe the rules and regulations in college. The hours we keep. Locked up at night. I'm not sure I'll last myself.'

'All very well for you to say, Parson Smart. But what's going to become of me?'

'You'll soon be seventeen years old, Ross. The world is out there waiting for you. Do what you will. You've got the head start on the rest of us.'

Cashel thought hard about what Ben had said. He was shav-ing himself with a new razor he'd bought, letting his side whiskers grow down to the level of his mouth, thinking that would make him look older. How he wished he had dark hair, he thought idly, like Hogan and Buckley, not muddy, fair hair, thick though it might be . . . The lather on his cheeks and chin looked like a white beard and made him imagine himself older – thirty, forty, married, a father with children of his own. But that exist-ence seemed remote, an impossible postulation. His time spent in the 99th and his experiences at Waterloo and afterwards seemed like a kind of dark chasm in his life. The person he had been in 1814 and the person he now was in 1816 seemed unrelated. Something – innocence? – had been lost and he wondered vaguely what might replace it. Still, he thought, he would procrastinate a while longer. Life at the Glebe was easy and he felt better each day, putting on weight, indulging himself, being spoilt by the ministrations of a mother who thought she had lost her son for ever.

Procrastination came to an end in the New Year of 1817, when, after dinner, Elspeth took him aside.

'Sir Guy is back from India,' she said. 'I had a letter today.'

'Back at Stillwell Court, I assume.'

'Yes,' she said. 'And he wants to see you. He wants you to go to Ireland.'

Cashel did not commit to going. The complicated double life of Sir Guy Stillwell was obviously continuing. Lady Evangeline had not died, despite every prognosis, and so the secret juggling of Sir Guy's two families had necessarily to be maintained. Cashel deliberated for a few days, resisting his mother's encouragement, but in the end capitulated, not so much because he wanted to see this man who was his natural father but because it was something to do – a catalyst. But what reaction would the catalyst provoke? he wondered.

It took him five days to travel from Oxford – first the coach to Bristol where he spent a night; then the overnight packet to Dublin, then the coach to Cork with another night en route. He loitered a day in Cork, booking a room in a cheap hotel, suddenly anxious about this encounter. He needed to gather his thoughts, to think of the demeanour he would present, how he would conduct himself with Sir Guy and Rosamond and Hester. His mother had underlined the severe importance of giving nothing away – not the merest hint – of their life at the Glebe. Cashel felt burdened by this multitude of pressures – of maintaining the pretence that he was still the orphaned nephew of Elspeth Soutar – and wondered if perhaps it had been a wise decision to come to Stillwell Court after all . . .

He took a car from Cork to Castlemountallen. He paid his sixpence and climbed up to the lateral bench that ran along the side and found himself between a priest and a fat woman. A thin drizzle was falling and he was glad of his beaver top hat. The car made its steady way north, the clip-clopping of the horse's hooves a kind of metronomic punctuation, marking out the yards and miles to Stillwell Court, stopping at towns and villages – Fermoy, Ballyhooly and Doneraile – where some travellers descended and other ones joined. The priest was talkative and smoked his pipe continuously, intrigued to discover that Cashel was a veteran of Waterloo. 'A great victory, glory be to God,' he said without much conviction. Cashel let him prattle on about his parish and its tiresome problems, glad to be distracted.

When he stepped off the car at Castlemountallen, memories began effortlessly to intrude. He retrieved his valise and, without thinking, knew exactly the road to take that would lead him to Stillwell Court and its demesne.

It was nearly dusk when he walked down the main, east, drive to the house. He realized it had been almost a full decade since he'd last seen it, yet its absolute familiarity pressed in on him disconcertingly. This place had been his home, constant and irrevocable it had seemed at the time, not somewhere that could be forgotten or easily eradicated by time passing. His infancy, his early childhood, had occurred here against this timeless background. As a toddler he had run about the parterre, chased by the girls; he and his mother had said their prayers and sung hymns in the servants' hall every Sunday for as long as he could remember. Stillwell Court was stitched into his very being, as was Glanmire Cottage. As the facade of the Court loomed larger before him he realized that this place was 'home' to him – if anyone really had a home in life, he thought.

He felt nervous as he beat the heavy door-knocker on its brass bolt. He was expected, he knew, but he still felt strangely unmanned, very unsure. He had no real idea of what was about to occur.

★

70

'Well, that seemed to pass off excellently well,' Sir Guy said, lowering his voice, as Rosamond and Hester left the dining room for the drawing room.

He passed Cashel a silver tray with a selection of cigars and cheroots and poured him a brimming glass of port.

'And I have to thank you, Cashel, for your superb dissimulation. I appreciate it. Only you and I know the amount of . . . of discretion required, here.'

'I do, sir,' Cashel said, taking the smallest cigar he could find. 'I don't want to do anything that might make things more difficult or untoward, even by mischance.'

'You did very well. The girls are delighted to see you – they don't suspect a thing, I can tell.'

Cashel lit his cigar from a candle. Sir Guy chose a longer, larger cigar and, before he lit it from a taper, there was the usual fussy preparation, clipping, piercing, thorough inspection of the glowing end – before the two of them were engulfed in heavy layers of grey smoke.

Cashel took a huge gulp of his port. Now that they were alone, his anxieties returned. His old friend inebriation had to come to his rescue.

'Let me talk frankly to you, man to man, Cashel. My particular problem,' Sir Guy said confidentially, 'is that my wife is not sufficiently insane. Would that she were fully deranged . . .' He paused. 'Paradoxically, life would be easier. However, her moments of lucidity give me pause, and give her – power.' He drew on his cigar. 'Be very careful if you chance to speak to her. She's not what she seems – don't be taken in. However, if my new Indian ventures prosper then that will give me some latitude – power of my own – and everything will be well. But I need to wait a year or two until I can be sure.'

Cashel wondered if he should ask about these 'Indian ventures' but he was more interested in another glass of port. He reached for the decanter.

Sir Guy went on – he was being very honest, Cashel noted – telling him that without Lady Evangeline's family and their considerable wealth the Stillwells would be bankrupt and Stillwell Court would have to be sold, 'No doubt to some upstart Corkonian merchant who would redesign it after his common fashion.' No, everything was precarious; maintaining the unsteady status quo occupied his every waking hour. How he wished to be back at the Glebe but he had to play a clever, holding game. Cashel would understand, he hoped.

Cashel did, and emptied his second glass. It was excellent port – no expense spared, there. He wasn't in fact that sympathetic, he registered. Sir Guy had made the difficult choices that dominated his life and he had to live with them, however complicated and fraught they were.

'Anyway, enough of my travails. What about you, Cashel, my boy? What's next for the Waterloo man?'

'What was it like at Waterloo?' Rosamond asked as they took a stroll through the park the next day.

Cashel could hardly respond, his headache was so violently present, pounding, throbbing. He and Sir Guy had emptied the entire decanter of port the night before.

'Well—' he began.

'To think,' Hester interrupted, 'that our Cash-cash-coo was a brave soldier in a famous battle.'

'I was a drummer-boy,' Cashel said. 'Not a general.'

'And you were gravely wounded,' Rosamond said. 'Poor old thing.'

'When you go to war you must expect—'

'Did you meet any winsome French maidens on your military manoeuvres?'

'No, I did not, Miss Hester, the minx.'

She punched his shoulder and stuck out her tongue at him. The three of them had quickly restored their childhood raillery. These young women, Rosamond twenty-five, Hester, twenty-three, were his half-sisters now, not frosty, distant chatelaines – little did they know.

'How is your aunt?' Rosamond asked. 'Dear Elspeth. How we miss her.'

'Very well. She asks to be fondly remembered to you both.'

'She made us what we are, Cashel. And that's no silly joke. We loved her dearly. Isn't that true, Hester?'

'Yes. Thank the Lord for Elspeth Soutar, I say.'

'She feels the same for you,' Cashel said, suddenly stupidly tearful. 'Shall we go riding?' he suggested spontaneously, keen to change the subject.

'Cashel Greville! You on a horse?'

'It has been known.'

It was upon a horse – a horse, walking – that Cashel sat, relatively secure, when Sir Guy asked him, two days later, what he was going to do next in his life. Sir Guy rode easily alongside him. They were progressing up the long avenue cut through the beech woods north of Stillwell Court. It was a day of clear weather and he could hear a turtle dove's murmured jubilation in the trees somewhere.

'To be honest, sir, I have no idea. I thought perhaps of the university – Oxford.'

'But what about travel? See the world, as I advised you.'

'That would be wonderful, but one needs funds.'

Sir Guy nodded. Clearly no funds were available to pay for a jaunt through Europe at the moment.

'You were a soldier. You're a decorated soldier. What about the army?'

'I'm on a two-year pension, sir. "Unfit for service". I can't rejoin the Ninety-ninth or any other line regiment.'

'True. Bit of a problem.' Sir Guy was thinking hard. 'But . . . Ah-ha! – there is another army that would welcome you.'

'What army?'

'The Honourable East India Company Army!' He slapped his thigh with a crack, so pleased he was by his idea. 'I made important contacts on my trip. Oh, yes, fellows falling over themselves

73

to do me favours. I can buy you a commission – not that expensive, you'd be surprised. You'll be an officer on a salary – and, more importantly, you'll see the Oriental world.' He smiled. 'That's the answer. I tell you, Cashel, India is a marvel, an Aladdin's cave. You'll never forget it.'

Glanmire Cottage was occupied by some new family. Smoke was coming from its chimney. Cashel decided that he didn't want to revisit it – maybe another day – and he plodded on along the lane heading for the Doolins'.

But the Doolin cabin was derelict, its turf roof half-fallen in and no pigs or livestock to be seen. He went further along the lane to ask what had happened to the family, and spoke to a toothless old man who was stacking peat by his front door.

'Yes, yes, the Doolins have gone. Two year ago.'

'Where did they go?'

'To America, like everybody else around here. Except their boy, the clever one – what's his name? He went to London.'

'Lorcan?'

'That's the one. He stole the family brain, that lad. The rest shipped out for the "Promised Land". Good luck to them.' He seemed to find this notion very amusing.

Cashel tramped back towards the Court. Somehow the Doolins' emigration suddenly made him recognize the attractiveness of Sir Guy's offer, its appositeness in his current situation. Yes, change was good. Real, dramatic change even better. The idea of being an officer in the Indian army took hold of him. Maybe this was the direction his life should follow after all.

He let the idea and its ramifications preoccupy him over the next few days. He went to a country ball and danced with Hester; he spent an afternoon shooting snipe on the estate that marched with Stillwell Court but found the noise of the shotguns disturbing, making him jump with every detonation; he went riding, uneasily, with Rosamond who laughed at his manifest lack of horsemanship; he enjoyed his dinners with the family, and the occasional guests – and all the time ideas were circling in his head: the army, travel, India, an escape, a future . . .

He was walking around the Court's sizeable rose garden, still pondering the possibilities, when he rounded a corner by a dense yew hedge and found himself confronting Lady Evangeline, supported by two nurses as she tottered along the brick pathways between the beds.

Cashel stepped back but she had seen him.

'Who's there?' she called in her high, croaking, bird-like voice. 'Let me see who you are.'

'It's me, Lady Stillwell. Cashel Greville.'

He stepped forward into full view. Lady Evangeline was dressed in a coat of some sort of stiff charcoal-coloured fabric and had her bonnet tied tightly beneath her chin. Her beady, rheumy eyes scrutinized Cashel in a way that made him doubt Rosamond and Hester's repeated diagnosis that their mother had lost her mind.

'Greville? You're the boy from Glanmire Cottage.'

'Yes, m'lady. That's me. Come to visit.'

'Yes, Cashel Greville. Yes . . . And what's become of your aunt?'

'She's very well. Living in England, now.'

'Good. Out of sight is out of mind.'

What did that mean? Cashel wondered. And, talking of 'mind', there seemed nothing wrong with the old lady's.

She made the nurses bring her closer to him and she peered in his face as if there were something to be read in his features. He tried not to flinch.

'You've turned into a handsome young fellow.'

'I'll happily take the compliment, ma'am.'

'I thought you a milksop. A stupid boy, when you lived here.'

'Maybe I was. You probably had every reason.'

'What're you doing here at the Court? Now?'

'Paying my respects, m'lady. I wanted to see Rosamond and Hester again. I was passing and—'

'Are you staying at the house?'

'I'm returning to England this very day,' Cashel lied, ducking her question. This interrogation was beginning to worry him.

'Good. Well, we have met again, Cashel Greville. I hope you thrive and prosper. I doubt there will be another encounter.'

'I hope there will be many more, Lady Stillwell,' he said vaguely but she had turned her back and nudged her nurses into motion and was now on her unsteady way, shuffling up the paths between the rose beds. He watched her progress for a while, then turned away himself and left the garden.

Strangely, that meeting made his mind up for him, though he couldn't really analyse why that should be the case. It was as if Lady Stillwell had sensed the huge secrets in the family, running like a poisonous undercurrent beneath the surface of their ordered, privileged, aristocratic life. Her daughters claimed she was already mad as a hatter but that conversation he had just engaged in had been both forensic and very sane, Cashel thought. And he thought further: maybe it would be an advantage to be far away from these secrets, to have a life alone, lived on his terms, and shed all these half-truths, lies and pretences that seemed to cluster around him whatever he did. Let me find my own way, he thought. Let me go to India.

In fact, it cost Sir Guy Stillwell £350 to buy Cashel a commission as a lieutenant in the Madras Presidency Army of the Honourable East India Company. (It would have cost at least twice that in a mid-level English army regiment, Cashel was aware.) Two months later, Cashel and Sir Guy stood in Sir Guy's tailors' rooms in London's Savile Row as Cashel was measured to confirm the fit of his various uniforms – dress, undress and service – required as a lieutenant in the 5th Madras (European) Light Infantry.

Cashel was looking at himself reflected in the full-length cheval-glass, wearing a gold-braided red hussar jacket with gold epaulettes, a black leather stock that showed beneath it the frill of his shirt front, and tight white breeches with slim Hessian black boots to the mid-shin. The tailor gently placed the stovepipe shako with the black ostrich-feather trim on Cashel's head.

'These are very fine uniforms,' Sir Guy observed drily. 'If a little flamboyant.'

'I feel that I'm about to go on stage in some ludicrous masque,' Cashel said.

Sir Guy laughed.

'But everyone else will look the same, Cashel. It's not old England – it's the Orient. Wait till you see it. You'll feel very at home in your finery.'

'Thank you, sir,' Cashel said sincerely. 'I've a feeling that perhaps this new chapter in my life might be the making of me.'

They spent Cashel's final night in England in Sir Guy's club, Brydges', just off St James's Street. The club was in a handsome house, newly built and paid for by the members. There was a great crowd gathered in the gaming room around the whist tables where vast sums of money were reputedly being wagered on the cards. Consequently, Cashel and Sir Guy had the drawing room pretty much to themselves. Some old fellow was snoozing in a corner. Another man was trying to read a newspaper by the light of an Arnal lamp.

Sir Guy had ordered two bottles of claret during their supper in the dining room – duck and green peas followed by apple dumpling – and was now calling for more brandy, telling the club servant to leave the decanter by their chairs. Sir Guy seemed mellowed and relaxed by the alcohol, reaching out to pat Cashel on the knee from time to time, as if to emphasize a point. Cashel, feeling chilly, went to stand with his back to the fire and, presently, Sir Guy joined him there. Cashel could tell he was close to drunkenness.

'I've never told your mother this,' Sir Guy said, swirling the brandy in his glass. 'But when I was first married to Lady Evangeline, we conceived a child – a boy. Who was duly born . . .' He paused. 'I had a son for two days and then he died.'

Cashel wasn't sure if any comment was required of him at this juncture, so he said nothing and sipped his brandy.

'Then the girls arrived, bless them, but my dead son – we called him Guy, also – haunted me.' He reached over and squeezed Cashel's upper arm, strongly.

'So when you were born . . . You can imagine how I felt.'

'I think I can,' Cashel said carefully. This information was gravid with implications.

'And perhaps you can imagine how I feel now. Standing here with you – my son.'

There were tears in his eyes – brandy-tears, Cashel knew – but what could he say in the face of this revelation?

'It's an honour, sir,' he mumbled. He felt confused: suddenly the pretence, the artifice of their relationship was briefly exposed in its strange rawness. Better late than never, Cashel supposed.

Sir Guy turned away to hide his emotion. He cleared his throat, as if resetting the timbre of his voice.

'I hope you know, Cashel, that I hold you in high regard. I mean, what you've achieved on your own – what you've survived, by God. Nothing in my life is equivalent to your experiences at Waterloo. Nothing. You're everything I could wish a son of mine to be – and, I swear to you, I will recognize you as my son, one day, when circumstances permit.'

Cashel stood in the doorway of his bungalow at Fort Blenheim, looking blankly at the dusty, beaten expanse of the huge parade ground in front of him as the setting sun gilded everything a fiery orange. He would have to stop writing his letter now. He sat down at the table on the veranda and read it through as a bugle sounded the Last Post and the flag of the Madras Presidency was lowered by a couple of sepoys. He took a drag on his cheroot and stubbed it out, half-smoked, before tossing the butt to the gardener, Malawo, who was watering the canna lilies by the front steps.

'Thank you, Lieutenant Ross, sir,' Malawo said and tucked the butt away in his loincloth for later. Cashel picked up his pen and began to reread his letter to Ben Smart.

Fort Blenheim
Ooty
Madras
India

3rd February 1818

My dear Ben,

　You'll be amused to hear that I rise at five o'clock – in the morning,
if you please – for the first parade of the day. Orders are read.
Companies report their numbers and then we bathe, dress and sit down
to a substantial breakfast, something in the Scotch style. Porridge, eggs
in various ways, bacon, rice and other vegetables. The rest of the
morning is taken up with lounging about, reading, some useful study,
perhaps. Most of my fellow officers seem to feel it's time for the first
siesta of the day. Indolence reigns until about eleven o'clock when we
might pay visits to friends – married friends, preferably, so we may
gain some sense of the fairer sex. We use our palanquins – or bandies,
as our little gigs are known – as it's too hot for riding or walking. Then
tiffin, as it's called – mainly fruits (very abundant here), some breads
and sweet cakes. Then, after another hour or so of repose, our grooms
bring our horses and we venture forth for rides or drives until sunset,
when we dress again and sit down to dinner at around seven o'clock.
Though, after tiffin, I always feel stuffed like a capon. Maybe a slice of
ham or some coast mutton (curried) and cheese from England. We
drink whatever is available – I bought a dozen bottles of Madeira for
forty shillings – perhaps enjoy a game of cards. I hear some regiments
encourage games of cricket – but not the 5th Madras (Europeans). By
ten o'clock most people are in bed. We live like nabobs – unless some
alarum calls us military types to be roused – this I've yet to experience,
I have to say. All the same, my £700 a year does not go far. It costs £50
per annum to maintain a horse out here and my syce receives ten pence
a day. Then there's the gardener and the girl who cleans our bungalow.
Luckily, I board with a fellow subaltern who is a rich man and who has
higher standards than I aim for and is happy for me to share them.
Anyway, you can rest assured that the empire is in safe hands and the
band of brothers that we are mucks along as well as we can manage.

I remain your affectionate friend,
Cashel Greville

Then he remembered to add the 'Ross'. He put his pen and ink and paper away and stood and stretched and marvelled at the sunset's blazing ostentation – orange, grey, streaks of pale blue, some shadings of crimson. How many sunsets had he seen at Ooty? he wondered idly. Two hundred? Must be more, he calculated. He had arrived in India in June 1817 and it was now February 1818. Good Lord, he thought: had he only been here eight months? It seemed like eight years.

The voyage from England had been a form of preparation – an apprenticeship – for the *ennui* that he now realized was to be the constant in his soldiering life in the Madras Presidency. It had taken twelve weeks to sail to the Cape where they rested a week on shore while their vessel was refitted and revictualled. Then another ten weeks to Bombay. Under six months was an unusually swift voyage, he had been told. It had been uneventful and calm, almost all the way, and the days on board blurred effortlessly into one another. He had enjoyed a chaste flirtation of sorts with a clever young woman, Miss Cicely Hynes, but neither took it seriously. It was a mutual pastime. She was going out to be married to the Resident of some distant Bengal province. He was going soldiering – or so he thought.

At least he was in Ooty, where it was always spring – verdant, hilly Ooty, the Switzerland of southern India, and the hill station where the Madras Presidency of the East India Company moved in summer to escape the enervating heat of the plains. And here in Fort Blenheim, a mile or so outside town on Westbury Road by the government brick fields, was the barracks and headquarters of the 5th Madras (European) Light Infantry. He supposed he should count his blessings but he was becoming overwhelmed by the torpor of barracks life. Thank God, he said to himself, for his friendship with Dr Rhys Freemantle. Without Dr Freemantle, he wondered if he could—

'Where's the damned gin, Ross?' came a shout from inside the bungalow. The question came from his fellow lieutenant and lodger, the Hon. Deveron Gilchrist-Baird. Cashel knew what he would be doing – looking at his face in a mirror.

'In a bucket of cold water in the pantry,' he called back.

Gilchrist-Baird was blue-eyed and blonde but his face had an odd pinched, deprived look that made him seem older than his twenty-two years. Some hellish misdemeanour had caused him to be cashiered from his Guards' regiment (Coldstream) – he refused to relate the nature of his sin – and he was serving out a temporary banishment here in Madras. In the fullness of time he would inherit a baronetcy, several fine properties and a sizeable income, so none of the other officers in the 5th Madras felt very sorry for him.

In fact, they were both semi-pariah figures in the regiment, Cashel had quickly realized – Deveron for his featherbedded wealth and aristocratic connections and Cashel because he was a Waterloo man. The renown of the appellation, and the medal, made the HEIC officers shifty and resentful. That Cashel had actually been present on the battlefield on 18 June 1815, and had been gravely wounded fighting for his country, and had been given a medal and a pension in recognition of this fact, marked him out in their eyes as a bona-fide warrior-hero, a type of personage that they manifestly weren't. They assumed, entirely wrongly, that Cashel looked at his fellow officers in the 5th Madras with disguised contempt – disguised, but contempt all the same.

This insecurity was related to the fact that the 5th Madras had not been on active service since 1803 (their last hostile engagement had been in the Second Anglo-Maratha War at the small battle of Asigarh Fort). Most of the subsequent military engagements in India had been undertaken by the Bengal and Bombay Presidencies. At first Cashel had taken pains to reassure his fellow officers that this was not the case, that he was proud and happy to be an officer in the 5th Madras (European) Light Infantry, but they didn't seem to believe his protestations. And now, after eight months of sloth, he didn't care – God rot the lot of them, he thought.

Cashel wandered inside. Deveron was pouring himself a gin

and wine, a concoction of his own devising, and contemplating his face in a looking-glass, pushing at his lips. Cashel accepted a glass of gin.

'Thought I might grow a 'tache,' Deveron said. 'What d'you think, Ross?'

'Excellent idea.'

'I do envy you your side whiskers, you hairy devil.'

'Grow whiskers, then.'

'I'm too fair. They'll look like bum fluff.'

'Then so will your moustache.'

'Ah. But I can dye my moustache.'

'Then you can dye your blonde whiskers.'

'True. True . . .'

Cashel drank his gin down, relishing the burn, and thinking he could easily go insane if these conversations persisted. He pulled on his jacket and buttoned it up.

'I'm off,' he said. 'Playing chess with the doctor if anyone should come seeking me.'

'What do you see in that dreadful bore?' Gilchrist-Baird asked. 'Not an amusing fellow, our doctor.'

'But a very good chess-player – that's the point.'

He strode across the parade ground towards the fort's gate, an ornamental structure set in its high earthwork boundary, acknowledging the salute of the sentries, two men from his own company – Melrose and Goodwin – and headed down Hadfield Road towards the lake where many of the married officers had their pretty homes in well-tended gardens with names like Woodside, Erin Cottage and Walpole Hall.

Dr Freemantle's house, Lakeview, where he lived with his wife, Letitia, and their two children, seemed a little island of normality in the eccentric world of the 5th Madras.

Freemantle won every game of chess they played together but Cashel didn't care – it was the mental exercise of the game that he relished, an antidote to his turgid life, and it ate up two hours of the evening. And he enjoyed the doctor's wry analysis of his colleagues, and his good advice. Freemantle was a neat, spry man with thinning hair and trimmed whiskers that were showing signs of grey. He was patient and unflustered as a person, though Cashel sometimes wondered if this was a carapace he'd erected to protect himself from the vicissitudes of barrack life. In his case, as he whispered to Cashel, it was the preponderance of venereal diseases amongst the troops – officers and other ranks – that made him despair. 'Sometimes I long for a cholera epidemic,' he once confided, 'if only to keep the men from their whores and concubines.'

He regularly begged Cashel not to succumb to temptation and he made a powerful case for abstinence, telling him, graphically, of the awful consequences of the pox and its noxious affiliates. 'Fascilis Decensus Averno' was a Latin motto he constantly repeated. Easy is the descent to hell. Cashel was affected by his seriousness. He could restrain himself – and there was always the tried and tested option whenever he felt frustrated.

Freemantle was standing in his front garden, picking dead flowers off a hibiscus shrub, and looking up as the first bats began to swoop and flutter around his head.

'Glad you could make it, Cashel,' he said – they were on first-name terms when they knew they wouldn't be overheard. 'I thought you'd be caught up in the general alarm.'

'What alarm?'

'Haven't you heard? The regiment's off to Ceylon. A request from the governor there. Needs more troops.'

'Ceylon? What's happening?'

'It's the Third Kandy War, man. You're going to put down a rebellion.'

They moved to the veranda where candles burned beside the chessboard.

'How come you know this and I don't?' Cashel asked.

Freemantle explained. An orderly (with the clap) from Colonel Mirrilees's staff had told him.

'There are no secrets when your breeches are down at your ankles and your penis is on fire,' Freemantle said evenly, as he set out the pieces on the board.

'Yes. I suppose not,' Cashel admitted, not wanting to dwell on the image.

'Two companies are being sent, apparently,' Freemantle added.

'Why only two?'

'Because half the regiment is out of action with the pox, the clap, herpes, syphilis, crabs, worms, pubic lice, you name it.'

Cashel wondered if his company, the left-flank company, would be selected. He hoped so but he put it out of his mind as they concentrated on the game for half an hour.

He was doing better than usual tonight, he thought, aware that he was making Freemantle think, forcing him to take time before he moved. Cashel pushed his knight forward to threaten Freemantle's remaining rook.

'Any idea when we might be leaving?' he asked.

'Imminently,' Freemantle said. 'Check.'

The next morning, Cashel, Gilchrist-Baird and Captain Poe – their company commander – were briefed by Major Prendergast and Colonel Mirrilees. Everything Dr Freemantle had prefigured the night before was confirmed. Two companies of the regiment were being combined into one makeshift large one of about a hundred and eighty men. Captain Poe would take command of this new company, assisted by Cashel and Gilchrist-Baird as his lieutenants. Major Prendergast would become brevet commanding officer in Ceylon as Colonel Mirrilees was not fit enough to travel. He would not specify the reason beyond saying, 'Trouble in the waterworks department.' He coughed, winced and then smiled weakly. 'All the glory will go to you fellows.'

Colonel Mirrilees outlined the situation in Ceylon, as far as he knew it. The Third Kandy War, like its two predecessors, was another attempt by the East India Company to subjugate and control the mountainous central provinces of Ceylon, whose capital was the city of Kandy. The British colonizers were well established in the maritime regions of the island but had found it difficult to usurp the two thousand years of Kandyan self-rule, however eccentric and autocratic that rule might be. A rebellion had broken out and a government official, a Mr Wilson, had been brutally slain and decapitated. British forces were attacked when they tried to enter the mountain kingdom. The Kandyans were arming themselves and blockading the few roads into the central provinces. It was time that they were punished, Mirrilees added, time they were made aware of who really held the reins of power in Ceylon.

Nothing moved fast in India, Cashel now knew. By the time the regiment marched to the coast, embarked on their transports and sailed to Trincomalee on the eastern side of Ceylon it was early April and, to their vague disappointment, they learned that the rebels' ardour for the fight was showing clear signs of lack of zeal.

Captain Poe was particularly furious. 'Why send us all this way if there's to be no fighting?' he demanded. 'Shocking waste of time.'

They made camp at Trincomalee and assessed the situation. This side of Ceylon reminded Cashel of Ooty and the Nilgiri Hills amongst which it nestled. Beyond the coastline, densely forested mountains rose up with very few roads and tracks into the interior. It was a difficult terrain for military operations, that much was instantly clear. Guerrilla-style rebels, as the new appellation went, even poorly armed, held the advantage. On their reconnaissance patrols Cashel saw that the thickly wooded hills and ravines were effectively impenetrable. Here and there were little villages of huts made from straw, bamboo and mud with a few paddy fields and bullocks grazing in thick-grassed meadows.

Captain Poe was a small, agitated, pugnacious man who had given his adult life to the Madras army. He barely bothered to conceal his disdain for Cashel and Gilchrist-Baird – two interlopers, as he described them to their faces, jumping the promotional queue with their purchased commissions. Poe was a man in his mid-forties yet still a mere captain. These 'boy' lieutenants reminded him forcibly of his own lack of progress and advancement. How could he ever arrive at Major Prendergast's level, let alone Mirrilees's? He had, it was rumoured, a native wife and several children in Ooty – though he was discreet and kept them well hidden.

But he was warlike keenness personified and at his urging, a week after they had established camp at Trincomalee, the company set off into the mountainous Kandyan provinces on its punitive mission. Nearly two hundred hot, sweaty European soldiers in their thick red jackets toiling along jungle paths, followed by their baggage train of Malay lascars. As they climbed higher into the mountain ranges the heat and humidity mercifully diminished, though they were reminded of their jeopardy when they were attacked on day three by invisible archers and two men died, both hit in the throat by multi-barbed arrows.

Everyone raced off the road to take shelter behind trees, the baggage train abandoned, the dead left behind. Cashel had his pistol in his hand though he could see nothing but vegetation. Occasionally there was a massive detonation and a hail of shot, as if from a small cannon, shredded leaves and brought down branches.

The men began to fire at random back into the trees. Poe shouted, 'Cease fire!' to no avail. There were a couple more explosions but the arrows diminished. The fire from the muskets, even un-aimed, Cashel thought, must have made the rebels aware of the size of the force. When all was silent, Cashel stepped carefully out into the roadway and went to examine the dead men. Both thoroughly dead, he saw. One with his hand around the arrow shaft stuck in his throat, as if he was on the point of pulling it out before the poison struck. Cashel blindly fired his pistol into the forest, in a gesture of anger and frustration. And it brought a few arrows in riposte, but the attackers were moving away – he could hear distant calling and shouting as they retreated.

Then suddenly he was knocked off his feet, as if he had been tripped up, kicked from behind. He fell, winded, then scrambled to his feet again. An arrow was buried in the heel of his boot. Sunk an inch deep into the leather layers. Cashel took his boot off and wrenched it out carefully. There was some kind of brown paste on the arrow head . . .

Poe came running up to see.

'Damn lucky, Ross,' he said. 'One inch higher and you'd be joining those poor sods.' He gestured at the dead men.

Cashel dropped the arrow and kicked it into the bushes by the side of the track.

'You're right,' he said, feeling a little shaky. 'Damn lucky.'

This setback stoked Poe's martial ire even more and he forced the column onwards towards their first targeted village, marching fourteen hours a day, deep into Matale province.

He sent Cashel and ten men into the village, even though it had clearly been abandoned. Cashel wandered through the narrow alleyways, past the round mud huts with their thatched roofs, and saw nothing apart from a few scrawny hens and feral cats. The livestock corrals were all empty. Cashel and his men emerged with the booty of one ancient *gingal*, a crude form of musket with a barrel of one inch in diameter, so heavy it had to be shot resting on a tripod. This was the type of gun that had fired on them during their ambush. The British soldiers called it a 'Grasshopper gun'; it was an extremely ineffective weapon, but for Captain Poe it was all the proof he needed.

'They've run away,' Cashel said. 'They knew we were coming.'

'But they left their weapons.'

'Weapon. I don't think it'll even fire. It's completely rusted.'

'I don't care. Set the village ablaze,' Poe ordered.

Cashel remonstrated in a conciliatory manner. What would be the point? What would we gain?

'That is my order, Lieutenant.'

Cashel conveyed Poe's instructions to his men and they duly commenced setting fire to the thatched roofs. The 5th Madras looked on as the village smouldered then erupted into flame. Thick smoke rose into the sky.

'They'll know exactly where we are, sir,' Cashel pointed out.

'And that's exactly what I want them to know,' Poe said, unperturbed. 'They'll know we're here, hard on their trail.'

They made camp by the village, now burned out, a charred ruin, embers glowing as night fell. They caught the few chickens and cooked them.

That night Cashel and Deveron Gilchrist-Baird discussed the day's events.

'I'd say don't disagree with him on anything,' Gilchrist-Baird said, licking his fingers free of chicken fat. 'That's my advice. Just do what he wants. He's an angry, small, disappointed man. The worst type. I know his sort.'

'I suppose so,' Cashel said. 'But when you're confronted with rank stupidity what're you meant to do?'

'Keep your mouth shut and look the other way. Best piece of advice I was ever given.'

They marched on another two days into the high forests. On the second day, Gilchrist-Baird said he felt unconscionably ill – he was certainly very pale and sweating copiously. He was sent back to Trincomalee on a palanquin carried by six lascars. Cashel proceeded onwards with Poe.

That night they camped in a forest clearing and picquets were posted. Cashel now had the tent to himself. His servant, a shrewd Scot called Ewan Dingwall, brought him his supper of salt beef and rice.

'What's going on, sir?' Dingwall asked. 'What's the plan?'

'The plan is to find the rebels and defeat them.'

'They sent another ten sick men back today.'

'We're still a formidable force, Dingwall.'

'We're certainly that, sir. I'd be scared rigid.'

Later that night, Poe sent for him and Cashel made his way to Poe's tent. Several candles were lit and Cashel saw a native man there, bare-chested in a long loincloth, glossy with sweat, trembling. The company's Vedda translator – a schoolteacher from Kandy called Dambulla – told them what this man was saying.

'There is a village, one day from here, with many guns and a chief.'

Cashel could see Poe stiffen with anticipation.

'A chief? Will this man guide us there?'

88

There was some conversation and then Dambulla said, 'This man will show you where the village is – but he wants to be paid first.'

'We'll pay him,' Poe said, 'if he comes with us and leads us to the village.'

This was agreed, as far as Cashel could tell, and Dambulla took the man away. Cashel turned to Poe.

'Looks very much like a trap to me, sir. Did you see the state that fellow was in? Shaking, trembling.'

'There's no trap that can catch me, Ross. This man, this turn-coat, will be with us, close to us. He doesn't want to die – which he surely will if he leads us into an ambush.'

'The company is down to one hundred and thirty men, sir. That's a third gone in a few days.'

'The weak third. The strong two thirds remain.' Poe gave one of his weird twisted smiles, as if he were trying out a new facial expression. 'That includes you and me, Ross. Gilchrist-Baird couldn't make the team selection.'

Two days later, at dawn, Cashel stood at the edge of a lush grassy meadow, hidden in the treeline, looking out at a sizeable village. Smoke from cooking fires rose into the air, donkeys brayed, cocks crowed. Another ordinary start to another ordinary day. The village was stirring, but the 5th Madras was on their doorstep.

Cashel had outlined a potential plan of how to attack and subdue the village and Poe, to his surprise, instantly approved it.

'You're the experienced man, Ross,' he said. 'I've never been in battle, never been under fire, apart from that little skirmish the other day. Can you believe it?'

For a moment Cashel felt a wave of sympathy for the small man. Then Poe began spontaneously to attack Gilchrist-Baird's character so viciously that Cashel felt bound to defend him.

'You're all the same,' Poe said disgustedly. 'You types stick together, no matter what.'

However, he still decided to follow Cashel's plan.

They had divided their forces. Cashel, with a hundred men, faced the village across the meadow in a classic skirmishing line. Poe and his thirty or so had skirted around the village and positioned themselves in the dense bamboo grove at the rear.

Cashel waved his men forward. They formed two lines six feet apart. The men in the front, kneeling, the men behind, standing, muskets raised, loaded, flint-hammers fully cocked, ready to fire. He waved them forward again and the standing men advanced through the line of kneeling men and knelt in their turn. The men now behind stood up.

The old drummer-boy in Cashel made him hear in his head the drumbeat instructions he would have given to trigger these manoeuvres. Once again, the standing men advanced through the kneeling men and knelt down. Cashel indicated that everybody should now be on their knees in the thick grass. They were fifty yards from the village. One hundred muskets were ready to fire.

Now they were waiting for Poe and his men to attack the village from behind. They were to charge in, screaming and shouting, create a ruckus and drive the armed rebels into the meadow where Cashel and his skirmishers would pick them off or capture them.

Cashel felt both excited and strangely calm. Maybe it was the cool peacefulness of the early morning that was keeping his heartbeat regular. He looked left and right and saw his men all ready, tense. They could fire two volleys of fifty shots each. After one rank had fired it would reload while the rank behind did the firing. They had plenty of cartridges. It took a trained soldier a minute to fire and reload a Brown Bess musket – he had done it himself hundreds of times – so every thirty seconds there would be a volley of fifty musket balls. Elite French cavalry at Waterloo couldn't withstand that. How would a few dozen Kandyan rebels fare?

Suddenly he heard Poe's men attacking at the rear of the village. Shots, screams, yells, commotion. Within seconds a large group of men and boys, thirty or so, armed with muskets and bows and arrows, ran out from the village. Cashel gave the order for his men to stand and level their muskets. Cashel fired his pistol into the air and the villagers stopped abruptly, as if obeying an order. Dambulla the interpreter screamed at them to drop their weapons and lie on the ground. They complied – only two men at the rear made a dash for the trees but they were brought down by sharpshooters on the right wing.

Cashel advanced carefully through the long grass towards the men. Poe had been vindicated, he supposed. A big village – that would no doubt be set on fire, later – thirty men and boys held as prisoners and a good haul of muskets. Perhaps there was a chieftain amongst them.

Cashel looked at the men lying on the ground. Small and slim, bare-chested with long cloth skirts gathered at the knee. Some of the boys looked as young as thirteen or fourteen. Cashel's soldiers began to collect the firearms and bows and arrows. Poe and his troop then emerged from the village leading away livestock – cows, oxen, goats – as from the houses came a strange sound of ululations and wailing: the women and girls left behind, Cashel assumed.

'What's the name of this village?' he asked Dambulla, who in turn asked a man and was told it was called Lewella. The Battle of Lewella Village, Cashel thought wryly. It must have lasted all of five minutes.

Poe left his train of captured animals and strode over to the prisoners. He was breathing heavily and Cashel saw that he was flushed and sweating. He looked at the Kandyan men lying quietly on the ground, their heads down.

'A good morning's work, Ross.'

'A conclusive victory, sir. Bravo.'

'Exactly. Now kill them all.'

Cashel paused.

'Kill who?'

'The prisoners – these men, here. Order your men to shoot them.'

He turned to Dambulla and told him to make the prisoners get to their feet. Dambulla did so and, slowly, the men stood up. A few raised their arms.

'They've surrendered, sir.'

'So what? They're savages. I want them dead, all of them.'

'Please think about what you're asking our men to do.'

'I have,' Poe said, staring at Cashel. 'We have to move on. How can we retain, transport, feed and ultimately imprison these villagers? Impossible.'

'Rope them up, tie them together. You'll only need a couple of guards. March them back to Trincomalee. Downhill all the way.'

'No. The Kandyans are systematically treacherous. They only understand one thing: power and power's retribution.'

'With respect, sir. Since when were you an expert on Kandyan mores?'

Poe stepped forward and put his sharp, seamed face close to Cashel's. He had to look up and that seemed to provoke him. He spoke in a low voice, with a slight tremble.

'I don't care about your fancy words – you Irish cunt. You have been given your order. Carry it out.'

Cashel sighed, deliberately loudly, and glanced around. Some of the soldiers of the 5th were standing close by, looking concerned. They had heard what Poe had said to him.

'I refuse,' Cashel said, raising his voice.

'You refuse to obey my order.'

'I do.'

'Hand me your sword.'

Cashel unsheathed his sword and handed it to Poe, hilt first. He wondered for a second if Poe was going to run him through but, no, instead he tried to break the sword across his knee, and failed. Cashel wondered what had inspired this histrionic gesture. Poe tried a couple more times with the same lack of success. The sword was good Sheffield steel and had cost twenty guineas.

'May I?' Cashel said and took the sword from Poe. He snapped it in two over his own knee, knowing that the trick was to make the break near the hilt, not in the middle of the blade. He dropped the two pieces on the flattened grass by Poe's feet.

'Consider yourself under arrest for court martial,' Poe said harshly, the muscles in his face alive with involuntary movement.

Cashel turned and walked away towards the treeline. As he did so he heard the first shots being fired and the screams and agonized pleadings of the villagers. He put his fingers in his ears as the firing continued. Not the Battle of Lewella Village, then; the Massacre of Lewella Village, instead.

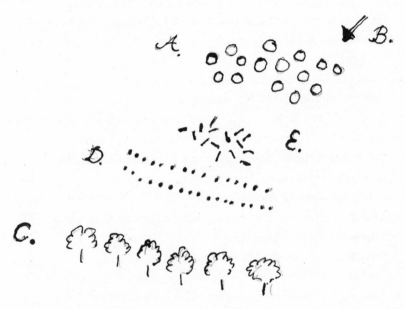

The Massacre of Lewella Village. A. Lewella village. B. Capt. Poe's company attacks. C. Treeline at the forest edge. D. Lt. Ross's skirmish line. E. Massacred villagers.

Colonel Mirrilees sighed, looking troubled.

'It's a bad business,' he said wearily. He looked a little jaundiced, Cashel thought. There was a glass of powdery white liquid on his desk that he took small sips from every minute or so.

'There's no avoiding the issue,' he said, almost exasperated. 'You did flagrantly disobey the order of a superior officer on the battlefield. In front of witnesses, moreover.'

'As any honourable man would, sir, I trust. We are not trained as soldiers to butcher people who have surrendered and laid down their arms.'

'These natives had attacked our column. Killed our men. Captain Poe felt it was too much of a risk.'

'That is arrant nonsense, sir. They were lying on the ground, terrified. We had gathered up their weapons. They were unarmed prisoners.'

Colonel Mirrilees heaved himself out of his chair and shuffled across his office to look out over the parade ground at Fort Blenheim, shaking his head and audibly tut-tutting.

'Poe is to be promoted to Major, to become my second in command now Major Prendergast has succumbed to the yellow fever, alas.'*

'Oh. I see,' Cashel said. This was not welcome news.

'You can understand the problem.'

'I don't, I'm afraid, sir. Captain Poe – Major Poe – is a callous murderer. He committed an atrocity outside that village. I refused to help him conceal that brutal reality. As simple as that.'

'It's not simple, Ross. It's damned complicated.'

'It's a question of morality, sir.'

Colonel Mirrilees smiled vaguely at him as if he didn't fully recognize the word.

'And there's the other factor,' he added.

'What other factor?'

'You're a Waterloo man, Ross. The only one in this regiment. We can hardly have you pilloried as a prisoner in the dock.'

Cashel said nothing. Waterloo again . . .

Colonel Mirrilees regained his desk, sat down carefully and took a sip of his cloudy liquid.

'Here's what I'm going to do, Ross. Dr Freemantle will write a certificate confirming that you are too ill to continue as an officer in this regiment and recommending that you be sent back to

---

* Over 90 per cent of the British casualties of the Third Kandyan War were caused by disease rather than enemy action.

England on indefinite leave. You'll be on half-pay for two years and then you may sell on or resign your commission.'

'Sir, I don't think that's the best—'

'Say nothing, Ross. This is not a discussion, it's a state of affairs. Think about it. The alternative is a court martial. You yourself candidly admit you refused to obey Poe's direct order on the field of battle. It's cut and dried, man. The Company will be very keen to avoid scandal, therefore, doubtless, everything will happen *in camera*. But God knows what your sentence would be.'

Cashel had to recognize the logic and sheer *force majeure* of this argument.

'Very well. I will book passage to England, sir.'

'Wise man, Ross. But don't waste any time. I suggest you quit Ooty before nightfall. Leave Major Poe to me.'

5

The Waterloo man was back at Waterloo. Cashel stood staring at the battered, blackened ruins of Chateau Hougoumont and its numerous outbuildings, then looked north to the ridge a mile or so away. He set off, trudging along a cart track between tall fields of rye – tall as a man – and ascended a gentle slope to the ridge line. Here the track diverged and he couldn't remember whether it was the one to his left or the one to his right that was the place where the French lancers had charged at him. Up here on the ridge there were no markers or handy trees to allow him to gain any sense of his bearings or trigger his memories.

'Greville! This way! This is where it happened, you slack fellow!'

He looked round to see John-Henry Croker pushing his way out of a rye field. He had the point of a French lance sticking out three feet from his chest—

Cashel woke up, abruptly, blinking, throat dry. He sat in the pulsing darkness on the edge of his bed for a moment, shaking his head to disperse the dream, and then reached below him for the pot, hauled up his nightshirt and pissed.

He wanted and needed light after that dream. He fumbled for his tinderbox and when he found it struck steel and flint to drop sparks on the dry charcloth, then blew gently on the glow. When there was a flare of flame he lit a taper from it and the candle on his bedside table, closing his box tightly to extinguish the charcloth flicker. He stood and pushed the pot back under the bed with his foot.

Now that he could see, he picked up his candle and walked carefully across the room to the table where the remains of his evening meal were still to be cleared away. He poured sour wine from a near-empty carafe into a glass and sat down. He drank, then ate a piece of pie crust and a couple of grapes and drank more wine, a bit shaken.

He knew why he was dreaming of Waterloo. Still troubled by the image in his head of poor, skewered Croker, he went to the window, opened it and pushed back the shutters to look out over the silvery Arno and the dark buildings of Pisa below him. He could see no moon but it was shining somewhere, obliquely, reflecting on the river that was high from floodwater, flowing swiftly. He looked at the glittering surge and flow and his mind began to settle.

His voyage back from India had taken almost six months. The ship – named the prosaic *Jane* – was full of packed tea chests and empty hogsheads of India Pale Ale being returned to the brewers in England, and the mixed aromas from this cargo seemed to fill every cabin and stateroom on board. There were few passengers, most of them returning soldiers with chronic ailments of some kind or other, victims of India's climate and disease: sunstroke, dysentery, cholera, yellow fever, dipsomania, breakdown and the rest. Cashel – the one healthy man apart from the crew – kept himself to himself as much as he politely could and wrote up a detailed account of his experiences in the Third Kandyan War, just in case he was ever called upon to defend his actions on the fateful day.*

The one person he came to know was a consumptive army chaplain called Cornelius Poynter, who was being 'sent home to die', as Poynter calmly analysed his situation. He was spectrally gaunt and seemed decades older than his thirty-eight years but he was a genial and learned companion and they spent many hours together on the *Jane*'s foredeck talking about India and books they had read and – with due caution – Cashel told him of his unusual family situation. Poynter would interrupt their conversation to cough into a large handkerchief and then studiously examine the expectoration with a frown, fold the handkerchief away and continue as if nothing had happened. Cashel tried to

* Much of this document has survived and was used as the basis for the events described in Chapter 4.

use the evidence of his illness to challenge Poynter's faith but Poynter responded with a stoical calm. None of us knows when or how we will be called to the Lord, he would reply evenly to Cashel's provocative atheistical sallies. They became good companions on the long voyage.

About five weeks out from Bombay, Poynter was observed by a member of the crew on the night dog-watch, two hours before dawn, staggering uncertainly as he moved across the decks. He was then seen to throw himself overboard. The alarm was raised, the *Jane* heaved-to, a cutter was launched, but no trace of his body was found and the voyage resumed. A note was found in Poynter's cabin, detailing his solemn decision to end his life (he had suffered a haemorrhage in the night and realized he would not see England). Cashel was strangely affected by this brave act – though, he wondered, had Poynter not voluntarily consigned himself to hell by his suicide? What would he have said to that? The other consequence was that Poynter had bequeathed him his trunkful of books. Cashel suddenly found himself the owner of a small, eclectic library of some sixty-seven volumes.

They were becalmed for three weeks in the Indian Ocean and Cashel began to read. The hours, days, weeks passed in a concentrated frenzy of study. He read his way through Shakespeare, Dante, Milton, Spenser. He read Spinoza, Ariosto and Montaigne. The *Jane* was close to running out of food and water by the time they arrived at the Cape and, while they provisioned, Cashel continued his impromptu education. As they reached the coast of Europe he felt he had spent the equivalent of three years at university, so varied and intense had been his reading programme of literature and philosophy. Then, on this second portion of the long journey home, half of a mizzen mast was broken away and lost during a violent storm in the Bay of Biscay and they put in to the port of Brest to make running repairs.

And it was while they waited at Brest that Cashel suddenly changed his mind about returning to England. He was not in disgrace, exactly, but the circumstances of his imminent and unexpected return would have to be explained – and he would rather not have to disclose them just yet. He thought of Sir Guy's puzzled consternation — perhaps even embarrassment. Everything to do with Cashel's Indian army career had gone wrong and he didn't feel this was the moment to analyse why or to start again. Travel – Sir Guy had always advocated it – see the world while you can. This was why he had gone to India, after all, so perhaps continuing his travels was an outcome to be desired . . .

There was a Dutch cargo vessel full of fresh-cut Brittany timber bound for Ostend and Cashel paid for a berth on it. He had his cabin trunks moved from the *Jane* and stowed on the *Vredewold* and the next day they made sail, Cashel's mood both eased and grew enthusiastic. He had his military passport and about £150 safe in his bank in London, a sum that that was being steadily though modestly replenished by his lieutenant's half-pay (four shillings a day) for the next year, at least; and he knew there was always the possibility of selling on his commission in the 5th Madras Foot for another £350 or so, when required. He could, if he lived thriftily and modestly, easily fund his peregrinations for two or even three years.

From Ostend all Europe lay before him and he had the idea that he might even attempt to write a book about his travels. This thought had come to him as he had, to his vague surprise, thoroughly enjoyed writing up his account of his Indian military life and his adventures in the Third Kandyan War. The words had come easily to him, he found, and he wrote with an unaccustomed fluency. Perhaps that was what he would become – a writer – and his first book would be *An Account of a Journey through Europe* by Cashel Greville Ross. He could see it in his mind's eye, the tight, neat leather-bound volume – a burnished scarlet, or sombre green – and he could imagine handing a copy to his mother and Sir Guy. A perfect vindication of his decision to set out on the road, incognito.

He wrote to his bank in London (Brookes & Co.) and asked for a letter of credit for £50 to be forwarded to the poste restante in Ostend. As soon as that arrived he could embark on his travels. He would arrange for other letters of credit to be despatched to the cities he planned to visit when required. He would travel by foot, also, he thought, at least for part of the time. Perhaps he might even buy a horse and, whenever he wanted to move faster, there were coaches to be had. Wherever he stopped, a simple inn would suffice, simple food also, expenses kept to a minimum. He felt an immense relief at this decision he'd taken and a growing excitement. He wasn't even twenty-one, yet he'd already lived to the full – who knew what awaited him down the road?

Once he was in funds – his letter of credit having arrived – he set about equipping himself. He bought two pairs of stout boots and leather gaiters, a greatcoat, a capacious shagreen satchel, a small double-barrelled flintlock pistol with a switch bayonet and a money belt to wear under his shirt. He reduced his possessions to essentials – shirts, breeches, stockings, jackets – that could be easily carried in a portmanteau with a strap that allowed him to sling it across his shoulders. He stored his two cabin trunks and Cornelius Poynter's library of books, along with his uniforms and Indian memorabilia, in an Ostend warehouse, paying for two years in advance. If and when he returned to England he could make sure it was via Ostend in order to reclaim his possessions. He regarded this measure as a guarantee of his intent. He would see a great deal in his two years of travelling – by the time he returned to Ostend he would surely have his book written. And the opening chapter of that book, he determined, would be entitled 'Waterloo Revisited'.

He took a coach from Ostend to Brussels and hired a horse for the day to carry him out to the battlefield. The road from Brussels to Waterloo was busy with gigs and barouches and omnibuses – 'touristes de guerre', an old man told him at the inn where he breakfasted on a couple of pork chops with greasy fried bread, washed down with a pot of porter. There were many souvenirs from the battle available for purchase, he was informed, and was shown a collection of suspiciously shiny swords and cuirasses, reputedly recovered days after the battle, and an assortment of plumed helmets – 'veritable Eenglish, monsieur' – that had never been worn by any member of an English regiment.

He left his horse at the inn and walked out into the country-side, feeling very strange. As he looked about him, it was as if no battle had ever taken place here in these placid fields of unfenced farmland. It was a cool sunny day in early autumn. The squares of corn and rye were close to being harvested, the trees still in full leaf. He walked along a lane from the hamlet of La Haye for a mile or so until he reached the chateau of Hougoumont, effect-ively the whole front line of the battlefield where the opposing armies had faced each other.

Only at Hougoumont were there signs of the severe fighting that had taken place and, of course, the eventual conflagration of the castle and its outbuildings. Cashel remembered his first sight-ing of the thick pillar of smoke that could be seen from the 99th's resting place, as they waited for their orders. He had read accounts of the long day's fighting at Hougoumont and he himself had seen the piles of bodies of the French soldiers stacked like timber at the foot of the chateau's walls. But what he had witnessed was only a moment in the day's conflict around the buildings. Now the chateau and its farm stood there, solid, battered, with black traces of soot on some roofless gables, but the roses had regrown and climbed the stonework and the pale grass was thick where the bodies of the French soldiers had lain.

On the way to Hougoumont he kept coming across ragged, barefoot boys who tried aggressively to sell him brass buttons and musket balls. He knew these tawdry artefacts were designed for gullible tourists and he waved the urchins away peremptorily. Now that he was at the chateau, he could position himself accu-rately and he headed off, northwards, up the slope of the ridge and eventually came to the field where the 99th had been ordered to wait. Of course, that day, five years before, the corn had been flattened like a carpet. Now bleached barley grew there, gently wind-combed.

He walked around until he found the lane where Croker had died and he had been wounded. He wandered up and down it, letting the memories congregate, scuffing at pebbles with his boots, wondering if he might find some trace of that shrill, terrifying moment – a shred of cloth, a nail from a hoof, a shattered remnant of canister shot. For a second, he thought he had come across one of Croker's teeth, bashed from his mouth by a scavenger's hammer, but, as he held it in his fingertips, he realized it was just a small piece of quartz, tooth-sized.

He tramped back to the inn feeling a strange nagging crepitation at the back of his left thigh, as if the scar of his wound was remembering its inception. In a ditch at the junction of the Brussels–Charleroi road he found a rusty belt buckle and a musket ball with a clear groove in it, as if it had been fired and had hit something unyielding. He put them in his pocket – proper souvenirs of the day he'd experienced, authenticity guaranteed.

Back in Brussels that evening he considered his journey through Europe begun and wrote up his account of his meanderings over the battlefield. He travelled to Amsterdam and then to Paris where he saw the year out and celebrated his twenty-first birthday. In the early spring of 1821 he set out for the south, heading down the Loire valley – often on foot, averaging twenty miles a day. He spent a month in Périgueux and then walked two days to Bergerac before taking an offer to sail on a *gabarre* down the Dordogne river to the confluence with the Gironde and Bordeaux. Summer found him in Grenoble and then in Geneva. Before the snows arrived, he traversed the Alps and wintered in Milan, renting a small top-floor apartment with a distant view of the Duomo. He diligently wrote the details down and his notebooks were regularly replenished.

He was not a gregarious traveller, he confessed to himself, but he had more than enough encounters with other people in the coaches he boarded and the inns and hotels he resided in to satisfy any craving for society he might have wished for. In Poitiers he kissed a young chambermaid, shy and nervous, a pale blonde wraith of a girl who promised to return secretly to his room later that night – and never did. He left for Limoges on the coach at dawn the next day. Between Périgueux and Bergerac, asleep at night in an oak wood, not far from the road, he was awakened by voices and the cracking of twigs under boots as people seemed to be gathering around him in the darkness. He fired his pistol into the air and scared the miscreants off.

In Geneva he sold on his commission in the 5th Madras Foot for 300 sovereigns to an Englishman who declared it would be the saving of his dissolute, wastrel son. Cashel deposited the gold coins in a Geneva bank and took a letter of credit with him on his journey south, suddenly feeling rich.

But despite his adventures and his encounters on the road, for the most part he kept his own company; and his thoughts, inevitably, ranged back over the life he had led so far. In Paris he had become friendly with a Russian libertarian called Dimitri Karlinsky, who rented the room below his and who constantly preached the doctrine that a person, and that person's nature and character, was formed entirely during the first ten years of his or her life. 'You are now what you were then,' Dimitri would intone, pointing a bony finger at him. 'There is no escape, I'm sorry.' Cashel disagreed, laughing at its inapplicability to himself, but the apothegm stayed with him and he found himself often questioning his own being and personality in the many hours he spent alone.

Who was he? What was he? What was the 'were' that constituted his present 'are'? He was the bastard son of an Anglo-Irish Protestant aristocrat and a Scottish governess. Almost his whole life had been posited on elaborate lies concocted by his father and his mother, conniving together to deceive him. Was his nature, this person that he now was, travelling freely through Europe, no more than a flimsy pretence, a scrim of convenient falsehoods woven to maintain a pretentious social norm? If that was the case, if that was what he 'was', how was he henceforth to reconstitute the current 'I am'?

These questions nagged at him during solitary moments on his travels. He decided that, given he'd been born in a nest of lies, then the fledgling that he was should only fly in an atmosphere of truth. The old edict of 'Be true to yourself' would be adulterated and replaced by 'Be true to the person you want to be from now on.' The 'you are' would overwhelm and supersede the 'you were', or so he instructed himself. Karlinsky's theory would be proved wrong.

Milan became his base from which, having explored the city, he ventured further – to Mantova and Verona, to the lakes around Como and as far north as Locarno. A trip to Venice was cancelled because of flooding. Venice could wait. He was happy in his high Milanese apartment with the view. His new solvency allowed him some modest luxuries. A frock coat, a pair of fine leather boots to the knee, some silk shirts, visits to barbers, to cafés, to the opera. He was living well, he told himself, like a gentleman of modest means.

While he was in Bordeaux, and also in Geneva, he wrote letters to his mother that made it seem he was still trapped in the unending boredom of cantonment life in India. Before leaving Ooty, he had made an arrangement with Dr Freemantle that he would send him these letters – and that Dr Freemantle, in turn, would then forward them on to Oxford, with the frankings, scribbled annotations and postmarks that these long trajectories accumulated. It could take anything from six to nine months for a letter from India to reach England, after all, if indeed it ever arrived. He made sure that his vicarious, inventive accounts were chatty and bland. There was nothing in these missives that would give rise to any suspicion that he was not still serving with the 5th Madras. He would admit to the subterfuge in the fullness of time, he told himself, knowing it would be more easily forgiven if he had a published book as mollification. As long as Sir Guy and Elspeth thought he was well and thriving in Ooty he could pursue his adventures in Europe with something of a clear conscience.

In the spring of 1822, Cashel found himself tiring of Milan and its environs so he moved first to Florence and then to Pisa. He thought that after a brief sojourn in Pisa he would perhaps travel south to Rome, Naples and Sicily; or, alternatively, westwards, to France and then Iberia – Spain and Portugal.

Florence was abnormally busy, he found, full of chattering, meandering visitors, mainly English, and many Americans also, and so, when he moved to Pisa, he found the city much more congenial. 'Dull, learned Pisa', as some disappointed wit had dubbed it, suited him perfectly. The city was stuck in its slow decline, centuries old, cut off from the sea and prosperity by the relentless silting-up of the marshes of the Arno's estuary. Its glory days may have been gone but, to Cashel's eyes, its shabby, fading beauty was unimpaired.

He took a small suite of rooms in a tavern called the Albergo Tinto on the southern bank of the Lung' Arno close by the Ponte Fortenza. His bedroom was separated from the dining–living area by double doors. He could order food from the *albergo*'s kitchens, his fire was laid each day and his bed linen was changed as requested. After he had explored Pisa and seen its celebrated sights – notably the Piazza del Duomo and the leaning bell tower ('To which every visitor promptly directs his steps') – he began to venture beyond the city's walls, strolling in the Pisan hills and sea-bathing at Il Gombo. He spent two days in Lucca and walked the ramparts by moonlight. From Lucca, he took a two-horse cab to Pistoia for the day.

Despite all this diversion he was beginning to have some doubts about the book he was writing. The vocabulary of sightseeing seemed to him to be limited and repetitive: the 'impressive cathedral', the 'fertile plains', the 'agreeable ancient town', the 'tolerable trattoria'. He was finding it hard to be original. In Pistoia, reputedly where pistols had been invented, he had a gunsmith overhaul his double-barrelled flintlock while he sauntered aimlessly around the streets. His brain was inert; he could think of no new way of describing the place. Pistoia would appear the same as every other ancient town he had visited on his travels.

Back in Pisa he wondered where to go next – where he might find some inspiration. His thoughts were turning to Spain and Portugal but he had not been to Rome and surely that was the *sine qua non* of any visit to Italy. He went to the English bank in Pisa, McKay & Hooker, and with his letter of credit drew out enough money to last him for a month. He thought idly of sailing from Genoa to Marseilles, to save time, then making his way along the coast to Barcelona and the Catalan towns and villages around it. The notion of travel, of new vistas and experiences, began to stir him again. Maybe all was not lost.

He was walking along the Via san Martino, returning to the Albergo Tinto, when he heard a woman's voice cry out in English, 'Stop, thief!' And around the corner careered a boy of about fourteen or fifteen, sprinting hard, with something clutched in his right hand.

Cashel instinctively stuck out a leg and the boy went flying, sprawling on the ground. Cashel knelt on his back and, with one hand, grabbed his hair and pushed his face into the paving and, with the other, prised a small beaded reticule from his grasp. He stood up and let the boy struggle shakily to his feet before booting him firmly in the arse and sending him crashing into the wall opposite. The boy yelped in pain, limped away up an alley and disappeared.

Cashel turned and saw two flustered ladies hurrying along to meet him.

'Got it!' he said and held out the bag.

'Thank you, sir! Bless you, sir, for your quick thinking!' the younger and neater of the two exclaimed. She had an open smiling face marred only by a long, slightly out-of-proportion nose. She took the bag from him gratefully.

'Are you all right, sir?' the other woman asked. 'Your reactions were astonishingly quick.' She was tall and a little on the heavy side, he saw, and she had one of those wide, stiff, inert faces, noticeably expressionless, displaying no sign of shock or excitement, despite being so recently robbed.

'I heard your shout – then the rascal appeared. He's the one who'll have a few bruises,' he said. This produced a smile in the tall young woman.

Cashel gave a little bow and introduced himself.

'I'm Cashel Ross,' he said.

'I'm Mrs Williams,' said the woman whose bag had been stolen. 'And this is my friend, Mrs Shelley.'

Cashel suggested that he walk them back to their residence in case the urchin should return with accomplices and they were very glad to accept his offer. And, as it turned out, where they lived was very close to the Albergo Tinto, at the eastern end of Pisa close to the city wall. They were renting two floors of a large plain palazzo called Tre Palazzi di Chiesa. Mrs Shelley and her family lived on the top floor; Mrs Williams and hers on the ground floor.

'Delighted to have been of service,' Cashel said. 'Here you are, safe and sound.'

'Are you from Ireland, sir?' Mrs Shelley asked. 'I can hear an Irish tone to your voice.'

'Yes. I was born and raised in Ireland, indeed. Well, raised there for a while. In County Cork. Now my family lives in Oxford.'

'Will you dine with us tonight, Mr Ross?' Mrs Williams asked. 'It seems the least we can do – to say thank you to our knight in shining armour.'

'Do please agree,' Mrs Shelley added.

No, Cashel thought, needing a quick and convincing excuse. Then he said, yes, it would be a pleasure. He could do with some company apart from his own, he realized, and it would be good to experience some society – English society – again.

Cashel had the chambermaid run a smoothing iron over his frock coat and replace a missing button on the fall-front of his tightest pantaloons. There was a patch on the knee but he would pass muster in candlelight. He combed his hair – it was growing long and soon he'd have to tie it back with a ribbon, he thought. He pulled up his collar and plumped out his stock. Yes, he would pass muster, though of course he was beginning to regret his quick acceptance of the invitation. Still, he rebuked himself, there would be plenty of time for solitude later, if he wanted it.

They were dining in the Shelley apartments on the top floor of the palazzo. Many candles burned and he could see as dusk fell that the view south through the wide windows carried as far as the sea. They ate a very good leg of mutton with brown potatoes – he might have been dining in England, Cashel thought.

Mr Shelley turned out to be a tall young man, almost as tall as Cashel, though emaciated and slightly stooped. His thick

dark-blonde hair was shot with grey and his face was very freck-
led and marred with many small lesions from sunburn. He had a
curiously reedy, contralto voice and, when he smiled, displayed
as crooked a set of teeth as Cashel had seen in a youngish man.

Very quickly it was made clear, by some politely pointed
remarks made by Mrs Shelley, that her husband was a literary
man, a poet of some renown.

Cashel begged forgiveness for his ignorance.

'I've been away in India,' he explained. 'In the army, these last
few years. I don't even know who the King of England is.'

'George the fourth, if you wish to know, Mr Ross. God bless
his obese majesty,' Mrs Shelley said to general laughter.

Cashel, of course, did know that George IV was now the new
King of England, but smiled politely. He suspected that the Shelleys and the Williamses took him for something of a simpleton,
not a scholar.

'The Indian army?' Mr Williams interjected. He was a handsome, open-featured, smiling man – maybe as much of a simpleton
as me, Cashel thought, before going on to explain that he had been
a lieutenant in the Madras army. The 5th Madras (European) Light
Infantry, he elaborated at Williams's prompting.

'And I was in the Eighth Light Dragoons of the Bengal army!'
Williams exclaimed.

After that, everything changed. It was as if he had presented
some form of passport to the company. Williams was an Indian
army man, and so was Ross, and by definition that made him a
good fellow. Cashel was quizzed, with genuine curiosity, about
his life abroad and his military experience. And then came the
great revelation – Waterloo. Even Mr Shelley stared at him
respectfully with his big restless eyes, as if he couldn't believe he
had a Waterloo veteran sitting a few feet away at his very table.

'Albé has to meet Mr Ross. Has to,' he said, his voice cracking
with emphasis. 'Without question. But we must surprise him. I
need to see his face when he learns you were at Waterloo, Mr Ross.'

There was overwhelming mirthful concurrence at this
suggestion.

'And who is this Albé, pray?' Cashel asked.

'Do excuse us,' Mrs Shelley said. 'It's our nickname for Lord Byron. L.B. Hence Albé.'

'Lord Byron is in Pisa?' Cashel said, astonished. He had heard of Lord Byron – who hadn't? He had even read *Childe Harold's Pilgrimage*, one of the books in Poynter's bequest.

Shelley pointed to a window in the north wall that looked over the Arno.

'About one hundred yards away, on the other side of the river,' he said. 'The Palazzo Lanfranchi.'

'Good grief,' Cashel said. 'Byron in Pisa. Who'd have thought?'

'We dine with him every Wednesday,' Shelley went on, suddenly animated. 'Do say you'll join us, Mr Ross. I guarantee you'll not be disappointed.'

Albergo Tinto
Pisa

21ˢᵗ March 1822

My dear Ben, *

  Last night I dined with Lord Byron, no less, here in Pisa. I told you in my last missive how by chance I fell in with the Shelley/Williams families. They, of course, know Lord B who has moved to a grand palazzo across the Arno from my taverna and hosts a dinner for the Shelleys and company every Wednesday night. It's a ten-minute stroll thither. So off we went – Mr & Mrs Williams, Mr & Mrs Shelley and yours truly. As we approached Lord B's palazzo, Shelley took me by the arm and drew me aside and told me that Lord B was very particular about rank and how he was to be addressed. It was always 'Lord' Byron – no simple 'Byron' would be tolerated – and he preferred 'My lord' and 'Your lordship' etc. to 'Sir'. Fine, says I, 'Lord Byron' it shall be.

  The palazzo is all white marble with its wide steps and a jetty to the river. Inside it is filled with animals walking free – birds, cats, dogs,

---

* There is an existing draft of this letter to Benjamin Smart. Cashel wanted it preserved, clearly.

apes – even peacocks. We made our way up to the piano nobile where
LB greeted us. He is quite short and, not to put too fine a point on it,
very plump. His face is plump, his hands are plump, his fingers are
plump. Hair receding, also. He introduced us to his mistress, Contessa
Guiccioli, very young, 18–20, I'd say, who matches her paramour in
plumpness but, however, is very beautiful with it, speaking hardly a
word of English but, looking at her very ample figure, let's say its
noticeable prominences, it is not her anglophony that explains her
attraction to LB, I would venture.

Anyway, we were plied with as much claret (good) as we could
consume and sweetmeats (indifferent) and then led into the dining
room. We ate well – three types of fowl – and the conversation ranged
widely. Shelley and LB talking mainly of literature whereas Williams
and I reminisced further about our army lives in India. He is the most
agreeable man and his simple, good spirit casts an unflattering light on
the complexities of Shelley's nature and the vanities of Albé's (as the
party call him behind his back).

Then when Shelley told Byron that I had been at Waterloo, and had
even been wounded on the battlefield, his Lordship was suddenly all
interest and summoned me to move my chair and sit beside him so we
could converse without interruption. He wanted to know all about
Waterloo (he had visited the battlefield in 1816, it turned out) and my
campaigning in the Kandy war.

What more can I tell you about him? He has a leaning-forward,
hurried, curious walk that Shelley told me was an attempt to
disguise a deformity to his left foot and the limp that this produces.
Beneath the plumpness he is handsome enough, I suppose, and there
is a certain sneering dissoluteness to his physiognomy. He is very
clever and cutting and very rich, Shelley says, with an income of
£4,000 per annum, not counting his book sales. Shelley confessed that
he makes do on a humble £1,000 a year, poor fellow. We talked at
length about soldiering and firing muskets and skirmishing and what
precisely it was like to be wounded by a lance. He almost seemed
jealous of my experiences and my wound. He has invited me to his
target-shooting party outside the city walls next week – of which
more later, when it occurs. He was relaxed and intimate with me at

this juncture (we had both consumed a lot of wine) then matters turned a little sour.

ME: Do you have Scottish blood, Lord Byron?

LB: Not a drop. Why do you ask?

ME: I can hear a Scottish lilt in your voice from time to time – a hint of a brogue.

LB: That's impossible. How could I have a Scottish accent? Absurd!

ME: Ah-ha. You mock me, Lord Byron! I know I have an Irish accent. We Celts can sniff each other out.

LB: You are quite mistaken, Ross. I assure you I am as English as Melbury pie.

Then off he abruptly went in search of his pulchritudinous mistress and I was left alone, conscious I had made some vast social blunder. I told Shelley what had transpired and he winced. It's true, Shelley said. Byron was born above a shop in Aberdeen. When he inherited his title and came to England to school he was roundly mocked for his Scottish accent and he's striven to eradicate all traces of it ever since. Shelley admitted that he had noticed the brogue, also, particularly late in the evening when the wine took effect.

So, dear Ben, there was my innocent <u>faux pas</u>. Will LB ever speak to me again? We wandered homeward in merry mood and I related my outcasting to Mrs Shelley who laughed loudly at my misprision. 'Serves him right,' she said forcefully. 'Albé may be the most famous poet in England but he is also the most sensitive to social distinctions. He can talk for hours about dukes and earls and lords and baronets and their various degrees of importance.' I begin to warm to Mrs Shelley, despite her somewhat stern and coldly observant manner. I was astonished to discover she is barely older than I am – only twenty-four years old. I thought she was the same age as Shelley – who is in his thirtieth year, I now know. When Mary Shelley's face is animated and she laughs you can see her youth – and her beauty – but in repose her face almost miraculously ages. By the way, it is apparent that all is not harmonious in the Shelley marriage.

Now you know, Ben, how my life is in society in Pisa. Shelley and Williams have invited me to go sailing with them in their little skiff on

the Arno and the canals of the Marezza and this very morning a note
came from LB reminding me of our shooting party. Clearly I have not
been cast beyond the pale. I will write anon when I have more
adventures to relate.

   I remain yr. affectionate friend,
   Cashel Ross

Cashel, Shelley and Williams met at the entrance of Byron's palazzo. There were two other men present, a Signor Gamba, the brother of Byron's mistress, and a so-called Count Taaffe. Horses were provided and they all rode off southwards – followed by servants on mules – through the Porto Fiorentina and into the countryside beyond the city. Cashel noticed that Byron had two pistols in his belt and another two holstered by the pommel of his saddle. Eventually they arrived at a farm about an hour's ride from Pisa where Byron was clearly known. Money was handed over and they made their way to a makeshift firing range in a meadow by a field of young maize. They fired their pistols at a selection of targets – bottles and stones and half-crown pieces hammered into staves of wood.

Byron was a good shot, Cashel saw, and there was a clear competition in marksmanship between him and Shelley. The servants laid out food and drink on blankets on the ground. When his turn came Cashel loosed off a few balls at the positioned bottles but he found the reports of the pistols and the rank smell of gunpowder an unfortunate trigger for his memories – he knew he would be back dreaming of the battle that night.

He stood with Shelley watching Byron and Taaffe load their pistols and wager who would hit the half-crown.

'Why does Lord Byron shoot at targets? He could shoot at game – ducks and geese, and the like,' Cashel asked.

'Byron wants to go to war,' Shelley said. 'He wants to be a warrior, a hero – more than anything. These excursions are a form of preparation for when that day comes. But at the moment he's a warrior without an enemy which, between you and me, Ross, makes his company a little tiresome, sometimes.'

'What about you, Shelley? Do you want to go to war?'

'I have no desire to aim at, shoot at, hit, wound or kill a fellow human being,' he said. 'But Albé must be . . .' He paused. 'Accommodated.' He lowered his voice. 'We've plans to start a journal together and we need his investment.' He smiled wearily. 'So we go to dine. We come out here and shoot at empty bottles.'

Shelley was more relaxed on the water in his little canvas skiff with its lug-sail. Cashel registered the improvement in his mood when he went out sailing with him and Williams some days later, coasting down the Arno to the wide bay and lunching at the Bagni di Pisa. For all his enthusiasm Shelley was an angular and awkward presence in the little boat and Williams, an expert sailor, often had to order him to sit down and stop moving around, as they were shipping water and there was a risk of capsizing.

When they stopped for lunch Cashel asked Shelley about London publishers – explaining about his travel journal – and Shelley warned him to be very selective. He talked about his current dissatisfactions with his own publisher, one Charles Ollier. 'Both inefficient and a thief,' he said harshly, adding that in London publishers were ten-a-penny. The key ambition was to achieve as large an advance as possible because, once the book was published and sold, he would hear nothing but lies. Don't accept a share-of-profits contract, he advised; it was little more than a licence to steal. Mrs Shelley could give him a few hints, he said. She was asking for an advance of £500 for her next novel.

Cashel returned with Shelley and Williams to the Tre Palazzi for supper and there he found a new guest, a young woman, introduced as a Miss Clairmont – Mary Shelley's stepsister, apparently – come to visit from Florence where she was living. She was small and dark, with a hairstyle of tight curls ringed around her pale face. She wasn't as beautiful as her stepsister but she had an energy and vivacity about her that Mary Shelley lacked. Cashel was aware of her taking him in and then saying, 'To meet a man actually taller than Shelley – remarkable!'

Cashel smiled at the compliment.

'Are you a swimmer, Mr Ross?' she asked.

'I am, indeed. I learned to swim as a child in Ireland on the Blackwater river, in County Cork. I love swimming.'

'So do I, now I've learned. I learned to swim this last year, at Leghorn.'

She went on to explain how at Leghorn the city council had built wooden baths out in the bay, constructing a jetty leading to screened, separate bathing areas for men and women. She had been taught to swim there but now she preferred the sea itself.

'Shelley can barely swim. Mary refuses. Mr Williams is a swimmer like you, Mrs Williams not. Lord Byron, of course, is a great swimmer. A legendary one.'

'Perhaps this could be a new division for the human race,' Cashel said. 'We are either swimmers or non-swimmers.'

Then Shelley appeared and she turned all her focus upon him, almost ignoring Cashel, hogging Shelley's attention ardently, talking endlessly about some translation of Goethe's *Faust* that she was undertaking.

Mary Shelley left the room to attend to their little son, Percy Florence, who had a fever and was calling plaintively for her. Cashel decided it was an opportune moment for him to leave and bade goodnight to Miss Clairmont who, now that he was departing, seemed suddenly friendlier.

'I hope we haven't driven you away with all our talk of Goethe,' she said. 'Pray excuse me, Mr Ross. My enthusiasms are my social undoing, time and again.' She laid a hand briefly upon his arm by way of apology and smiled warmly at him. Cashel assured her she had by no means driven him away. He had to leave as he was planning a trip to Genoa and from there to Nice – more chapters for his book of travels – and he had to depart very early in the morning.

'But you will return, I hope,' she said. 'We must become friends.'

'I'll be back before the end of the month, I'm sure,' Cashel said, and meant it. There was something about this Miss Clairmont, this Claire Clairmont, that was strangely alluring, now that she had noticed him again and her brown eyes were fixed on him.

Shelley descended the stairs with Cashel and walked out onto the street with him; they paused for a moment, looking at the silvery Arno as it flowed silently by.

'We're searching for a house – a house by the sea for the summer,' Shelley said. 'And Williams and I are having a boat built at Genoa, a proper boat, big enough to sail across the Mediterranean to Africa, if we feel like it. You must join us, Ross.'

'I'm something of a landlubber, to be honest,' Cashel said. 'And I'd better be on my way if this book of mine is ever going to be written.'

'Linger here through the summer,' Shelley urged. 'It can be very congenial. And, I assure you, it'll be better away from Pisa and a certain noble person's presence, if you catch my drift.'

Cashel did; he said the point was well made and promised he'd be back.

In fact, Cashel was away for more than three weeks on his journey to Genoa, which he enjoyed, and Nice, which he didn't enjoy as much. Nice, now back in the Kingdom of Piedmont after a couple of decades of being French, seemed unsettled as a result of its national changes of identity, if such a thing could be said of a place, he thought. Perhaps it was because the city itself was also visibly changing: it was becoming prosperous as a winter resort for wealthy aristocrats, and that too seemed conflicting. The smart buildings on the seafront – the new hustle and bustle – were at odds with the sleepy old town around the port. Still, it gave him material for another chapter and he was pleased with what he had written, for once. He began to realize that perhaps travel books were only interesting when things went wrong or were arduous, or when expectations weren't lived up to. Trouble-free voyaging was dull. And it was dull being on his own again, he noted. His brief exposure to society in Pisa had been invigorating and now that he was a solitary traveller once more he found his thoughts turning homeward: wondering how his mother was, what Hogan and Buckley were up to. And how Elspeth would love to hear of his encounters with Lord Byron!

Cashel was back in Pisa towards the end of April and disappointed to find that the Shelleys and the Williamses were gone from Tre Palazzi. He didn't bother to inform Lord Byron of his presence in the city. He resumed his solitary, anonymous life with real pleasure and spent his time reworking the chapters of his book in the light of the new revelation he'd experienced in Nice. Sourness was all. Everything seemed much more interesting when seen through jaundiced eyes.

Then a scrawled hand-delivered letter came from Shelley to the Albergo Tinto.

Lerici

28th April 1822

My dear Ross –

In haste. May I ask of you an important, personal favour? In my study in Tre Palazzi hidden beneath the cushion of the chair at the desk you will find a pigskin attaché case. I would be for ever in your debt if you could retrieve it and bring it to me at Casa Magni, San Terenzo (next to Lerici). Please do not tell anyone of this service you are doing for me.

Sincerely yours,
PBS

Cashel duly went to Tre Palazzi and the concierge took him upstairs to Shelley's apartments on the top floor. He found the pigskin attaché case exactly where indicated and took it back to the Albergo Tinto where, of course, he thoroughly examined its contents.

They were intimate letters from a woman who signed herself 'C' and were addressed to a 'Mr Joseph Jones' at the poste restante, Pisa. It took no real sleuthing to determine that these were letters between Miss Claire Clairmont and Shelley. They referred to secret nights spent in Leghorn together and were generally long expressions of intense feelings, of ardour, of rapture, of frustration, of impossible dreams of escape to new lives – the stuff of all love letters between clandestine lovers throughout history, Cashel supposed. However, having opted to do the favour for Shelley he now had to carry it out. He could see how devastating it would be if these letters were read by Mary, given the unhappy state of their marriage, even if there was nothing specific in them about any lovemaking that had taken place during these Leghorn visits – though it was the clear inference. One's naivety would have to be adamantine to choose to believe that these two adults had not physically consummated their evident obsession with each other, Cashel realized.

He hired a Tilbury gig and drove it the several miles to Lerici, taking the best part of a day – the road was bad – to reach the little port on the gulf of La Spezia. When he finally arrived, the Shelleys and the Williamses seemed genuinely delighted to see him. They were living in a large isolated boathouse called Casa Magni right on the rocky seashore. To one side on a headland was the small village of San Terenzo with its ruined castle and the cupola of its church, visible above the pine trees and scrub that lined the low cliffs which rose up behind the house. Across the bay from Casa Magni was Lerici with its more splendid castle and its secure harbour.

The house was spacious and the two families – with their three tiny children – lived on the upper floor above the five arched bays that fronted the sea where the boats had once been stored. The servants' quarters were at the rear. The main attraction of Casa Magni was the large wide terrace that gave off the living rooms, with an unimprovable view of the bay and the rocky islands and the sea beyond. It was a noisy, hugger-mugger ménage, Cashel saw, and he was given a windowless room the size of a pantry next to the kitchen. He had arrived at sunset and had no choice but to spend the night there.

Shelley took him aside after their supper and, in his mean room, Cashel discreetly handed him the attaché case, taking it from his travelling bag. Shelley removed the letters, glanced at them and then briskly tore them into small pieces. He handed them back to Cashel.

'Would you be so good as to dispose of these for me, please, Ross? Burn them, bury them.' He seemed in a strange mood, troubled and agitated.

'Of course,' Cashel said, thrusting the scraps into a pocket. 'But, if you can tell me why – I'd like to know the reason.'

Shelley rubbed his eyes, as if the light from the solitary candle was making them ache.

'Have you met Miss Clairmont?' he asked. 'My sister-in-law?'

Cashel politely replied that he had – in Pisa, in Shelley's own apartments, in fact – and recalled the encounter for him that Shelley now seemed to remember, when prompted. Then Shelley told him that, some several years ago, when Claire was very young, only sixteen, she had had a 'liaison' with Lord Byron, as a result of which a child had been born, a daughter called Allegra. The child duly became the ward of Lord Byron and he had placed her in a convent not far from Pisa. But Byron had banned Claire from visiting her daughter.

'And now,' Shelley said abjectly, 'little Allegra has died. Two weeks ago. From typhus. She was five years old.'

Shelley's face hardened and Cashel now understood his strange behaviour. Claire, Shelley went on, was not surprisingly undergoing a tumultuous emotional crisis, in a state that vacillated between raging fury and abject misery.

'Claire and I,' he confessed, 'are unusually close. We have always written to each other, constantly. Those letters you brought me were from her. They contain . . .' He paused. 'Candid expressions of her feelings for me.' He paused again. 'That might easily be misinterpreted. My wife, Mrs Shelley, is with child. We've lost two children already in our short marriage, poor little William and Clara. I can't risk anything upsetting her, d'you see. If she ever read these—'

'Please, Shelley. Tell me nothing more,' Cashel interrupted diplomatically. 'I'm happy to have played my little part – especially if it eases stress and strain.'

Shelley took his hand and shook it warmly. For a moment Cashel thought he might embrace him.

'You're a true friend, Ross. By God, I wish I had a few more friends like you.'

After one night in Casa Magni, Cashel decided he had to move out. He had never known more sleepless, wailing and demanding babies. And, as if in adult counterpoint, the Shelleys had a domestic staff that seemed to have been recruited from disputatious mountebanks, arguing or shrieking loudly into the night, banging pots and pans to emphasize a point – or to inflict bodily harm, for all he knew – from their quarters just beyond the kitchen.

He made an excuse to move to Lerici where he took rooms in a taverna. He could hire a boat and row from the harbour to Casa Magni in half an hour or walk around to the house via a coastal path – though that took longer – whenever he felt like visiting. The bay was calm, the early summer weather ideal and the new Shelley boat was imminent. Better to be on the coast in Lerici than in broiling Pisa, Cashel thought. And he was told that Miss Clairmont was expected back in early June . . .

As it turned out, Cashel deliberately didn't go to Casa Magni every day, even though he was invited. The atmosphere in the house was uncertain – sometimes full of good cheer, sometimes full of nervy, agitated undercurrents. When he did row across the bay, he would appear unannounced – giving a warning 'Hulloo!' to alert the residents. He only spent as much time with the Shelleys and the Williamses as he wanted.

In fact, it turned out to be an ideal plan. The irregular visits suited him and the Casa Magni couples were always pleased to see him. He began to enjoy the stimulating company that the Shelleys provided – the Williamses were simply genial and welcoming. He realized that regular, undemanding human contact was something he had missed in his wanderings. The little children – when they weren't fractious or crying – were charming and beguiling. Percy Florence was not yet three; Medwin Williams was two and Rosalind Williams had just celebrated her first birthday. Playing with them on the beach and amongst the rock pools reminded him of the days when he'd frolicked with Hogan and Buckley, his little brothers. Of course, he had heard nothing from the family since he had left India. He hoped his convoluted correspondence via Dr Freemantle was arriving safely in Oxford.

He began to instil habits of his own into his trajectory from Lerici to Casa Magni. Instead of going directly to the house he would stop at one of the small crescent beaches set between the rocky outcrops of the shoreline – completely out of sight of the house – and bathe. He would drag his boat onto the sand, strip off and swim to a rocky atoll some hundred yards offshore, swim around it once or twice and head back. He would dry himself with a linen sheet, dress, comb his hair and row on to Casa Magni, full of energy and good spirits, in time for luncheon on the terrace. He often brought wine or salami sausage or cheese as his contribution to the long and idle meal. It was, in a way, a perfect holiday – and one that fitted into his schedule. When he wearied of chatter and children he would climb into his rowing boat and disappear. Percy Florence – a curious, sweet child – would always ask him if he was coming back and began to call him Cash.

One day in early June he arrived at Casa Magni to discover that Claire Clairmont had returned to the family. When they had a moment alone on the terrace after lunch, sitting at the table amongst the empty plates and wine glasses – Shelley in his study, Mary and the Williamses on the beach below the house with the children – Cashel made a point of referring to Claire's daughter's tragic death.

'I'm so sorry for your distress and unhappiness, Miss Clairmont,' he said. 'I can't imagine how hard it must be for you.'

'It is hard,' she said. 'Very hard, indeed.' Then she added with real venom, 'But I hope it's harder for *him*.' She would not mention Byron's name. 'My agonies are diminished somewhat by the thought of the ravening guilt and shame that I assume – that I hope – he is feeling.'

Cashel could see how her rage at Byron was assuaging her grief. She went on to tell him, in a sudden candid outpouring, of the history of her relationship with Byron. Their time in Italy with the Shelleys, Allegra's birth, their estrangement and her separation from her own child. 'Where does such coldness and hostility come from?' she asked rhetorically. 'What kind of man will not let a mother see her child?' Cashel nodded and listened. 'And now she's dead and he weeps and wails. It disgusts me.'

Cashel kept his counsel, aware that he was becoming privy to too many secrets swarming amongst the Shelleys. Shelley and Mary, Shelley and Claire, Mary and Claire, Shelley and Byron, Claire and Byron – all complex, turbulent and fraught relationships amongst these privileged people. Only Ned and Jane Williams offered sunny and untrammelled company, seemingly unaffected by the swirling currents of emotion stirred by the poets and their companions.

Then Claire's mood suddenly switched and she smiled at him.

'I'm so pleased to see you here, Mr Ross. You can't believe the pleasure it gives me to think of you as part of our little community.'

She reached spontaneously for his hand and held it for a second, squeezing hard. Then she pressed her lips briefly to his knuckles.

'I feel you are a true friend,' she said softly. 'I hope, likewise, I can be a true friend to you.'

She stood up, smiled again, and left the terrace. He heard her calling to the children down below.

He looked at the back of his hand where she had kissed him. There was a little gleam of saliva on his knuckle. Something made him lick it off. He was beginning to understand the nature of Claire Clairmont's potent and surprising effect on men. First Lord Byron, then Shelley, and now – perhaps – Cashel Ross . . .

Shelley and Williams began to spend more time travelling to Genoa to check on the progress of their schooner that was being built there – the *Don Juan*, so-called – leaving Casa Magni to the three women, the children and the always cantankerous servants. Consequently, Cashel was encouraged to visit more often during the Genoa absences and was always offered a bed for the night. But he preferred to return to Lerici and his room in the taverna.

By now Mary Shelley had announced to the company what Cashel already knew privately – that she was with child again. The prospective arrival of a new baby so soon after the death of another child both ameliorated and heightened the shifting atmosphere of the house on the bay: Claire reminded of her loss; Mary hoping for a trouble-free birth after the death of her other children. New life provoking both unhappy memories and extra worries for the future. Nothing was straightforward at Casa Magni.

One morning, having promised to visit earlier than usual, Cashel pulled in to his usual beach and dragged his rowing boat onto the sand. He now regarded the exertions of his morning swim as essential to maintaining his equilibrium and good humour during the long day with the Shelleys and Williamses. He stripped off his clothes, folded and laid them on the thwart in the boat and swam out to his rocky island. Having vigorously circumnavigated it a few times until his chest was heaving and his arms were aching, he swam back, ready for anything.

He sloshed out of the water and walked to the boat – but his clothes were no longer there.

He stood there, naked, wondering, alarmed. Some urchin or goatherd from San Terenzo, he surmised wildly, had seized the opportunity of acquiring a new jacket and a pair of buckled shoes. In a bewildered fury he walked aimlessly to and fro along the small beach as if his clothes would miraculously reappear. Then he felt a kind of hot panic descend on him. What could he do now? He supposed he could row back to Lerici harbour and ask one of the fishermen there to provide him with temporary covering until he could regain his room. But the shame, the embarrassment. At least it would—

'Are these what you're looking for, Mr Ross?'

He turned to see Miss Clairmont standing there, holding out his bundle of clothes. He swiftly covered his nakedness with spread palms. She was wearing a 'swimming costume', he supposed – a pink outfit, trimmed with purple, with baggy pantaloons and a jacket with frilled and gathered sleeves.

'I came to the beach to go swimming and found these abandoned clothes,' she said, perfectly calm.

Cashel's confusion had in no way diminished. True, he was covering his cock and balls with his hands but he knew full well that she had observed him emerge from the water and rove around the beach with his 'manhood' unselfconsciously on display.

'Shall we swim together, Mr Ross?' she asked. There was no hint of coquettishness in her voice.

'With pleasure,' Cashel said, turning and immediately reentering the water to waist height. He began to relax a little.

Miss Clairmont deposited his clothes where she'd found them and waded in to join him.

'I swim to that rock and back,' he said. 'Is it too far for you?'

'Not with you by my side.'

So they swam out to the rocky island, chatting as they went, Miss Clairmont telling him of the enormous woman who had taught her to swim at Leghorn.

'You would think that someone so fat would sink to the bottom in a moment but her surprising buoyancy gave me every confidence.'

'Really? Most interesting.'

'See how well I swim, Mr Ross. Isn't it the most wonderful sensation?'

'It is. It is, indeed.'

When they returned to the beach Cashel stayed in the water – waist deep – as Miss Clairmont stepped onto the sand, her heavy, soaking costume hanging from her slight frame in dripping swags.

'How convenient your boat is,' she said, and quickly removed her sodden costume, hanging it on the freeboard to dry.

Cashel felt his throat contract as he stood there watching her walk down the beach towards him, pausing at the water's edge, letting the wavelets wet her ankles.

'Now that we're both naked,' she said, with a slight smile, 'I think it's safe for you to come out of the water, sir.'

*

They made love on his linen sheet. Then they lay for a while in each other's arms while the sun dried them. She kissed his shoulder and said he tasted deliciously of salt.

'I can't tell you how wonderful it is to be held. To be safe and cherished in another's arms,' she said. 'To be held close with warmth and strong feeling.' She paused. 'After everything I've been through.'

He kissed her mouth and her tongue flickered against his.

'Let's meet here again tomorrow, shall we?' she said softly and Cashel agreed.

'We must be very, very careful and discreet,' she said. 'Shelley must not have the slightest clue.'

'Of course,' Cashel said, suddenly gaining a sense of what this licentiousness might actually be about. Was Shelley to be made jealous? Was this another dangerous Casa Magni game?

'They expect me to go and swim,' she said. 'Those at the house. They know it's my new passion, after Leghorn. No one is surprised to see me set off in the morning in my costume.'

Cashel thought.

'Then it would be better if you return, as normal,' he said. 'And, say, half an hour later I innocently arrive in my boat.'

'I see you're a practised conspirator, Cashel Ross. I must call you Cashel and you must call me Claire – but only on our beach. In the world of our beach.'

'I do understand the necessary precautions, you know,' he said, kissing her small breasts and then running his hand down her belly to touch the dense dark triangle of hair between her thighs. 'I'm not a benighted idiot.'

He pressed his hardening cock against her leg and she wriggled round to face him.

'You don't have to return just yet, do you?' he asked.

And so, for a few mornings – five in total, he counted – they met secretly at their beach and swam and then made love. Claire would dress and walk back to the house and half an hour later Cashel's 'Hullooo!' would announce his arrival at Casa Magni and the day

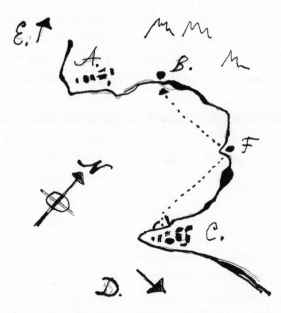

The bay at Lerici. A. The village of San Terenzo. B. Casa Magni. C. The port and township of Lerici. D. Towards Viareggio and Pisa. E. Towards La Spezia. F. The beach where Cashel used to swim.

would continue as it always did: eating, drinking, fishing, reading, talking. And always 'Miss Clairmont' and 'Mr Ross'.

A week later Shelley's slim schooner arrived from the Genoa boatyard and, as Shelley said, they had their 'perfect plaything for the summer'. The beach trysts ended when Claire returned to Florence for a fortnight and Cashel had the chance to join Shelley and Williams on the narrow, graceful sloop.

With its great mass of sail the *Don Juan* could, with a favourable wind, out-speed anything in the Gulf of La Spezia. Landlubber Cashel was occasionally enjoined to haul on a rope but most of the time he sat with Jane Williams – who sang and played on a guitar that Shelley had bought her – as her husband and Shelley familiarized themselves with the seaworthiness and handling of the boat. Jane Williams had a melodious, throaty voice and as she sang, with dusk approaching, while they steered their way easily back under half-sail to Casa Magni (where the listless and nauseous Mary waited for them), the warm nights seemed to breathe a kind of magic. Jane's husky voice, the creak of timbers, the idle slap of water on the narrow prow, the first stars appearing in the evening sky, the prospect of dinner and wine and animated conversation before them, made Cashel forget the surging tensions in the household and for once he saw what Shelley meant with his talk of a 'community of souls'.

As for Cashel himself, he was missing Claire and their carnal beach encounters. He would ask, as casually as possible, when she might be returning from Florence, but he received no definite answer. Jane Williams remarked to him that it was astonishing how 'tranquil' Claire was and how well she was bearing her awful loss. Cashel felt bound to agree.

But the household's fragile, vulnerable nature couldn't be held at bay for long. Cashel rowed round to the house one afternoon – much later than usual – and, receiving no answer to his usual call, beached his boat and went unannounced upstairs to the first floor, where he surprised Shelley and Jane Williams in a passionate kiss – an ardent, full-blooded kiss, Jane's arms tight around his neck.

Unobserved, Cashel stood, struck still for a second in the doorway. Shelley's hand was roving vigorously under Jane Williams's skirts as they kissed. Cashel stepped quietly back into the shadow of the landing but he was instantly aware that Shelley had now seen him. Their eyes connected. Cashel raised a hand – a simple gesture that he hoped was eloquent, as it was meant to convey so much. Yes, I saw what I saw; but I do not judge; and I will tell no one. Then he disappeared quickly down to the beach. Once there, he shouted again, lustily, and beat upon a doorpost to announce his specious arrival. Shelley called down to him and he came up to the terrace to find them both at opposite ends of the long table where they dined. He ignored their evident tense fluster, and chatted breezily about a near miss with a fishing boat that had occurred as he had rowed his way over. Then, two nights later, Mary Shelley miscarried her three-month foetus and nearly died. It was a tumultuous and highly dangerous situation, by all accounts, with Mary suffering copious bleeding and only the quick thinking of Shelley, who had plunged her in a bath of iced water, had managed to save her life. But the shock and deep dismay could not be dispelled and all the apparent harmony in the household fled for good.

Cashel missed all the drama as he had gone back to Pisa, not confident he could maintain the clever act that he was now required to deliver after what he had seen – particularly regarding decent, honest, ignorant Ned Williams. In any event, he had to visit his bank for more funds and needed to retrieve his mail from the poste restante. When he returned to Lerici towards the end of June everything had changed. Claire was now staying in the house and when he quietly suggested a morning 'swim' she said it was too hot for swimming now. True enough, the June sun was scorching and relentless, but he knew that wasn't the reason. Mary Shelley was now a semi-invalid, mourning another dead child. Only the Williamses were congenial – they were Ned, Jane and Cashel to each other, now – but the coldest welcome he received was from Shelley himself.

Cashel was on the shore outside the villa, preparing to row himself back to Lerici, when Shelley approached him. Cashel imagined he was going to give him a helping hand to shove the boat out into the lapping waves but he was immediately aware that Shelley's countenance was stern and hostile.

'What is it, Shelley? Is there a problem?'

'I think you should keep your distance from Miss Clairmont,' he said abruptly, his reedy voice rising to a screech when he mentioned her name.

'I don't understand,' Cashel said. 'What do you mean by "distance"?'

'I believe you both go swimming together.'

'Not at my invitation. Claire – Miss Clairmont – asked to join me.'

'I don't think it's seemly.'

Cashel laughed.

'I assume that's an attempt at humour,' he said drily. 'You – of all people – giving advice on what's seemly.'

'She's part of my family,' Shelley went on, ignoring the sarcasm. 'I must look out for her welfare.'

Cashel was thinking hard, now.

'Who told you we went swimming?'

'Claire herself. She said you swam naked.'

Cashel understood, now. Claire's subtle manipulations were under way.

'You've been warned, Ross,' Shelley insisted. 'Keep a respectable, proper distance.'

'You want all the women for yourself, do you, Shelley?'

'What do you mean?'

'First there's Mrs Williams. As you know, I witnessed your unusually fervid embrace. And I've read Miss Clairmont's letters to you. And you already have your wife. So – Mary, Claire and Jane. All for Percy Bysshe.'

Shelley had coloured markedly at this, his sun-mottled skin darkening as the blood flushed his features. He was about to speak but Cashel held up a hand to stop him.

'I'll hear no more of "warnings" from you, sir. Miss Clairmont is a mature young woman and, indeed, a free agent. She may see whomever and do whatever she wishes.' Cashel paused. 'If we choose to swim together, then we shall. And damn you for your insolence.'

They looked at each other for a second or too, in silence, then Cashel turned and pushed his boat off and hopped into it, pushing it further out with an oar.

'Good evening to you, Shelley.' He raised his voice. 'I'll gladly leave you to your harem. I won't be troubling you again.'

Shelley turned away without a further word and strode back to Casa Magni.

As he rowed back to Lerici, Cashel felt saddened by the hostility of their exchange. He had liked Shelley – and responded to his sudden enthusiasms and wild energies. Even though he could barely understand the man's poetry, apart from a few short lyrics, he was aware of his active, challenging intellect, his robust questioning of the world and its hierarchies. For a while he had thought that the amity was reciprocated. But, thinking further, he realized that Lord Byron was now back close at hand in Leghorn, with his own new ship, the *Bolivar*, bigger and better than the *Don Juan*, of course. And when Byron was close by, his looming, competitive presence always unsettled Shelley, making him possessive and acrimonious – unusually insecure.

Cashel reefed his boat to a bollard on the breakwater at Lerici and wandered gloomily back to his taverna, contemplating an evening of strenuous inebriation, his old friend. It was time to begin to think about packing up and leaving Pisa, he reckoned, time to recommence his wanderings. A few more chapters of his *magnum opus* demanding reluctantly to be written.

Some days later a scribbled note from Claire Clairmont was delivered by a servant to the Albergo Tinto. It was barely legible:

> *Shelley and Williams lost at sea. The <u>Don Juan</u> sunk in the gulf in a storm. We are all inconsolable. Do not forget us – do not forget me. In despair.*
>   <u>*Dein geliebter Fisch.*</u>*

He had been on the point of leaving Pisa, his bags packed for Rome and Naples, having decided that the right decision was to make his book as Italian as possible. Now Cashel was in sudden, destabilizing shock. Shelley and Ned Williams drowned? . . . It seemed both a preposterous and an impossible fate. And he was instantly nagged and embittered by the memory that he and Shelley had parted in a mood of such bad feeling. Then, shortly after Claire's note, came a letter from Lord Byron asking him to call. Apparently, the bodies of Shelley and Williams had been found and, in line with the strict quarantine laws in the Tuscan kingdom, they had been buried on the beach where they had been washed up and were not allowed to be moved for fear of

---

* Your beloved fish. This dashed-off note survives, suitably water-damaged.

pestilence and infection. Byron wrote that they were to be burned *in situ* and asked for Cashel's help.

Cashel visited the three grieving women in Tre Palazzi and offered his solemn and heartfelt condolences. It was immediately obvious that all trace of sexual interest between him and Claire was now absolutely a thing of the past. She was polite and distant, thanked him for coming and for his offer of help. Mary Shelley and Jane Williams were in deep grief, barely able to talk. Cashel wondered why Claire had bothered to write to him: '*Dein geliebter Fisch*'. Another self-regarding, spurious cry for attention, swiftly forgotten.

Byron had also returned to Pisa and was reinstalled at the Casa Lanfranchi. Byron gave him more information. Shelley and Williams and a boat boy had sailed the *Don Juan* to Leghorn to meet a friend, Leigh Hunt, and Byron, with whom they were planning to start up a journal. Shelley was keen to return to Casa Magni and, despite the local sailors' best advice, he set sail with Williams and the boat boy on a stormy afternoon, dark clouds looming. The *Don Juan* was last sighted by a fisherman, beating fast for Leghorn in 'heavy seas'.

Byron's mood was troubled and melancholy as he recounted the story. He kept asking, 'Why?'

'Why did they not wait? Why? These squalls in the gulf pass in a day.'

'Williams was a good sailor. I used to sail with them both.'

'Yet they were under full rig with a storm coming.' He pointed at Cashel. 'Shelley's madness, I tell you. That's what did for them. Shelley would have insisted. Overruled Williams's sensible seamanship. Faster, faster. And look what happened. Fool.'

Cashel told him he would gladly accompany him and the others to organize and supervise the gruesome *auto-da-fé* of Shelley's cremation. He hired his usual Tilbury gig and followed Byron's vast coach-and-four as it rumbled down to the coast towards Viareggio in early August.

There on the shore by Viareggio, on the wide sandy beach, they met Captain Trelawny, the master of the *Bolivar*, and a couple of other friends of Byron and Shelley whom Cashel didn't know. Trelawny had ordered the swift construction of a kind of high, narrow metal bedstead upon which the disinterred remains of Shelley's body were to be set above a stacked pile of dry logs (Williams's body had been cremated in the same manner the day before).

Everything was in place when Cashel walked down with Byron to the makeshift pyre on the seashore. Cashel looked with some revulsion at Shelley's remains on its thin iron bed. Most of the exposed parts of Shelley's body – his face, neck and hands – had been eaten away by fish and other sea creatures during its many days in the gulf before the body had finally been washed ashore, and what visible flesh remained had a curious, putrefying, blue-grey hue. As the firewood was lit below the iron griddle, Byron, visibly upset, suddenly said he would not stay and, with Trelawny, went to swim out to the *Bolivar*, anchored some hundreds of yards offshore. It was a hot sun-blasting day and, once the fire had been lit, Cashel watched the shimmering heat-haze trembling and vibrating above the flames as the body burned fiercely. A Shelleyan image of the soul departing the charred, blistering flesh, Cashel thought. He didn't linger much longer himself, but walked up to the coastal road to watch from afar and talk with the coachmen and the half-dozen dragoons who had been despatched from Pisa to deal with any sightseers – though there were none.

When Byron returned from his swim he asked Cashel to join the party at Viareggio where they planned to dine but Cashel said he had to return to Pisa. Somehow, he felt that it would be wrong to try and preserve a fond conversational, reminiscing memory of whatever modest relationship he had had with Shelley – at once fleeting and strangely intimate – and he wanted to be away from Byron with his operatic, self-obsessed grief. He rode his gig homewards in a sober mood. The perfect summer had turned sinisterly, disastrously sour.

Yet, back in Pisa, still hastening to be away on his travels, Cashel found Byron constantly demanded his company. Now he was invited to the palazzo on an almost daily basis to dine, drink and play billiards and, ostensibly, advise Byron on a scheme he was concocting to go to Greece to fight in the war of liberation against the Turks.

Byron played billiards with difficulty, wincing and cursing. He had been terribly burned by the sun on his impromptu, ill-conceived, long swim to the *Bolivar* at the height of the afternoon's heat. He had salve and thin bandages all over his neck, shoulders, back and chest.

'I've stripped pages of skin off my body,' he told Cashel, 'whole manuscripts of integument.'

Cashel sympathized.

'Come with us to Greece, Ross. You're a soldier. I'm a poet. We need men like you in the struggle.'

'My soldiering days are over, my lord.'

Byron eventually gave up trying to persuade him and then he would turn the conversation to Shelley, particularly when he had drunk a great deal.

'Shelley or Byron, Ross?' he said, his voice slurring somewhat. 'Who will survive? Byron or Shelley?'

'I've no idea. Why not both?'

'No, not both. It will be me, I'm sure. You must agree. I speak to the heart, to the testicles, to the viscera. Shelley is all intellectual mind, all . . .' He gestured vaguely. 'All generalization, all faery-land.'

'Was it not the Stoics, my lord, who said, "Posterity is not our business"?'

'I don't give a bucketful of farts for your Stoics, Ross,' Byron said, topping up their glasses. 'I'm talking about longevity, literary longevity. We read Shakespeare, not Tourneur. We read Smollett, not Fielding. So it will be with me and Shelley. Poor, doomed fellow.'

'I'm sure you're right, my lord.'

But Byron was obsessed and, as he became drunker, literature retreated and personalities came to the fore.

'Were you aware, Ross, of how obsessed Shelley was with social rank?'

'I can't say I was. He always seemed—'

'Shelley once said to me – he said this to my very face, can you credit it? – he said, "You were born above a shop in Aberdeen, Lord Byron. And look at you now." I mean to say . . .' Byron took a gulp of his wine. 'It was a deliberate slur. An insulting attempt to put me down. I hadn't realized until that moment how much rank meant to him. I don't think – correct me if I'm wrong – I don't think he could ever get over that I was a peer of the realm and he was only the son of a provincial baronet.' Byron leant forward, holding both arms out as if in supplication, and for a moment Cashel thought he might fall out of his chair. 'I don't think Shelley could ever come to terms with the fact that I was superior to him – in society. I don't mean as a poet – he always granted me that. He knew that I was the greater artist. But he couldn't live with the fact that he was inferior to me, socially speaking. In terms of rank.'

'Is it important – now, I mean?' Cashel said. 'Now that he's dead and gone? All that is irrelevant, surely.'

'No, no! No, it's important – vitally, crucially important – in every aspect of a person's life. But you wouldn't understand that, Ross – with no disrespect – being the kind of person you are. Given the lower level of society that you hail from. These factors don't apply to you in the same way.'

'That's very true, Lord Byron.'

Eventually, Cashel announced his departure for Rome and Byron insisted they send him off with a lavish *conversazione*. It was the last gesture Cashel wished for but there was no way of reasonably refusing it without causing lasting offence. In later life, he sometimes wondered what his fate would have been had he politely turned the honour down and simply gone away and travelled to Rome . . .

6

Lord Byron's *conversazione* for Il Signor Cashel Greville Ross took place in late August 1822, in the two main salons of the Palazzo Lanfranchi that overlooked the Arno. Cashel had bought a new topcoat and silk stockings, had been closely shaved and had his hair cut and pompadoured with a scented oil. However, it was immediately apparent when he arrived, was announced and then moved unrecognized through the throng – there were over a hundred people noisily gathered in the rooms – that this *conversazione* was in fact all to do with Lord Byron and he, Cashel, was an irrelevance.

Since the invitation had been extended to Cashel, Byron had decided to leave Pisa and the Kingdom of Tuscany with the Contessa Guiccioli. Her family, the Gambas, were being exiled – Cashel had no idea why – and Genoa was chosen as a safe haven as it was in the Kingdom of Piedmont-Sardinia. Consequently the purpose of the evening's gathering was in fact to signal Byron's farewell to Pisan society and really had nothing to do any more with Il Signor Cashel Ross's impending expedition to Rome and points south. Cashel felt a bit of a fool but Byron was being particularly amiable and so he relaxed and decided to try and enjoy himself. What did it matter, anyway? he thought to himself.

Byron drew him aside into an alcove where they could talk quietly.

'While you were at Casa Magni,' he asked, 'did you meet Miss Clairmont?'

'I did. Yes.'

'How did you find her?'

'Very . . . Personable.'

'You know about our sordid history, don't you?'

Cashel paused and thought quickly before replying.

'I did hear something of it from Shelley.'

'You don't want to believe everything Shelley said. Poor drowned sod.' Byron's face hardened. 'He was always on Claire's side, anyway. In every sense.'

A servant topped up Cashel's glass of wine from a silver jug.

'Miss Clairmont was—' Cashel began but Byron interrupted him.

'You know she came scampering after me when she was only sixteen?' he said. 'I mean, even by my standards, it was brazen. Let's both go to an inn out of town, she said. It was her idea.'

'That I didn't know,' Cashel said carefully.

'People like to forget that – more often than is supposed – the women are the instigators. It's not always us whoreson, mangy men. People forget that women like a bit of tooling, also.'

'It's an interesting point,' Cashel observed diplomatically. 'I've heard it said before.'

Byron looked at him knowingly.

'So, Ross, you met Miss Clairmont, the fetching Claire . . . Did anything ensue?'

'*Ah, mio Byron. Eccoti qui.*'

They both turned to see Byron's diminutive mistress. Contessa Guiccioli stood there, smiling delightedly, with another tall young woman standing just behind her.

Byron greeted the Contessa and her friend. He seemed to know her vaguely.

He then pushed Cashel forward towards this young woman, hands on his shoulders, speaking in his reasonably good but heavily accented Italian.

'Contessa, I would like you to meet my brave warrior friend – *mio coraggioso amico guerriero*,' he repeated. 'A true man at arms, Signor Ross. Signor Ross, please meet the Contessa Rezzo.'

'*Lei è la mia cugina preferita,*' La Guiccioli added proudly.

Cashel turned to greet the tall young woman standing behind the petite Guiccioli and gave a little bow of the head, feeling Byron's palm-thwack of encouragement on his shoulder as he and his Contessa wandered off, leaving Cashel to this new one. He smiled at her politely.

And then it happened.

They looked at each other intently, despite the polite bored smiles pasted on their faces. Cashel felt a variety of reactions – his chest inflated dramatically and, simultaneously, a spasm tremored deep in his bowels.

'Very pleased to meet you,' he managed to say, almost forgetting his Italian.

'Perhaps I should salute you – as a brave warrior,' she added in English with an unusual accent that Cashel couldn't initially place. 'Shalute' was how she pronounced the word.

Cashel shrugged, smiling.

'Lord Byron – you know how he is.' All the while he was taking in her appearance, fastidiously, instantly.

She was unusually tall and slim and young – maybe only seventeen or eighteen years old, he calculated. She had one of those long thin faces and sleepy, long-lidded eyes. A slightly hooked nose, he saw, and an upper lip marginally fuller than the lower, as well as a strong chin. She had dark auburn hair held up in complicated, braided coils, an auburn offset to good effect by the shimmering ice-blue silk of her gown. It seemed very flimsy, transparent enough to reveal the white silk chemise underneath. She had a wide darker blue ribbon tight beneath her breasts, as if holding them up. Her exposed skin was very white. Her neck and chest, her arms . . .

'I'm sorry,' he said, clearing his throat. 'I didn't catch your name.'

'I'll throw it to you again,' she said, deadpan. 'Ready?'

Cashel nodded. Smiled faintly.

'I am the Contessa Raphaella Rezzo.'

Cashel gave his little bow once more. Raphaella. Raphaella and Cashel. Cashel and Raphaella.

'So, are you a real soldier?' she asked. 'Or just a chocolate soldier?'

'I was a real soldier. But now I'm a writer.'

'A writer? So am I. Isn't that interesting?'

Cashel wondered if she were mocking him.

'But I'm a writer who has yet to be published,' he confessed.

'That makes another thing we have in common,' she said, smiling.

Cashel was finding it hard to compose himself. He felt like a schoolboy before her sardonic, clear-eyed gaze.

'I was a soldier at the Battle of Waterloo,' he said, playing his trump card. 'Lord Byron always brings it up.'

'Not only a warrior but a survivor.'

Cashel, wordless, drained his wine and showed his empty glass to a servant passing with the wine flagon. He paused to refill it.

'Yes, I survived, but not unscathed, alas.'

She politely asked him what had happened and he swiftly told her, adding a few martial embellishments. She didn't seem particularly impressed.

'My husband is a soldier, also – *was* a soldier. I'm glad he's stopped.' She lifted a sweetmeat from a passing tray, popped it in her mouth and chewed, looking at him intently.

Cashel focused his gaze to meet hers. He would not flinch.

'What book is it that you're writing?' he asked.

'A book on social etiquette. I've lived in many cities in many countries. What about you?'

'I'm writing a book about my travels through Europe.'

'Another one? Hasn't the world had enough?' She was blunt.

'Well, every experience of travel is unique, surely. Like social etiquette.'

'Do you think my book would be more original than yours?'

'Who can say? We'll only know when they're written and published,' he said, gratified that his weak sally at least provoked a smile – two thin parentheses briefly appeared on either side of her intriguing lips.

He drank wine from his glass, playing for time, feeling awkward, inarticulate, watching her pick a crumb from the corner of her mouth.

'What are you staring at?' she said, flicking it floorward.

'Nothing, nothing.'

Silence. They stood looking at each other. She was in control of this conversation, without question, Cashel thought.

'Do you know Lord Byron well?' he asked, instantly regretting the predictable tedium of his question.

'No. I was living in Bologna when he was living in Ravenna. And when we moved back to Ravenna he came to Pisa. But I know the Contessa – who is not my cousin, by the way,' she added. 'For her, "cousin" is a term of affection, not blood.'

'Dutch,' Cashel said.

'Dutch?'

'Your accent. I can hear it now. When you speak English your accent is Dutch.'

'Yes. Perhaps because my mother was Dutch. Mmm?' She smiled condescendingly. 'She taught me English. And then we lived in England for a while. My father was an ambassador. He was Italian, however.'

She turned and called for some wine and they stood there for a moment, drinking, looking at each other.

Cashel knew that she knew what he was thinking. And he knew – as an animal knows – that he had found his mate. He need look no further, ever. The Contessa Raphaella Rezzo was ideal, perfect. He almost laughed at the revelation – and its absurdity. Life was cruel, he was thinking. Fate engineered these encounters, provoked the life-altering realization and then instantly humiliated you with the impossibility of its ever happening. If only he was someone of more—

'Where are you living, here in Pisa?' she asked. 'With Lord Byron?'

'No.' He explained that he was staying at the Albergo Tinto preparing to journey south, in the next day or two, to Rome and Naples. 'For my book,' he added weakly. 'For what it's worth.'

'You should visit Ravenna,' she said. 'Before you go to Rome.'

'Why?'

'Because I live in Ravenna,' she said and wandered away into the noisy throng of his *conversazione*.

★

138

That night, back at the Albergo Tinto, his head thick with all the wine he had drunk, Cashel sat on his bed and tried to bring Raphaella Rezzo's face to mind. It duly shimmered and formed in perfect detail. The heavy-lidded eyes – what colour? How had he not noticed? – the imbalanced lips, the long, almost bony face. Not beautiful, exactly, but strong, individual. There was a kind of insolence about her particular beauty. Yes, that was it, insolent beauty – provocative, challenging. As if she was constantly weighing you up. Don't make a mistake. Don't make me think the less of you. It was a kind of wonderful torment, he thought. He felt a swoon come on him and he opened his eyes.

Be rational, he told himself. She's no goddess, no Venus incarnate. One little exaggeration of her physiognomy and she might look plain or lumpy. *Jolie laide,* as the French had it. But no – for him, everything cohered in the face of Raphaella Rezzo, everything coalesced: she was entirely, fascinatingly alluring as far as he was concerned. And then, like all young men who were drunk and obsessed with someone they had just met, he tried to imagine her naked – and failed.

The next morning a letter was delivered to the Tinto by a servant. Cashel broke the seal and unfolded it to find an address on a scrap of paper – Palazzo Rezzo, via Guidone, Ravenna – and also a tiny lock of scented hair tied with an aquamarine silk ribbon. He sniffed. Lavender? Rosewater? Opoponax? No, lavender, that was it. Charming, anyway. Then he looked again at the lock of hair, touched it with the palps of his fingers. He went downstairs to talk to the innkeeper, Adriano Buzza, whom he'd come to know quite well.

Adriano was a bald, middle-aged, worldly man going to fat. A former dandy, his previous self was still manifest in a sharply waxed moustache and very bright clothes.

'Oh, yes,' Adriano said, handing back the lock. 'Obviously <u>peli pubici</u>. It's normal.'

'How can it be normal to send a cutting of pubic hair to someone you have just met?'

'It's a tradition, here, Signor Ross. A sign – an indication, you

139

know,' Adriano added a little patronizingly, like a rakish uncle talking to his gauche nephew. 'When this sort of token is sent to a man it means that the person who sent it – the *signora* or *signorina* – is happy for you to . . .' He searched for a euphemism. '*Per piatare la tua carota*', as the saying goes in Pisa.'

Cashel mentally, unthinkingly, translated the phrase into English. The meaning was obvious.

'It's a signal,' he said.

'*Esattamente*. It's a clear invitation, my very lucky young friend.'

Cashel took a diligence from Pisa to Bologna. After a night in Bologna he hired a two-horse, open cabriolet – in the interests of speed – and was driven swiftly to Ravenna in a few hours.

After Pisa, Ravenna seemed to him something of a poor relation. It was yet another ancient city whose port had moved further and further away through centuries of a silting river delta and, consequently, steadily deprived the once-coastal town of its prosperity and significance. Despite its unrivalled collection of Byzantine churches and basilicas the place seemed to his eyes, as he surveyed it for the first time, somewhat shabby and uncared-for, all peeling stucco and gimcrack scaffoldings in every street and alleyway. Still, he had not come to Ravenna as a tourist.

He found an inn near the centre, the Albergo Massimo, close to the post office and the theatre, where as usual he rented two rooms on the top floor, as far away as possible from the noise of the taverna and ristorante on the ground floor. He had no idea how long he would be staying but his mood was charged with anticipation after the letter he'd received and its exceptional contents. It seemed such an assured and confident incitement from someone so young. He could only suppose she knew exactly what she was doing.

He had a formal letter of introduction delivered to the Palazzo Rezzo. Snr. Cashel Ross presents his compliments – arrival in Ravenna – residing at the Albergo Massimo – sincere regards. He waited to see what would happen next. Within twenty-four hours an invitation came – a little note, unsealed – though somewhat formal. La Contessa Rezzo would be attending the theatre on the following evening and would be happy to make Il Signor Ross's reacquaintance in the interval. And so Cashel went to the theatre.

He had only brought his smartest clothes with him from Pisa – he wanted to make an impression, after all. He took care to dress himself as close to the height of fashion as he could manage. He wore his navy-blue short jacket with brass buttons, his striped Cossack trousers, and his upturned collar thrust as high as comfort would allow, secured with a white silk stock. The theatre was crowded and hot and the opera – some tale of matricide and filial despair – was both overwrought and boring. He was only interested in the interval.

When it duly arrived he mingled with the chattering nobility and bourgeoisie of Ravenna, wandering through the crowded corridors and the small salons alert in the hope of spotting Contessa Rezzo. He saw her standing with her back to a wall, close to a sconce with three candles burning that cast a warm, shifting light on her hair, burnishing its auburn into a kind of deep glossy chestnut. On seeing her, he felt the authentic body-disturbance of lungs and viscera, the attendant lightness of head, the genital tightening and quiver of acute sensual recognition. He had never been so convinced of the rightness of a course of action in his life. Imagine if he had ignored the invitation and travelled on to Rome to add another chapter to his boring book. What folly would that have been? he thought. He felt as though he was on the brink of some enormous change in his life. Nothing would be the same after Ravenna.

He moved closer to the small crowd of people surrounding Raphaella. Her gown was of the latest style, he could see: a loosely draped lemon-yellow dress with a broad silver ribbon tight below her breasts, as if demarcating them from her slender torso, presenting them to the world as the first point of interest of her ensemble. Above her white gloves her arms were bare, her neck and chest likewise. Cashel, entranced, hovered closer, made eye contact, raised his hand in greeting and was called forward with feigned, delighted surprise and introduced to the company. Il Signor Ross, from England, who speaks excellent Italian and is a close friend of Lord Byron. That was the key that opened the Ravenna door. Cashel learned very quickly that the city had been honoured by Lord Byron's presence for some two years. Prompted, he told stories of the death of Shelley and Lord Byron's abject grief. He felt himself the cynosure of all attention.

'*Bravo*,' Raphaella whispered as they filed back into the amphitheatre to take their seats for the second half. 'I'll send a messenger to the *albergo* tomorrow.'

She glanced left and right and, unobserved, reached behind him and squeezed his buttock.

'We just have to be very prudent and patient. You understand?'

Cashel said, yes, perfectly. But he didn't care – as far as he was concerned there was nothing *to* understand. He now saw that his whole life had been leading him towards Ravenna. Its complexity of forking paths, diversions, doublings back, inadvertent decisions and happenstance had somehow conspired to place him at this moment in the Teatro Municipale and beside this astonishing, mesmerizing woman. He was convinced that he had arrived at his life's climacteric – its ripening, its turning point.

Cashel began to be invited out, because, he sensed, he was a cut-price Byron substitute. Ravenna society was keen to have another English 'writer' within its walls – and one who could speak Italian, furthermore – and he found himself very much in demand. Birthday celebrations, feast days, marriages, anniversaries, *conversazioni*, visits to the theatre and concerts all seemed to require his presence. And he was happy to accept each and every invitation because that, so far, was the only way he could see Raphaella.

There was a moment, after the christening of a Rezzo relative's child, when, walking out behind everybody else, they miraculously found themselves alone in the gloomy narthex of a church and, without a word to each other, they kissed. Only for a few seconds – and yet for days afterwards Cashel was convinced he could still recall absolutely the impress of their lips, the firm softness of hers, the slight clash of teeth, the touching of tongues, the thin filament of saliva that hung, curved, glistening between their mouths for a second as they pulled apart, startled by their own intensity.

'Soon,' she whispered. 'I'm arranging everything. It will happen soon.'

They wrote to each other, in English, as if it were their private cypher. Every day Raphaella's African page, Timoteo, would come to the Massimo with a note containing instructions. The theatre and concerts became their preferred meeting places because, in a crowd, or in semi-darkness, they could send messages between their eyes and, if no one was looking, could squeeze hands, touch a knuckle to a cheek, press thigh against thigh.

Timoteo became their go-between and, inevitably, their confidant. He had a small slim figure and was maybe twelve or thirteen years old, Cashel guessed. He wore a dramatic red-and-black striped uniform, with a large 'R' on the breast, and carried a sheathed dagger and a pistol on his belt. He had no idea where in Africa he had come from – 'A green land with a wide river' was all he could recall in his strong Ravennate accent. He had been 'given' to Raphaella when she was fourteen and he had become an essential part of her life, utterly trustworthy and beholden.

He came to the Massimo each day and would drop off his missive and collect anything that Cashel wanted to send in return. The procedure worked well – they were in daily, clandestine communication – but, after a few weeks, with Cashel now fully integrated into Ravenna society, there was a sense in him that consummation of their relationship was becoming very overdue.

'We cannot continue like this,' Cashel wrote to her. 'I'm being driven to the edge of madness.'

'I know, I know, my dearest,' she replied. 'But I have to choose the right time. It must be proficient.' He assumed she meant propitious.

What was propitious and what would change everything was the meeting between Cashel and Raphaella's husband, Count

Giacomo Rezzo. Cashel found it strange that they had yet to encounter each other in one of Ravenna's innumerable social gatherings. But all was made clear – shockingly clear – when, finally, Timoteo brought him the note setting out the arrangements for the first meeting.

This was to occur at Count Giacomo's birthday celebrations. The count was holding a small soirée to commemorate his sixty-seventh birthday. Some fifty people were invited to the Palazzo Rezzo, including Il Signor Ross. He dressed as smartly as his wardrobe would allow and even pinned his Waterloo Medal to the revere of his topcoat – his talisman, his good-luck charm. He strolled from the Massimo through the streets of Ravenna to the palazzo, allowing himself a hint of swagger in his progress, feeling good in his tall hat, though as he approached the palazzo some nervousness returned. Rush torches blazed on either side of the main door. Liveried servants lined the stairs.

In the salon, Raphaella led him through the other guests and presented him to an elderly grey-haired and grey-bearded gentleman in a bath chair. There was a lavishly embroidered throw over his lap. Cashel bowed and he was introduced by Raphaella. Count Rezzo himself.

'So, you are friendship with Milord Byron. A very complex-icated man,' Count Rezzo said in faltering English.

Cashel agreed, switching to Italian which made the count seem to relax. A chair was brought and Cashel sat beside him to continue their Byron conversation. The count explained that his legs and his right arm were paralysed as the result of apoplexy suffered some three years previously. Cashel sympathized, but was somewhat baffled. This man, handsome old devil as he must once have been, was close to fifty years Raphaella's senior. Half his body was paralysed – did that apply to his cock? Cashel found himself pruriently speculating. And, moreover, why would the delicious, clever, alluring young Raphaella attach herself to this wreck, this half-ruined figure, this shadow of a man, as his wife?

After five further minutes of polite, solicitous conversation he took his leave as others were beginning to queue up to speak to the count. As he wandered away, Cashel realized that the count had not asked him one question about himself – the Lord Byron imprimatur had obviously been sufficient.

Cashel asked a servant for brandy, was given a glass and wandered out onto the wide landing that gave on to the palazzo's splendid curved marble staircase. Another manservant was wiping down the balustrade with a damp cloth. The babble of conversation from the salon behind him was now overlaid with music from a flute and a cello.

'How did that go?' Raphaella breathed in his ear.

Cashel turned. Raphaella stood close to him, the arrangement of her hair looser, her lips gleaming wet, excited somehow. He felt overwhelmed, suddenly, by her proximity, her strange beauty.

'What? Oh, he seemed perfectly amiable. How old is he again?'

'Sixty-seven. You should have seen him before his apoplexy, like a man of forty.'

'He's almost fifty years older than you. Old enough to be your grandfather.'

'What does that matter?'

'Never mind. Do you love him?' he asked, rather astonished at his audacity.

'Of course not. But I like him. He's kind, considerate to me. He's happy that I'm his wife. And I brought much property to the Rezzo family with our marriage.'

'Right. I see. Maybe that explains his good nature.'

She ignored him.

'But, now that you two have met, everything will change. Everything'll be different.'

'Why? How?'

'Because he now knows who you are. It's so important.'

Cashel exhaled and gulped at his brandy, deciding to surrender himself to whatever was required of him.

'But I still don't really understand,' he said. 'Now that he knows who I am – how does that affect you and me?'

She smiled, glanced around and seeing that no one was observing (the balustrade-cleaning manservant had disappeared below, round the stairway's great curve) she kissed Cashel's cheek and licked his earlobe. He felt weak, hollowed out.

'I'll send Timoteo to you tomorrow. All will be explained.'

The message duly came the next day and Cashel read his instructions carefully. Raphaella was going to the theatre for a performance of Il Barbiere di Siviglia but Cashel should not come. In the interval she would say to her companions that she was feeling sick and was going home. Cashel should be waiting at the junction of Via Marianna and Via Secca from ten o'clock onwards.

Cashel positioned himself at the junction half an hour earlier, sensing that tonight was the night, that the watershed in his relationship with Raphaella was about to arrive. He paced about, patiently, somewhat amazed at her organizational powers, her skilful overseeing of strategy and tactics.

Autumn was well advanced and the air was chilly. He turned up the collar of his overcoat and blew warm breath on his numb fingers, looking down the near-empty street that was the Via Marianna waiting for the noise of a coach. Shortly after ten o'clock he saw a two-horse brougham appear with the curtains drawn at the windows, Timoteo in the driving seat. He hauled on the reins when he saw Cashel and they greeted each other, circumspectly, before Cashel opened the door and stepped into the carriage.

Raphaella was there waiting, in a dress of dazzling blue and silver, a thick shawl around her shoulders. They kissed. Cashel's face was now warm, flushed with excitement.

'We've at least one hour before the opera ends,' Raphaella said. 'Then maybe we can have another twenty minutes or so before I have to be back at the palazzo.'

She knocked on the ceiling and the brougham moved off.

They reached for each other and kissed again with more urgency and feeling. He pushed back her shawl to kiss her neck, he squeezed her breasts.

'Wait,' she said. 'Wait until we are out of the town.'

They left Ravenna by the Porta Serrata and turned off the north road into a lane with young woodland on either side.

Timoteo stepped down from his driver's seat and Raphaella told him to go for a walk for an hour.

'I have no clock, Contessa,' he said.

'Count to five thousand,' she said and Timoteo disappeared into the darkness.

There were two lit candles burning in glass lantern-boxes inside the carriage. Raphaella blew one out and they fell upon each other. Cashel squirmed and tugged at his breeches, frantically undoing buttons, and his hot, hard cock sprang free.

Raphaella hauled up her blue-and-silver skirts to reveal her pale naked thighs above her gartered silk stockings and the dark 'V' of her pudenda. The carriage was small and Cashel had to kneel on the floor in front of her to manoeuvre himself into the right position. She shifted to accommodate him, reached for his cock and guided him home.

Cashel felt he might faint, his head reeling, but he couldn't ignore the painful pressure on his knees and the unsought-for mental image of Timoteo in his red-and-black uniform wandering the extra-mural lanes of Ravenna counting to five thousand.

Still, he thought, as he pushed himself deeper inside her, this was the 'congress' he had been dreaming of for weeks and weeks. He was finally making love to the woman he adored even though it was in a brougham parked in a country lane and the springs were squeaking and he could feel wax from the tilted candle dripping hotly onto the back of his stabilizing hand.

He came, shuddered, collapsed, buried his head in her neck and felt tears in his eyes. Raphaella – gasping a little, her mouth open – gently pushed him to one side and they sat together on the brougham's seat and rearranged their clothing. Cashel relit the second candle and in the soft glow of the flame all the uncomfortable pragmatism of their sexual encounter receded. He took her in his arms, his throat thick with emotion. Wordless, he touched her face incredulously. She kissed his fingertips.

'What now?' he managed to say. 'What do we do now?'

'We will meet,' she said. 'I've many ideas.'

'Not in carriages, please.'

'Maybe it's the easiest solution, you know.'

'Whatever you say.' Cashel felt frustrated. 'But,' he said, 'when we meet with others present it'll be a kind of hell. Pretending, being polite, all the while staring at each other, remembering.'

'No, my sweetheart, believe me – I have a solution. We can be together and alone. Alone in the world, our world.'

'That's all I want, all I desire—'

'Trust me. I've thought of everything.'

Outside, Timoteo coughed politely. He had counted to five thousand.

Winter set in. A fire was lit in Cashel's sitting room every morning. Snow fell on the plains of the Po river valley. Raphaella's grand strategy was still unrealized so they made do with their carriage encounters until it could be plausibly engineered.

It was a love affair, Cashel supposed, but it felt baulked by their necessary precautions, half-functioning. When they were together, however, he forgot his frustrations.

One night, on their way back from another dark country lane, Raphaella made Timoteo stop the carriage by Dante's tomb and she gave Cashel a copy of *La Divina Commedia*, inscribed '*C from R. Sempre*'.

Cashel had read Dante's masterpiece on the journey back from India, a blank verse 1805 translation by one Rev. Henry Francis Cary, part of Cornelius Poynton's literary bequest to him. He looked at Raphaella's small block of a book, bound in black calfskin with a gold dentelle, and felt strangely moved by the association, remembering Poynton with his friendly, tolerant manner – and his maritime suicide.

'Do you think we're like Paolo and Francesca?' Cashel asked, suddenly recalling Dante's two slaughtered lovers, banished to hell for their adultery, battered for ever by ceaseless, tumultuous winds, whirling them endlessly through their circle of hell.

'Nobody's going to come and kill us, *carissimo*. But we are a bit like them, that's true. We do love each other like Paolo and Francesca.'

While he waited for their promised 'world' to appear, Cashel visited every church and basilica in Ravenna. He made notes for his travel book, little sketches of details in San Vitale and San Nazario e Celso and many more. One problem arose in that no bank in Ravenna would accept his letters of credit so he had to travel to Bologna from time to time when his funds ran low. Bologna was added to the book and its chapter grew.

Now that his carriage encounters with Raphaella were happening more regularly he began to take more care of his personal cleanliness. Once a week he would order up a deep basin of hot water, strip off and wash his entire body with soap and a scrap of flannel cloth. He kept further small squares of this cloth to wipe himself when he defecated. He knew that most men simply tucked their shirt tails into their buttock cleft and forgot about the inevitable staining. What on earth did women do? he found himself wondering. Now, in the cramped space of the carriage, he was down to his shirt, breeches round his ankles, and he felt self-conscious. Raphaella always smelt so sweet, so lavender-scented and clean. So he bought a perfume for himself from an apothecary – a lemony, tart-smelling scent – that he sprinkled on his clothes. He went to a barber every two days to be shaved. He wanted nothing rank or unseemly about his meetings with Raphaella. He wanted them to be as pure as possible.

And in the New Year of 1823 circumstances changed dramatically for the better. There was a masked carnival due to take place in the streets of Ravenna. Cashel bought a beak-nosed mask and joined the raucous, gaudy crowds in the piazza in front of the theatre. Timoteo had delivered the latest set of instructions to him and he stood waiting at the designated corner of the square, watching the strolling lutenists and trumpeters, the jugglers and the stilt-walkers and the surging, liberated, anonymous Ravennesi, all determined to enjoy themselves. The mood was both gay and edgy. Fun could evolve into sinful fun – and, with luck, all kinds of further mayhem and mischief. The taverns were open, and food and heated wine was being served from braziers; people were dancing spontaneously, and shouts and whoops of applause echoed round the piazza.

He felt a tug at his elbow and turned to see a face like a white moon surmounted by scarlet feathers.

'Follow me,' said Raphaella's voice, and they slipped down an alleyway that led towards the Duomo.

'Have you candles?' she asked.

'Yes. And tinder.'

She was leading him by the hand – heedlessly – and then Cashel remembered they were both masked and therefore anonymous like the rest of the frolicking townsfolk. Which was the defining point of masked carnivals, Cashel realized – all licence was therefore possible.

They came to a shuttered house. Raphaella had a key for a side door and when she opened it they stepped inside to a dark hall. Cashel took out his tinderbox, applied flint to steel, caught a flame and lit one of the candles he had brought with him in his pocket. Now that they could see, Raphaella took off her mask, as did he, and they kissed.

'Come on, upstairs,' she said and they climbed up to the first floor.

'Where are we?' Cashel asked.

'The house of a friend.'

'Who is this friend?'

'It doesn't matter.'

She opened the door to a room. Cashel lit more candles and they could see that it contained a large, canopied bed. A fire had been laid in the fireplace and Cashel lit that too. Raphaella threw off her cloak and found a flagon of red wine and two glasses placed for them in the cupboard of a dresser. They kissed, they drank, they waited until the fire took and, for the first time, they both removed all their clothes, exulted for a moment in their fire-lit nakedness, and fell into the hard bed.

As spring advanced a new ploy presented itself. Between Ravenna and the coast and Ravenna's slowly distancing port was a dense pine forest, La Pineta. In the depths of La Pineta the Rezzo family had a hunting lodge. It was made entirely of wood, though painted a creamy white to resemble stone, and looked like a small classical gatehouse, Cashel supposed. One storey, a porch, two Doric pillars. The paint was flaking and some of the walls showed signs of damp but it wasn't hard to make it comfortable enough. Cashel spent two days sweeping it clean and left a feral cat locked inside to deal with the mice. He bought a soft goose-down mattress, linen sheets and a quilt, a chamber pot and some basic provisions and, as the days lengthened, Raphaella discovered the joys of equitation. She would go out into the countryside to ride with Timoteo, now her groom, accompanying her.

Cashel rented a horse from a livery yard and made sure he was always at the lodge an hour or so before Raphaella and Timoteo were due to arrive. Sometimes he lit a small fire before they came, if the day was chilly. Timoteo looked after the horses while Cashel and Raphaella made themselves at home.

They had never really spent more than an hour alone together, Cashel realized. Two hours during the carnival had been the exception. Moreover there were periods of time – a week, ten days – when she refused to see him. Cashel realized these absences were based on calculations when she'd be most fertile. She told him, when confronted by his deduction, that her menses were very regular and reliable. And she did not want to become pregnant with his child just at this moment of their lives. His lover's fervour set aside, Cashel had to agree – it was a wise precaution. He was beginning to see his life in Ravenna as an opera – and he had seen dozens of operas since arriving in the city – but one plotted and constructed, with all its narrative wiles and swerves, by the librettist Raphaella Rezzo.

Cashel realized that his travel book, his *Journal of a Tour*, was becoming thick and unwieldy. Ravenna had been exhaustively dissected, Bologna was not far behind – and he had visited Bagnacavallo, Ferrara and Imola and written them up as well. He had run out of adjectives to describe tombs and basilicas and rolling countryside. Everything in his life with Raphaella seemed to have reached a point of bothersome stasis. Where were they going? What were they going to do? And then Count Rezzo came to the rescue.

The count had another, minor, apoplectic attack and for some days lost the power of speech – then recovered it, perfectly. But the warning was heeded and his physicians suggested a course of treatment and convalescence at the warm baths in the Bagni di Pisa. He would take the waters daily, receive massages, be bled, eat a diet based on rice and milk and, he was assured, he would make a remarkable recovery. The count and his entourage left for Pisa and so, in the early summer of 1823, the Palazzo Rezzo became a free state for Raphaella and Cashel.

The count would be absent for at least two months. Raphaella planned two visits to Pisa during his cure – it was her pleasurable, uxorious duty, naturally, the least she could do. However, for the first time in their love affair, Cashel and Raphaella could approximate to the status of man and wife. They could spend entire nights together. Cashel had a key to a side entrance of the palazzo that led to a stairway that, in turn, led to a landing off which Raphaella's apartments lay. Timoteo stood guard. Cashel didn't roam the palazzo but he wasn't stupid enough to imagine that the servants didn't know exactly what was going on. After a night with Raphaella he would slip out at dawn, with Timoteo's connivance, as the household began to stir. Again, even with this liberty, Raphaella insisted on the strict adherence to her menstrual cycle. Cashel returned to the Albergo Massimo until the delivered note summoned him back to the palazzo again. Everything was wonderful – even though his amatory life became almost routine, now the count was absent – but the routine did not diminish its ardency.

One evening around midnight, after a long session of strenuous lovemaking, they caught their breath. Naked, they drank wine, ate grapes, bread and cheese, tore drumsticks off a roast chicken and regathered their depleted energies.

Cashel slipped out of bed, pulled on a heavy velvet dressing gown and went to sit in a chair by a window. He opened it an inch or two and allowed the breeze to cool the sweat on his throat and brow. From where he sat he had an oblique but perfect view of Raphaella lying naked amongst the sheets and strewn pillows.

Cashel lit a small cigar from a candle and topped up his glass of wine. Raphaella also liked to smoke after lovemaking when she was spent, contented, somewhat drunk. It was a secret pleasure she enjoyed – her maid had taught her, she said.

She smoked a perfumed tobacco in an elegant tiny-bowled white clay pipe with a fragile, long stem almost eighteen inches long. She tamped tobacco into the bowl – no bigger than a thimble – and lit it from a taper held to a candle, drawing the smoke deep into her throat through the long stem and exhaling steadily through pouted lips. The smoke was cool, she explained, its journey through the long, thin pipe-clay absorbing all heat. 'I just need a little,' she said. 'Two or three puffs. It calms me. Makes me relax.'

Cashel watched her. He felt his body shiver, covered for a second in goose-bumps – and he realized this was a physical manifestation of his mood. He was experiencing happiness, a kind of earthly bliss. He was happy, he recognized, and he decided to register this moment in his personal history, to fix it for ever in his mind, as a vindication and a solace. He put down his cigar and stared at her, like a cartographer, charting her every move, noting every detail. He was sitting at the ideal angle to the bed and could survey her entire body as she lay with one leg raised, knee bent at a sharp angle, and he could see her small breasts and the dark hair of her sex as she luxuriated.

Later, he would analyse and re-analyse the powerful erotic effect of this tableau. It was the preposterous, fragile long-stemmed pipe that made it sensually resonate – so odd and inappropriate to the scene, like a baton in her hand – but it was the pipe that made the orthodox naked odalisque that was Raphaella now transfixingly exotic and unique. She was indifferent to his gaze, however, concentrating on the effect of the tobacco and, as she shifted, raising her other leg to give her purchase to turn and hold the pipe-bowl again to the candle flame, showing him her slender buttocks with their shadowed furrow, he felt himself to be an invisible voyeur, as if Raphaella were lying naked in bed believing herself to be entirely alone. Because this indifference made her seem guileless it was all the more potent. Cashel felt himself becoming massively aroused as he looked on. He stood, letting his gown fall to the floor, and strode naked towards the bed. Now Raphaella was aware of his presence and she turned to see him standing there.

She smiled – it was more of a wide grin.

'And what do *you* want?' she asked. She put away her pipe.

The new, easy domesticity of their relationship – whole nights spent together, breakfasts in the morning, all fear of discovery gone – disappeared abruptly when Count Rezzo returned from his cure at Bagni di Pisa. It was back to the occasional hour or two in the hunting lodge that, now summer had arrived, was becoming increasingly and uncomfortably hot and fly-pestered.

Cashel didn't really care: time spent with Raphaella was all he craved – but she was becoming fussier and more demanding. They concocted a scheme to rent a house on the road to Florence but, after some investigation, Raphaella became convinced they would be discovered and the plan was abandoned. They resorted, reluctantly, to their tried-and-tested encounters in the carriage.

One night in September, the carriage was parked on the road by the canal that ran south of the city towards the coast and the port. Timoteo was sitting on the bank looking at the turbid water and counting to five thousand, as usual. Cashel and Raphaella lounged back on the carriage seat in their disarrayed clothing, drinking wine, the candles flickering in the warm breeze coming through the open windows.

Cashel turned and kissed her cheek.

'Do you remember how we knew?' Cashel whispered. 'From that first moment. How we knew something was going to happen. I've never experienced anything like this – this feeling.'

'I know,' she said simply. 'How do you explain how you feel like that – I mean, simultaneously? Without a word spoken . . .

From the instant that I saw you in Lord Byron's house, something was already happening between us. Isn't that strange?'

'It was as if something – I don't know – magical, somehow
other-worldly, was happening,' he said. 'Very strange and very
wonderful. But – what're we going to do about it? We're young.
We can't spend the rest of our life like this, meeting in a carriage
every now and then.'

'I know, I know. Don't worry,' she said. 'I have a plan. Everything's going to change for us. For our future.'

He kissed her gently, not having a remote idea of what she was
talking about, happy to let the idea – the concept of a plan that
would bring about change – drift there in the sultry, heady atmosphere of their carriage, happy to believe in her confidence, her
determination.

A week of abstinence went by. Cashel knew the reason: careful, prudent Raphaella and her fertility calculations. Then
Timoteo presented himself at the Massimo.

'I am to conduct you, *signore*,' he said, though the usual note
was not proffered.

'Fine. Right. Is the count away?'

'I will take you to the palazzo, *signore*.'

Cashel, a bit mystified, followed the little page through the
streets of Ravenna. People glanced at him – was he recognized
now? he wondered. He had been living in the city for months.
Did they make the connection between the tall Englishman and
the diminutive African page with a large 'R' on his tunic? Did
they make the connection between the Englishman and the
Contessa . . .?

Timoteo led him through the palazzo's main doors. They
crossed the hall and climbed the wide staircase to the *piano nobile*.
Cashel was by now vaguely troubled. This was all very public –
was Raphaella trying to make some kind of point?

Timoteo showed him into the grand salon on the first floor
and gave a little bow of farewell. Another manservant took over
and Cashel followed him across the marble floor towards the
giant fireplace before which, in a carved wooden chair almost

like a throne, sat Count Rezzo himself. His useless feet had been placed on a small stool and were not quite aligned. His dead hand was carefully resting on a carved snarling griffon at the end of the chair's arm. With his good hand the count gestured for Cashel to sit on a stool that was six inches lower than his seat. It was an audience, clearly, and Cashel felt his apprehension grow.

They spoke careful Italian to each other, formalities at first. How was the cure at the Bagni di Pisa? Most helpful. It would be cooler by the sea, Cashel observed. The summer had been very hot in Ravenna. The count replied that he did not mind heat, it made him feel better; his enemy was the cold. So far, so banal, Cashel thought, and began to relax a little.

'I'm very grateful to you, sir,' Count Rezzo said with a smile. His grey beard had been neatly trimmed and when he smiled Cashel saw many gaps in his teeth. He was an old man, after all.

'Grateful for what, Count Rezzo?'

'For your discretion with *la contessa*.'

Cashel felt as if he had been struck by some invisible force. He managed not to jolt in his seat, stiffening inwardly.

'I don't understand.'

'I know about your . . . liaison with the countess.'

He had used the word *legame* and as Cashel caught the inference he felt the heat grow in his cheeks. The count held up his hand to stop him saying anything.

'There was no insult to my dignity – that is what I appreciate. Hence my gratitude.'

'I feel I should—' Cashel stopped. 'How do you know?'

'Contessa Raphaella has told me, of course. Everything, every detail.'

Cashel said nothing.

'Which is why I'm very happy for you to become the countess's *cavaliere servante*.'

'What is a *cavaliere servante*?'

'It means you don't have to hide any more. You need have no fear about being seen in public with the countess – always maintaining decorum, of course. You can travel together, go to the theatre, the opera, together and – as long as discretion is observed – you could continue your . . .' he paused. 'Your special friendship. The world will know that I know and that I have given this dispensation.' He pointed at his legs and his inert arm. 'How could I have any objection, anyway? She is a young, vital, beautiful woman. It would be absurd of me to hold her to a set of ancient marriage vows. No, this is the civilized solution.'

Cashel was wordless, his face still flushed with the embarrassment. *La soluzione civilizzata . . .*

He stood up and stepped back.

'Thank you, sir. There is nothing more to be said.'

'You know, you remind me of him,' the count smiled amiably.

'Who?'

'The first one.'

'The first what?'

'The first *cavaliere servante* that she had.'

'I'm sorry, I don't—'

'Didn't she tell you? He was tall and fair, like you. A nice young man. He died of a fever.'

The count explained. He had suffered his attack of apoplexy only three months after he and Raphaella had been married. As he was no longer capable of being a proper husband, he urged her to acquire a *cavaliere* and she met a young man from Milano. The arrangement was ideal until the young fellow died suddenly.

'And now,' he pointed at Cashel. 'Here you are. The very image – except you're English.'

Cashel bowed, turned and left. He walked slowly back to the Massimo where he ordered a bottle of brandy to be sent to his rooms. He sat for an hour or so, drinking to no effect, his mind a raging confusion of shock, betrayal and shame. He took out pen, ink and paper and, after a few drafts, wrote a terse letter to Raphaella, in English.

Contessa –
   Your husband has spoken to me and offered me a proposition. I choose not to reply to him, however – but to you. I will not become your

second *cavaliere servante*. I will not degrade myself by becoming your next prostitute, your succubus, your English Cyprian. I have told you many times that I loved you beyond life itself – and yet you treat me as your plaything, your toy, your pet lover to be displayed in public. I can never forgive you for your betrayal of my love for you.

Addio per sempre.
Cashel Greville Ross

He folded and sealed the letter and then packed his bags and settled his account with the innkeeper. He didn't sleep that night, his brain a frenzy of activity as he ran through the months of his life with Raphaella searching for signs of her unfeeling pragmatism. How had he managed to misinterpret so monstrously the love he thought she had for him? Was it just lust? How had he come to believe in such a false reading of her nature? This was her 'plan', obviously. To persuade the count to grant him, Cashel, the status in the household of official *cavaliere servante* – number two. No doubt in the fullness of time there would be a number three when she grew tired of him. Another tall, fair-haired young man. It made him want to weep, rage, vomit.

After two hours of tossing and turning he pulled on his clothes and his boots and, grabbing his coat, walked out into the dark city streets. Better to keep walking than lie in bed tormenting himself, he thought. He wandered aimlessly until he found himself somewhere he recognized – the church of San Francesco – where he walked towards the set of iron gates by the side and peered through the bars at Dante's tomb. He had been there many times – once with Raphaella – and, though he couldn't see it in the darkness he knew there was a half-lifesize statue in bas-relief of the poet, set above a sarcophagus.

He stood there for a while, in a spirit of vague supplication to Dante's shade, brooding on his own private *purgatorio*. The perfect fool, cast out from *paradiso* by his complacent lover, Raphaella. What would Dante have done with this story of misguided, heartfelt love and callous negotiation . . .? Cashel raked his throat and spat in the street, feeling a nausea overtake him. He had to leave this cursèd place, he told himself. Get out of Ravenna and never return.

When Timoteo called at the inn, as usual, in the morning, Cashel handed him the letter and the copy of *La Divina Commedia* that Raphaella had given him.

'Take these to the contessa,' he said. 'And tell her that I've suddenly been obliged to return to England – immediately.'

'Of course, sir. When will you return?'

Cashel gave Timoteo a gold sovereign, to the boy's astonishment.

'I'll be sure to let her know – say that to her. Thank you, Timoteo, you're the only true person in Ravenna. I will always think of you as my friend.'

7

Arles
France

20th February 1824

Dearest Mother,

Thank you for your letter. I'm glad to report that my convalescence continues and I am almost completely recovered from the after-effects of my Indian fever, but my doctors advise me to continue to reside in the south where the winters are mild. Life here is tedious and uneventful. I will probably stay on here in Arles until the spring and try to complete my book of travels. I'm sufficiently in funds and can live very simply and cheaply here. Write to me at the poste-restante, Arles, Bouches du Rhone, France. The mail seems very reliable.

Do give my best regards to Sir Guy, Hogan and Buckley.

I remain your loving son,
Cashel Ross

Cashel took his letter to the post office the next day and had it franked. Then he returned to the café where he had left his horse in a back alley. The sky was dense with grey cloud and a nagging, chill wind was blowing. He ate a late breakfast of jellied eggs and a few hunks of bread washed down with a bowl of coffee, then mounted up and left Arles through the Porte de la Cavalerie, plodding back along the road to Fontvieille before turning off into the lane that led to the farm – la Ferme de la Vache Noire – his current home.

He led his horse to the stable and left it in its stall. The boy, Jaufret, would deal with it. He crossed the yard to the house and saw Clotilda coming back from her toilet on the midden behind the barn. He waved hello at her but she just glanced at him and clumped on by in her heavy clogs. Clotilda made no effort to disguise her suspicion of him; he had no idea why, as he was perfectly civil to her and the family. He pushed open the door – maybe it was because they had to rent out their farmhouse to survive, he reasoned. The family was grudgingly grateful for the money he gave them and annoyed that they needed it.

In the house, he raked the coals of the fire back to life and threw on some logs. His manuscript was spread out on the table in the main room, with his quills and ink, but he didn't feel like writing any more today. He sat down in an armchair in front of the fire and stared at the flames as they began to flicker and stir, clutching at the dry logs with their sharp orange fingers. He could stare at a fire for hours, he knew – a whole night, if he had a glass in his hand and a bottle nearby. He eased his shoulders and bowed his back, feeling the ache still lingering there, like rheumatism, but much better than in the past. He went in search of wine.

He hadn't felt truly well in himself, he realized, for weeks, for months – not since leaving Ravenna, to be honest. Sometimes he felt feverish, other times struck with massive lethargy, and he experienced odd pains on his left side, in his chest. He remembered how Shelley had always complained about a mysterious pain in his side that was never diagnosed. Another troubled soul, he thought. He suspected that these random illnesses were all symptoms of the turbulence in his mind, of his profound unhappiness.

He had travelled from Ravenna to Pisa and collected the rest of his belongings that he had stored at the Albergo Tinto and then had taken a diligence to Genoa, planning on resuming his old itinerary – a boat to Marseilles and then on into Spain. But in Marseilles he had felt so ill that he had summoned a doctor to the hotel where he was staying who for some reason had decided to bleed him, several times.

While he was recuperating at the hotel, heavily dosed with laudanum after his bleedings, he had a somewhat delirious conversation with another guest who was raving about the astonishing beauty of the women of Arles – *les Arlesiennes*. I need beauty, Cashel had told himself, and promptly decided to go to Arles, not that far away. So he took a coach to the ancient, crumbling town on the broad, brown Rhône river, with its Roman arena and narrow cobbled streets of decrepit, weed-badged houses.

And he did indeed see plenty of Arlesiennes – in their lace bodices and shawls, their hair made up in double chignons wrapped around a curious flag-like ribbon – but could not see their reputed beauty. It was not their fault, he knew. He was blind to beauty because of the beauty who had betrayed him.

However, as he brooded bitterly on what he now termed Raphaella's treachery, slivers of self-doubt began to insert themselves in his mind and to agitate him. Why had he been so precipitate? Perhaps, he found himself thinking, he should have let a day or two go by before fleeing the city like a terrified refugee escaping a marauding horde. Why did he always have to act so spontaneously, he wondered, driven by absolute conviction? Absolute convictions could all too easily be wrong – as his own life had demonstrated . . . He put the suggestion to himself that he should consider returning to Ravenna – at least for a proper confrontation with her, the betrayer, the traitress, face to face. But then he rebuked himself. No, that would make him a true lapdog, a cowering spaniel, a desperate and sad man. He had done absolutely the right thing, had behaved with cold and proper dignity. He would not demean himself.

Also, apart from his chronic, undiagnosable ill-health, other more pragmatic matters demanded his attention. His half-pay from the regiment had now ceased and his modest remaining capital had to be carefully husbanded. No more hotel life, he reasoned. No more dinners in restaurants.

Through a local lawyer he found out that there was a farm-house to rent for very reasonable rates about an hour's ride from the town. He went to visit and found a large, simple, two-storey farmhouse. It was larger than he needed but seemed comfortable and had been recently whitewashed inside; a few sticks of solid furniture were also provided. For a little extra money he could have the use of one of the farm nags housed in the stables. The farmer and his family had moved into a capacious stone barn across the yard. The farmer, a widower, was a wizened, toothless old man called Silvan Couderc. He had two grown-up unmarried daughters – Clotilda and Limoun – and a simple teenaged son called Jaufret. The daughters, Cashel was informed, would cook, shop, launder and clean the house when required for a few extra francs.

It was actually an ideal situation, he soon realized. The family – who spoke Occitan to each other – kept themselves to themselves. If Cashel wanted something he went to the barn and called out and one or other of them would diffidently emerge. He had never set foot in the dark, fetid barn and had no idea of the living arrangements within.

In a very short time, Cashel felt surprisingly established. Bread was brought to him every two days. If he wanted hot food he asked Clotilda to roast a chicken or make a stew but he hadn't much of an appetite and was happy with cheese and cold meats most of the time. He brought big green demijohns of rough red wine and a few bottles of eau de vie and spent his days rewriting his *Journal of a Tour*. But he couldn't stop thinking of Raphaella and their time together in Ravenna.

He went over and over their encounters, social and sexual, with a kind of mania, trying to see the origins of what he now called the Great Betrayal. He was beset with doubts, of course. Had he been too impulsive? Might it not have been better to accuse her face to face, to humiliate her more? How would she have reacted to his letter? Shrugged and torn it up? Laughed? Had a momentary spasm of guilt? The obsessive questionings and re-imaginings began to overwhelm him, to make him doubt his sanity, sometimes. Then one day, spontaneously, he decided to write it all down as a way of exorcizing himself, of clearing his mind. He selected a new sheet of paper and began to write a thinly fictionalized account of his love affair with Raphaella Rezzo.

He realized the inspiration lay in his late-night visit to Dante's tomb and he reread his English translation of the *Commedia*, seeking out the story of Paolo and Francesca. This new version of the doomed lovers was, he decided, to be set in contemporary London. He called their English incarnations 'Paul' and 'Frances' and simply related through them the events that he had experienced with Raphaella – though with the obligatory decorum. Soon he had covered over a dozen pages and he could sense the story taking on its own energies and inspiration. He set aside the *Journal* to concentrate on this new fiction.

It was interesting, he noted, how after a couple of weeks of writing his health began to improve and, feeling in better spirits, he decided to end the charade that he was still in India, soldiering, and had written to his mother, telling her that he had had a bad dose of 'Yellow Jack' fever, had been invalided out of the regiment and had returned to Europe to recuperate and convalesce. He had received a swift reply – full of concern – thanking him for his letters from India and offering to send a letter of credit if his funds were running low. A correspondence had now begun and that made him feel better about himself, also. He was in no hurry to return to his old life, he knew; he would winter on in Vache Noire and see how he felt when summer came around.

That evening, Cashel dined on stale bread and hard cheese washed down with a pint or so of red wine from his demijohn. He lit two candles, thinking he might read, but instead he looked at the fire and drank more wine, wondering morosely what would become of him. He went to bed in a fug of mild self-pity and intoxication and, snuffing out his candles, lay there in the dark thinking – as he did every night – of Raphaella. And, again, he dutifully tried to stoke up his rage against her but all he could feel was the loss, what had gone from his life and how it was so diminished without her presence.

The image of her lying naked in bed, guileless, heedless, pleasantly exhausted, the thin, white-clay pipe in her hands like a fragile wand, continued to haunt him. The way she had shifted her weight and raised the other knee to give her purchase so she could turn towards the candle . . . Cashel heard himself groan through his erotic doze and then was startled by a powerful knocking at his front door.

He jerked out of his reverie. Had something happened to the Couderc family? Was the barn ablaze? He fumbled with his tinderbox – the knocking continuing – made fire, lit a candle and walked through to the front door, pulling on his greatcoat over his nightshirt, his loaded pistol snug in his pocket.

'*C'est qui dehors?*' he shouted.

'Are you an Englishman?' came a voice from outside.

'Yes, I am.'

'Thank the crucified Jesus. I'm an Englishman, also – but in dire need of help.'

Cashel carefully unlocked the door, his hand in his pocket feeling for the butt of his pistol.

A lean, handsome, neat figure of a young man stood there, a bandage round his face. He spoke in a rush.

'Do forgive the late hour and the disturbance. My name is Brooke Mason. I'm an artist and I am dying of the toothache. I was told that there was an Englishman living at Vache Noire. Any Englishman will have laudanum, thought I, in my hour of need. Do not disappoint me, sir, I beg you.'

'I do have laudanum.'

'I knew it! I knew it! Thank the Holy Carpenter!'

Cashel showed him in, sat him by the smouldering fire which he revived with a couple of logs, lit more candles, poured the man a glass of eau de vie and went in search of his supply of laudanum. In fact, he had four bottles of the syrup in his medicinal chest. Since he had been bled in Marseilles and had had recourse to the miracle drug, he had thought it as well to lay in a stock as he was going to be living in the countryside.

He poured some laudanum into a small glass, handed it to Mr Brooke Mason and watched him drink, rinse the liquor around his mouth and then swallow. He asked for a refill that went down in one go.

'It is wonderful, powerful, efficacious stuff, there's no doubt,'

Mason said. He followed up the laudanum with a slug of eau de vie.

Cashel took a look at his visitor, who he reckoned was about thirty years old. He had a thin set of whiskers and an agitated manner – his hands always in motion, touching his face, gesturing, scratching sudden itches. Cashel introduced himself. Mason stood and bowed.

'I would sacrifice a child in thanks to you, Mr Ross – had I a child. But I am sincerely, everlastingly beholden to you. I feel remarkably better. The pain is entirely supportable, now.' He looked around the room. 'I walked ten miles to reach you. Sometimes, when you're in desperation, all you need is a fellow countryman. And – look – you've saved me. I've been on a rack of pain, sir. A boiling griddle of agony.'

Cashel said he was welcome to stay the night, if he wished. There must be a tooth-puller in Arles, or a barber-dentist, who could relieve him of his problem in the morning. Most graciously kind, Mason said. Find me a dry corner and I'll gladly sleep there. Cashel took him upstairs to a room where there was a straw mattress on the floor, gave him the rest of the laudanum bottle, furnished him with a clean chamber pot, and they said goodnight.

The next morning, in the front room before the fire, Cashel reached cautiously into the back of Mason's mouth with his thumb and forefinger and, with a sharp tug, pulled out a molar. Mason spat blood and pus into a dish for two minutes, rinsed the new cavity with eau de vie, took another swig of laudanum and proclaimed himself free of the toothache. One of mankind's cruellest curses, he said. Animals don't get toothache, so why do we? God's malice, he said. Pure malice.

Brooke Mason, now fully recovered, made Cashel a proposition. He needed a place to stay and thought that the room he had slept in the night before was all he required, despite the fact that it was very mouse-ridden. But he didn't care about mice – live and let live. He suggested a rent of ten shillings a week or whatever the

French equivalent was. He was more than prepared to buy his share of wine and victuals.

'You won't see much of me in the day,' Mason said, 'as I'm out and about earning my living, but I'll usually be back before nightfall.'

Cashel agreed without further thought. It would be good to have some company – even eccentric company. He was keen to have some distraction, wary of his night thoughts, and a trickle of rent would boost his diminishing funds.

'What's the work that takes you away all day?' Cashel asked.

'My art business,' Mason said, then added, 'I commission art and I am paid for it.' He smiled. 'All will be explained.'

Mason walked back to his previous abode to retrieve his horse – he would not tell Cashel where he had been living. If he has a horse, why didn't he ride here? Cashel asked himself. But he had already registered that Brooke Mason was a complicated fellow. His accent was patrician but his clothes were shabby and much repaired. His cravat was greasy and his collar dirty and unstarched. However, Cashel didn't care: diverting company and ten shillings a week was no great penance.

Mason returned, mid-afternoon, on a big-bellied, wheezing mare with two artist's easels strapped to the saddle. He threw down a big leather bag and said, 'There you have it, Ross. The worldly goods of Brooke Mason.'

Over dinner – a beefsteak grilled on the coals of the fire with some potatoes cooked in goose fat – Mason explained his particular profession. He showed Cashel a dozen, very capable watercolours of various buildings – grand houses, chateaux, churches, hunting lodges and the like. They were well achieved, finely detailed, Cashel thought, and he congratulated the artist.

'Oh, no. I didn't do them. I bought them – a job lot – from this down-on-his-luck artist in Paris. But the thing is, I pass them off as my own work – that's the key thing.'

Mason explained. He saw a house – a small chateau, a *chartreuse*, a *maison de maître*, a presbytery – and introduced himself to the owners. He showed them his 'work' and offered to render their own dwelling in the same style.

'I name a very modest price,' he said, 'and that draws them in. Then I ask for a small advance – to buy paper, paint, frames, what-have-you – and tell them I'll be back on the morrow to immortalize their humble or not-so-humble home.' He smiled. 'They always pay. I take their money and travel on down my lonely road.'

'You never return?'

'Never. Of course, after a few days, the ruse becomes apparent – but I'm long gone.'

Cashel said nothing – it was theft, effectively, fraudulent extortion.

Mason sensed his covert condemnation and launched into a convoluted history of his life as if that would explain why he had to resort to such wiles. His father had died when Mason was a young man and his mother – a very merry widow, he said – had swiftly married again to a rich cotton merchant who nurtured a warm affection for young Brooke. This man had two daughters, in their early twenties, who now became Mason's stepsisters.

'I should never have fornicated with them, Ross. That was my colossal error.'

'You had them both?'

'Yes. Not simultaneously, of course. But the second, for some vain reason, confessed to the first – who confessed in turn to the second – and then the two of them confessed to their father.'

Mason was banished to Paris where he 'got into another scrape or two', lost all his money and then came up with his 'art-commissioning' scheme. He had spent the last two years meandering southwards from Paris ('I made a small fortune in the Loire valley') and had wound up here, near Arles and the shores of the Mediterranean.

'I have to keep moving, Ross, that's the disadvantage to my scheme. Which is why I'm so happy to have found you and your farmhouse. I think I might do very well in the environs of Arles and, if I do, so shall you.'

'I've no issue with that, Mason.'

Mason tugged at one of his scanty whiskers and scratched his nose vigorously.

'My life's well remunerated but it's not without its complications.' He sighed. 'I'll have a drop more of that wine, my dear friend, if I may.'

Cashel took Mason's glass over to the demijohn and refilled it. He offered Mason one of his cigars and the two of them lit up with a spill from the fire. They sat back in their chairs, drinking and smoking, and Cashel felt his spirits rise. He hadn't thought about Raphaella for at least two hours. Mason was clearly an unscrupulous, strange man, Cashel recognized, but he was engaging company all the same.

'What's going on in the world, Ross, do you know? I haven't seen a newspaper in months.'

'Neither have I. In Arles, the other day, I heard that Simón Bolívar was made the President of Peru.'

'Damned socialist. Any wars going on?'

'We are fighting the Ashanti in the Gold Coast, I have heard, also.'

'Where's that?'

'West Africa.'

'Good. Far away. Any wars in Europe?'

'Not that I know of.'

'Even better. Don't want to get caught up in a war.'

'No. To be avoided.'

An amiable routine established itself at Vache Noire. Mason went forth in the morning (in a carefully paint-spattered top-coat) on his horse with his easels lashed to the saddle and his watercolour samples in a bag slung over his shoulder. Cashel would work at his novel about himself and Raphaella, that he had now decided to call *Nihil*. He had taken it from a phrase attributed to Catullus – *Nihil est tam acerbum quam amor perditus*. Nothing is as painful as love destroyed, was his harsh translation. He had pondered *Amor Perditus* as a title but felt that the one terse word more powerfully conveyed his bitterness and misery.

Of course, the more he thought of Raphaella and the more he wrote about her – and himself, and the two of them – the more the torment grew. He would lie in bed at night and picture her in precise and perfect detail. Her face, her hair, her eyes, her lips, her wrists, her breasts, her long legs, her toes. Sometimes he heard himself spontaneously and audibly groaning.

Perhaps it was the presence of Mason and his artistic pretensions that made Cashel now wish that he had some image of Raphaella: a portrait, a silhouette, a cameo, a miniature, even a drawing, a sketch – some physical reproduction of her that would instantly trigger the memories of the pleasures they had shared, the love they had shared. Or that they had seemed to share . . . Why, he asked himself, had he not commissioned a portrait, a miniature, even, as a memento? Because, you fool, he answered himself, you left Ravenna as if the plague or some other deadly pestilence had arrived. You left Ravenna, you fool, when at the time you had no intention of ever leaving it, when you saw Raphaella whenever you wished and had no need of a simulacrum. Cashel's inveighing against himself continued – the absence of a portrait was another regret to add to the small mountain of regrets that was beginning to form in his mind. He forced himself to think anew of the wrong she had done him – her callous arrogance, her carnal opportunism – and for a while the regrets were subdued.

He was glad of the distraction that Mason's presence as his lodger provided. As night approached, Mason would return with his day's 'commissions' – sometimes just one or two, sometimes half a dozen and, on one miraculous Saturday, he returned with ten. No day seemed to go by without someone being duped and dunned. He paid the rent of his upstairs room in advance and was generous in buying provisions. It was clear that his knavery worked very well. Nobody knew where this itinerant painter was living and because the sums he bilked were relatively modest – no one was seriously out of pocket – people cursed him, he supposed, but did nothing more. It was hardly worth it for a few francs.

They ate well, they drank well. Mason was a source of amusing anecdotes. He occasionally asked for a glass of laudanum – to ease his aching tooth cavity, he said – and Cashel happily raided his supplies. Then, a few weeks into their new life together as landlord and tenant, Mason asked if Cashel knew of a brothel in Arles. Cashel knew of two, he said. Well, we must pay one of them a visit, Mason said, claiming that he was beginning to feel ill and he knew it was the result of an absence of sexual activity.

That evening they rode together into Arles and went to number 1 rue du Bout. There were two reception rooms in the large, bourgeois house – one plain and bare for working folk, and one all velvet and leather with a chandelier, a bar and a man at the piano. This salon was for the richer clients – most of them were soldiers, Zouave officers from the garrison at Arles. There were up to a dozen 'girls' circulating as drinks – absinthe, some kind of cheap champagne, brandy – were purchased at the bar while the client made his selection before climbing the stairway to the bedroom floor.

Mason wasted no time and went upstairs with his choice – a beefy young woman in a revealing version of the Arlesienne costume. Cashel said he wasn't interested.

'Come on, man, live a little,' Mason insisted.

'You have to understand, Mason. I was an officer in the Indian army. Every European had the pox. The regimental doctor himself told me that five out of six officers had the pox or some equivalent. I saw the effects with my own eyes – hence my prudence.'

Mason was intrigued.

'You were in the Indian army? Bengal?'

'Madras.'

'You're a dark horse, Ross,' he chuckled. 'Who'd have thought? You'll have to tell me more.'

He went upstairs. Cashel politely declined the solicitations of the professional Arlesiennes, ordered more brandy, listened to the pianist playing polkas and thought, inevitably, about Raphaella.

Spring passed, uneventfully. The air warmed and there began to be a few days of full summer heat, blue distance starting to be perceived. Cashel's financial worries had disappeared what with Mason paying his rent faultlessly on time, in advance. He was doing a 'roaring trade', he said, expanding his portfolio to include churches, presbyteries, monasteries and the like. The priests were mad with vanity, he said, and he was thinking of offering a portrait service, if only he could find some specimen drawings or canvases to pass off as his own.

Cashel was approaching the final chapters of *Nihil* though he was struggling with the end. He was considering having Paul kill himself after Frances's perfidy – perhaps drown himself or fling himself over some beetling cliff. Inspired by Mason's regular brothel visiting he had written a chapter in which Paul goes to a house of ill-repute, expressly to expunge memories of Frances, but finds himself unable to perform (memories of Frances's body achingly present in his mind) and flees the scene in tears, even more of a broken man.

One afternoon – Mason was out for the day, as usual, though he was now ranging further afield searching for clients – there was a knock at the door. A dark-suited burly man with a dense beard stood there, wearing a tricorn hat. He said he was looking for an Englishman, an artist called Mason – did he live here by any chance?

Cashel knew instantly that he should deny any knowledge of this 'Mason' and he did so convincingly. The man went away, seemingly placated.

Mason was unperturbed.

'There's bound to be the odd unsatisfied customer who'll come after me. Occupational hazard. All they've got to go on is "Englishman", so you might get a few more enquiries to see if you're the one in question. Won't be a problem.' He smiled. 'That's why it's so useful I'm staying with you. It confuses people. You're my perfect disguise, Ross.'

But Mason's insouciance became more of a problem when, one morning in the kitchen, Cashel heard lighter footsteps on the stairs down from the upper floor and Monsieur Couderc's younger daughter, Limoun, appeared, smiled briefly, and left without a word. Mason appeared two minutes later.

He confessed that he'd smuggled her upstairs into his room when Cashel was preoccupied.

'I offered her two francs, on the off-chance, and she said yes, instantly. You should avail yourself, Ross. These country girls know a few tricks.'

Cashel kept his temper, just.

'This is really not acceptable behaviour, Mason,' he said. 'It changes my relationship with the family – completely. I may be your landlord but Couderc is mine. And here you are jouncing his daughter – the younger one. How old can she be?'

'He'll be glad of the supplementary income, believe me, old chap. Now, what's for breakfast? I could eat a polar bear.'

But Cashel was becoming troubled. The anarchic force that was Brooke Mason was now disturbing the tranquil pool of his life at Vache Noire. Two more men came to the door in the next fortnight seeking the 'English artist'. Limoun confronted Cashel in the farmhouse and raised her skirt to show him what was beneath, informing him, in her accented French, that she was available for five francs. Cashel laughed harshly and shooed her out.

A day later Silvan Couderc himself approached him in the yard and said that if the other Englishman wanted Limoun on a regular basis then the money should be paid to him, not her. Also, Clotilda was available, if he – Cashel – or the other Englishman were interested, but she would be more expensive as she was a virgin. Cashel said no, and apologized sincerely. He felt ashamed. He wondered if he could persuade Mason to move on before the whole Couderc family was irretrievably corrupted.

Then, one evening, Mason returned with a swollen eye and a cut on his cheek and wouldn't explain how it had happened.

'Have you got a firearm in the house, Ross? A pistol, a shotgun?'

Cashel showed him his double-barrelled pistol.

'May I borrow it?'

'Why?'

'There's a man I want to frighten. To convince him of my utter ruthlessness.'

Cashel handed over his pistol and Mason rode off into the night, returning some two hours later. He handed the pistol back.

'Not discharged, you'll notice. But it did the trick.' He paused, tugged at his whiskers (one of his constant twitchy gestures) and seemed about to say something.

'What is it?' Cashel prompted.

'I'm afraid I'm going to have to move on. I seem to have overstayed my welcome in the Arles region.'

'What's happened?'

'Let's just say things have got a little out of control. I'll be gone before dawn, don't worry.'

They sat up late that night, smoking and drinking the last of Mason's brandy. Mason – usually so carefree – seemed untypically troubled. What exactly had he done? Cashel wondered.

'I've got to go far away,' he said, staring at the fire. 'I've got to disappear – so I was thinking of Venezuela. Somebody told me that they want English gentlemen to emigrate there. They're offering vast tracts of land for next to nothing.'

'Venezuela? Why not go to Italy?'

'Because I can be found in Italy,' he said mysteriously. Then he turned his full attention on Cashel.

'Come with me, Ross. You and me in Venezuela. We could be kings, emperors, satraps, demigods!'

'No, thank you, Mason. I have a novel to finish.'

When Cashel woke the next morning, Brooke Mason was gone. There was a brief note on the table explaining that he had taken Cashel's pistol and he apologized for being a week in arrears for the rent of the room. A postscript said that if anyone came looking for him Cashel should say he had gone to Morocco. Not to breathe a word about Venezuela.

★

At first Cashel was relieved Mason had gone. Then as the summer progressed he found he rather missed his exotic company. The Couderc family treated him with injured aloofness, as if he had ruined some promising potential in their lives. Moreover, he was stuck with his novel – he couldn't finish it, try as he might – and now alone and left to his own devices he began to feel increasingly unsettled. He needed some dramatic resolution, he realized, not just for *Nihil* but for himself. He began again to regret leaving Ravenna so precipitously. He should have confronted Raphaella – seen her with his own eyes as she attempted her explanations and evasions. Now he felt troubled by the lack of answers to his questions. He had been too hasty, too impulsive – that was clear to him, now. It was one of his faults, he knew. Too often he acted without thinking, driven onwards by pure feeling, not pausing to analyse situations from all angles, weigh things up, soberly, thoughtfully. And he began to think that if he could see Raphaella again he would at least have an end to the episode, to the love affair – and maybe that would provide him with an authentic end to *Nihil*, also. Hiding, brooding, obsessively going over events in his recent history was the wrong sort of life to be living. It became evident to him as summer ended and the autumn winds began to blow over the Rhône estuary that he needed, absolutely, to go back to Ravenna.

He bade a warm farewell to the Coudercs at the end of September, to which they coolly responded, unmoved by his departure and taking the money he gave them as if it were their due, though Jaufret Couderc generously offered to drive him into Arles to pick up the stagecoach to Marseilles. He helped Cashel load his trunks and bundles into the pony and trap and they trotted off down the lane together.

Jaufret was a solemn, quiet lad of about eighteen, Cashel guessed, who had a big lumpy face, as if his features were still being formed and eventually a proper nose, cheekbones and chin would appear, fixed finally for adulthood. He was trying to grow a moustache without much success.

Halfway to Arles he spoke, unprompted.

'Monsieur Ross, I have a favour to ask you,' he said in his twangingly accented French.

'Of course, Jaufret.'

'Take me with you on your travels. I could be your manservant.'

Cashel felt a pang. The Couderc family were beginning to disintegrate. The Brooke Mason effect.

'I cannot pay you. I have very little money.'

'All I need is some bread to eat and water to drink.'

'Your father wouldn't be pleased.'

'It's because of my father that I have to leave. And my sisters. You see, they make me—'

Cashel stopped him; he didn't want to know.

'I'm sorry, Jaufret, it's impossible.' He paused. 'But if I ever have some money, I'll send for you.'

'Thank you, *monsieur*. I will wait for your call with impatience.'

Jaufret seemed very cheered, almost exhilarated by this false vision of his future. Cashel felt more guilt accumulate: why had he made the offer? Fool. He should have kept quiet. But that was the flaw in his nature, he was coming to realize – he was too decent a man; always trying to please, to be liked. He had to become more self-serving and ruthless, like Brooke Mason.

Cashel stood with his baggage outside the Hôtel de la Lice, that acted as the coach depot in Arles, and, with very mixed feelings, watched Jaufret drive away back to Vache Noire and the rest of his life. He turned and gave Cashel a cheery wave, a big smile on his face.

And so Cashel retraced his steps to Ravenna. Packet from Marseilles to Genoa. Diligence from Genoa to Bologna. A hired chaise to drive him from Bologna to Ravenna. As he crossed the plain approaching the city he felt his apprehension mount. He had left Raphaella just over a year ago and he wondered how she would feel to have him back. Perhaps he should have written, he now thought – too late for that, however. And what would he say if she chose to meet him? She might not, of course – only now did he think of that possibility. Should he apologize? But she was the one in the wrong – all he had given her was untrammelled devotion. He now even began to doubt the wisdom of returning, feeling the acid burn of indigestion – always a sign of tension within him – and took a sip of brandy from the small silver flask he carried in a pocket. He looked out at the sunlit countryside unrolling before him, at the harvested cornfields, briefly cloud-shadowed, at the thin poplars swaying in the stiff breeze, and told himself to take everything one hour at a time. His impulsive heart had made him quit Ravenna and now it had urged him back again. Was that another mistake? There was nothing to be done about that, now.

He was able to find a room at the Albergo Massimo where he was welcomed as a familiar. He changed out of his dusty travelling clothes, combed his hair and applied some eau de Cologne and, without more ado, headed out and walked through the streets of the city towards the Palazzo Rezzo.

He saw at once, as he approached, that something was amiss. The heavy double main doors were closed and barred and every window facing the street was shuttered. Weeds were growing in the fissures of the marble steps. Perhaps the Rezzo entourage had decamped to Bologna . . . But the air of a neglected, unmaintained building was inescapable. The palazzo looked abandoned.

He walked down the side alleyway to the rear of the main building where the stables, outhouses and the kitchens were. Here also the gates into the back courtyard were shut with heavy chains. A stray dog sniffed at some scraps of rubbish, barked once at him and loped off. A dead cat lay in a gutter. He cupped his hands around his mouth and shouted for someone to receive him. Silence. A passer-by told him the palazzo had been empty for nine months. Nine months! He shouted again and saw a high shutter swing open. It was closed and then, moments later, the door to the kitchens opened and Timoteo stepped out.

Timoteo transformed, however. His hair was woolly and untrimmed, his smart striped uniform rank and unwashed, the 'R' on the tunic front almost illegible. No jewelled dagger or pistol hung from his belt. He was pleased to see Cashel, however, and smiled widely,

'*Signor Ross! Come stai?*'

'What's happened, Timoteo? Where is everyone?'

The boy came to the gates and told him. Count Rezzo had died, a month after Cashel had left. Timoteo pointed to his head. His brain died very suddenly, he said. The count's son (from his first marriage), Gianfranco Rezzo, lived in Rome and had no desire to move to Ravenna and cared nothing about the palazzo. Anything valuable was removed and the place was locked up. What was worse, Timoteo complained, was that the new Count Rezzo never sent any money. Buildings didn't look after themselves. The roof leaked. There was rot in some beams. Timoteo, a caretaker and his wife were the only staff remaining. It was impossible to look after a building of this size without money. Even after these few months it was beginning to fall apart. What were they—

'But the contessa? Where is she?'

'She is in Milan, sir. With her husband.'

'Husband?' Cashel felt sick. He put the back of his hand to his mouth.

'She married Count Mazzolino. Count Ludovico Mazzolino. A very rich man. You should see his palazzo in Milan, Signor Ross. It makes this one look like a hovel by the roadside.'

'Why aren't you with the contessa?'

'I went there with her when she was to be married to the count but I was not welcome in the household. So I was sent back here. The contessa writes to me, from time to time. She promises me I can return when she has persuaded her husband.'

Cashel was thinking hard as Timoteo talked on. The wedding had taken place three months after Count Rezzo's death. She hadn't waited long, he thought, with some bitterness. Timoteo was saying something.

'What's that?' Cashel asked him to repeat his information.

'In her last letter – she told me about the baby.'

'How can she have a baby . . .?'

'No. She's with child, sir. The baby will be born at Christmas.'

Cashel's calculation was immediate. The child was not his – not *their* child. A child for rich Count Mazzolino. He felt a shroud of cynical resignation descend on him. It was absurdly typical, he thought, how easily passion obscured clear vision. At least he had an ending for *Nihil*, now, and a suitably apt one.

Timoteo's hand reached through the bars of the gate and gripped his sleeve.

'Please, Signor Ross, take me into your household. You know me. You know you can trust me. I'm not wanted here – I'm forgotten. I can come and work for you, sir.'

'I have no household, Timoteo. I'm a poor man.'

Timoteo looked at him blankly, then incredulously.

'How can you be poor, sir?'

'Believe me, I am. I'm poor in everything that life has to offer. All riches have passed me by.'

He smiled ruefully at the truth of this statement, shrugged, squeezed Timoteo's outstretched hand and said farewell. He turned and walked slowly back to the *albergo* trying to take everything in – all dreams gone, shattered, his life truly empty now.

Back at the *albergo*, the innkeeper greeted him warmly. He had remembered that they had property for him that he'd left behind after his last stay. Oh, yes, and a letter, he said. He went to fetch the items. The property was *La Divina Commedia*, now returned with an accompanying letter. He recognized Raphaella's handwriting and went upstairs to his room to read it. His hands were shaking as he broke the seal and unfolded the single sheet. He saw that it was in English. Written in a fervid outpouring, her familiar handwriting jagged, the paper torn by the impress of the pen, the page blotted and dark with scorings-out.

Ravenna

September 1823

How can you be so cruel to me? How can you be so cruel after everything we have experienced together? What kind of ~~man~~ *being are*

you? Everything was planned and would have worked. I do not
understand what you mean by my 'second' <u>cavaliere servante</u>. ~~You were~~
~~the only person who~~ There was no other person in my life before I met
you. As you know my marriage to Count Rezzo was a convenience, a
transaction between two families as is completely normal in our society
in this country. ~~What have you done?~~ We could have been together
without fear, whenever we wanted, without hiding. And now you have
suddenly gone from my life – vanished. I have no idea where you are or
how to communicate with you. You might as well be dead. ~~You are~~
~~dead to me to all intents and~~ You have made a terrible, terrible, terrible,
awful, mistake that will haunt us for ever. You have destroyed
something absolutely beautiful. You have left me. You have left me
alone.

   <u>Addio per sempre</u>, as you say.

   Raphaella*

Cashel gave something between a dry heave and a choking
sob. He felt he was about to vomit and ran to the window, fling-
ing it open and spitting phlegm outside. He took a gulp from his
flask – hoping to quell the panicked, trembling shock he was
experiencing. He sat down on the bed, his brain furiously turning
over – madly deducing, slowly comprehending.

Of course, of course – now it was utterly clear. Count Rezzo
had lied to him. There had never been a 'tall, fair-haired young
man' who resembled him and who had been the 'first' *cavaliere
servante*. The fiction must have been the result of a crippled old
man's spite, a cuckold's resentment and jealousy. It was an
attempt to poison and undermine a recognized social convention
that allowed an old man's young wife to keep a lover – in public –
and therefore be a permanent rebuke to, and reminder of, the old
man's paralysed impotence. So the count lied and confected a

---

* This letter has survived. The deletions have been transcribed as accurately as
possible.

barbed, evil, bitter calumny – a destructive piece of false information to damage and disturb his replacement husband.

But the lie would only work if the fool to whom it was directed believed it. Or cared about it. Tragic fool, indeed. Cashel swore at himself, in real despair, as the other realizations crowded in with hindsight. The count had died only a month after he had left Ravenna. Had he, Cashel, been in Ravenna as the recognized *cavaliere servante*, what then? What kind of life might he and Raphaella have lived together, free of the constraints of her marriage to the count? Raphaella could have made her choice, unimpeded. They loved each other with a wanton passion that was only just under control. What new freedoms might they have enjoyed? Where might they have decided to live together? Nothing tied them to Italy . . . And he had thrown that all away with his absurd, headstrong dignity, his pure and haughty self-regard, his perceived personal hurt – so quick, so selfishly eager to believe that the woman he loved was manipulating and false.

He groaned out loud, unable and unwilling to calculate the consequences of his abject foolishness, to imagine the world he might have lived in. It was a bleak, tormenting realization and he knew that he would have to live with this knowledge for ever. He had wilfully, crassly, in a moment of madness, lost *everything* he held dear. He had, he realized, ruined his life.

8

Cashel handed his mother the small package, wrapped in manuscript paper and tied with string. Elspeth took it, smiling.

'A present for you, Mother.'

'But it's not even close to my birthday.'

'I can give you a present if I want, can't I? I don't need a reason.'

She unwrapped it and weighed the solid leather-bound book in her hand, marvelling.

'Oh, Cashel. I don't believe it.'

'Finally, yes. I had it properly bound. The public will have to settle for quarter-bound with marbled boards.'

'It's beautiful.' Her voice quavered. She swallowed.

She leant forward and kissed his cheek. Cashel felt tears in his eyes – his mother's pure affection had that effect on him.

She opened the book to the title page and read out loud.

' "*High-Ways and By-Ways. The Journal of a Tour through France and Italy. Including a Walk over the Battlefield of Waterloo and some Recollections of Lord Byron and Shelley*".' She looked up. '*By Cashel Greville Ross, Esquire (proud honouree of the Waterloo Medal), London 1826.*'

'It's a bit of a mouthful, I admit,' Cashel said.

'I don't think so,' she said. 'It's what you need to know when you're thinking of buying a book by a new author.'

'Well, at least you and Sir Guy – Father – will see I haven't been wasting my time.'

'He'll be prouder than I am. I'm just sorry he can't be here.'

Cashel smiled sympathetically. The situation at Stillwell Court hadn't changed. Sir Guy was continuing to live his double life. Sir Guy Stillwell, Bart., in Ireland; Mr Pelham Ross, Esquire, in Oxford. It wasn't easy. Lady Stillwell, drifting deeper into insanity, looked as though she'd live to be a hundred, his mother had told him. The estate was massively in debt, land had to be sold, the remaining farms and tenants closely administered to maximize income. He was spending more time in County Cork than he was with his Oxford family.

Elspeth was turning the book over in her hands.

'I can't believe you came to know Lord Byron.'

'Well, just a little. My publisher insisted that it be mentioned in the title.'

His publisher was Purvis Yelverton, of the firm Yelverton & Bale. A man who saw in Byron's untimely death in 1824 an unforeseen but massive publishing opportunity. 'His name *must* be in the title, Ross. I insist,' Yelverton had said. 'And stick that arse Shelley in while you're at it.' He didn't need to add that the book would not be published otherwise.

Cashel felt a bit cheapened by the ploy but he was sure Albé would understand. The news of Byron's death had shaken him, coming so soon after Shelley's. It gave the summer and the months they'd spent together a malevolent aftertaste and made him wonder if there had been portents to be spotted. He remembered Shelley saying that Byron was a warrior without an enemy – and now some fever in the Eastern Mediterranean had got the better of him. Perhaps, Cashel consoled himself, these reminiscences were a good thing – to keep the old Byron alive in people's minds.

He smiled at his mother.

'Where are the boys?'

He had coached down to Oxford that day and would stay the night. This was only his second visit home since he'd returned from the Continent and he had missed them the previous time.

'Buckley's at his college. Hogan should be here soon. He knows you're coming.'

Buckley was in his first year studying Divinity at Merton College. Hogan had become apprenticed to a horse dealer called Enoch Starkie, who ran a sort of stud farm near Iffley. Starkie sold horses to the English army, in the main, and did good business through the endless demand for coach and carrier horses.

They also operated a thriving knackery. Hogan was earning a living, Elspeth told him, though it was clear she would rather it wasn't in the horse trade.

At almost nineteen years old, Hogan and Buckley were now young men, it rather shocked Cashel to realize, their age reminding him of just how long he had been away from his home and his family, of how much he'd experienced since Sir Guy saw him off to India in 1817 . . .

He heard the front door open and Hogan Ross presently sauntered into the room. He was swarthy, darkened by his work outdoors, and his hair was unfashionably long and tousled. A lean young man – not as tall as Cashel – with pale brown eyes, the colour of ale, Cashel thought. He looked like a prosperous ruffian, with the same nervy, shifty comportment about him that he'd had as a boy. He had a worn beaver-skin topper in his hands that he tossed on a sofa, the better to embrace his brother.

'The prodigal returns,' Hogan said with a thin smile. 'Have we fatted calf for supper, Mother?'

'Look. He's brought his book with him,' Elspeth said, and handed it over.

Hogan glanced at the title page.

' "*Cashel Greville Ross, Esquire*". Are you getting a bit grand for us provincials, Cashel?' He gave him back the book. 'I'll be sure to buy a copy meself, don't worry.'

Buckley joined them for an early supper. He had to return to his college by eight o'clock. Cashel felt more at ease with diffident, sweet Buckley, slighter than Hogan, and with a gentle, serious manner. No twins were less twin-like, Cashel thought, seeing an almost Manichaean separation in their natures. Apart from their eyes – both Hogan and Buckley had brown eyes. Cashel's were pale blue. Guy Stillwell eyes.

After their supper of baked sole and a leg of mutton, Buckley returned to his college and Hogan and Cashel sat on in the dining room sharing a decanter of port.

'I doff my cap to you, Cashel,' Hogan said, miming the gesture, almost blurting the compliment out. 'I admire you for what you've done and I'm not too proud to admit it.'

'Admire me for what?'

'For getting out. For going your own sweet way. For writing a bloody book.'

'It's not as simple as that.'

'Have you ever met someone?' Hogan said, leaning forward confidentially. 'I mean, have you fallen in love with a lass? I haven't.'

Cashel paused before answering. Shall I tell him? he wondered. But the mood was strangely warm – it wasn't like bluff, confident Hogan to be so open and confiding.

'I did meet someone. In Italy – a wonderful, beautiful, unique young woman . . .' Cashel felt his throat tighten, choked with sudden, instinctive emotion. Here he was talking blithely to Hogan about the woman he had loved – and lost. 'But I messed it all up. My fault, entirely. I ruined everything and lost her. I'm not sure I'll ever get over it, to tell the truth.'

'Maybe it's her loss,' Hogan said loyally. 'I'd look at it from that angle, if I were you.' He raised his glass. 'Here's to you, Cash. And, remember, if you ever need a helping hand, you can call on your little brother.'

Cashel smiled and they clinked glasses.

'I'm not just saying it to curry favour, mind,' Hogan went on. 'I'm here, if you need me – for anything.'

'I won't forget,' Cashel said. 'Thanks, Hogan. It means a lot.'

On the coach back to London the next day – the eleven o'clock *Retaliator* – Cashel found his thoughts returning to Raphaella, prompted by his confession to Hogan. He thought about her every day, he realized, as some memory, some recalled image, came to mind unbidden. And he dreamt about her. Many times he had considered writing to her in Milan but realized it would be pointless. She was married again; her first child would be a toddler and there might have been a second, for all he knew. What would a letter from him achieve? The genie would not go back in the lamp – too much time had passed. Too much silence.

He thought back to his long morose journey northwards through Europe. He hadn't hurried. The year had turned by the time he reached Ostend and retrieved his stored belongings and Cornelius Poynter's library. He wrote to his mother and Sir Guy from London, telling them he was fully recovered, in excellent health and renting rooms in Soho where he was occupied in finishing his travel book.

He found a suite of three furnished rooms on the top floor of a house in Meard Street, Soho, number 35. It was a proper lodging house with a landlady – a Mrs Ackerman – and was well run. Full board, half board, breakfast only, no board, were all offered at descending rates. Cashel, having checked his funds, elected for 'breakfast only' plus chambermaid service. His chamber pot was emptied, his fire cleaned and laid each day, his bed linen changed monthly – laundry services were extra.

There were four other lodgers in 35 Meard Street. Sometimes Cashel met one or two at breakfast; he often heard them on the stairs as they came and went, and one – a Mr Greenstock – occasionally practised the fiddle (badly) to everyone's general irritation.

Once, when Cashel had a headache and wanted to sleep it off he found the scraping of the Greenstock fiddle too insistent and went down one floor to ask if the gentleman might be so kind as to postpone his repetitions. Arthur Greenstock was a huge young man, in his late twenties, tall and portly with an untrimmed beard and a marked shortness of breath. He was, he happily confessed, a jobbing writer and having apologized for the noise of his fiddle – it looked like a child's toy in his big hands – he invited Cashel into his rooms for a glass of rum, sugar and hot water, 'the only reliable headache cure'. He wrote hack journalism for half a dozen newspapers, letters for illiterates, advertising copy, pamphlets for any organization that required a manifesto, and did a certain amount of clerking in law courts and Parliament when journalistic assignments were in short supply. Anything that could be written in an hour or two – he was your man. He was impressed when Cashel told him he'd been writing *Journal of a Tour* for several years and asked if he might read a chapter or two. Cashel gave him his opening pages – about his visit to the battlefield of Waterloo.

Greenstock was enthused, so he said, and thought that the book should definitely be published if the rest was of the same standard. He knew any number of publishers, he said, and it would be a pleasure to be of service. Cashel was very happy to accept the favour.

It was Greenstock's introduction that led him to Purvis Yelverton of Yelverton & Bale.

The publisher's office was to be found in Cripplegate, in the east of London. Cashel took a growler across the city and told the driver to wait – he'd get double the fare if he waited – as the area was not salubrious. They stopped in Postern Street and Cashel alighted and saw the sign for White Cross Court where the Yelverton & Bale office was located. Filthy, near-naked urchins stared at him as he crossed the road. There was a skeletal dead horse lying in the gutter with crows picking listlessly at it. With some trepidation he walked down the alley that led to the court.

There he found a butcher's, a turner's workshop and a button-mould maker – and a sign that directed him up some rickety wooden stairs to the first floor above.

Yelverton & Bale's office, however, was in noticeable contrast to its environs. A fire blazed in the fireplace, there were Oriental rugs on the floor, and many prominently labelled portraits of writers on the wainscoted walls – Cashel spotted Shakespeare, Dante, Mrs Burney, Dean Swift, Alexander Pope and Dr Johnson amongst others – as if there was some benefit accruing to the firm from this ad hoc association. In any event, seeing illustrious fellow writers, Cashel relaxed somewhat.

Purvis Yelverton was a gaunt, jaundiced man in his fifties with scant hair and teeth, yet he was well dressed with a matching daffodil-yellow cravat and waistcoat and black velvet slippers on his feet. He was an unctuous and fluent speaker, also, though his toothlessness made him lisp occasionally.

He accepted Cashel's manuscript eagerly and, while quizzing

him on the length and location of his travels, sat up in his seat when Lord Byron was mentioned.

'You knew Lord Byron?'

'I knew him for a few months in 1822. I spent some time alone with him. We conversed—'

'I will publish your *Tour*, sir.'

'But you haven't read it.'

'I don't need to. You're obviously highly literate if you were a friend of Lord Byron. He does appear in the account, I assume?'

'Yes. There are a few pages—'

'Then I would advise expanding on them. Any minutiae will be most valuable.'

'But, I think—'

'Excellent. I will offer you fifty pounds, sir. I'll have my clerk draw up a contract.'

Yelverton went to a cabinet and took out a cut-glass decanter and two glasses.

'Madeira?'

'Thank you.'

He and Cashel drank to the success of *Journal of a Tour through France and Italy*. Cashel reflected: first there had been the Waterloo dividend; now it seemed that his slight connection to Lord Byron was to be his *passe-partout*. No matter – he would do whatever was necessary. With some careful husbandry, £50 plus his savings would keep him secure for a couple of years. And so his career as a published author looked like beginning. He walked back to his waiting carriage in buoyant spirits.

Cashel stepped down from the Oxford coach in Fleet Street. It was already dark. Six hours from Oxford to London! or so the coachman had loudly boasted at the inn. More like eight or nine, Cashel thought. There had been a long queue at the turnpike to pay the toll and then the carrier wagons had blocked the road as they waited for their turn at the weighbridge. It was by no means the 'fast run' promised. Still, here he was back in London. He stretched, easing his jangled bones. He would walk back to Soho, he thought – these coaches were damned expensive. Fleet Street had gaslight but he would prefer the company and solidarity of others once the luminosity was left behind.

'Who's going west?' he called out.

He found a couple of men and a woman with a child who were prepared to walk with him together as a group. Off the lighted thoroughfares a solitary pedestrian, at night, was at risk from footpads and gangs of feral children. The sooner the entire city had gas, the safer, he thought.

He split off from the party at Drury Lane and then turned down Long Acre, heading for Soho, always looking carefully about him. There was a stiff breeze blowing and a number of the oil lamps at street corners had blown out. He would have felt safer with his little pistol on him but bloody Brooke Mason had purloined it in Arles and he'd never bothered to re-arm himself. Perhaps he should buy himself a little purse-gun, as they were called.

He came safely to 35 Meard Street and, taking a lit candle from the hallway, went upstairs to his rooms. Mrs Ackerman had propped a letter on his mantel above the fireplace. He lit the fire with a spill, had a piss in his pot, took out his bottle of brandy from the cupboard, poured himself a glass and sat down to read his letter. It was from Yelverton.

My dear Ross –

Success! No sooner is <u>High-Ways and By-Ways</u> published than you are invited to the most select artistic salon in London. Mrs Davenport desires your company at 4 p.m. on the Thursday next at 10 Hill Street, Mayfair. Toot le Mond will be there so dress to the nines. These are the gates to literary paradise, Ross, make no mistake. Word will spread like locusts on fire.

Sincerely yours,
Purvis Yelverton

Cashel went downstairs with his bottle of brandy and rapped on Greenstock's door.

'Come!'

Cashel made himself comfortable in an armchair before Green-stock's meagre fire and surrendered the bottle to his host. He showed him the letter.

'Mrs Davenport's salon. A waste of precious time?'

'No, no. She's a presence, definitely. Very rich, very ambitious to make her mark. Do not prevaricate, my son. Mrs Davenport is worth it.'

'Yelverton encourages me, also.'

'Yelverton knows what's what. He's absolutely right.' Green-stock smiled and topped up their glasses. 'I'd go like a shot but they'd never invite the likes of me. You'll eat and drink well and meet some of your distinguished peers.' He tapped Cashel's knee. 'This is how you get in the swim, these days, Ross. Chit-chat – babble, blather, small talk.'

'Right,' Cashel said, feeling a little spasm of excitement. 'I shall enter the lion's den.'

Ben Smart agreed with Arthur Greenstock's assessment when Cashel met him two days later. They were in a chop house on the Strand. Ben had grown a moustache and whiskers and put on weight. He was now the deputy editor of a daily paper (Monday to Friday) called the *London Star*. It was a curious mix of news, radical Whig-biased opinion – sometimes – with a sea-soning of speculative gossip and general flyting. It was very successful, its circulation growing. They lamented Prime Minis-ter Canning's sudden death and were violently opposed to the banning of mantraps against poachers. Such were the *Star*'s shifting, unpredictable priorities. Ben said they were worried about the recent arrival of the *London Standard* – how many newspapers could one city support? He slurped down a dozen oysters and then called for turtle soup.

'Ben, please. I don't care about the *London Standard*. What about Mrs Davenport's "At Home"?'

'Well, yes . . . It's a good idea. *La crème de la crème*, I suppose. If she takes you up – if you're seen there – it'll make a difference.

But don't be corrupted. Don't forget your old friends. Try the pickled salmon, Cashel. It's delicious.'

Mrs Ethalinda Davenport's 'At Home' took place in her Mayfair house on Hill Street, close to Berkeley Square, an imposing, grey-bricked, five-storey mansion with a mews behind. Gaslights burned in the porch. Carriages and cabs were already arriving and departing, Cashel saw, having walked from Soho in squeaking patent leather shoes. He was shaved, barbered, perfumed and punctual. He felt oddly nervous, as if he were the guest of honour.

To his surprise, he spotted Purvis Yelverton waiting for him in the small crowd of onlookers by the spectacular front door. Cashel went over to him.

'I didn't know you were coming, Mr Yelverton.'

'I'm not invited. I just wanted to make sure you appeared. Be forward, Ross. You want to be noticed. Don't lurk in corners.'

'I'll do my best.'

'There's a lot hanging on this, my boy. A lot.'

He urged Cashel in.

Cashel entered, gave his name to a footman and was directed up the sweeping grand staircase to the next floor where he offered up his name again to a major-domo figure in a red coat who boomingly announced him to the assembled crowd.

'Mr Cashel Greville Ross!'

Nobody paid the least attention and Cashel wandered into a huge room, like a ballroom or a reception salon in a palace, hearing other names announced behind him, and looking around, curiously, as the room swiftly began to fill up. The floor was glossy parquet and upon it were grouped a dozen clusters of chairs and sofas, couches and chaises longues. The walls were so burdened with paintings that the puce silk wallpaper behind them was scarcely visible. In a corner, tables were set with silver Russian samovars for tea; footmen patrolled with trays of coffee, almond biscuits and green-stemmed glasses of Moselle. Soon there were about fifty or sixty people in the room and the clamour of excited conversation filled the air.

Cashel, despite Yelverton's injunction, lurked in a corner with a glass of Moselle, scrutinizing faces. He didn't recognize anyone. He wandered along the far wall looking at the paintings and came to a halt in front of a portrait of an elderly man in a grey wig. Wigs – yes, men used to wear them – how peculiar.

Yelverton had told him that Mrs Davenport had 'tearlessly' buried three husbands, the last of whom – Mr Davenport – had become extremely rich through the network of canals he had constructed and owned in the north of England. A canal magnate, then, who had then made another fortune speculating on stocks and shares until he had suddenly died, leaving his vast wealth to his wife and three children. As the children were all under the age of responsibility the control of the Davenport millions had fallen to their mother.

A large mansion had been acquired in fashionable Mayfair and quickly renamed Davenport House. Mrs Davenport, an authoress herself – she had written a little book about her late husband, *Sydney Davenport: A Life of Canals* – established her residence in London and was determined to make her intellectual presence felt. A Davenport scholarship had been established at the Academy of Music for young composers. Her bounty and patronage extended to fellow writers in the form of semi-anonymous subventions. Samuel Coleridge, it was rumoured, was a notable beneficiary – and who had paid the lease on William Hazlitt's house in York Street? But her greatest success was her swiftly famous 'At Home's, every second Thursday of the month in Hill Street. Mrs Davenport was a force for good, everyone agreed, hoping the force might extend in their direction one day.

Cashel moved away from his corner and, sipping some more Moselle, wandered through the room, speaking to no one, not recognizing any fellow writers. He heard Wordsworth's name mentioned. Was he present? What did he look like, anyway? He wished Arthur Greenstock were here to point out the luminaries. More and more people were arriving, many of whom seemed to know each other. The room was becoming distinctly crowded and he began to wonder when he could politely leave, as he helped himself to his third glass of Moselle. He realized he had no idea, either, of what his hostess looked like.

'Mr Ross? Can it be you?'

Cashel turned, blinked, and in the next moment just recognized Mary Shelley.

'Mrs Shelley. What a pleasure.'

'And mine too. I can't believe it!'

Her expressionless and sullen features were suddenly, genuinely animated and Cashel saw the young woman he had briefly known in Pisa and Lerici – another lifetime ago, he felt. As they talked and reminisced Cashel began to feel more relaxed. Here was another author whom he knew – he was ever so slightly in the swim, after all. And Mary Shelley did seem delighted by the encounter. She asked him how he knew Mrs Davenport and Cashel told her about the publication of *High-Ways and By-Ways*, realizing, as he informed her, that he had written many pages about Shelley. Not with asperity but with a certain honesty, describing the Shelley that he, Cashel, had experienced. He felt a little sick.

'I must acquire *High-Ways* immediately.'

'Don't waste your time. It's a very amateur production—'

'Mrs Shelley, here you are, bless you, my dear.'

The accent was a Yorkshire one, though with genteel modulations. Mary Shelley turned to greet Mrs Davenport and introduced Cashel.

'Mr Ross, a dear friend, spent much of Shelley's last summer with us in Italy.'

Cashel immediately felt Mrs Davenport's interest focus strongly on him.

In Yelverton's description she was a 'damn'd clever and a damn'd handsome woman'. She appeared to be in her forties and had a strong, hawkish face with flared nostrils, as if she had just inhaled lungfuls of air. There were great clusters of tight ringlets hanging on either side of her face, like bookends, or drapes that were yet to be drawn. She had an exceptionally long, dancer's neck that made her head seem a kind of bust on a pedestal, like a deity or Roman empress. She was tall and broad-shouldered with a prominent bosom – there was no other proper description, Cashel realized – the adjective validated by the way her dress was designed to present it: the tiny cinched waist, great puffed sleeves, the glimpse of transparent chemise revealing the flesh beneath.

Cashel gave a little bow; Mary Shelley smiled and excused herself and he found himself the recipient of Mrs Davenport's full attention. She asked him the title of his book and he told her – but she seemed not to recall it. She frowned.

'Is that the new one about Byron and Shelley?'

'Amongst other subjects.'

'I have it!' she said triumphantly. 'I will read it!'

She asked him to remind her of his name and he did so.

'Are you Irish? You have an Irish sway to your voice.'

'I was born in Ireland and grew up there. The brogue tends to linger. I must—'

'How do you like London life?' she asked, lowering her voice.

'Well enough. I suppose it is the place to be for a writer, after all.'

She touched his arm with her fan, smiling. Conspirators.

'Well said, Mr Ross. My feelings exactly.'

And then she swept away. Cashel selected yet another glass of Moselle from a passing servant. At least Yelverton will be pleased, he thought, draining it, leaving it on a table, and easing his way through the throng and down the grand staircase to the front door.

And Yelverton was right. Mrs Davenport's interest in him paid off. His book, his modest *High-Ways and By-Ways*, became talked about for a few weeks. Many people bought it and claimed to have read it. It went into a second and then a third edition. There was an excellent notice in the *Morning Chronicle* – '*Mr Ross writes in a nice, clean prose unmuffled by the affectionate bromides of traditional guidebooks*' – and a patronizing reference in the *Edinburgh Review* – '*the latest, trifling lodestar of London flim-flammery and tittle-tattle'* – all fuel to the fire of temporary renown. Mrs Davenport sent him a handwritten note inviting him to her next 'literary conventicle' as she wittily described her 'At Home'.

'You've arrived, man!' Yelverton exclaimed when Cashel showed him the missive. Cashel returned to Hill Street and found that, thanks to Mrs Davenport, people now wanted to talk to him and took an interest in him. Yelverton announced in a letter that there would be a fourth edition of *HBABW*, as he referred to it now.

Cashel realized he had been 'taken up' by Mrs Davenport. He was the latest young writer to be discussed and assessed in London society and wherever its reverberations and ripples spread – whether to Bath or Brighton, Edinburgh or York. His mother sent him a cutting from the *Oxfordshire Bugle*. Sir Guy wrote to congratulate him on his 'tremendous success' and claimed he was the talk of Cork and Dublin. Greenstock said the 'bubble reputation' was all very well but had he made any money from his short-lived celebrity?

The answer was no. He went to see Yelverton in White Cross Court. The publisher poured him a glass of port.

'You don't understand the business, Ross. I'm still out of pocket, if I may be blunt. You always lose money on a first book, I'm sorry to inform you. Always. It's a cross we publishers must bear. What we need – how we capitalize on any success of the first – is the second.'

'Well,' Cashel said. 'I have a second book, as it happens. All written.'

Yelverton looked genuinely shocked for a moment, then recovered himself.

'More travels? Please, no more travels. They are becoming *passé*—'

'It's a novel.'

That changed everything. Cashel sent Yelverton the manuscript of *Nihil* and he read it in a day. Cashel was summoned back to White Cross Court.

'It's strong stuff, Ross. Might be risky for me.'

'There's one condition, Mr Yelverton. It must be published anonymously.'

'Oh. Good. I like that. Excellent idea – I was about to suggest that myself.'

Yelverton offered £100. After consultation with Greenstock and Ben, Cashel counter-proposed £200, remembering Shelley's advice. Yelverton agreed instantly, fuelling Cashel's suspicions. He declined to sign the contract immediately and took it back to Meard Street for Greenstock to scrutinize. Greenstock advised that he accept the offer. Ben Smart proposed an emendation to the document, suggesting that a coda be added stipulating that, after the £200 had been redeemed, then Cashel should insist on – demand – a 50 per cent share of the subsequent profits. The profit-sharing model was an acceptable one and many authors were coming to favour it. As he was therefore setting no precedent, Yelverton could hardly object, although – after an initial fit of outrage, disappointment and disgust – he offered only 10 per cent. They eventually settled on 30 and the contract was adjusted and notarized. Cashel banked the £200 at Brookes & Co. He was beginning to feel well-to-do again.

Mrs Davenport returned to her Yorkshire country house for the Christmas season and Cashel's literary life went into abeyance, to some degree. He revised the manuscript of *Nihil*, made a fair copy and delivered it to the publisher's offices early in the New Year. He had decided that the anonymity would be slightly adjusted: it would be *Nihil, by A Lover*. Yelverton could hardly conceal his glee. The book would be published in the summer. 'Start on the next one,' he encouraged. 'You're on your way, Ross. Mark my words. There'll be no stopping you.'

Cashel felt the surge of enthusiasm himself and began to ponder what he might write next. He went up various blind alleys and returned. He was not inspired – inspiration was not his strong point – and he began to doubt if he had the imaginative powers required to be an author of fiction. For a while he dallied with the idea of writing about his own peculiar childhood – cleverly disguised, of course – and telling the story of Elspeth Soutar, Sir

Guy Stillwell and their unacknowledged child, Cashel Greville. But he reasoned that if the subterfuge was exposed he might as well plunge a stiletto in his mother's heart. The idea stayed with him, however, and the fact that it did told him something important about his artistic nature. He realized he could only write about himself, about what he had personally experienced or witnessed – he couldn't live in another, fictional body. But if he decided to tell his mother's story, then the deception would have to be impenetrable. Was the risk worth taking . . .?

Nihil, by A Lover was published in June 1828. By July everyone was talking about it. Ben Smart told him that he had turned down a dozen articles claiming to have identified the author. Only Ben, Greenstock and Yelverton knew the truth and, somewhat amazingly, Cashel's anonymity was sustained. As the speculation grew more fevered – Hazlitt? Leigh Hunt? Maturin (posthumously)? Scott (surely not)? – so the sales increased. *Nihil* had been published in a deluxe edition of dark navy leather, with the title and author's name inlaid in gilt, price a hefty ten shillings and sixpence.

In that summer of 1828, for a brief few weeks, *Nihil* and the identity of its author was the subject of endless conversation at Mrs Davenport's 'At Home' afternoons. Cashel would stand in the corner of the huge drawing room and count the number of copies he could see in people's hands. It had become a kind of parlour game, clearly, with guests parsing the text looking for clues, and that chit-chat and tittle-tattle drove the sales onwards. Who was this 'Paul'? Who could this 'Frances' be? Which one of them might have written the thing, indeed? Why was the author hiding behind that tantalizing pseudonym and who was he?

Cashel was accosted by Mrs Davenport on this very subject during one afternoon's 'At Home'. She now knew exactly who he was and she said she had greatly enjoyed *High-Ways and By-Ways*. That particular day she had done something different to her hair and had abandoned the usual tiny bonnet that perched to one side on her head. Now two braided loops framed her ears and a set of bejewelled combs held the complicated twists and folds of her coiffure firmly in place at the back of her head. Her ensemble was as fashionable as ever – he could not believe how small the diameter of her waist was – and Cashel kept his eyes fixed on hers as she spoke to him.

'I'll ask you straight away, Mr Ross. Do you know who the author of *Nihil* is? You have the same publisher.'

'Like the rest of the world, I haven't a clue.'

'Have you read it?'

'Not yet.'

'Why not? The whole of London has read it.'

'I'm struggling with my own next book,' Cashel explained.

'I've a strange feeling that you know, sir,' she said a little coquettishly.

'I would whisper it to you if I did, Mrs Davenport.'

'You can whisper anything you like in my ear, Mr Ross, any time you want to share a secret.'

This was a little forward, Cashel thought, but, then again, Mrs Davenport had a Yorkshire-woman's reputation for candour and plain speaking.

'How do you find your Mr Yelverton, your publisher?' she said, changing the subject.

'I'm relatively content. A least he doesn't owe me money.'

She laughed – a throaty, strangely delighted laugh.

'That day will come, I'm sure.' She looked at him knowingly and sauntered off.

Cashel asked a footman for a glass of port. Something had just changed, he thought. He and Mrs Davenport had just entered a higher plane of familiarity, it seemed, and he wondered what it might betoken . . .

Despite his worries and his better judgement, Cashel – in some desperation – started on his novel and the whole Stillwell Court conspiracy. He made his mother Spanish, Sir Guy an English lord, and relocated events from County Cork to the Lake District – but he found the necessary artifice counterproductive to creation.

He often dined with Ben Smart in Fleet Street on a Friday night when the last issue of that week's *London Star* had been run off. Ben always had a fiendish appetite on him and would order two pies and sometimes a third after his usual appetizer of a dozen oysters. This particular evening, he was eating while Cashel moaned about how badly his new novel was going.

'What's the title?' Ben asked, signalling for a waiter to refill his port and water.

'*The Governess.*'

Ben feigned a yawn.

'I'm sorry, that won't do, Cashel, my friend. It does not titillate. I think *The Wanton Governess* would work better.'

'Impossible,' Cashel groaned. 'For reasons I can't explain.'

'You won't need to write another novel, anyway,' Ben said. 'You can live off what you're going to make from—' He looked around and lowered his voice. 'From *Nothing*, let's say, paradoxically.'

'Really? Do you think so?'

Ben quoted him sums of money that other modish, fast-selling books had delivered to their authors. It could be hundreds, possibly thousands, he said. Cashel felt his mood change – thinking of Lord Byron's sales.

'Do you want me to try and find out?' Ben asked. He outlined a plan whereby he would go to Yelverton's printers to see if the man would give a speculative quote for the printing of the *London Star*. As he, Ben, was the deputy editor it would seem entirely plausible – he could spin some story about escalating costs making the editors look for alternatives to their current printers. A pretence, but the idea would enthuse any potential competitor – and then he could 'innocently' enquire how *Nihil* was doing. Cashel gave his permission as he was curious. Yelverton was being very vague about sales.

Mrs Davenport squeezed Cashel's arm as he was on the point of retrieving his cane and top hat from the manservant in charge of the garde-robe. It was dusk and time to be heading home to Soho.

'Mr Ross,' she said. 'Can I persuade you to stay and dine with me? Just a light supper. I've some questions I wish to put to you.'

'With pleasure,' Cashel said and handed back his cane and hat.

They dined in a small third-floor parlour with painted panels. A butler was present, supervising the serving of the meal by a couple of footmen. They had a lobster salad and then a slice of raised pie with pickled vegetables washed down with an excellent claret.

The ostensible object of the exercise was that Mrs Davenport was, she said, thinking of writing another book. She asked him practical, pragmatic questions about how many words he wrote in a day, the presentation of the manuscript, the delay between galley proofs and the finished book.

Cashel grew steadily more suspicious. She must have known the answer to these questions, surely? Why quiz a young author who had only recently been published?

Mrs Davenport called for a decanter of brandy and some coffee and dismissed the butler when they were brought to the table. They drank and chatted. Then she asked to be excused and went behind a folding screen set in a corner of the room. Cashel tried not to think about what in fact was going on out of sight. He heard her skirts being rearranged and then she emerged.

'Do avail yourself of the commode, Mr Ross, if you've a need. I do hate to leave the room in the middle of a fascinating conversation.'

Cashel said he was fine, thank you.

She poured them both more brandy and looked him in the eye.

'It's you, isn't it?'

'Me? What? What am I?'

'The author of *Nihil*.' She smiled confidently at him. 'Your secret's safe, don't worry.' She tapped his knuckles with a teaspoon. 'But don't deny it.'

It was a strange relief not to do so.

'How do you know?' he said.

'Mr Yelverton told me.'

'Ah.'

Bastard Yelverton, Cashel thought.

'Why would he do that?'

'I can be very persuasive,' she said, pointedly rubbing her thumb against her first two fingers. 'Anyway, congratulations. You and your book are on everyone's lips. Now – this is the real purpose of our little supper – tell me all about it. Is it all true?'

Cashel half-confessed. He knew that the best lies always had an element of truth in them. He said it was not his story but his brother's, and he had begged for anonymity. She fired more questions at him until the clock on the mantel chimed eleven.

'Good Lord! Is that the hour? Where do you live, Mr Ross? Covent Garden?'

'Soho.'

'You must stay the night here and return to Soho at your leisure in the morning.' She rang the bell and gave instructions for a small fire to be lit in the Blue Room.

Cashel protested. 'Really, there's no need—'

'No, no. I've kept you very late with all my questions. I insist.'

The Blue Room turned out to be sumptuous and immaculate. Panelled walls, painted blue. Stained floor with a thick Persian rug (predominantly blue). There was a commode behind a screen, as in the dining room. The bed was extremely high, as high as his chest, and heaped with pillows. The room's two windows looked out onto the mews at the rear of the house. There were two three-candle candelabra lit on either side of the bed. Cashel undressed, leaving only his shirt on, and blew out the candles on one candelabrum. He lay in the bed, knowing that something was going to happen – something sexual. The incident with the commode had been a kind of test, he assumed, a provocation. He ordered his brain not to speculate.

Suddenly she was in the room, having come silently through a small flush door concealed by a cupboard. She slipped off her silk gown to reveal a sheer, ivory satin nightdress.

'Here I am, Cashel Ross. In this room I am Ethalinda and you may call me Etha. Please be quiet as my son is sleeping in the room below.'

She climbed into the high bed and Cashel noted the slope and sway of her heavy breasts beneath the satin. He was feeling a mounting panic – a panic to do with him, not Mrs Davenport – and as he drew her into his arms and felt her warm body press against him a form of despair overtook him. They kissed and Cashel realized that the last lips he had kissed had been Raphaella's. He rolled out of bed.

'Mrs Davenport – Etha – forgive me. I can't do it. I'm sorry. It's my fault – it's because I'm in love with another woman. I can't betray her.'

He walked to the window, feeling a nausea rise in him as tears welled. How absurd. How stupid.

'You're "Paul", of course,' Mrs Davenport said in her patient, sensible, Yorkshire tones.

'Yes.'

'And who is "Frances", pray?'

'A woman – a young woman – called Raphaella. Whom I met in Italy, in Ravenna.'

'Ah. The long Ravenna chapter in *High-Ways* is explained,' she said. 'And you say you're still in love with her.'

'I suppose I must be.'

'You're a very romantic fellow, aren't you, Cashel.'

'Possibly. I'm confused. Please, Etha, I think you're a marvellous, wondrous—'

'Yes, yes. Very wondrous. Come to bed, Cashel. Let's sleep the night together, at least. I'd like that – I haven't shared a bed with a man for two years or more.'

She held back the counterpane for him and he climbed into bed again.

'Say nothing,' she continued. 'Let's have a good night's sleep and we'll see how we feel in the morning.'

As she had confidently predicted, Cashel succumbed to Mrs Davenport early in the morning. Warm in the bed in her arms, half-asleep, it was impossible not to go through with the act, he told himself, pure animal instinct dominating him, in control. I am a young man, a virile young man, he told himself as she slipped out of his room through her secret door. But he stayed away from Hill Street when her invitation came for the next 'At Home'.* He couldn't trust himself. It was absurd, he knew, but he felt that he had betrayed Raphaella.

Cashel sometimes thought that Ben Smart was growing stouter before his eyes. They were in a chop house on the Strand. Ben was eating veal cutlets and mashed potato with gravy, which was all very well, but he'd already consumed a cheese soufflé and cod with oyster sauce. He had just returned from the visit to Yelverton's printers in Greenwich. The ruse had worked perfectly.

'No, it was astonishing,' Ben said, sawing at a chop. 'The books were stacked there, ready to be shipped. Great mountains of them. I asked how many. A thousand, I was told. And there was an order for a thousand more.' He popped the square of veal in his mouth and chewed.

'My God,' Cashel said.

Ben pointed his fork at Cashel.

'Then I asked him how many he'd printed in total and he said seven thousand. Seven thousand with an order for a thousand more.'

Cashel did a quick calculation. Say eight thousand books at ten shillings each. Four thousand pounds. How much did a bookseller take? What was Yelverton's profit? His brain refused to deliver a figure.

'What did Yelverton pay you?'

'Two hundred pounds.'

'I reckon he must owe you several hundred more. Six hundred, say, at least. And there's more to come. And the book is obviously

* In fact, there were only two more of Mrs Davenport's celebrated salons. In 1828 she met a man richer than Sydney Davenport, married him and left London. He was Haddon Raikes (1773–1845) who was worth millions from his many coal mines. Their fifty-room mansion, Raikes Hall near Harrogate (now a National Trust property), is where Mrs Davenport made her home for the rest of her life. She died in 1862.

still selling away.' Ben put his knife and fork down. 'He's stealing from you, Cashel. Simple as that. He's been in profit for months.'

'What do I do?'

'You have a contract on the share-of-profits model. Enforce it. Hold him to it.'

Cashel felt a rush of emotions: pleasure that his book was so successful; rage that he'd been so grievously defrauded; helplessness over what to do next.

'Beard him, Cashel. Confront him. This is your money, not his. He signed the contract, just as you did.'

Cashel went out to Cripplegate with Arthur Greenstock who was introduced to Yelverton as his 'associate' but there for moral support and to act as witness to anything Yelverton might say; his considerable bulk in the publisher's office was also an extra, solid reassurance. Greenstock refused the offer of a chair and stood by the window that looked over White Cross Court, his arms folded across his chest, staring intently at Yelverton as he spoke. He did accept a glass of sherry when it was proposed, however.

Yelverton was disarming – amiability itself.

'Yes, yes, of course, I won't hide it from you, Ross. It's been a great success. No, a triumph. I mean it – seriously, yes, yes, of course. And you will receive your reward. But – before I pay you I must pay my printers, and, luckily for you, they're still printing *Nihil*.'

He explained how if he settled his account with the printers and then went back to them with another order their rates would rise dramatically. That's why he couldn't pay them until the demand for the book was over.

'Why?' Cashel asked.

'Because they're thieves. All printers are devilish thieves. You only have control over them if you withhold payment.'

'What about Mr Ross's contract with you?' Greenstock interjected. 'You're withholding payment to him. It's legally binding.'

'Yes, yes, of course. Yes, yes. You want your money, Ross, I understand that. So let me see if I can make your life easier until I can get the printers off my back.' He rummaged in his desk.

'Permit me to introduce you to a Mr Forbes Harkin. A very good friend and sleeping partner of Yelverton and Bale. Everything will be sorted out.'

He reached for a pen, dipped it in ink and scribbled a name and address on the back of his visiting card, handing it to Cashel. Greenstock stepped forward and intercepted it.

'Harkin Brothers. That's a bank,' he said.

'Precisely, Mr Greenstock. Mr Forbes Harkin will advance the money due to Ross, here. I will stand surety to the amount.'

'But banks demand interest on their loans,' Greenstock said sternly.

'Of course, yes, yes. Of course, yes. A modest percentage and very short term. Six months, no more, I'd say. The interest will seem inconsequential. Tell you what – I will cover the interest myself.' He smiled, showing his few brown teeth. 'Can't say fairer than that, can you?' He poured them more sherry. 'Most authors never arrive at this happy position, Ross. Another indication of your success. Lucky man, lucky man.'

Arthur Greenstock was still somewhat suspicious as they analysed the meeting later in a tavern in Soho called the Lockpenny. Cashel paid for their lunch as a sign of his gratitude.

'Did you notice how he kept saying "Yes, yes, of course, yes, yes"?' Greenstock said. 'Strange verbal tic – as if everything in the world was in order and self-evident.'

'Well, I suppose Mr Forbes Harkin will be the proof of the Yelverton pudding,' Cashel said and called for another round of rum and water for them both.

Harkin Brothers, Bankers, was to be found in a tall thin building on Knightrider Street in the City, like a slim novel shelved between two thick ledgers. The ground floor was full of industrious clerks at their high desks and at the rear of the room was a vast iron-and-brass safe the size of a garden shed, as if to say to any casual visitor, 'Yes, you're right, this is a bank!' Cashel was led upstairs to Mr Forbes Harkin's office, from which a view of the top half of St Paul's dome could be perceived through the surprisingly clean windows.

Forbes Harkin was a slim, serious-looking bald man with a stiff-pointed white wisp of a beard growing from his chin that looked as though it had been stuck there as a prank. The room was functional: a desk, a rug, two wooden filing cabinets and an etching of a man in a clerical-style collar above the mantel. A small fire burned in a grate beneath the portrait.

'Is that John Milton?' Cashel asked, studying the likeness.

'It is, as a matter of fact,' Mr Harkin said with a faint smile. 'He was a customer of our bank in its earliest incarnation.' He waved Cashel to a chair across the desk from his own and took his seat. 'We do a lot of our business with the print trade and publishers – not so many writers, these days, alas.' He picked up a letter from his blotter. 'Mr Yelverton has laid out your good fortune in great detail. Congratulations.'

'Thank you.'

'As a result of Mr Yelverton's guarantees we are prepared to advance you a loan of one thousand pounds for a period of six months.'

'My God!'

'Your book has exceeded all expectations, apparently. In six months, Mr Yelverton assures us, you'll be in a position to redeem the loan – and be left with considerable change from your accumulated earnings.'

'Really?'

'Which is why our terms of interest are so modest – a mere ten per cent. Mr Yelverton will cover that, of course.'

'Of course, yes, yes.'

'Do you have an account with a bank, sir?'

'Yes. Brookes and Company.'

'Very able.' Mr Harkin nodded, opened a drawer and handed Cashel a prepared letter of credit. 'Don't delay in presenting this to your bank. In case Mr Yelverton changes his mind.' Mr Harkin spread his hands. 'That is a joke, by the way.'

'Yes, of course. Yes.'

Cashel wandered along Knightrider Street in something of a daze, heading in a general westward direction. He was a rich man – for the first time in his life. As rich as Percy Shelley with his thousand a year, he told himself, while recognizing that he didn't actually feel any different from the relatively poor man he was accustomed to being. But, with this bounty, he resolved that he was going to change his circumstances, the way he lived. He felt he needed the physical manifestations of his good fortune. What was the point in merely carrying on with his old way of life when he had so much money in the bank?

Cashel didn't waste any time in this new remodelling of his status quo. He took a ten-year lease on a terraced house – number 23 Bond Street, Chelsea. He bought a covered curricle and a young horse to pull it, renting a stable and a yard around the corner from Bond Street to house them. He made a gift of £100 each to Hogan and Buckley and bought his mother a diamond clip.

He acquired a live-in housekeeper and manservant (a young married couple called John and Isabella Proudfoot) who occupied number 23's basement floor, paying them one pound ten shillings a week, all found. He went to a tailor and rejuvenated his wardrobe. He joined Sir Guy's club in Pall Mall, Brydges', and made himself dine there at least three times a week to justify the subscription. He also worked in the club's library on *The Governess*. He swiftly developed a fondness for playing whist and won and lost in equal measure at the club's tables. He was a cautious gambler, however, and kept an account of his balance, managing to keep his losses to an acceptable minimum. He allowed himself to feel that, finally, and somewhat astonishingly, his life was 'good'.

In the New Year his mother informed him that Sir Guy was unwell and so Cashel travelled to Ireland to visit him at Stillwell Court. He was shocked to see his father – confined to bed, gaunt and worryingly pale. It was a challenge for him to breathe properly, he could see, Sir Guy's chest and shoulders rising effortfully with each inhalation.

'There's something wrong with my heart,' he told Cashel. 'Not working to best capacity. If I walk upstairs I have to sit down for ten minutes. Once summer arrives and the weather warms up I'll be much better, so Dr Killigrew informs me.' He coughed and Cashel could see how it pained him. 'Pour me a glass of that cordial, will you, Cashel? It does seem to help. God knows what's in it.'

Cashel told him of his good fortune and how his book was continuing to sell in cheaper editions. Sir Guy asked for news of his Oxford family and any London gossip. As Cashel chatted away he kept telling himself that the wheezing invalid in the bed opposite was his father. But, strangely, he found that concept as hard to grasp as the certain knowledge that he was now a rich man. Why were these facts so hard to integrate into his sense of himself? Why couldn't he acknowledge the genealogical reality? Perhaps, he thought, the first stories we tell ourselves about our lives when we are young and forging our personalities are the ones we find hardest to relinquish. Would he always be the orphan boy, raised by his loving aunt, victim of a seafaring tragedy that had claimed the lives of his mother and father? Was this the narrative that gave him the bedrock of his being, however false it had turned out to be? And when the facts emerged or changed – that he was the bastard son of an Anglo-Irish baronet, or that he was the wealthy owner of a house in Chelsea with servants and a horse and carriage – why did that reality seem chimerical, somehow? Why did this tangible, verifiable state of affairs seem alien from the person who was Cashel Greville Ross? Even the name he went by was a construct.

Having left Sir Guy after an hour, seeing that he was tiring, Cashel wandered about the parterre at Stillwell Court. He felt somewhat disturbed and reflective, pondering these questions and emotions and found – to his vague surprise – that his thoughts had begun to congregate around his memories of Raphaella. Not just an orphan boy, turned bastard son; not just a young soldier turned successful writer; but also a man in love, with love freely given back. That situation was as much a part of the definition of the person he was as anything else. And he was still a man in love, he told himself, even though his stupid, impulsive pride had made the love suddenly impossible. He stood still in the shock of a revelation: his love for Raphaella still defined him, as much as the colour of his eyes did. And with that revelation came the immediate conviction that he should write the sequel to *Nihil* and call it *Amor Retribuit – Love Requited*. There and then, he resolved to go to Milan, find Raphaella and, somehow, win her back.

Back in London, Cashel began to make concrete plans. He would travel to Milan, rent a property there and establish himself as an English gentleman of means – now that he had his new financial security – and see how he could infiltrate the circle of Count Mazzolino. Once Raphaella saw him, he knew, everything would change. All the powerful emotions they had shared would be immediately present again – irresistible. But an unwelcome warning voice in his head told him, Remember, she's married. Remember she's had a child, maybe another, by now. It didn't matter, he responded to his cautious self, all that was required on his part was action – whatever the reaction might be was unknowable, but there would be one.

Then, one morning, going to the post office, he found a letter waiting from Harkin Brothers, Bankers. His six-month loan had fallen due and *'the prompt repayment of £1,100 would be gratefully appreciated. We remain, sir, your most humble and obedient etc., etc.'*

Cashel felt a lurch of panic. This was not how events were meant to play out. Where was Yelverton's accounting of monies due? He had promised a full statement in six months. Moreover, he, Yelverton, had volunteered to pay the interest so why was he being dunned for it? No, no – Yelverton had to repay this loan or else give him the funds that were due to him so that he could settle everything with Harkin. He had to confront his publisher himself.

As he stepped into White Cross Court, Cashel felt his foreboding in a series of physical effects – a coldness at the centre of his being, a sudden thirst, a smear of sweat on his brow. Yet there was the stairway, there was the familiar sign: *'Yelverton & Bale, Publishers'*. He climbed the rickety staircase thinking it had always been rickety. But the door to the office was locked; the brass let-terbox and door-knocker were tarnished black. The blinds at the windows were down.

He descended the stairs and went into the button-mould maker's shop where a tired, white-haired man in a leather apron told him wearily that Yelverton had decamped over two months ago. The tired man was Yelverton's landlord and there was a year's rent owing. Cashel felt sick.

'What about the partner? The sign says "Yelverton and Bale".' Where is this Mr Bale?'

'There is none,' the landlord said. 'There never has been.'

Cashel went to his bank – Brookes in Newgate Street behind St Paul's – and asked to be given the balance of his account. The clerk returned with a ledger and showed him that his account stood in credit to the sum of £187.7s.8d. Cashel made the quick calculation: even if he offered every penny he had, he would still owe Harkin Brothers, Bankers, something over £900.

Back at 23 Bond Street, he composed a relaxed, informal letter asking if Mr Harkin might be so obliging as to extend the period of his loan for another six months. He was writing his next novel, he said, which showed every sign of exceeding the revenues gen-erated by his last, and the extension would be greatly appreciated. I remain, sir, your most obedient servant, etc., etc.

He needed some time, he realized. Time was the most pre-cious commodity at the moment. He was solvent, in a sense, and he could take himself off to Milan with the funds he had. *Nihil* had sold in its thousands and any publisher would buy the sequel and pay handsomely for it. Surely Harkin could see the sense in extending the loan?

Cashel left the house with John Proudfoot a few mornings later, heading for the stables in the mews, full of new resolve. Having heard nothing from Forbes Harkin, Cashel thought a per-sonal visit was the answer – man to man, eye to eye. Integrity was better demonstrated by physical presence – far more effective than formulaic words penned in ink.

Two men in identical brown overcoats and tall hats were

approaching from the other end of Bond Street. Cashel noticed that one of the men looked as if he was carrying some sort of cudgel in his hand.

'Watch out for those fellows, John,' Cashel warned quietly.

'Mr Ross, sir?' one of the overcoats addressed him as they drew near.

'Yes. What can I do for you gentlemen?'

The other man tucked a sheet of paper into the breast pocket of Cashel's topcoat.

'You've been summoned, Mr Ross. We're here to take you to the magistrate's court in Westminster.'

These brown-overcoated men were bailiffs, Cashel realized.

'How dare you! Summoned for what?'

'For debt, sir. Seems you owe a certain person a great deal of money.'

9

Every morning when Cashel woke he would say to himself, 'I am in prison. I am a prisoner.' And yet the Marshalsea – the 'New' Marshalsea to be precise – was very unlike a prison in every sense of the word as it was commonly understood and Cashel was very unlike an archetypal prisoner. Visitors came and went; he had no cell but instead a small room that he furnished and decorated himself, and if he wanted anything – food, drink, sex – it was there if he had money to pay for it. Yet – despite this licence – in subtle ways his felony, his custodial life, his punishment, was always being gently reinforced, come what may. Whatever small freedoms he had, whatever privileges, had to be bought while money lasted. And, while he was relatively comfortably incarcerated, he was still in a prison and that incarceration had no end – until the debt was paid and the creditor satisfied.

The entrance to the New Marshalsea prison was on Borough High Street in Southwark. Once through the main gates you were faced with what looked like a house with two doors. The door on the right led you to a long, thin, paved quadrangle with high fifteen-foot walls topped by *chevaux de frise* spikes. These high walls enclosed a crude barrack-like building – a four-storey undecorated block that contained fifty or so rooms, about ten feet square, off a series of staircases or closes, so-called. These were the rooms for the imprisoned debtors – the 'collegians' as they drily dubbed themselves. Solitary space could be purchased for two shillings and sixpence and if you were a solvent debtor (strange oxymoron) you could live in some comfort. If you were poor you might find yourself sharing the small room with three or four other indebted souls. The great majority of the prisoners were men but there were always half a dozen, or a dozen, women. Fallen women in the main, free to fall further in the Marshalsea.

Beyond the barrack-block were the privies and a smaller, lower building that housed the taproom – where beer and food could be purchased – and a 'snuggery' where they could be consumed. Beyond this building was another cruder prison, separated by a wall, known as the Admiralty Yard, that contained convicted smugglers and others who had fallen foul of the excise men. The collegians and the smugglers rarely mixed.

Cashel's £900 debt to Harkin Brothers made him one of the largest debtors in the Marshalsea and generated a certain notoriety. But because he still had funds in his own bank he was able to purchase a room of his own. Visitors were permitted between 8 a.m. and 10 p.m. Cashel and John Proudfoot painted his room – white walls, dark blue ceiling – and set up a green Venetian blind over the barred window. A bed, a table, a chair, some etchings and a bookshelf were salvaged from the house in Bond Street before the bailiffs moved in and the lease was foreclosed. Once a week Isabella Proudfoot would give the room a sweep and a dust and do whatever shopping and laundering was required. Everyone assumed that Cashel would be free within a matter of weeks.

However, for all these domestic comforts, Cashel settled in to his new quarters with real despondency, not remotely sure of how he was ever going to repay Harkin. The lease on the house had gone, his furniture and his horse and carriage as well, but their re-sale would barely make inroads into the debt – where interest was also steadily accruing. While he was still in funds at Brookes & Co. he could live as well as the Marshalsea allowed but the bigger problem seemed insuperable. Only Harkin, paid off, satisfied, could bring about the crucial change in his circumstances.

He had several visitors in the early weeks of his confinement. Both Hogan and Buckley came up from Oxford. Ben Smart and Arthur Greenstock popped in once a week for a drink and a chat in the snuggery. Cashel had written to his mother outlining his problems in all outraged candour but had forbidden her mentioning anything of what had happened to Sir Guy. Cashel knew how seriously unwell he was, not to mention his own ongoing and considerable financial crisis at Stillwell Court. There was no need to break his back with Cashel's final straw. He wondered, even, if Sir Guy could have raised the £900 – he was mortgaged to the full.*

The only solution to his predicament lay with Yelverton, it was clear. He had stolen Cashel's lawfully earned money. If Yelverton could be found then perhaps he could be 'persuaded' to pay up . . .

He suggested this course of action to Hogan on his second visit. Cashel was impressed with his brother's righteous anger on his behalf while he reluctantly noted the cleverness of Yelverton's scheme at the same time. Cashel suggested that Hogan might sniff around Cripplegate and see if the publisher had unwittingly left a trail; if he had confided with someone about his new whereabouts. Where had Yelverton lived? Was there a Mrs Yelverton? A family or any dependants? They might know where he had disappeared to.

Hogan was very keen to help.

'And if I find him, Cash, I'll do for him – I swear.'

'Get my money first, please.'

Ben Smart also agreed to do some investigating and very quickly discovered that Yelverton had perpetrated the same fraud with two other of his authors – but not to Cashel's degree of indebtedness. Harkin had, in good faith, advanced loans to these two authors at Yelverton's asking – pro-tem, a question of waiting a few weeks – but for sums of £80 and £120. In this way the financial burden of modest literary success was transferred from publisher to banker.

'It's quite a clever scheme,' Ben said. 'You have to admit. The author is paid, the author is pleased, the author spends – then discovers that he's in debt to a bank, not a publisher.'

* It gives some measure of the scale of Cashel's debt when one considers that the basic annual salary paid to the resident surgeon at the Marshalsea at that time was £50 per annum. He was not, admittedly, a medical practitioner of the highest quality but it was nonetheless an acceptable salary.

'I refuse to admit it,' Cashel said. 'It's disgraceful.'

However, it was obvious, Ben analysed, that the degree of success with *Nihil* was incomparable. He thought that *Nihil* must have grossed several thousand pounds over its many editions – far beyond anything that Yelverton & Bale had ever experienced – and the temptation had proved too great. It was too much to share with author and printers (they hadn't been paid, either, naturally) so he had absconded with his loot.

'But where?' Cashel asked futilely.

'Somewhere in Europe, no doubt,' Ben said with a hopeless shrug. 'That's where all thieves and debtors go.'

Cashel painted small white stars on his dark blue ceiling at the prison and he would lie in bed imagining he was looking at a night sky above him. Sometimes the wavering candle flame seemed to make the stars wink and twinkle and the illusion became almost perfect.

Cashel glumly celebrated his thirtieth birthday in the Marshalsea. He and Arthur Greenstock went to the taproom, bought two pots of beer and sat as close to the small fire in the snuggery as they could without burning their trouser-cuffs. Newspapers were provided here but Cashel couldn't be bothered with reading them. They were full of analysis of 'Reform' – the extension of the franchise. What did he care for Reform? The only reform he was interested in was one that affected his situation.

Greenstock had brought a small pint flask of gin and he added a slug to their watery porter. He could sense Cashel's glum mood.

'Happy birthday, Ross. If I had a spare nine hundred pounds I'd give it to you.' He made a face. 'I do blame myself – a bit.'

'You weren't to know Yelverton was a villain.'

'But I suggested him to you.'

'And it was a good suggestion. I made the judgement to sell my books to Yelverton on my own. And, look, both of them were successful. Any author would be delighted.'

'Except . . .' Greenstock looked troubled, as if he were wrestling with a thorny philosophical dilemma. 'You had great success – and look where it got you. That's what bothers me. Success brought you to prison.'

'It wasn't your fault and it wasn't mine. I fell in with a clever thief.'

Just then a wan-looking man wandered up to them, somewhat sheepishly. Cashel had seen him in the yard. He was one of the 'scavengers', so-called. Impoverished debtors, they paid their way by doing the worst jobs in the prison, including emptying the privies when the night soil was collected, and lived off charitable monies. He was on the bottom rung of the Marshalsea ladder. The man was extremely thin with lank long brown hair tied behind his head with a greasy ribbon, and a patched greatcoat buttoned to the neck that flapped around his ankles.

'Apologies for troubling you, gents,' he said. 'I can tell from your conversation you're educated men and I wonder if you might be interested in this.' He produced a folded pamphlet from his pocket and held it out. 'Yours for sixpence.'

Cashel looked at it.

'COR-ISM. A New Religion of the Heart.'

'Cor is the Latin for heart,' the man explained.

'Cor blimey,' Greenstock said sarcastically.

'Tell us about this Cor-ism,' Cashel said. The man had an open, honest face, despite its stark thinness, and a dark scab at the corner of his mouth.

He tapped his head.

'People think all the answers are in here – with the brain. Reason, intelligence, deduction. They think thinking will solve all problems.' He put his hand over his heart. 'But no – the answers are here. Your heart will tell you what is right or wrong. Your best guide through life – this vale of tears – is not your brain but your heart.' He shook the pamphlet. 'It's explained here in more academic detail. But that's the essence.'

'And thus, your heart, sir, led you to the Marshalsea,' Greenstock said scathingly. 'Your Cor-guide.'

The man stiffened, almost offended.

'I don't claim Cor-ism will spare you from the corruption and evil in this world, or the iniquities of your fellow man,' he said reasonably. 'Nothing can protect you from that.' He gestured at the others sitting in the snuggery. 'Ask these people, here. But when it comes to choosing your own way it's as true a method as you'll find.'

Cashel fished in his pocket for some coins and bought the man's pamphlet.

'Thank you, sir,' the man said. 'May I know your name?'

Cashel told him.

'And I am Ebenezer Farley.' He smiled. 'No doubt our paths will cross again.'

That night, by the light of two candles, Cashel read the pamphlet. The philosophy was almost endearingly simple, namely that the heart was the root of all instinct, whereas the brain, with its propensity to rationalize and analyse, actually stifled instinct. Cor-ism led its adherents back to the simple, innate knowledge of what was good and bad, right and wrong, that every human being possessed as a birthright. Various authorities were presented to back up the theory and Cashel recognized some – Plato, Aristotle, St Augustine – but not others. When in doubt about anything, Farley advocated, listen to your heart and follow its dictates unswervingly. Cor-ists would be astonished at how straightforward and fulfilling their lives would become.

'Trite homilies,' Cashel said to himself and tossed the pamphlet on the fire – and then immediately retrieved it before it ignited. Something about Farley's modest thesis made a strange impression on him. He found himself returning to moments in his own life and the mistakes he had made. If only he had listened to his heart, he found himself thinking, then he might still be with Raphaella. For God's sake! Every decision he had made in Ravenna had been wrong – so disastrously wrong. And it was his brain that had led him to those fatal, irreversible conclusions, he could see that. His brain. Too much thinking; too much irate, convoluted speculation leading to false conclusions. Maybe there was some deeper truth in Farley's homespun ruminations, after all . . .

He sought Farley out and bought him a pot of ale and sat him down in the snuggery. Farley's debt of £43 was modest – the rent owing on a meeting-house he had leased in Spitalfields where his Cor-ist flock were meant to gather for instruction and mutual support – but didn't, in any numbers that could support him. Farley was from Bristol – he had a West Country burr to his voice – and was married with five children. In the Marshalsea he slept in a room with four other scavengers. Every penny he scrounged and could spare, every sixpence for a pamphlet, was sent to his wife and children. His case was very different from Cashel's but just as hopeless.

Cashel led him back into the taproom for another pot. There was a pile of rabbit pies on the counter made by a turnkey's wife. Cashel offered to buy him one.

'I don't eat the flesh of any animal,' Farley said. 'But I will take some bread and cheese, thank you kindly.'

They began to meet most days in the taproom, Cashel finding Farley a sympathetic and intelligent man, becoming more and more impressed with his quiet, long-suffering zeal. He gave him money so his wife and children could take the stagecoach from Bristol and visit. He paid two shillings and sixpence to evict the 'chum' from the room next door and installed Farley as his neighbour. He lent Farley some of his clothes and paid to have the man's hair cut. Slowly but surely, as the winter of 1830 transformed itself into the spring of 1831, they became companions and then friends.

Then Hogan came to the Marshalsea with news of Yelverton.

'I found this woman in Cripplegate,' he told Cashel. 'She claimed to be Yelverton's housekeeper but it was clear she was his slut.' Hogan's face was expressionless. 'Yelverton lived with her and then left her in the lurch as well, when he ran off. She had no idea – suddenly he just disappeared, she told me. Then, this last month, she gets a letter from him. From Paris. No address, of course – poste restante. I managed to persuade her to write back, to keep up a correspondence. That's how we'll find him.'

'How did you do that?'

'I can be very persuasive, Cash – if need be.'

Cashel didn't ask any more questions. But he noticed that his brother seemed even more tense than usual by this discovery; wound up like a grandfather clock, over-keyed, over-ticking, running fast. He said he was very happy to be doing this sleuthing for Cashel – more than happy – and that he was going to find Yelverton. He knew it, he felt it in his bones.

His expression changed and he paused before screwing up his eyes and shaking his head, as if a fly was buzzing round him.

'That hundred pound you gave me, Cashel,' he said quietly. 'You weren't to know, but it saved my life. Out of the blue, like that, one hundred pound . . . Came in the nick of time. The very nick. I won't forget that – which is why I'll find that cunt Yelverton for you and get you out of this sink.'

Cashel was touched by Hogan's fierce commitment, realizing, at the same time, that he hardly knew his brothers. Buckley was easier to be with and to understand – a mild-mannered, educated man, if opaque. Hogan, by contrast, seemed to be driven by some kind of wild, demonic force. There was energy there that broke out to a degree that seemed almost destructive. Still, perhaps that very energy was what was required to snare Purvis Yelverton.

In their moments in the taproom, Cashel told Farley about his twin younger brothers, reminiscing, pondering their differing natures. He and Farley were spending time together on a daily basis now that their rooms were adjacent. Farley told him that he had a dream of leaving England – 'The Land of Disappointment' – and of going to live abroad with his family and enjoying a simple, trouble-free life organized by the principles of Cor-ism; perhaps, he ventured, even founding a small community of like-minded individuals. A community that was self-sustaining, mutually beneficial, without avarice, without rank.

'No aristocracy,' Farley said with feeling. 'No overseeing, dominating government. A place of fairness, equality and tolerance, everyone helping everyone else.'

'Is that not a fantasy, Ebenezer?' Cashel asked. They were on first-name terms now.

'Who's to say, until it's put to the test?' He pointed a straight, accusatory finger at Cashel. 'It's an alternative to what we have. Isn't that a better option? Look at your sad and desperate case, Cashel. You were betrayed by a professional man and hounded into prison by another professional man. Are you content to live in a system that allows that to come to pass? Wouldn't you prefer to live under conditions that you establish, administrate and control with values that you subscribe to? Isn't that better? Why should that be a fantasy?'

Cashel agreed, a bit shaken by Farley's vehemence. And then he suddenly remembered something Brooke Mason had told him about, in Arles, when they were living together. Where was it? In South America? Venezuela. Yes, Venezuela, that was it.

'A man I knew told me that you could buy land in Venezuela for next to nothing,' Cashel said, now recalling Mason's enthusiasm. 'Hundreds of acres. They want European settlers there, apparently. Desperately, this man told me. They're giving the land away.'

'Venezuela? South America? I'd go there – to be free. Yes, so I would. Imagine, Cashel. We buy the land. We build a house – houses. Maybe your brother Hogan will join us and build a house also. Suddenly we'd have a small community. We'd share what we produced, we'd help each other, we'd live by our own morality.'

The 'Venezuela Scheme', as it came to be known, began to occupy all their conversations. Ben Smart brought them a map of Venezuela and provided details of transportation to Caracas, the capital, and information on climate and geography. Even Arthur Greenstock, being apprised of the scheme, said he might be interested in joining them as soon as the practicalities were clear.

Farley, for his part, became more and more enthused, writing to his wife and children to tell them of the plan and their prospective new life. He suggested to Cashel that they should call their new community – wherever in Venezuela they established it – 'Libertania'. And in this community they would be a 'Panocracy' – a group of people where no individual had authority over another and where all decisions were taken by democratic vote: men, women and children at the age of reason. The plans became more detailed. The Farley house would have to be the largest because of the size of the family. Cashel, Hogan and Greenstock would have simpler, smaller houses – until one or the other married and started their own family. In Cashel's mind the scheme began to take on an almost physical reality – he could see a gentle valley, a dammed stream, comfortable wooden houses with farm tracks between them, planted fields and vegetable gardens, children playing. It was a beguiling vision but there was one significant problem.

For all his searching, Ben Smart could find no trace of this generous offer made by the Venezuelan government to putative European settlers. In fact, as far as Ben could determine, there was no demand for any more European settlers in Venezuela. Indeed, there was no cheap land available and the climate, sanitary conditions and attendant risks to health in the tropics made the prospect of settling there 'demanding', to say the least.

He broke this news to Cashel, alone, on one of his regular visits, bringing in a basket of foodstuffs and smuggling in a bottle of brandy. Cashel sent down to the taproom for a kettle of boiling water and they made themselves a pot of tea fortified with the liquor.

'I'm sorry to demolish your dreams,' Ben said. 'But have a look at this. Seems far more sensible.' He showed Cashel a clipping he had scissored from the *London Star*. It was an advertisement placed by a land agent in Massachusetts, United States, one Sam M. Goodforth, advertising prime farms and farmland for sale in the counties surrounding the city of Boston. There was land for sale from a price of £2 an acre and a list of working farms for sale of various sizes for sums ranging from £200 to £400, depending on the acreage and its quality and the various commodities included.

All very reasonable and feasible, Cashel thought. Then he checked his speculations. What was he thinking? He was sitting in his cell in a prison with substantial debts still unpaid. Why was he tormenting himself with these visions of a new life? He felt his despondency gather round him like dark smoke. But no, he thought, it was even more important to have these dreams and ambitions. The powers that be could lock you in a room and deny you your freedom but they couldn't stop you thinking and hoping.

Thus encouraged, Cashel immediately wrote to Goodforth in Massachusetts asking for more information about a farm in a small town called New Banbury, in Middlesex County. It was called Willow Creek Farm – 120 acres, with a barn, a stream and a substantial pond. Certain items of farm machinery were included in the purchase. A plough, a buggy, stabling for horses, a chicken run, a piggery, assorted spades, hoes and mattocks. All for £325.

Cashel chose his moment with Farley to show the prospectus he'd received from Goodforth (who was prepared to reduce the price to £300 in the interests of a quick sale).

'The great advantage,' Cashel said to Farley, 'is that we don't have to learn Spanish. We would be in a wider society very like our own – yet a republic. No king, no dukes and duchesses.'

'A slave-owning republic,' Farley said. 'I cannot live there.'

'Not in Massachusetts, Ebenezer. There are no slaves there.'

Farley pressed the claims of Venezuela. Cashel explained what Ben Smart had discovered. Farley's face registered his reluctant disillusionment almost as if he were on stage, acting.

Cashel pointed to the map.

'You, Mrs Farley and the children would live in the farmhouse. I would build a comfortable cabin, here, for instance – on the far side of the pond. There's plenty of room for Hogan and Greenstock to construct their own dwellings. One hundred and twenty acres, Ebenezer . . . We would be a village in no time. Libertania Village, Middlesex County, Massachusetts. What do you say?'

'Aye,' Farley said, a wistful look on his face. 'Have you got a spare three hundred pound?'

Cashel managed a rueful laugh but he was undeniably stirred by the idea. An existing farm, a barn and some agricultural equipment. There would be no building of houses, no striking out into virgin jungle and clearing it. No hazards to health that weren't to be found in England. This scheme was feasible.

And it was a fact that was underscored by a visit to the Marshalsea by the Farley family. Mrs Farley – Sophronia – daughter Lydia (fourteen) and the four sons: Thornton, Leigh, Barnaby and the baby, Fortunatus, aged three. Sophronia Farley looked careworn and exhausted by the daily struggle of how to put bread on the table for herself and her offspring. Lydia was a slim, striking girl, but very shy, her eyes always lowered. Thornton and Leigh were already big lads for their ages of twelve and eleven. Suddenly Cashel could envisage the community of Libertania. Eight people already – and a workforce, able bodies that would grow abler. Let a couple of years go by, Cashel thought, and these children would be strong and capable. There would be a small clan of like-minded folk, all with the same purpose in life. Listen to your heart, he told himself: keep thinking, planning, speculating – everything is possible.

They managed a kind of celebratory feast in his room: pigeon pie with a thick wine sauce, half a Stilton and a jug of harvest beer. Cashel raised his tankard to their enterprise, to Libertania.

'All we need now,' he said, 'is for my brother to find our Mr Yelverton.'

Hotel Louisiane
Paris

14th August 1831

Dear Cashel,

I leave Paris this evening but will post this before I go. It should arrive in London before I do. I have good and bad news. First, the good news – I have found Yelverton.

The woman in Cripplegate that I mentioned (her name is Sarah Dobbs) started, at my pecuniary urging, an intermittent correspondence with Yelverton that has lasted some months now. He evidently has some vague amatory feelings for her, judging from his replies, and is experiencing some remorse that he had to abandon her. He never gave his address; all letters from Miss Dobbs being sent to the main post office in Paris.

However, he obviously welcomed the communication and I made sure Sarah complained a great deal about her circumstances. Yelverton became more forthcoming and began to give away clues, notably that he was living in a rather select area of the city. And then, in one recent letter, he complained about the endless noise caused by the construction of a large shop – a milliners on three floors – that was 'behind my house'. He said he would send for Miss Dobbs as soon as it was finished, not long off, apparently. I thought this gave me enough to be going on and took myself off to Paris three weeks ago.

At the Hôtel de Ville it was easy to discover the information that there was a large emporium being constructed at the corner of the rue St Antoine and the rue de Birague. I went to visit and saw that the site backed onto the Place Royale (formerly Place des Vosges). I instantly assumed that this was where Yelverton was living. In the square I made enquiries about the abode of Monsieur Yelverton. The name provoked no reaction. So then I asked about 'Un Gentleman Anglais' and was told that a Monsieur Bale lived in number 42. He was living in some style, I can inform you. The house – a hôtel particulier, as they call them, was splendid and the barouche that carried M. Bale hither and thither was equally splendid – black lacquer with gold trim and pulled by a pair of white horses.

I waited in the square for some days, assuming I had made the proper identification (I had your description of the man). He spent every night away from his house, dressed to the nines. After the third night, seeing him return very late, I decided to try my luck.

As he dismissed his coachman and before he could reach the door to his apartments I drew near and called out, 'Mr Yelverton, is that you?' He turned – a reflex – and then realized his error. I approached. 'Excuse me,' he said. 'I am Mr Bale.' He had the slight lisp you spoke of. 'I'm looking for a Mr Yelverton,' says I. 'I have news from a Miss Sarah Dobbs.' Again there was the natural reaction. 'I'm a friend of Miss Dobbs,' I said. 'I know of no Miss Dobbs,' said he and took out his door-keys.

That's when I struck him with my blackjack and he went down. I covered his mouth and dragged him into the centre of the park where the gaslight didn't reach. I threw water on him from a fountain and gave him a kick that brought him around fast enough. He was whimpering and wailing like a girl so I gave him another kick to shut him up.

I said, 'I'm here for Cashel Ross's money, you thieving cunt' – and here's the bad news. There is no money as such. All of it is tied up in his property, his furnishings and paintings, his carriage and so forth. Each night he goes gambling and loses, he says. He's already living on credit, having mortgaged the hôtel. He had a few francs on him and I removed them from his person as well as his gold watch and his cufflinks. He was gibbering and pissing his pantaloons, by now, swearing he had no money to pay you back. He wasn't lying to me, Cashel, I swear – you get to tell if a man is being truthful or lying in my trade. So I broke both his legs – I stamped on his knees a few times with my heavy boots (and heard the satisfying crack, confirming the job well done) and left him lying there, screaming his lungs out. It's a damn big dark square – I'm not sure anyone would like to venture in at that late hour looking for the source of the noise. You won't receive what you're due, I'm afraid to say, but Purvis Yelverton will never walk easy, if he can walk at all, and will never forget your name.

I shall return via Rotterdam in case there's any hue and cry in Paris. I'll pawn his watch and cufflinks there so there will be something to give you. I'm sorry, Cashel. I wanted to kill the scoundrel there and then but I was sure you wouldn't approve.

Ever your affectionate and grateful brother,
Hogan Ross

Cashel put the letter down and smoothed it flat, somewhat shocked at Hogan's stark and brutal narrative of his encounter with Yelverton. Cashel felt almost sorry for him – an elderly man with two badly broken knees was not going to enjoy his dotage. Or my money, Cashel thought, his mind hardening as he realized that Yelverton's Parisian spree meant that the end of the Marshalsea chapter of his life was not imminent. Even if Hogan could have forced £500 out of him, say, he could have begun a negotiation with Harkin, and maybe set out a timetable of repayment. Only Harkin could spring him from the Marshalsea, now, he realized. The dreams of Libertania Farm would have to wait.

But how long would the wait be? He felt his hopes dim, like a guttering candle, no matter how hard he tried to dismiss the brute fact of Yelverton's insolvency from his mind. Libertania couldn't be magicked into existence. It was real – not some fond chimera – bricks and mortar required, husbandry, investment of time and hard work and money. How could he maintain any confidence in the face of these inescapable realities?

And then, early in the New Year of 1832, Sir Guy Stillwell died – and everything changed.

Cashel was brought the news by Buckley. Sir Guy's heart had finally given out, he said. Stillwell Court was to be sold, with its farms, and the debts paid off. Lady Stillwell and Rosamond would go to live with Hester and her family in Dublin.* They were well provided for. But there was a secret codicil to the will that Sir Guy had written in his last months. Only the lawyers were to see it. The Glebe, Oxford, was left to Mrs Elspeth Ross with a capital sum of £5,000.

'I don't know where that money came from, but it's real,' Buckley said. 'Mother will be secure. And she can now sell the Glebe – it's too big for her, anyway, costs a fortune to keep up. A nice cottage with a housekeeper is all she needs. And he left us money, Cashel. Me and Hogan are to get five hundred each.'

---

* Stillwell Court was bought and sold three times before being demolished in 1932 by a Cork building firm (Aloysius Byrne & Sons Ltd) for its stone and lead. Only the keeper's cottage remains as a symbol of the house's former grandeur.

'What about me?' Cashel blurted out, not thinking – then felt some shame. Sir Guy had expended more than £500 on him over the years.

'Sorry, Cash. Sorry – I was about to say. Forgive my excitement. You've been left two thousand.'

'Two thousand . . .?' He felt a roaring in his ears, as if his blood were boiling. Harkin could be paid in full. There would be more than enough to buy Willow Creek Farm – and to pay for the voyage to America for himself and the Farley family. Libertania was suddenly a reality.

He stood up, shakily, and embraced Buckley, tears in his eyes. Buckley was also moved, knowing the consequences of this astonishing good fortune. He thumped Cashel on the back.

'We'll get you out of here, Cash. All will be well again.'

Cashel rummaged in his cupboard and found the brandy bottle. He poured them both a glass. They drank and he poured again. New energies were rising in him.

'God bless our father, Buck. Good old Sir Guy.'

'Hogan's doing a jig of joy, I can tell you,' Buckley said. 'Everything changes for him. Everything.'

'What about you, Buckley?'

'With that capital I can buy a nice living – easy. Become a parson. No impediment now.'

Cashel shook his head, still taking the news in.

'Funny the way things turn out, isn't it?'

They both knew what Cashel was talking about. The illicit love between a Scottish governess and an Anglo-Irish baronet had, in the end, provided for their three illegitimate sons in ways they could never have imagined.

'Thank the Lord,' Buckley said, reaching for the brandy again. 'Thank the Good Lord above.'

If Cashel's benefaction had brought tears to his eyes it made Ebenezer Farley weep openly. Cashel had told him he would repay his debt, make a down-payment to the land agent Goodforth for Willow Creek Farm and provide the packet tickets for the Farley family to sail to America. Farley's gratitude was almost too much to bear – he swore to repay him but Cashel refused, urging him to think of it as an investment in an ideal, a humane philosophy, a new way of living. There were to be no debts in Libertania.

However, there were the months of probate to be waited through, and the complexities of the negotiations with Harkin Brothers and Farley's landlord to be resolved. The Marshalsea confinement had a finite end but the place still had to be endured. Cashel told himself to be patient – a few more months were going to make no difference. He and Farley made detailed plans, contemplated ways of making the farm pay for itself, investigated the nature of the soil, the weather conditions in New England and the types of crop that flourished there. Time passed slowly, the wait grated, but it was not time wasted, he told himself.

Then, one bright morning in April 1832, Cashel and Farley stepped through the Marshalsea gates onto Borough High Street as free, solvent men.

Sophronia Farley was waiting for them. She took Cashel's hand in hers and kissed it, half-curtseying as if he were visiting royalty. Cashel saw them both off on the coach to Bristol. The Farleys had plenty of time to sort out their affairs. It had been decided by then that Cashel would be the advance guard – he would sail to Boston, finalize the acquisition of the farm and make sure that essential provisions, tools and equipment were in place. Two months later the Farleys would set out to join him. If all went to plan they would be established in New Banbury in the height of the summer, able to judge what prospects the farm had to offer (Cashel having sufficient funds to support them in this initial period). They would plant and sow what was required in the autumn and slowly but surely establish the nature of their new lives. Farley had a cousin who was interested in joining them and Arthur Greenstock's scepticism was diminishing rapidly, as he saw their plans take realistic shape. He too was keen to experience what the New World had to offer.

'Keen' wasn't a powerful enough word for Cashel's state of mind. It was bitterness, bad feeling and frustration that was driving him away from England and her corrupt complacencies. Since leaving the Marshalsea he had found himself brooding more on the injustices he'd experienced. He had been defrauded, true, but the fact that he'd then been designated a criminal as a result of that first fraud made him nauseous with anger. He had spent over two years in the Marshalsea prison, duped by a clever man, then cornered by an unscrupulous one, and he still had no share of his profits from *Nihil*.

He felt that he now wanted a new life in a new place governed by new principles – it was as simple as that. All his real happiness, he realized, thinking of Raphaella, all his confidence and self-belief, had been engendered while he was 'abroad', far from John Bull's islands. Travel may broaden the mind, he thought, but it can also be your saviour, the making of a person.

He bade farewell to his mother – grieving, black-clad – and his two brothers, promising them all regular letters. Hogan was also showing signs of interest in the American adventure. Cashel caught the coach to Liverpool with his few possessions. He was setting sail for the 'Land of the Free' on 2nd June with his head brimming with ideas and new prospects, his being alive with high-spirited anticipation. 'Libertania Farm', he felt strangely sure, would live up to her name in every degree. He was going to build his house and live in it. In a bizarre, paradoxical way, he had the sensation that his life was only just beginning.

10

The winter of 1836–7 had been unusually severe and protracted. The first snows had fallen in early December and even now, in March, it was thick on the ground, still four inches or more, hard with a frozen surface rime that crackled like glass breaking under the spinning wheels of the buggy whenever it wandered off the rutted way that other carts and buggies had made on the road between New Banbury and Concord. Cashel sat huddled on the driving seat, reins in one gloved fist, the other rammed deep in a pocket. He was wearing his heaviest greatcoat and scarf, with another scarf tied under his chin holding his felt hat tight on his head. He could feel his feet and his fingertips numbing. Not far to go now. Get the fire blazing and some grog down him.

He drove into the farm and pulled up outside the barn, noticing that there was smoke coming from the lad Ignatz's cabin set just behind and beside it. He unharnessed the horse, Amelia, led her to her loose box and threw off the bales of hay and sacks of meal he'd bought in New Banbury. The cow was in its byre, the pig in the sty, the hens in their coop – all was well with the world. He saw that Ignatz had managed to claw out some turnips and mangelwurzels from their frozen beds and had piled them in a sheltered corner to slowly thaw out. He was a kind of practical genius, was Ignatz, Cashel thought, not for the first time. He seemed capable of doing anything well – shoeing a horse, building a wall, ploughing a field. He felt weak when he tried to imagine life here at Willow Creek without him.

He tramped through the slush to the farmhouse and let himself in. He had $50 in his pocket from the firm that cut the ice blocks off the pond and reckoned that was worth celebrating. He removed his coat, scarves and hat, kicked off his boots and chucked logs on the fire – a fire that had been burning against the ferocious cold since October last, he realized, without ceasing. He stuck a poker in amongst the logs, shook them up and left it there to heat up. He lit candles. He took the sack of provisions into the kitchen and dumped them on the deal table. The range was nicely warm. He put the parcelled joints of meat in the meat safe and, finding his slippers, went back to the parlour.

There, he poured himself a good measure of corn whiskey into a pewter cup, the sour-mash that they made hereabouts, fetched the poker from the fire and wiped it off with a damp rag before placing its glowing end into the whiskey. There was a sizzle and he caught the grainy, malty smell off the smoking liquor as it suddenly heated up. He took a careful sip and felt the agreeable burn down his throat. Then he closed the interior shutters against the advancing dusk.

He took a spill from a jar on the mantel, lit it from the fire and touched the flame to the wick of his oil lamp. The soft white light spread through the room. It was one of the few luxuries he had bought himself, once the farm was his – a 'student' lamp, so-called, because it made reading easy with its steady luminosity. The other luxury had been a new percussion-cap fowling piece. A most efficient weapon. He had become a good shot – wild turkey, snipe, partridge, duck. He and Ignatz ate a lot of fowls.

He sat down in the big leather armchair in front of the fire and lit one of his small cigars, sipping at his warm bourbon. He felt the big house enfold him, with its dark rooms on three floors, many unused, but solid and secure, like a vast carapace, as big as the Glebe in Oxford, he calculated. Home – but a big house for a single man. He had offered the top floor to Ignatz but he politely declined, preferring the privacy of his little cabin with its iron stove. Anyway, it was probably all for the good that the boss and the help didn't live under the same roof.

He heard the distant lowing of the cow – maybe Ignatz was milking it – and, closing his eyes, let the sound take him back those few years to his voyage out. It was the strangest thing to associate with the Atlantic Ocean, he knew, but it was an instant memory-provoker for him. There had been two cows on the *Lady Amelia*, the private packet ship of the Hughes Line that had ferried him and two hundred other souls to the United States of America – you could hear the cows mooing throughout the ship. 'Fresh milk on board,' the Hughes Line prospectus had said: 'The _Lady Amelia_, 400 tons, Capt. Thomas Arbuthnot, just returned from Boston (21 days).'

Cashel had made the decision to travel steerage –'Tween Decks – to save money and he made sure he arrived in Liverpool two days before the advertised departure to secure his berth. The sleeping quarters on board were mixed, but he had been told that a lower bunk was essential and that it should be as close to the middle of the ship as possible to minimize the effects of the pitching and tossing of the vessel. He unrolled his straw mattress and laid out his blankets on his bunk – no more than a wide wooden shelf, in reality, with a raised side to prevent the occupant falling out. He stowed his bags of essential provisions and took his two trunks to the hold. Discreetly, he found the ship's cook and paid him five shillings for the private provision of victuals once they were at sea – another tip he had been given. The wealthier cabin passengers on the aft decks had their own kitchen and dining room where they were served by stewards. Cashel had brought his own food supply as well – tea, coffee, bacon, salt beef and oats for porridge – but he wasn't prepared to cook and feed himself for the entire voyage.

He went up on deck and watched his fellow emigrants arriving, labouring up the gangway, burdened by their worldly possessions. Young men alone, like him; families, some with newborn babies; a few older folks going to join their children, no doubt. From their accents he could tell that most of them were Irish or Scots and then came twenty pauper-women from County Mayo – who were to be lodged together, kept apart from the other passengers, in separate quarters behind a temporary bulkhead. They were dressed in identical long caramel-coloured capes and white bonnets. All young women, they were patently excited by the prospect of the voyage and the new life that awaited them.

As he watched them arrive, more and more toiling up the gangway, he began to wonder if he had made a mistake. Perhaps he should have booked a personal cabin. His economy identified him with these poor, needy people, Britain's rabblement and impoverished unwanted being exported to a new country desperate for man- and woman-power. He should be wearing a sign, he thought: '*I am a farmer. I own a farm in America.*' Then he chided himself for his pomposity. He had saved ten pounds by travelling steerage – and ten pounds would buy a lot of dollars in Massachusetts.

At the appointed hour the *Lady Amelia* was cast off and headed out to sea with full sail set on her three masts. The private packet ships offered more amenities for the price of a ticket – three quarts of water a day, a portion of biscuits and meal, all included. Basic rations, but no passenger would starve as they often had in the old days of emigration. Now there was a market and competition – money was to be made. There was even a surgeon on board the *Lady Amelia*, so the prospectus claimed, but no one had been able to identify the individual. They were not convicts on their way to Van Diemen's Land, after all, so these advertisements seemed to underline – they were men and women voluntarily seeking to make new lives for themselves and the Hughes Line packet was proud to be part of this enterprise and adventure.

For all that, Cashel could see that many of his fellow passengers were abjectly poor. Dirty, badly clothed, barely prepared for the voyage and what lay ahead of them. He gave away his daily ration of biscuits to a ragged, starveling family – the McDaids – who, with their four children, slept in the wooden platforms around his. The children seemed cowed and silent, wondering and confused by this new environment they found themselves in. Hector McDaid, the father, was a cooper, he told Cashel. His landlord had generously subsidized the family's ticket to Boston. Was it generosity – or a disguised eviction? Cashel wondered. Hector McDaid had no idea what awaited him in the United States, he confessed, but it had to be better than the life he had been living in Glasgow. Anything was better than what he and the family had to endure.

The days at sea passed slowly. The weather was fair. Cashel spent time in his bunk reading books on animal husbandry and treatises on cereal crops – making careful notes. Luckily Farley was a hundred times more competent. The son of a tanner, he had grown up surrounded by animals and Cashel fully intended to leave most of the practicalities of farming in his hands. However, *he* had bought the farm, after all, not Farley, and it would be absurdly complacent not to know what was going on in his fields.

Some days were benignly sunny and Cashel spent more time up on deck, making steady circuits to give him some exercise. There was always a queue at the water closets as the mixed accommodation made the use of chamber pots inappropriate for adults. The poorer émigrés could earn a few pence keeping these cabinets clean, rinsing the closets out with chloride of lime, an odour that Cashel for ever after associated with defecation. There were queues also for the deck stoves where meals could be cooked. When he found an opportunity Cashel would fry bacon or make some porridge, but he was well fed, clandestinely, by the cabin passengers' cook who would slip him a covered skillet containing a stew or some slices of mutton on a bed of potatoes or a hunk of rabbit pie or beefsteak pudding. Anything he couldn't consume went to the McDaid family.

Three and a half weeks after setting forth from Liverpool the *Lady Amelia* hove to in Boston harbour. They were told they would disembark the next morning, carried ashore by steam paddle-boats. Cashel stood at the taffrail looking at the lights of the city behind the crowded masts of the vessels berthed at the wharves. He felt excited and apprehensive at the same time. Everything was prepared: he had his letters of credit, he had cash to exchange for dollars, he had his contact's address in the city and the prospect of a four-hour drive to his farm in New Banbury. He would take his time, he decided. He would find a comfortable hotel, have a proper wash and a shave and a substantial meal or two before he went to meet the land agent. After all, he reasoned, he had the rest of his life before him.

After breakfast – he was staying at the Hanover Hotel on the corner of Boyleston and Clarendon Street – Cashel had his luggage and trunks loaded into a hack and was driven to the office of Goodforth Realty on Devonshire Street.

To Cashel's eyes Boston looked very like a provincial English town picked up and set down on a low promontory or peninsula, jutting out into its wide, island-dotted bay. There was an old town with narrow streets and clustered buildings, grimy warehouses and grain stores – a bit like Portsmouth's Southsea that he remembered from his soldiering days – with, beyond the rooftops, the aerial woodland of hundreds of masts and spars of innumerable vessels. But beyond that old town, the North End, broader boulevards had been built with grander brick and stone buildings, churches, spires, cupolas, parks, some evidence of tree-planting. On either side was water – coves and creeks – and silty marshland. But the place was busy and carriages rattled down the wide streets and the pavements were filled with the bustle of people going energetically about their business. A provincial town with a hint of a capital city about it, then. Money was being made here, he could tell. Pillared buildings, tall porticos, commercial advertisements everywhere, gilded carriages drawn by glossy horses, men and women in the most fashionable clothes.

At Devonshire Street he met Mr Sam M. Goodforth himself, who proposed to drive him to New Banbury in his new two-horse Surrey. Goodforth was a small, neat fellow in a tight suit – a few years younger than Cashel – who had a surprisingly dense blonde moustache that seemed to strangely imbalance his face and head, as if the moustache had been transplanted from a larger, more powerful man.

'We'll be there in no time, sir,' he said with a broad, genuine smile. And as promised, the Surrey and its two horses moved at a fair clip. They crossed the Charles river and they soon left the city behind them. Cashel noted the superior quality of the turnpike, the ride was smooth, the Surrey well sprung. Goodforth was a talkative companion and very curious about England and Europe – he had never left the United States, he confessed. He was full of questions and amazed at the extent of Cashel's travels.

'Have you ever been on a railroad, Mr Ross?'

'I have not, not yet, anyway.'

'You have them everywhere now in England, I believe.'

'Well, not everywhere. But I saw the rail*way* – that's what we call them – that exists between Manchester and Liverpool when I went to board my ship.'

'There's talk of building one here – between Lowell and Boston.'

'It's the coming thing, so they say.'

'But if my Surrey can go faster than a locomotive, what's the point?'

'But can your Surrey pull carriages full of tons of goods, and dozens of people?'

'You make the argument very clear, Mr Ross.'

They stopped at a roadside tavern in Concord, ate a pie and drank some ale and then headed on to New Banbury.

New Banbury was like a smaller version of Concord, Cashel saw. There was a courthouse and a church on a central square. There was a jail and a school, a windmill, a general store and some livery stables. The houses were of brick and wooden boards, simple constructions set out in large gardens. It had turned out to be a warm, sunny day and Cashel removed his coat – Goodforth followed his lead – as they drove on to Willow Creek Farm, some two miles out of town off the public road between New Banbury and Stow.

Cashel felt his heartbeat increase as they pulled in to the property. The place looked very overgrown and unkempt. Goodforth explained: the owner, a Mr Watts, had upped and offed to Georgia in the gold rush of the previous year. The farm had been effectively abandoned for some eighteen months, hence the urgency to sell. Mr Watts had been an unsuccessful prospector, thus far, and was in need of funds.

The house was about twenty years old, a plain, weathered, two-storey, boxy construction made of boards set on a wooden frame with a large central chimney. Cashel counted five windows on the facade and four on the gable end that was visible. Set at ninety degrees to the house was a barn of almost the same size, also clapboard, half-closed, half-open, and with a labourer's cabin just behind. Here there was a weed-choked vegetable garden and a small orchard of apple, pear and quince trees.

Goodforth led Cashel up a small rise that revealed a long thin pond, approximately one hundred yards long by thirty wide. Along one side of the pond was a low overhang of rock-face and what looked like a cave of some size. The other bank was filled with thick unmown meadow and once-tilled fields that had gone to seed. In fact there wasn't a great deal of arable land, as Goodforth explained; most of the acreage was wooded – pines, hickory, sumac and a few clumps of ancient oaks. Beyond the overhanging cliff was an area of semi-fertile land of scrub oak.

'You'll get a lot of cordwood from that,' Goodforth said, pointing. 'Oh, yeah.'

Cashel then inspected the house, with its empty and dusty rooms. The big brick fireplace, the mantel at head height, dominated the main parlour. All the furniture in here had been cleared out but there was a table and chair in the kitchen and a long black range stood there, untouched.

'In the barn you've got stabling, a byre, a sty. Little corral in back of the cabin,' Goodforth said. 'It's a real nice property, Mr

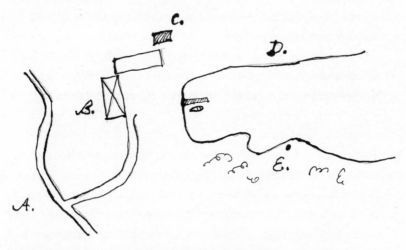

Willow Creek Farm. A. Road to New Banbury. B. Farmhouse (X) and barn. C. Ignatz's cabin. D. Willow Creek Pond. E. The cave.

Ross, especially at this price. I imagine you'll quintuple your money once the railroad reaches out here.'

Cashel held out his hand.

'I'll take it, Mr Goodforth. Lock, stock and scrub oak.'

Willow Creek Farm
New Banbury
Middlesex County
Massachusetts

23rd July 1832

My dear Farley,

I write in haste as I want you to receive this letter before you set sail for the United States. The farm is perfect! I've made camp in the house and set about giving the rooms a coat of whitewash. There is plenty of space for us all – even a small cabin with a stove where I shall live until I can plan and build something more substantial. I've bought a piebald horse to pull the buggy and the plough and some sticks of furniture. I'll await your arrival so we can make further plans regarding the domestic aspects. There are six rooms on the upper floor that will serve as bedrooms for you, Mrs Farley and the children.

To be frank, the land is neglected and somewhat run wild. We will have our work cut out initially to make it good but there is no hurry. New Banbury can provide us with everything we need and a little further away are the larger towns of Stow and Concord. Boston can be reached in a few hours and the road is good. Here included is a rough plan of the property to give you an idea – I've tried my best to draw everything to scale.

I have a warm and elated feeling about Willow Creek – soon to be re-christened Libertania Farm. The most remarkable feature is the pond. The water is uncommonly limpid, and reflects the blue of the sky in the most enchanting manner. You can see the sand beneath quite clearly and the fish that swim in it – mainly perch and shiners, I am told. The water is very clear when poured into a glass and very potable. In winter, Mr Goodforth told me, there is money to be made selling the ice in great blocks. On one side there is a little sand bar in front of a low limestone cliff face that boasts a long cool cave. The rock must have been quarried by aboriginals for a man can stand upright in it to a depth of twenty paces. The children will be enchanted by it.

I will stop now and haste this to the post office. I know that you are due to sail on 10th September. Make sure you arrive in Liverpool two days earlier to secure your berths – near the middle of the ship, if possible – and bring as much food for the journey as you can carry. The Boston Pilot *announces the expected arrivals of the packet ships and they seem to be remarkably accurate. I will be waiting on the dockside to welcome you all. Give my fondest wishes to your wife and children.*

I remain, my dear Ebenezer,

your firm and affectionate friend,
Cashel Ross

Cashel folded the letter, sealed it and took it to the post office in Concord. The postmaster advised him to pay the postage in advance to make sure it had the most expeditious start possible on its journey. Cashel did so and saw the letter franked. While he was there he enquired about the poste restante facilities. He was waiting for letters from his mother, Hogan and his bank in London. He gave the postmaster his name and new address and somehow the simple act of doing so brought home the reality of what he had done and achieved. He felt a surge of emotion overcome him that made him sway on his feet for a second or two. He gripped the edge of the post office counter to steady himself.

'Are you well, sir?'

'I've never felt better. Thank you.'

Cashel knew the date of the Farleys' departure – he had paid for the passage himself – and the Atlantic crossing could be timed with some accuracy these days. However, he went to Boston early to meet the ship, not wanting to risk missing the family. He stayed at the Hanover Hotel again and, while he waited, treated himself to fine meals in fine restaurants. He walked in the Common. He wandered round an exhibition of wildlife paintings in the Gallery of Fine Arts behind the Athenaeum. He went to see *Paul Pry* at the theatre on Federal Street. The *Boston Pilot* predicted the arrival of the packet (the *Leviathan*) on 8th or 9th October.

In fact, it turned out to be the 9th. Cashel stood on the Long Wharf watching the first passengers emerge from the steamboats ferrying to and fro. After two hours it was clear that the Farley family had not arrived. Frustrated, he went to the harbourmaster's office where he was told that the passenger manifest from the *Leviathan* would be posted the next day.

Cashel duly returned and was baffled to discover that the Farleys had not been amongst the *Leviathan*'s 218 passengers. He didn't know what to do. He had given Farley money for the tickets and he knew that passage was booked for 10th September. Where were they? What had happened? He tried to curb the unwelcome feeling that he'd been cheated again and rebuked himself for his suspicions. Farley was not that kind of man – just because Yelverton had proved himself a lying rogue didn't mean that everyone else he had to deal with in his life was similarly duplicitous. There was nothing more he could do. If the Farleys had been detained for some reason and were coming on another packet ship they would have to make their own way to New Banbury. He couldn't wait in Boston at the wharfside, scrutinizing every set of passengers on every ship from England.

He went back to the farm and busied himself as he waited for their eventual arrival. He worked on the house, buying beds and some more essential pieces of furniture. He painted the kitchen. He harvested the fruit from the orchard and stored it in the scullery cupboards. He bought a fishing rod and tackle and began to catch fish in the pond. He introduced himself to his immediate neighbours – the Corcorans, the Van der Veens, the Bradshaws and the Eliots. They seemed decent, hard-working folk. The Corcorans were from Galway and hearing Cashel's accent welcomed him warmly as one of their own. He told all of them that he was awaiting the arrival of his partner and his family and that Willow Creek Farm would soon be alive and functioning again.

At the beginning of November he drove to Concord to buy seed potatoes. He had managed to plough the vegetable garden and wanted to have everything ready for the following spring.

'Ah, Mr Ross, good morning,' the postmaster said. He was a familiar face by now as letters were coming regularly from England. 'Just the one today,' he said and gave him a letter with handwriting he didn't recognize.

14 Clerk Street
Bristol

8th September 1831

Dere Mr Ross,

Please excus my ill-taut hand. I must convey to you the sad news that my hus-band, Ebenezer Farley, dyed of a sudden fever this last Thursday. He had been of fit and well health. We are all in despare. We cannot come to America without him. I do so apologyse. I have taken the mony you gave us to feed our children. God save us, Mr Ross. I will pay you back for you being so kind if I die in the effort. You are a good man to our family. I am so sorry that this terrible accident has be-fallen us. We are lost souls now and our dreams are only desastres.

With my cordial good wishes and may God bless you as he does not bless us.

Mrs Sophronia Farley

Cashel felt heart-sick at this devastating news. Poor Farley! Poor Ebenezer, the idealist, the dreamer! Life could be mercilessly cruel sometimes. So close to the voyage and the promises of this literal new world and to be struck down like this . . . Then he began to wonder. Darker speculations ensued. Had his good

nature been exploited, he asked himself, his trust undermined . . .?
But he rebuked himself sternly for his suspicions. No – the Farleys, of all people on this earth, would not steal from him. In fact,
this poignant letter alone – with its artless neologisms – proved
that the awful news was genuine. If they had merely wanted to
rob him of his money they would have simply done so – nothing
would be gained by composing and communicating a lie. Farley
was dead. The family was beleaguered and lost – and with that
loss the vision that was Libertania Farm came crashing down.
Cashel was on his own in America – he had to face that fact. He
began to wonder how he could survive.

Cashel threw the two-handed saw into the back of the buggy
and Ignatz waved him goodbye as he trotted off to return it to
the Corcorans. Of all his neighbours he had grown closest to
this family. They had a big, prosperous farm of nearly four hundred acres to the south of Willow Creek, and, during the taxing
early years on the farm, Cashel had only been able to survive
through the sale of twenty acres of pitch-pine wood to Shay
Corcoran, the patriarch. He was a widower and worked the
farm with his two sons, Devin and Murphy, both in their early
twenties. There was a younger daughter, Bríd, who was eighteen and ran the house and the domestic side. Shay Corcoran and
his late wife had emigrated to America in 1804 and his Galway
accent had remained strong and unmistakable, whereas the children had all been born after the parents' arrival and spoke like
New Englanders.

It took him only twenty minutes to drive to the Corcoran
farm, named Rockfell, and as he pulled up in front of the house –
grander than his with a long porch and two gable chimneys – he
could see Bríd hanging out washing on a line behind the
kitchen.

She dropped her bundle of clothes and came immediately to
meet him. She was a shy, dark-haired girl, with a round pallid
face. In fact, her skin was so pale it was a source of fascination to
Cashel. She had the sleeves of her dress rolled up and he could

see that her forearms were as white as her neck and cheeks – chalk white, white as writing paper, he thought.

'Mr Ross, how are you? Always a pleasure to see you.'

'Thank you, Miss Corcoran, I'm very well. I'm just returning this here saw.'

He lugged it over to the barn, Bríd walking with him.

'The men're all down in the south fields shearing sheep,' she said.

'I won't linger then—'

'Why don't you have a cup of coffee, Mr Ross. I've just set it to brew.'

Cashel sat on a cane chair on the porch, his hat on his knee, as Bríd poured coffee into a china mug. He knew she was attracted to him though she had never said anything or given any other tender indication. But he was aware from the way she smiled when she saw him and how she overcame her habitual diffidence in his presence, particularly when her father and brothers weren't around. The Corcorans were a devout Catholic family. There were daily family prayers, he knew, and a crucifix hung in every room. Bríd always wore her mother's gold cross at her throat. She was a sweet and efficient girl, Cashel was aware. Her mother had died when she was thirteen and she had replaced her at once, taking over the running of the household, cleaning, laundering, cooking meals for the Corcoran men, all robust, rangy types, at home in the outdoors.

As usual, Bríd was all curiosity when she had the chance to talk to him alone.

'I was just thinking, Mr Ross, what cities in Italy did you live in? How I'd love to go to Italy.'

'I lived in Milan and Pisa and Ravenna, mainly.'

'Pisa? Did you see the famous leaning tower?'

'I did. Many times. I must lend you the book I wrote about my travels.'

'That would be grand. Very kind of you. Which city did you like the best?'

'I, ah, I liked Ravenna best. Yes.'

'And why was that?'

He didn't have to answer because, just at that moment, Shay Corcoran appeared around the barn leading his horse.

'Here comes your father,' Cashel said, glad he didn't have to talk about Ravenna.

Shay Corcoran was a tall, lean man with dense white hair and whiskers, white as his daughter's skin. His left hand was deformed by arthritis into an awkward-looking claw. It caused him great pain, Bríd had confided once, but he never referred to it, never complained. They greeted each other respectfully. Cashel was very grateful to Corcoran – he had bought the pine-wood acres in 1833 without trying to bargain him down even though he must have been very aware that Cashel needed money badly. A fiercely honourable man, Cashel recognized: Corcoran's money for the woods had kept him and the farm afloat.

'It's a fine saw, that one,' Cashel said. 'Much obliged, Mr Corcoran.'

'Cutting timber?'

'It's a scheme that my man – Ignatz, you know him, the fellow that helps me – has come up with. We'll see if it works.'

Bríd resorted to her dutiful-daughter mode, poured her father a coffee from the pot and left them to talk about farming matters. In fact, Cashel often sought out the old man's advice. Rockfell was thriving. As they chatted, Cashel noticed how his own Irish brogue thickened, now exposed to Corcoran's Galway accent. Cashel had made a point of being vague about his antecedents, saying only that his family had moved to England from County Cork when he was a boy. Yet it was enough to make Corcoran warm to him – and his two sons happily followed their father's lead. Cashel was always welcome at Rockfell and they were free and helpful with their suggestions.

Cashel finished his coffee, made his farewells and headed back to Willow Creek. There was some heat in the spring air, he noticed – winter was over, so now was the time to initiate Ignatz's unusual scheme. Cashel was happy to go through with the experiment as it was clear that farming might just about sustain him but he was never going to turn a profit. Willow Creek had to be exploited in other ways.

Back at the farm, Cashel saw that Ignatz had laid out all the timber they had felled, long lengths of pine, twelve-foot logs, trimmed and neat. Ignatz was standing looking at the cut wood – he turned as Cashel approached.

'Have we cut enough?' Cashel asked.

'Enough to start with. Easy to cut more, if we need.'

'Good.'

'Twenty logs – so, ten supports.' Ignatz pointed at the area of the meadow by the pond that they had scythed close. 'Now we have to dig twenty holes,' he said.

The plan had been hatched at the end of the previous year. Just before autumn had truly set in Ignatz had approached him one day with a switch of vegetation in one hand. The plant was densely leaved, its leaf a bit like a maple or a plane, Cashel thought, and hanging from it were flowers, like soft green cones.

'What's this?' Cashel asked, sensing Ignatz's enthusiasm.

'I don't know the English word,' he said. 'In my country we call it *chmel*. For making beer.'

'Ah, yes. Hops, we call them.'

'Hops . . .' Ignatz tried the word out. 'Hops.'

'Where did you find it?'

'They are wild. In the woods. We have many.'

'What good are they?'

Ignatz smiled at him. A little sceptically, as if puzzled that Cashel couldn't come up with the answer himself.

'We can make beer,' Ignatz said. 'Ale. Beer. I know how to make it.'

'I like beer.'

'Mr Ross, please, not just for us. We can make a lot of beer.'

'Why would we do that?'

'To make money,' Ignatz said patiently and held up the plant. 'This *chmel*, this hop . . .' He sniffed it. 'It reminds me of the one we have at home in Bohemia.'

'And what advantage does that give us?'

'If I'm right it gives us a big advantage. Where I live we call this type of hop "Saaz". It can make a very special beer.' He paused. 'We have this hop. We have the beautiful water, we have the cave. I can make you a wonderful beer, sir. Better than any in America.'

'How do you know how to make beer?'

'I have a book, sir. A German book – everything is explained.'

Cashel laughed.

'All right. Let's do it, Ignatz, let's give it a go.'

'One warning. It takes three years.'

'Oh. Well, maybe not, then.'

'No, sir. We must do it. We start next year. Hops are very easy to grow. We make a place for them, we look after them, then, when the time is right, we harvest – and we make beer.'

And so the scheme for the Willow Creek hop yard was born.

After the shocking news of Ebenezer Farley's death in 1832 Cashel had almost thought of abandoning Willow Creek Farm. Clearly, Libertania was now never going to come to pass. He had even made a new sign – burned with a hot poker in a deal plank – that he had planned to hang at the farm's entrance to welcome the Farleys to their new life, their collective future. It was now placed on the mantel above the big fireplace, an *aide memoire* to what might have been.

But after some anguished, questioning reflection he decided to stay on and see if he could make a life for himself here in New England. Something about the big house and the translucent pond had spoken to him. He felt at ease in the place; he was glad his old life with its troubles was behind him; his neighbours were respectful and helpful. The proximity of New Banbury meant he would never feel isolated and alone in the 'wilderness'. He was not a pioneer launched on an arduous, distant journey to explore some *terra incognita*. There was a library in Concord; improving lectures were given in the meeting house; there were inns and taverns; there were shops that sold everything he needed from needles and thread to ploughshares and pickaxes. And Boston was only a day's coach journey away. There was every reason to forge on, he told himself.

But the first year had been difficult. He had to hire labourers to take the hay off the meadows. The first cow he bought died after two months. He didn't even attempt to plough the arable fields or sow any crops, but managed to make his vegetable garden flourish, after a fashion – potatoes, runner beans, peas, melons – and could almost feed himself. He was spending a lot of money equipping the place, however, hence the need to sell the twenty acres of woods to the Corcorans. His bank credit remained just about acceptable.

But by the spring of 1833 it was clear that he could no longer manage single-handedly. He needed help. He put up a notice in the town halls, churches and meeting halls of Stow, Concord and New Banbury advertising for an experienced agricultural labourer who could till fields, cope with livestock, prune fruit trees, etc., etc. – a jack of all trades, in other words. He offered $10 a week plus accommodation – he had made the cabin comfortable and the stove worked efficiently. Three months went by, however, without a single applicant. He wondered if he should increase the wage he had posited. Corcoran had said it was generous, but there were no takers.

And then one June evening he saw a young man walking down the farm track towards the house. He was very young indeed, Cashel saw, as they started talking. The young man spoke in a curious mixture of a guttural European accent with an overlay of twangy American tones. He was squat and powerfully built but his face was lean and angular with high cheekbones and large expressive brown eyes. His name, he said, was Ignatz Vlac and he would like to apply for the position advertised.

'May I ask your age, Mr Vlac?'

'I think I am eighteen – or perhaps twenty.'

'When were you born?'

'I don't know, sir. But I grew up in a country called Bohemia.'

'The name is familiar. Were your parents from Bohemia?'

'I never knew my parents. I was raised by my uncle. It was he who brought me to America about eight years ago.'

'Does he live nearby?'

'No. I don't know where he is. We have separated a long time ago.'

Cashel decided to stop asking questions. Listen to your heart, as Ebenezer Farley advised. Cashel liked the candour of Ignatz Vlac's replies – his instincts told him that this powerful young man with the sad and searching face might well prove to be the answer to his problems.

And it turned out that Ignatz, as Cashel was soon calling him, could do anything the farm required from mucking out stables to milking a cow – he had bought another, at Ignatz's suggestion. He could do metalwork and carpentry; he could cut down a tree and lay bricks; he could clean tack and find wild honey. There seemed no end to his capabilities. He suggested that Cashel also buy a mule to do the ploughing and – a mule having been acquired – the small fields around the pond were ploughed and sown. They planted Indian corn and turnips the first year. Half an acre was given over to clover for feed, and the meadows were cut for hay. Slowly but surely, Cashel learned from Ignatz's example as they worked together in the fields. Within a year they were self-sufficient. They took their sacks of corn to the mill in Concord and were paid real money for them.

They lived as amiable, respectful neighbours – Cashel in his big house, Ignatz in his basic cabin. Basic, but clean. Cashel called him Ignatz; Ignatz called him 'sir' or 'Mr Ross'. The proprieties between employer and employee were fully observed. Cashel offered him one day off a week but he declined. 'I take my rest at night while I sleep,' he said. 'We spend one third of our life asleep, not working. Why should we not be working for the other two thirds?' Cashel asked if that was a Bohemian saying but Ignatz claimed to have evolved this homespun philosophy himself.

Willow Creek Farm
New Banbury
Middlesex County
Massachusetts

15ᵗʰ May 1837

Dear Hogan,

I wonder if you could find and send me Alexander Moxley's <u>Cottage Economy</u> and also a farmer's almanack for the year 1837, if such a book exists. I need an English almanack because the American versions – easily had – are full of extraneous matter: how to tell the stars in the sky, the world's longest rivers so far discovered, the history of Ancient Egypt, astrological tables and the like. I seek only practical guidance: when to plant potatoes, when to tup sheep, how to store fresh picked strawberries and so forth.

Last week, Ignatz – my labourer – slaughtered our hog (whom we called Sam). He burned the hair off, then took out the innards and made hog's puddings and blood sausages. Then he cut the carcase up – souse, griskins, spare ribs, chines, cheeks and trotters. The house is full of meat. He took the two flitches and salted them with dry salt; then he smoked them, hanging the flitches in the chimney and burning hickory shavings beneath. We shall have sweet bacon until Christmas, he says. He stores the flitches in a box covered with the hickory ash – no flies or skipping maggots, he guarantees. He is a wonder-worker. I would not survive without him.

By the by, the great excitement here is that our neighbour's son, Devin Corcoran (I've told you all about the Corcorans, I think) is to be married to an Irish girl from Boston – just a year off the boat from Dublin. There will be a dance and music and general feasting for a hundred people, they say. It will be a welcome change as I have to report that it is a routine and yet d____d busy life out here at the farm and I confess I miss the entertainment that a city offers. When I tire of being a farmer I go into Boston for a couple of days, visit a bookseller, eat in a hotel restaurant, go to a theatre, wear my finest clothes. Boston is a fast-growing city, nothing like London, however, but I find I need the contrast with my life on the farm. Then after two days I find myself pining for the simple verities of country living and am glad to return.

Do give my fondest love to Mother and Buckley – and tell him I need news of his new parish. I will report on the great wedding feast.

Ever your affectionate bro.
Cashel

<u>*Postscriptum.*</u> *I forgot to tell you we are planning to make beer at the farm. Ignatz has found a species of feral hop that he says will make an exceptional brew. So we have built a hop yard and the plants grow to enormous height, two feet a week.*

We hack them back brutally and they grow again with renewed force. It takes three years before you can harvest the hops. Soon, Ignatz says, we shall be brewers.

Cashel drove to Boston and bought a wedding present of a tea service for Devin Corcoran and his bride, Caitlín. He saw a poor production of *Two Gentlemen of Verona* and, after he'd eaten and drunk, he took a hack to the North End of the city and was dropped at Ann Street that ran just behind the wharves on the harbour front. He was looking for a bawdyhouse and Ann Street, and the streets off it, had plenty, along with saloons and dance halls, small taverns and noisome basement brothels.

Two or three times a year Cashel felt the overpowering urge to hold a woman in his arms – a naked woman. To press his naked body to hers and see what happened. In the small lane close to Ann Street there were more opulent, pretentious establishments, so-called 'parlour houses', where music was played, drinks – including champagne – were served, the decor was sophisticated and the basic nature of the exchange that was being offered was disguised. Jugs and ewers were provided in the private rooms behind these front salons, so a customer could wash himself before putting his clothes back on.

It was always the last item on his Boston list and, as he remarked to himself on his journey home to New Banbury the next day, the visit always brought in its train a familiar melancholy, guilt, regret and anxiety. He had never forgotten Dr Freemantle's heartfelt injunction about prostitutes. *Facilis descensus Averno*. It is easy to descend to hell . . . But sometimes hell had to be visited. Dr Freemantle in Ooty! What world was that?

And as he drove back to the farm, thinking about what had happened the night before in the parlour house on Endicott Street, he found his mind turning inevitably to Raphaella. Memories made more anguished by his ignorance of her circumstances. Where was she? How was she? Was she happy? How many children did she have? Did she ever think of him as he thought of her? The questions came quick and fast, answerless. Years had gone by, he knew, and she had probably forgotten the incredible intensity of their love affair. But he hadn't. He would never forget her, he swore. What was that old saying? You will never forget your first love. It was true, every woman he saw who attracted him was measured, as a matter of reflex, against Raphaella. And yet he was aware that he would probably never see her again.

His absurd guilt about the night before returned – as if he'd betrayed her, betrayed the purity of their love. But he chided himself, Come on, Cashel, you're only human. You're only a man, a fairly young man. You have natural appetites – so what? – no need to be ashamed of yourself.

Cashel was dancing with Bríd. He was a bit drunk, he realized – too much corn whiskey. That and the jig they were dancing, all that bouncing about and whirling around, was making him feel even more light-headed. They were both out of breath, exhilarated, and he saw a look on Bríd's face that he had never witnessed before – sheer excitement, pleasure being taken, a kind of abandonment. He experienced a surge of crude lust for her, then – her youth, her white skin, her lips lightly rouged, two coins of flushed pinkness on her cheeks, the inhale and exhale of her chest under the pea-green silk bodice of her bridesmaid's gown.

The music ended and they all applauded the band – two fiddles, a squeeze-box and an upright piano. Cashel almost took

Bríd's hand as they walked off the wooden dance floor set beneath its open-sided tent.

'That was wonderful,' she said, still breathless. 'You fair whirled me off my feet, Mr Ross.'

'You have to call me Cashel at your brother's wedding.'

'Only if you call me Bríd.'

'Bríd, Bríd, Bríd.'

They laughed. And looked at each other.

'I'd better go and see how Father's getting on,' she said. 'I'll see you later, Cashel.'

He watched her go and then headed for the trestle table where all the drink was set out, much of it brought by the hundred or so guests. There was whiskey, rum, cider, a keg of ale. It had been quite a Corcoran show, Cashel thought. Two hogs spit-roasted on open fires, cold meats and puddings, everyone sitting down at long tables under another huge tent. Speeches, toasts, more speeches – and then the band had struck up. Cashel found a shot glass and filled it from a stone jar of corn whiskey. He took a gulp, feeling in a strange mood: excited by the dance and stirred by Bríd's—

'Y'all right, Cashel?'

He turned to see Devin Corcoran, the groom himself, very drunk, chewing a plug of tobacco, a glow of sweat on his forehead. He adjusted his position carefully, as if he might fall over. His cravat was coming loose and Cashel found it odd to see the young farmer pomaded and smart in frock-coat and shirt frill.

'Congratulations, Devin,' Cashel said. 'Great day. You've a lovely bride, there.'

'Married life awaits,' Devin said, squaring his shoulders. 'Yes, she's a winner, is Caitlín.'

They looked around the crowd of guests to see if Caitlín could be spotted, but saw no sign of her. There was Bríd, however, with her father. She glanced over at them and waved.

'Ah, Bríd. Bless her,' Devin said, smiling inanely. And unthinkingly spat a large rivulet of tobacco juice onto the grass.

There were candle lanterns set on the table now as evening

was advancing and Cashel took out his small cigar case and lit a cigar from the nearest flame. He offered one to Devin who took it gratefully, taking his quid of tobacco out of his mouth and tucking it in his waistcoat pocket. They smoked for a while, watching Bríd steer her father through the groups of guests, stopping to chat from time to time.

Cashel remembered that Corcoran had just been elected First Selectman of New Banbury – a kind of mayor, he supposed, though there were two other Selectmen besides him, running the town's municipal affairs – planning, administrating and legislating as the place grew ever larger. A big man in the neighbourhood now, Cashel thought, the immigrant makes good. He saw people come up to greet Corcoran with wide smiles, both congratulatory and supplicating. Bríd stood patiently beside him. Cashel noticed a small oval of sweat darkening the material of her green dress between her shoulder blades. Again he felt that quickening, that animal sensuousness she had mysteriously inspired. Like Claire Clairmont, he thought. Where had that memory suddenly come from . . .?

'Look at Bríd, there,' Devin said, his voice a little slurred, leaning in to him. 'Eighteen years old, a catch for any man. She'd make a grand wife.'

'Yes, I suppose she would,' Cashel said, not thinking.

'You should marry her yourself.'

'What?'

'Before some other fella plucks her from your grasp.'

Cashel laughed. 'I'm far too old for her,' he said. 'She must think of me as an old man.'

'She's soft on you, I tell you. Always talking about you.'

'Really?'

'Look, there's the new Mrs Corcoran signalling for her husband. I'd better run. Thanks for the cigar.'

Cashel stayed until dusk, talking to the people he knew, his neighbours, suddenly feeling part of the community – and drinking more. He ate a big slice of wedding cake to counter the whiskey but decided the time had come to leave before he fell over. He went to find the bride and groom to make his farewells but instead ran into Bríd, who was coming from the house.

'I'm off, Bríd. Full to bursting.'

'I'll walk you to your buggy,' she said.

They strolled round behind the big house to a mown field full of carriages – buggies, Surreys, driving cars, pony traps. Horses cropped grass in the gloaming, stamped their feet, ate from nosebags. Cashel found his buggy and picked up the reins, flipping them onto the seat. He turned to Bríd and felt his head reel – all that whiskey. Jesus.

'Thanks for the dance, Bríd. Highlight of the day.'

He took off his tall hat and caught her hand and kissed it in what he hoped was true cavalier fashion.

She looked round to see if they were alone and turned her gaze directly on him. Eye to eye.

'You can kiss my lips as well, if you want,' she said quietly.

Without thinking, Cashel leant forward and kissed her soft mouth. He felt her arms go around his neck and her body pressed against his.

They separated, breathless again, and somewhat astonished. He thought she looked inordinately beautiful in the dusk, seeing the girl in her vanishing to be replaced by the woman.

Listen to your heart, he thought.

'Would you marry me, Bríd?' he blurted out. 'Would you ever think of marrying an old fellow like me?'

'I'd like nothing better in the world. I swear,' she said instantly and smiled. 'And you're far from old, Cashel Ross.'

They kissed again, more passionately.

'Let's not wait, Cashel. No long engagement, please. I can't stand that woman my brother's married. I can't be in the house with her. You've saved my life . . .' She paused. 'My darling.'

Two days later, as Bríd and he had quickly planned, Cashel drove round to Rockfell Farm – having sent Ignatz ahead the day before with a note asking for a private meeting with Shay Corcoran.

Corcoran led Cashel into a small parlour at the rear of the house. It smelt of pipe smoke and there was a portrait of a severe-looking woman in old-fashioned clothes – the late Mrs Corcoran – in a gilt frame above the fireplace. Corcoran poured them both a drink of Irish whiskey, left over from the wedding party. They talked about the dry weather and the need for a good sousing of heavy rain. Corcoran lit his pipe, Cashel lit one of his small cigars and came to the point. He had grown very fond of Bríd over the few years they had been neighbours and he had sensed those feelings were reciprocated. He would like to request, with the greatest respect, the honour of her hand in marriage.

To Cashel's surprise, Corcoran beamed, stood up from his easy chair and shook his hand.

'It would make me very happy, Ross,' he said. 'Very happy. Of course, you'll understand I have to ask one vital question.'

'Please ask me anything.'

'Are you one of us? I'm assuming you are.'

'I'm sorry?'

'Are you a Roman Catholic? Do you believe in the Catholic God?'

Cashel blinked. Fool, he thought. Why hadn't he foreseen the question? With all the crucifixes in the house, he should have considered this.

'Alas, no. I was baptized a Protestant. I conform to the Protestant faith, though I have to confess, I'm not devout.'

'That's a great shame,' Corcoran said, his geniality leaving him suddenly. 'I won't have my daughter marry a Prod. I'm sorry, Ross.'

'Does Bríd have any say in the matter?'

'No, she does not.'

'Right.'

Again, Cashel spoke without thinking. 'What if I convert? What if I become a Roman Catholic?'

Corcoran smiled faintly, as if the answer had been obvious all along.

'Well, that changes everything. In that case, I'd be delighted to welcome you into the family.'

Father Standish O'Malley was the priest at St Aloysius Church on Chestnut Street, not far from Boston Common. Corcoran had suggested he go there to see about being admitted to the flock. Catholic churches in Puritan Boston were rare, Cashel realized. There was the Church of the Holy Cross on Franklin Street, the Catholic cathedral, and there was another church in Salem, but St Aloysius was only a few years old, a small wooden building that could take only two dozen worshippers and it was here that Shay Corcoran had directed him as the priest was an old friend, he said. There will be many more Catholic churches in Boston, Father O'Malley insisted calmly. Oh, yes – all the Irish are coming to Boston.

He received Cashel in his dark and shabby rooms in the 'presbytery' that was, in fact, his house, next door to the church. He was a burly man in his fifties with a sizeable belly and a dense grey beard. He wore oval rimless glasses that enlarged his rheumy eyes considerably, making his stare especially curious, Cashel thought. He felt he was under a microscope; Father O'Malley had a brusque no-nonsense manner that seemed to go well with the penetrating gaze. He sat Cashel down in an armchair in front of a small fire. It was September, and through the window Cashel could see a lime tree, its leaves beginning to turn.

'A few initial questions, Mr Ross.'

'Feel free to ask me anything.'

'No need to go that far. Where are you from?'

'My farm is near New Banbury, Middlesex County.'

'No, no, no. Where in Ireland? I can hear the trace of a Cork accent.'

'Yes, I grew up near Castlemountallen, County Cork.'

'And I'll wager you think you're much cleverer than the rest of us.'

'Certainly not.'

'Are you baptized?'

'Yes. But in the Protestant faith.'

'That will save the devil of a lot of time. Why do you want to become a Roman Catholic?'

'I want to marry a girl who's a Catholic.'

'That would be Bríd Corcoran?'

'Yes. Her father won't let me otherwise.'

'So, let's say it's more a matter of practicality rather than religious faith.'

'I think that would be fair.'

'Well, it'll speed everything up.' Father O'Malley stood. 'Will you join me in a little brandy, Mr Ross?'

'Thank you. I will, gladly.'

Cashel accepted a wine glass, quite full.

'Do you smoke a pipe, Mr Ross?'

'I smoke cheroots – a bad habit I picked up in India.'

'India, begad. What were you doing there?'

'I was in the Indian army.'

Father O'Malley's large eyes seemed to focus more intently on him having received that information. Cashel took out his neat cigar case and Father O'Malley took a cigar and lit it with a spill from the fire. He handed the spill to Cashel.

'Funny how a bit of brandy needs a whiff of tobacco.'

'They do seem to complement each other,' Cashel admitted.

'That's very Corkonian of you. There you go.'

'What do you mean by that, sir?'

'I mean that no one in Dublin would reply in that manner. I'm a Dubliner, you see.'

'I'm long out of County Cork. Almost thirty years.'

'Anyway, back to business. Are you an intelligent man?'

'I don't know. But I have written two books. Both published.'

'You're full of surprises, Mr Ross. One minute a soldier in India; the next, a published author. But this is good news. Intelligence guaranteed. Next question: do you believe in God's objective existence?'

Cashel thought for a second. Time to be prudent, he calculated. 'Yes.'

'That was my trick question.' Father O'Malley laughed heartily. 'Always a bit of a moment for the new recruits.' He smiled. 'We're almost there. Have you committed any Mortal Sins?'

'Yes.'

'Then go to confession and receive the Sacrament of Reconciliation.'

'Shall I confess to you?'

'I think not. I'll find you an available priest. Will you have another wee drop?'

'Thank you.'

'Any questions for me?' Father O'Malley asked as he topped up their glasses.

'How soon can I be received into the Church?'

'Any old Sunday Mass will do. There's a period of instruction – I'll take you through that. Then, after you've confessed, you will go to Mass – so you're in a state of grace, you see. Then you'll celebrate the Eucharist and – hey presto, abracadabra, alakazam – you've become a Roman Catholic and you can marry your lovely Catholic girl.'

'Oh. Right. Good.'

'Tell me, how is that old bastard Shay Corcoran?'

At Father O'Malley's suggestion Cashel went back to Boston several times for ostensible instruction – 'Just so it doesn't look like you're slipping in through the back door' – and, then, one Sunday in October, he went to confession followed by Mass, partook of Holy Communion – receiving a dry morsel of bread and a sip of bitter wine – and became a Roman Catholic. Shay Corcoran was his witness.

As they drove back together along the turnpike to Concord, Corcoran seemed in a particularly good mood.

'I'm pleased to have you as a son-in-law, Ross. Delighted that you're marrying Bríd. She's a quiet girl but a good one.'

'I couldn't be happier, sir.'

'And now our two farms are in the family, so to speak.'

'Indeed, they are. I hadn't thought about that. I suppose that we—'

'There's a lot we can do together. You have that ice revenue in the winter. That's a big advantage – we can make more of that. And we can help you with the cereals. And the meadows, and the woods.'

Cashel decided not to tell him about the beer scheme just yet.

'I look forward to our association, sir. I'll be a good husband to Bríd – you can be sure of that. I'm a lucky man.'

'A man makes his own luck, Ross.' Corcoran gave Cashel's knee a squeeze and grinned at him lewdly. 'And let's throw in a few grandchildren, shall we? A few more Corcoran boys won't go amiss.'

Willow Creek Farm
New Banbury
Middlesex County
Massachusetts

17th November 1837

My Dear Mother,

We remembered you at our wedding – and raised our glasses to the absent Ross family. It is my only sadness that you couldn't all be there. After the ceremony at St Aloysius we repaired to the Hanover Hotel where we all enjoyed an excellent dinner.

Bríd and I stayed in Boston for our Honeymoon (just a week long) and we savoured all the delights the city has to offer. It grows yearly more sophisticated, almost visibly expanding before one's eyes. There are concerts, lectures, plays and operas. We had a fine time.

You would be charmed by your daughter-in-law. She is young, modest but very capable. Already the farm exhibits the results of her energy and enthusiasm. And I have never eaten so well! Perhaps if our great (secret) plan succeeds as we hope we will travel to Europe – Bríd has never left the United States – and we'll come and stay with you in Oxford.

I am thriving here. The farm is beginning to earn its keep. My helpmate, Mr Ignatz Vlac, is a <u>sine qua non</u>. And now I am blessed with a lovely young wife. My cup overfloweth.

I send my fondest love to you and my brothers.

Ever your faithful and affectionate son,
Cashel

II

Cashel watched his daughters playing hide-and-seek in the hop yard. Maeve was four years old and had been born almost nine months to the day after his and Bríd's wedding – conceived in the Hanover Hotel, Cashel used to laugh – and Nessa joined her a year later. Maeve was fair like him; Nessa dark, like her mother. Would their natures echo their respective colourings? he found himself musing. He watched the excited children running through Ignatz's strange forest – the inverted 'V's of the poles now dense with green leaves, making the hop growth look like pine trees in a picture book.

Maeve ran up to him and hugged his legs.

'Papa! Papa! She's cheating. She says she's not looking but I know she's peeping out.'

'She's just a little girl, remember. Where's Mama?'

'She's praying.'

'Right.'

He looked up and saw Nora, their housemaid-cum-children's nurse, walking down from the house. He told her to keep an eye on the girls and to let them play for a while longer. He could be found in Ignatz's cabin, if required for anything.

In the cabin, Ignatz was at a table looking at charts with long columns of numbers on them. He stood when Cashel entered. He had recently grown a small pointed beard and Cashel thought it made him look more melancholy, for some reason – a sad cavalier.

On a stool by the desk was an eighteen-gallon kilderkin barrel of Willow Creek German Beer. The new season's brew.

'How is it?' Cashel asked.

'I say nothing. It's better if you taste it yourself.'

Ignatz turned the spigot that was set into the barrel and filled a wine glass with the beer. Cashel sipped – it was surprisingly cold, thanks to all the ice they had laid down in the cave where it was stored.

'Tastes good to me,' Cashel said.

'No. There's still something wrong.' Ignatz tapped his magic book. 'First, it should be an even more golden colouring. More rich gold. And the taste should be more sharp, more crisp.'

The book was *Die Kunst des Bierbrauens: physisch-chemisch-ökonomisch beschreiben*, by Franz Andreas Paupie, published in 1820. This is the bible, Ignatz insisted, for all beer-brewing in Bohemia.

'So what's the problem?'

They had lost a year when the hops were attacked by a severe mildew during the wet summer two years after they'd been planted. But they were brutally cut back and had regrown even more powerfully, the bines gripping and spiralling round the twelve-foot poles like hungry pythons, Cashel thought. The hops that were subsequently produced, Ignatz swore, were uncannily like the Saaz variety that they used in Bohemia. There was no reason not to produce the same level of excellence.

'It's not our hops – they are beautiful. It's not the water – the water is pure, as we can all see. Therefore, it must be the barley.'

Cashel bought the barley from the Corcorans.

'Could it be the yeast?' he asked, conscious of his ignorance.

'No,' Ignatz said definitively. 'The yeast is just the trigger that fires the gun. It's the barley. We have to find better barley.'

'All right,' Cashel said. 'Lots of folk round here grow barley. Let's go and take a look at what might be on offer. I'll explain to Corcoran – he'll be fine, I'm sure.'

As Ignatz harnessed the horse to the buggy, Cashel went into the house to fetch his hat. He saw that Bríd was on her knees on her prie-dieu in front of the small altar she had constructed in a corner of the main parlour. In the morning she sometimes prayed for two or three hours. There was an idealized painting of the haloed Virgin Mary, hands clasped, eyes looking yearningly upward at a dove, set on the wall over a small cupboard upon which two candles burned. She was still deep in her prayers, Cashel saw, eyes closed, head bowed, fingers moving slowly through her rosary beads.

He left her and slipped quietly into the kitchen. The girls were now at the table drinking milk and eating slices of bread and butter. Nora was washing plates in a bucket by the window. Cashel told them he'd be back at lunchtime.

He and Ignatz visited half a dozen farms in the New Banbury municipality that grew barley. Ignatz would take a handful of barley seed, sniff it, chew on one or two and make a judgement. Where the barley was still growing, unharvested, he would tear off the ears and pluck out a few kernels and chew them for a few seconds. He did not find what he was looking for. We'll have to look further afield, he said.

Cashel was impressed with his stringency, and said as much as they drove back to Willow Creek.

'I told you, Mr Ross. My uncle in Pilsen taught me everything. He worked in the breweries, a beer maker. He gave me this book when I came to America.'

'I thought you were a child when you came here,' Cashel said. 'Was that the same uncle who brought you here?'

'I was young, but not so young. And it was a different uncle.'

Cashel sensed he would unearth no more detail.

'Maybe tomorrow I'll take the buggy,' Ignatz said. 'I'll go a bit further – Stow, Sudbury.'

'Of course. Let's find our perfect barley – there's no point otherwise.'

Cashel was more than happy to let Ignatz take control. He had no option. Since the idea of brewing beer on the farm had been mooted, Cashel had been impressed both by his zeal and by his secrecy. Ignatz had let him watch part of the process – the malting, the mashing, the creation of the wort, the addition of the yeast, the fermentation. But he never told him where or how he bought or made the yeast he used. Nor would he tell him why he cut ice blocks from the pond in winter and lined the floor of the cave with the ice, like glass paving stones, which he then covered with a thick layer of sawdust transported from a timberyard in New Banbury.

They cave had always been cool – even on a hot summer's day – but now it was very chilled, a few degrees above freezing.

'Why does it have to be so cold in here?' Cashel asked.

'It's for the process. It's very important,' was all that Ignatz would tell him.

That evening, after Bríd had said her lengthy grace, they sat down to their meal. Cashel told her about the search for perfect barley but realized she wasn't interested. He asked her how she was feeling.

'I'm less troubled,' she said candidly. 'I feel calmer.'

Cashel smiled.

'That's good news, my dear. Take your time. The doctor said it wouldn't be a swift return to your old self.'

'I'll never return to my old self,' she said plainly.

It had been Nessa's birth that had created the problem. The parturition had been long and difficult. Bríd had lost blood and was very weak afterwards. What was more disturbing was that she seemed to have no interest in her new baby and remained effectively bedridden for months. A walk around the farmyard seemed to exhaust her for days. That was when Nora was employed to help with the girls.

Slowly but surely, Bríd emerged from her listless melancholy and started to resume some of the routines and habits of her own life but she still seemed, to Cashel's eyes, quite transformed – she had become a quieter, more preoccupied and sadder person. However, from time to time a kind of mad fury would erupt in her and she would rail against Cashel, calling him a 'useless man', a 'pathetic husband', a 'degenerate' and a 'corrupting influence on the family'. The fury subsided as quickly as it had detonated and then he would find her sitting in a corner weeping, but not from remorse – from misery, she said. Cashel didn't remonstrate or argue against her, accepting the tongue-lashing like a rock battered by a stormy sea, he told himself. The storm would surely pass and the sea would be calm again. And when she was restored,

Bríd performed her maternal duties as far as Nessa was concerned but it was obvious to Cashel – and Nora – that Maeve was her favourite. It was almost as if she blamed Nessa for this transformation in her personality.

Some months after Nessa was born, when Bríd seemed to be slowly sloughing off her inertia and invalidism, on the road to recovery, Cashel came into her bedroom one night – they had been sleeping apart – slipped off his nightshirt and climbed into bed with her. She became almost hysterical, in shock, not allowing him to touch her, repelled and appalled by his nakedness.

'I cannot have another child,' she said in a small strangled voice, once Cashel, now clothed, had calmed her down. 'I won't. I won't.'

And then, as if some mental dam had been breached, the religious phase began in earnest. Always devout, she now became obsessively so. The altar was created, the prie-dieu set before it, and she prayed there, silently, for hours at a time. Cashel arranged for a doctor to travel from Boston to see her but he came to no sensible diagnosis apart from generalities – vapours, nervous tension, hysteria. He recommended a regime of cold baths and types of patent broth that he had devised which would give her more energy, or so he said. After a week of forcing her to bathe and eat the broth it was apparent that the 'cure' was making her worse. Cashel ordered it stopped and allowed her to create the circumstances of the life she wanted to live. The girls were very young and, to them, this eccentricity soon became normal. Mama prayed – it was what she did most of the day – and then she turned her attention to them for a little while. Nora was jolly and they liked her. Cashel made an effort to spend more time with them in compensation for their mother but truth be told, he said to himself, the girls seemed fine.

At times, away from her religious devotions, Cashel could imagine she was the old Bríd, the sweet girl he had married. She ran the household, visited her family and neighbours, occupied herself with the girls, but Cashel always felt that this 'normal' behaviour was manufactured and that, somewhere else inside, another darker, suffering life was being endured whose only solace and comfort was in prayer.

All sexual relations, all intimacy between her and Cashel, had ceased since that night he had climbed into bed with her. She would flinch if he touched her inadvertently – and yet would dutifully profess her love and concern for him if he solicited it. Of course, I love and honour you, Cashel – you're my husband and the father of our beautiful children.

Cashel decided that the best and only course of action was to wait it out. He was busy with the farm and the hop yard and everything else associated with the 'beer scheme' and, after a while, he resumed his occasional trips to Boston, with its pleasures, licit and illicit. While he was away it was easier to forget the sham that his marriage had become.

Cashel looked across the table at Bríd and smiled. He was always smiling at her, no matter what he was thinking.

'There's a travelling circus coming to Sudbury. Shall we take the girls?'

'I have to ask this, Cashel – I'm sorry.'

'Ask what?'

'Is there drink in the house? Alcohol?'

'No. I cleared away all the bottles – as you asked me to.'

'I can't stop you drinking, I know. But I won't have my house defiled.'

'Of course. I understand your feelings. Don't worry. There's not a drop of alcohol in this house.'

He smiled again.

After dinner, Cashel went outside with a lantern. He entered the barn and took his bottle of brandy from its hiding place behind one of the woodpiles. He lit a cigar from the lantern flame and swigged directly from the bottle, trying to empty his mind. There was a half-moon shining in the almost clear sky, the thin clouds like shreds of chiffon or muslin. Below them the pond glimmered, a burnished silver in the moonglow. He drank again from the bottle and paced around. One of the farm dogs, Bruno, came up to him and he rubbed his ears. Good dog, go away, leave me alone.

He could see a light shining from Ignatz's cabin. For a moment, he thought about knocking on his door and asking him if he'd like a shot of brandy himself, but decided against it. Ignatz had beer on his mind, now that things were coming to a crucial stage, and it was all he wanted to talk about. Strange young fellow. Cashel put the bottle back in its secret place, ground out and flicked away his cigar butt, picked up the lantern and strolled back to his home.

'I've found our barley,' Ignatz said, trying not to show his exultation.

'Bravo! Where?'

'Out by Stow. Five Oaks Farm.'

'Five Oaks Farm,' Cashel repeated. 'I know that place. Apples, right?'

'Yes. It has one of the biggest orchards in the county,' Ignatz said. 'And, lucky for us, some barley fields. It's perfect.'

Cashel remembered. A year after he'd bought Willow Creek, Five Oaks Farm had been bought by a Mrs Frances Broome – separated or divorced from Mr Broome. She'd paid for the place with cash, no mortgages or loans, and moved in with her two young sons, quickly alienating her neighbours with her cool and imperious manner. Amongst the farming community they had taken to calling her 'Queen Victoria' behind her back, now that the young Queen had ascended to the British throne.

'Did you meet the woman?' Cashel asked. 'Did "Queen Victoria" deign to speak to you?'

'Yes. She's happy for us to buy whatever amount of barley we need. Fair price.'

'And this is the barley for you, yes? We can actually make beer.'

'And in quantity. Wait till you taste my beer, Mr Ross. It'll astonish you.'

The lad's excitement was contagious.

'I'm ready to be astonished, Ignatz. I could do with a bit of astonishment in my life.'

They drove over to Stow the next day. Ignatz had made proper calculations and knew exactly how many bushels of barley he needed. Cashel had a leather pouch of gold and silver dollars with him. He felt in something of a devil-may-care mood about this 'beer scheme' that Ignatz was so passionate about. He was beginning to think that a life without schemes was a life not worth living. All the planning, expense, prognostications and wishful thinking gave a focus beyond the familiar routines of daily life. In a way the success or failure of the enterprise was paradoxically irrelevant as it was the energies, mental and physical, congregating around it that made it worthwhile, gave it value. And, as if to demonstrate the truth of this proposition, he said to himself, Here I am on a warm September afternoon, with money in my pocket, driving to buy barley from a demanding, unpopular woman. The day is different from the day before – that was all that mattered.

He steered the buggy through large plantations of well-maintained apple orchard. Men were working amongst the trees, on ladders picking fruit. Five Oaks Farm itself was a surprisingly small old wooden house – square, classic saltbox style – but around it was a scatter of larger barns and new outbuildings. They pulled up in front of the main door and Ignatz asked a young boy where Mrs Broome could be found. Cashel was directed to a large orchard about half a mile away. He set off on foot, while Ignatz took the buggy round to the grain store.

The afternoon sun was hot and Cashel flipped his hands at the small black flies that danced annoyingly around his head. He saw a pony cart parked under an ancient oak tree and three empty wagons standing nearby waiting to be loaded. Just beyond, he could spot a woman with her back to him, checking on the apples that were being tipped from baskets into large wooden boxes. Mrs Frances Broome, no doubt.

Cashel removed his hat as he approached. The woman was wearing a straw bonnet pushed back on her head and a canvas duster-coat over her print dress. Beneath the long skirt he could see she had wooden clogs on her feet.

'Mrs Broome?'

She turned at the sound of her name and for a split second Cashel thought he might cry out. He coughed, cleared his throat and introduced himself. He apologized if he had startled her and looked at her again. No – it wasn't exactly Raphaella transferred into an older American farming woman, but Mrs Broome had the same type of long, mannish face and strong jaw that Raphaella had. There was a distinct look there, a similarity, that had caught him unawares. Her hair was a chestnut brown, like Raphaella's, but beginning to grey at the brow and temples. Her skin was tanned from the sunshine and there were thin lines on her forehead and at the corners of her mouth, bracketing her lips. She looked about his age: forty, forty-one or two. Cashel gave a little bow. Pleased to meet you, ma'am.

'Mr Ross, yes. You're the Englishman who bought Willow Creek. I had my eyes on that for a while. Wasn't quite big enough for my needs.'

He couldn't place her accent. Was there a tinge of the South? Mah eyes . . .

'What is it, Mr Ross?'

'Sorry. You reminded me of someone just for a moment. No matter.'

'We haven't met before, have we?'

'No. Definitely not.'

He realized he was staring at her again. She was smaller than Raphaella, but also with a trim, taut figure. They walked back together to the pony cart and he felt a shiver pass through him as memories crowded in, provoked by this unexpected catalyst of resemblance.

He rode with her on the cart back to the farmhouse. Ignatz was heaving sacks of barley into the buggy. Mrs Broome and Cashel went into the house.

She poured him a glass of sherry and then counted the money he'd paid her, twice. Ignatz and she had agreed at their first meeting on the amount of barley and what it would cost.

'Aren't you going to try and knock the price down, Mr Ross?

I'm kind of disappointed. I like a good wrangle – you get to know people faster.'

'My man says it's a fair price. He's the expert. Sometimes bargaining for the sake of bargaining is both impolite and futile.'

'You see, that's the Englishman in you speaking,' she said. 'You're not a fully assimilated American, I can tell. You've given yourself away.'

She laughed – a deep throaty laugh – as if delighted with her own sally, Cashel thought. An intelligent woman, he saw: worldly, confident in herself.

'I don't think I'd dare try and knock your price down, Mrs Broome. I wouldn't stand a chance.'

'And now you're flirting with me, Mr Ross. That's more American of you. Keep trying, you'll get there.' Her look was direct. She smiled. 'Anyway, it's only money. There are more important things in life, so I'm told.'

There was a little bitterness in her voice as she said these words, Cashel thought, watching her turn away and go to the fireplace where, to his vague surprise, she rolled herself a cigarette with tobacco taken from a jar on the shelf above the fire. She lit it from a candle flame and Cashel followed with one of his cigars. They sat down and smoked and chatted about their neighbours in Stow and New Banbury and which of them they both knew. Cashel noticed that, as she talked, she sat perched on the edge of her seat as if she were about to leap up at any moment. The young boy they'd met on arrival came in and was introduced as her son Clayton. There was another son upstairs, Whitaker, who was in bed with influenza.

'What're you going to do with my barley, Mr Ross?' she asked.

'Make beer. My brewer is very particular. Your barley is perfect, he says.'

She was curious. Cashel said the whole brewing process was in Ignatz's hands. He was just an investor, as it were, so to speak.

'I'll buy some off you,' she said. 'If it's any good.'

'If it's any good I'll *give* you some.'

'You have a deal, sir.'

She walked him to the buggy. Ignatz was in the driving seat, waiting. Cashel said goodbye, and thanked her for the sherry. She had left her bonnet in the house and, with a flat palm, shielded her eyes to make shade against the sun's glare, as if wanting a better look at him.

Cashel watched Ignatz malting the barley in a series of large copper vats, stirring the roasted mash around with a large wooden paddle. There had been a necessary and sizeable investment in the 'beer scheme' – not just the vats and the kiln but also the doubling of the hop yard. But Cashel was happy to provide the money. By curious chance it was Willow Creek pond that had become the source of the farm's solvency. Every winter a team came out from Boston with a couple of wagons and strange pieces of equipment and cut away, depending on the coldness of the season, around two tons of ice. The extremely cold winter that started in late 1839 prompted a visit from a man called Frederic Tudor who offered Cashel $150 for the exclusive rights to harvest all the ice he could from the pond. Tudor was an ice exporter, so he claimed. He shipped ice from New England ponds and rivers to the southern states of America; to the Caribbean; to Brazil and even to India. The reason why he was offering so much for Cashel's supply of frozen water was, he explained, because of Willow Creek ice's unusual transparency. This was ice that, when broken into small chunks, could be placed directly in the glass to chill a drink – a julep or white wine or a cobbler – which was a precious asset. Ice that was simply used for chilling could be dirty or opaque – ice that went directly into glasses was surprisingly rare. Cashel signed the contract and to a real extent it solved all his financial problems. He could make some more money selling the excess hay from the farm's meadows, but he barely broke even with his few fields of turnips or Indian corn. Cut grass and frozen water, he realized, paid for everything and the surplus that was available could happily be directed to Ignatz's beer project.

Cashel left Ignatz to his malting and wandered back to the house, his mind returning to his stimulating encounter with Mrs

Frances Broome. He was jerked back to reality by the sight of Maeve and Nessa running full pelt towards him. He swept them both up into his arms and kissed their cheeks. Tiny lithe girls, excited to be borne aloft.

'Can we go to the cave, Papa?' Maeve asked.

'Cave! Cave! Cave!' Nessa shouted into his ear.

He set them down and took their hands and they walked down to the pond. The magic pond, he thought, as its expanse slowly revealed itself to him, source of unsought-for bounty. Sometimes, he realized, what is outside your control provides control. Clear water and severe cold in winter equalled many dollars. He would not begrudge his good luck.

In the gloomy depths of the cave the girls thrilled to the cold, their breath condensing as they ran about. Cashel noted that Ignatz had already set out lines of curved supports for the barrels, butts and firkins that he had bought from a cooper in Fitchburg. Stillage, that's what this woodwork was called. There was a lot of stillage ready to receive its filled barrels. Suddenly, inspired by the shrieks of his daughters, he had a thrill of confidence about the beer adventure. There was a sureness of purpose about the way Ignatz had patiently gone about making certain everything was ideally just so, no compromises. The chill in the cave was remarkable given that it was a warm September day outside. He looked down at the layer of sawdust that covered the thick blocks of ice cut from the lake almost nine months ago. Well-insulated ice, blocks closely packed together and covered in thick layers of straw or sawdust, melted extremely slowly, it appeared. Slow enough to survive journeys halfway across the world. He thought back to his meeting with Frederic Tudor as they had stood on the small jetty looking out over the pond. 'Who would have thought that ice from a pond in Massachusetts would cool a nabob's lemonade in Bombay, Mr Ross?' Tudor had said. Cashel had been suitably amazed. The world was changing beyond his immediate, local horizons, he realized. Perhaps Ignatz's Willow Creek beer would bring that world to New Banbury . . .

Cashel called the girls back to him and they headed off up the sloping meadow to the house. Thinking about the beer and the barley they had bought made his mind return to Frances Broome again and her curious resemblance to Raphaella . . . Or was it just his fancy? Was he seeing a likeness that he wanted to be there? Seeing things he wished to see because his life with Bríd was so awkward, tense and unsatisfactory? Bríd and her delusions were making his memory as malleable as his imagination.

The girls were arguing hotly with each other and he spread his arms to hold them apart as a plan began to stir in his mind. Maybe he should verify or refute his fond imaginings; confirm or invalidate his Raphaella dreams. It would be an intriguing diversion, come what may.

The next day, Cashel idly asked Ignatz if he was sure he had enough barley and was informed that indeed he had – more than enough. Cashel suggested that maybe it was worth laying in a few more bushels, just in case. It could be safely stored, anyway – and what if Mrs Broome suddenly sold her stock? Ignatz shrugged – it's up to you, sir. Cashel harnessed the horse to the buggy and drove over to Five Oaks Farm. As he approached the house through the apple orchards he began to feel that familiar breathlessness of desire – the hollowed-out feeling in his chest that signalled sensuous anticipation. There was only one reason why he had come back. But at the farm he discovered she wasn't there. Her eldest son, the one who had been sickly – Whitaker – said she'd gone to Stow to a meeting with her lawyer. Cashel felt the deflation as powerfully as he had felt the anticipation. But, he thought, I can always go to Stow and find her. Whitaker told him the name of the lawyer.

As Cashel drove towards the town he began to feel both excited and foolish. Here he was, a forty-two-year-old married man with two children running around the countryside like an adolescent. But he knew he wouldn't turn back. He wanted – he needed – to see Frances Broome again.

Stow was a town very like New Banbury – somewhat larger and constantly expanding like all these New England municipalities. There were surveyors out and about plotting routes for the new railroads; land was being bought to accommodate them at very high prices; the need for cuttings and embankments being assessed, bridges planned, gradients measured, railroad stations and halts being posited. In Stow there were tin workers, cabinet-makers, two gristmills, three sawmills, two tanneries and at least four taverns. There was a Masonic Lodge and talk of establishing a Bank of Middlesex County. Credit on your doorstep. As Frederick Tudor had said, the world was changing fast and, Cashel thought, this transformation was nicely symbolized by the person of Frances Broome, herself – divorcée, successful farmer and controversial citizen.

Cashel pulled up his buggy across the street from the lawyer's office. By now the foolishness factor was considerably overwhelming his ardour. Still, here he was: he had obeyed his baser instincts – followed his heart – and he might as well see the encounter out, should it take place.

After half an hour, on the point of returning home, he saw her step out of the office and chat for a moment with the man he assumed was her lawyer. Then she made her farewells and strode away along the sidewalk towards her pony trap. Cashel jumped out of his buggy, ran up an alley, emerged a block further down, crossed the street and hailed her just as she was about to pull away.

'Mrs Broome, what a coincidence!'

She was more smartly dressed than the last time he had seen her. Her hair was elaborately pinned up beneath a small hat with a half-veil. She wore a short, embroidered jacket over her Eton-collared green tartan day-dress. Seeing her in her stepping-out finery he noted the handsome woman she was and registered, with a heart lurch, that she did indeed look like Raphaella – it wasn't just a fantasy of his own making. And he knew now – though he banished this thought from his mind – that he was lost.

He told her that he'd called by her farm to buy more barley. She suggested he follow her home and they could complete the transaction. At the farm, Cashel duly purchased six more bushels of barley for $12 and loaded them into his buggy. She invited him back to the house where she could present him with a proper bill of sale.

They sat in the parlour, business concluded, Cashel with a bourbon and water, Mrs Broome with her sherry. She rolled a cigarette and lit it from the fire.

'I wonder – I can see you staring – are you astonished to see me smoking, Mr Ross?'

'No. Not at all.'

'I grew up on a farm in Philadelphia. My father's foreman taught me to roll and smoke when I was twelve years old to keep the bugs off me in the fields.'

'Very wise. What kind of paper is that? I see it's printed.'

'These are pages from an old bible. A discarded bible, I should add. Now you are shocked.'

'It takes a lot to shock me, Mrs Broome. Seems very sensible to me – the practical use of something not wanted. Would you care to try one of my cheroots?' He took out his case.

'Leave it to the side there. I might have a go after supper.'

Cashel did so and lit his own.

'I don't suppose you've ever seen a woman smoking. But a lot of us do – in private – you'd be surprised. Why should this pleasure be for men only?'

'It's a fair point.'

'I wouldn't walk down Main Street in Stow with a cigarito in my hand but I can smoke freely in my own home, so I feel.'

'Actually, I did know a woman who smoked. In private, like you. In Italy, many years ago.'

'There you are. I will quote you.'

Cashel smiled and drank his whiskey, happy to be in her company. She told him a little about her upbringing – a farmer's daughter who had married another farmer.

'Is Mr Broome deceased?'

'I certainly hope so, but I have no news. All the same, I've two fine sons, thanks to his contribution – but that's all I owe him.'

Cashel didn't probe any further, sensing a wound that was still raw. She told him that after her father's death – her mother had predeceased him – she decided to settle further north. She had lived for a while in New York and then 'pined to be back on the land', she said, wanting her boys to be raised on a farm as she had been.

Cashel nodded and listened, wondering what the true story was, but he didn't really care. He was happy simply to be looking at that long, strong face, his memory working excitedly overtime.

When they had finished their drinks, she walked him out to his buggy. They watched her two sons playing with a puppy by one of the barns.

'I was told you're Irish, is that not so, Mr Ross?'

'Not entirely. But I was raised in Ireland as a child, in County Cork.'

'What brought you to New Banbury?'

'Misfortune at home, in London. I was cheated and betrayed. I needed pastures new.'

'Kind of like me. Rather, pastures familiar, in my case.'

'We should cultivate our gardens, so the philosopher told us, whatever misfortunes rain down upon the world.'

She laughed at that, her deep delighted laugh.

'And so we do. I'm going to remember those words, Mr Ross.'

He climbed into the buggy and picked up the reins.

Frances Broome rested her hand on his knee for a moment and looked him in the eye, a slight smile still registering on her face.

'You come by for extra barley any time you want,' she said, before turning and going back into the farmhouse.

Ignatz made his beer. The malted barley wort had yeast added to it; when it fermented, water was stirred in and the mixture was decanted into barrels that were placed in the chill of the cave by the pond. And then they waited for the alchemical process to magically take place.

While they waited, Cashel thought many times of paying

another visit to Frances Broome but restrained himself. Instead he wrote to Father O'Malley and asked him to come out to Willow Creek and talk to Bríd. He came and spent an hour alone with her before joining Cashel outside. Cashel offered him a brandy from his woodpile stash and they stood in the barn drinking from wine glasses and smoking cigars.

'I can't drink in the house,' Cashel explained. 'Mrs Ross won't have it. Apologies.'

'No, I understand. The temperance movement – the temperance zeal, the temperance fanaticism – gets stronger and stronger by the day.'

'Is she insane, Father?'

'It's not for me to diagnose,' he said. 'In fact, I should applaud her devotion, as a priest. I've seen nuns in love with the Blessed Virgin in the same way, but never a wife with two children.'

'It was very sudden – after Nessa's birth. She's never been the same since. Like she's become a different person.'

He topped up the priest's glass.

'I have heard,' Father O'Malley continued, 'that childbirth can provoke these . . .' He searched for the words. 'These mental convulsions. These strange passions.' He shrugged. 'I think you can do nothing more, Mr Ross. Go along with it. Don't fight her, if you know what I mean. Maybe time will heal her.'

'I feel I've lost her,' Cashel said, emotion in his voice. 'She's like a stranger, a different person from the sweet girl I married.'

'I'll pray for you both,' Father O'Malley said, emptying his glass. 'I'd better make my way back to Boston.' He smiled. 'Perhaps I might see you at Mass one of these days.'

'I am overdue, I admit.'

'You can make your confession.'

'I have nothing to confess.'

'Lucky man.'

A week after the priest's visit, Ignatz said they were ready to taste the beer. It had now been stored in the cold cave for two months. Ignatz brought out a small firkin and set it on a stool at the cave mouth. It was a sunny day in November and the low sun struck sharp shadows on the seams of the rock-face. The waters of the lake were perfectly calm, a pale unrippled blue. All around them the sumacs and the hickory were orange and deep yellow. Cashel had brought two crystal rummers down from the house – clear glass, as Ignatz had requested. He turned the spigot and filled the glasses. There was a modest head of foam but what struck Cashel – used to porter, stout and ale – was the colour of the beer. It was golden. He held the glass up to the light – more complex than golden, like clear honey infused with lemon sunlight, the essence of rich transparent light amber, gently carbonated, bubbles rising.

'Well, it certainly looks beautiful,' Cashel said. 'Good health, Ignatz.'

'*Prost.*'

They both drank big draughts of the beer. It was cold from the cave, slightly sour yet with a real, sharp taste of hops. It was like no beer Cashel had ever tasted.

'Good God,' he said. 'This is delicious. Wonderful! Ambrosia. The apotheosis of a beer, Ignatz. Congratulations!'

Ignatz smiled and closed his eyes, his delight and pride very obvious.

'I told you, Mr Ross. I told you we could brew something wonderful here.'

'But what is this? Is this Bohemian beer?'

'Pilsner, we call it. *Lager* – a German word. It means to store. *Das Bier wird gelagert.* It takes longer than ale or porter to be ready. And it has to be cold so it ferments from the bottom, not from the top, like other beers. That's why we need the cave and the ice. The conditions are perfect. The hops, the water, the barley, the cold cave.'

'But wait until people taste this . . .' Cashel was thinking. 'They won't want their watery ale any more.'

'*Genau.*' He nodded emphatically. 'I prophesied this to you, Mr Ross.'

'So you did, Ignatz, so you damn well did. I take my hat off to you.' He doffed an invisible hat.

'Thank you, sir.'

'We have to give it a name. Golden Beer?'

'No. I think something like a firm, a brewery. A name of a brand, something manufactured.'

Cashel thought.

'Willow Creek Beer? No. Doesn't sound right.'

'I have it, sir. We should call it "Rossbrau". Like we brought it from Bohemia.'

'Rossbrau . . . Rossbrau. I like it. Rossbrau it shall be.'*

Cashel filled a stone carboy with Rossbrau and took it up to Five Oaks Farm. Mrs Broome provided two pewter pots but Cashel asked for glasses. She found two etched tumblers and Cashel filled them with the lager. They toasted each other.

'It's called Rossbrau,' he said. 'The Golden Beer.'

They drank.

'I like it,' she said. 'It's got a nice sour taste, but not too sour. And it's cold, sharp.'

He topped up their glasses.

'Where are the boys, by the way?'

'At school. Where do you think on a Wednesday morning?'

They sat in front of the fire and drank some more. Cashel was telling her of their plans to sell the beer, feeling the alcohol going quickly to his head – or was it the anticipation of what he knew was about to occur?

After their third glass they stopped talking and looked at each other. Cashel stared at her. In his mood of pleasurable inebriation he felt he was sitting opposite an American Raphaella. He crossed over to her chair and knelt down. He took her hand.

'And what do you think you're up to, Mr Cashel Ross?'

'What do *you* think I'm up to, Mrs Frances Broome? May I?'

'All right. You have my permission.'

Cashel kissed her and moved his hand around her neck to press

* Rossbrau, it can be argued with some conviction, was the first lager beer to be brewed and commercially sold in the United States.

279

her mouth harder against his, feeling her lips flatten against his and her tongue gently part his teeth. They broke apart.

'Come with me,' she said, standing. 'I don't want to do it in the house.' She picked up a candlestick and lit the candle and Cashel followed her out through the kitchen (where she grabbed a key hanging from a hook on the wall) and around the big barn to a smaller wooden building with no windows. She unlocked the door.

Cashel stepped in. She locked the door behind them. The smell of apples was overpowering, like a sweet dense musk, almost chewable, he thought. She lit a candle-lantern that was sitting on a small table and, as the light grew, he saw that the large room was filled with stacks of slatted racks on which were placed apples by the thousand. Row upon row, not touching but very close. Long aisles of shelves, floor to ceiling. Like a library of apples, he thought, like an apple bank.

'What is this place?' he asked, following her down an aisle to the back of the barn.

'Apples for the winter. You can double the price if they haven't rotted.'

He heard a cat miaow and saw one – a big tom, he thought – lope away into the shifting shadows.

'We don't want mice eating our winter apples,' she said. 'Best mouser on the farm.'

She set the lantern on the floor. There was a canvas camp bed set up there, with a thick blanket, folded. She had prepared every-thing, confident the day would come when it would be useful, she said. They looked at each other. He took her in his arms again and they kissed. Frances Broome lay down on the bed and pulled up her skirts.

'Don't be tardy, Mr Ross,' she said. 'The boys will be home in an hour.'

Afterwards, they lay quietly in each other's arms in the narrow concavity of the camp bed.

'You knew this would happen, didn't you?' he asked.

'Yes. I think about five minutes after we met.'

'I see . . . Right . . . I had that feeling, too. Funny that. I mean, how you know. How you can just tell . . . What'll I call you?' He kissed her brow. 'Fran? Frances?'

'Not Fran. That's what he called me.'

'Who?'

'My unlamented former husband.'

'How about Frannie?'

She thought for a moment.

'I like that. But only you can call me by that name – in private.'

'Agreed. Good. Frannie.'

They eased themselves out of the camp bed and adjusted their clothing.

'Every time I smell or eat an apple, henceforth, I'm going to think about you,' Cashel said, picking one off a shelf, sniffing it and then taking a bite.

'We have to find some more congenial, more sophisticated place to meet,' she said. 'It can't be here. The boys must never be suspicious.'

'I know. Yes. You're right. Let me have a think.'

Cashel was quietly exultant, realizing that this encounter in the apple barn signalled the beginning of something new. There was a future for them both.

Back at Willow Creek, he acted as insouciantly as possible. Bríd was sewing by the fire. He could hear the girls playing outside. All was well with his Willow Creek world and he felt his guilt paint him black as he stood there, hat turning in his hands.

'How're you today, dear?' he asked.

'I'm always well, thanks be to God.' She crossed herself and paused. 'You smell of apples.'

Apples, he thought. The rank odour of sex, of adultery, of sin.

'I was looking to buy some,' he said quickly. 'Ignatz is thinking that we might make a cider.'

'Cider? Cider and beer. Are you going to corrupt the whole county?'

Cashel smiled and said nothing. He had the prospect of a

secret life, now, beyond the sad perimeter of Willow Creek Farm. He hung his hat by the door and went to find his daughters.

The Rectory
Claverleigh
Nr Lewes
Sussex

17th May 1846

My dear Cashel,

It is with heavy heart indeed that I have to inform you that our beloved mother was called to God this morning of a dropsical fever. It was very calm, she felt no pain, asleep with the medicinal draught the doctor had provided for her. One minute she was breathing, one minute next, she was not.

Of course, by the time you receive this, she will be long buried – here in the graveyard of my own church at Claverleigh. It makes everything easier, as you will understand. I can erase all complications arising from her unconventional life. The headstone will read: 'Mrs Elspeth Ross 1775–1846, beloved wife of Mr Pelham Ross Esq. of Oxford, (d.1832) adored mother of Cashel, Hogan and Buckley. RIP.' I think you'll agree this is both apt and prudent.

Hogan will come from Oxford for the funeral. We will be joined by Emily and our children. I feel sorrowed that she fell ill here on her annual visit but perhaps it was a blessing as she was surrounded by members of her family. Her grandchildren loved her and will miss her sorely.

Hogan is the executor of her will in your absence. The estate is not substantial and is to be divided equally between the three of us. I will leave it to Hogan to keep you informed of progress. The cottage and furniture in Woodstock will be sold and there are, I believe, some modest funds in the bank.

She is with God, Cashel. Her unique life is over. She was a wonderful, brave, extraordinary woman. I think only her three sons can appreciate the full validity of that judgement. We were lucky to have her as our mother.

My sympathy and sincere condolences. I know how close you and she were, before the Oxford years.

Your devoted, loving brother,
Buckley

Willow Creek Farm
New Banbury
Middx. County
Massachusetts

3rd July 1846

My dear brother Buckley,

God bless you for being with our dear mother at the moment of her demise. She and I in our recent correspondence had been planning for her to come to visit us in Massachusetts. She always told me she was in good health – and could happily withstand the voyage over. I very much wanted her to see the life I have made for myself over here, and of course to meet Mrs Ross – Brid – and the girls, her American grandchildren.

I confess I wept when I received your letter. You're correct in identifying the intense bond I had with her before we moved to Oxford and the Glebe years began. Our life together in Ireland was – what can I say? – both perplexing and wonderful. But is that just hindsight? I ask myself. One day I'll tell you everything that I remember about the strange circumstances we lived in at Stillwell Court and what took place between our mother and our father, Sir Guy, Mr Ross. She and I were two conspirators – one compelled, one unknowing – until you and Hogan were born and, in Oxford, a social equilibrium of sorts was established. Everything changed and we were able to live as a family for the world to see. But even then, her secret life, and my unwitting participation in it, made our connection different from the usual links between mother and son. I was her 'nephew' and you and Hogan were my 'cousins' for many years before the truth was out.

Sometimes, indeed, I wonder if that long dissimulation is what has made me the man I am today. Did everything in my life stem from that

artful pretence, that complicated lie that I had no idea we were living?
Forgive my passion, but your letter unleashed a turbulent flood of
powerful memories, not all of them gentle and loving. But she, of all
people, would understand my sentimental anguish. In her transgression
she made an audacious choice and had the courage to live by it. My
participation was, therefore, inevitable. Truly, by any standards, a
remarkable woman. We must count ourselves blessed that she was our
parent.

Do inform Hogan that I am standing by if there is anything
material I can do to ease the progress of probate. Does he need some
form of power of attorney from me? Or was provision made for him
given I was absent?

All's well here. I have become a successful brewer of German beer as
well as a farmer, you will be astonished to learn.

The American Rosses send their fondest love to their English cousins.

I remain your most affectionate brother,
Cashel

Cashel drove the horse and buggy to Concord on a Thursday morning and left them at the livery stable. Valise in hand, he walked to the railroad station in good time for the Fitchburg and Boston Railroad's 10.30 train to the city. He stood waiting on the platform thinking about the day ahead – and his various commissions – still somewhat amazed that he would be in Boston before noon. The world was whirling faster, that was for sure.

On the train – he travelled first class now that he used the railroad for his business: he was a comparatively wealthy man, after all – he took out the list Ignatz had prepared for him and the money orders from the bank in Stow that he was going to deposit in Boston. $635.17. And that was just the accounting for the last two months. He looked at the names on the piece of paper in his hands. Sudbury, Stow, Assabet, New Banbury, Concord, Bolton, Lincoln, Bedford, Westford, Littleton and a dozen more. The crosses beside each name designated the number of taverns in these townships that bought and sold Rossbrau's 'Golden German Beer'. Golden in every sense of the word. They had accounts with over forty inns and taverns and a few hotels. Cashel was travelling to Boston to bank the money and secure a new loan, if he could (and he was confident), to fund further expansion. They were planning to start selling in Fitchburg and Lowell next, now that they could transport butts and hogsheads by the railroad, but they needed new drays as well, a new bigger kiln to roast the barley, more men to help Ignatz. In fact, he was thinking of constructing a purpose-built brewery on a site at Willow Creek – no more making-do in the barn. Success breeds success, he said to himself, registering the cliché's validity and banality at the same time.

He had discussed the matter that very morning with Ignatz as they had watched two loaded drays, heavy with barrels, head out to towns in the locality. On each barrel Ignatz had stencilled, in blue capital letters, 'ROSSBRAU'. Cashel had felt an unusual pride watching them roll out. Folk liked this new German beer – he could even provide ice at a modest extra cost if they wanted to serve it chilled and keep it longer. The hop yard was twice as large as it had been. Other ale breweries were beginning to ask about his magical variety of hop. Everything was going as well as possible. Except his marriage . . .

Cashel smiled ruefully, stroked his chin and touched his black silk cravat with the tips of his fingers, then flicked a shred of lint off the revers of his swallowtail coat. He still liked to wear his collars high rather than folded down – it suited his features better, he thought. There was something dashing about the high collar. He was a man of his times, after all, nothing he could do about it. Doubtless it would all be old hat and very unfashionable in a year or two. He liked to be well dressed when he went into Boston. In addition to the business he had to transact he was going to meet Frannie, and spend a couple of days at a smart hotel to celebrate the fifth year of their love affair.

From the railroad depot Cashel took a hack to the Franklin House Hotel on Beacon Street, *fully gaslit with steam-heating* as it said on the advertisement. He was taken to his room on the top floor that provided a good view of the common, the public garden and the Mill Dam basin beyond. He gave the bellboy who had carried his bag a dime and told him to be sure to alert him when Mrs Broome had returned.

Frannie had come to Boston and booked in a day earlier, as usual. They were not careless. Either Frannie or Cashel would send the other a letter to say that they were planning a trip to Boston on such and such a date, mentioning the hotel that was to be their base in the city. Thus forewarned, it was not difficult to book separate rooms in the hotel and celebrate the delightful coincidence of finding themselves guests there at the same time. They tended to spend two or three days in the city, anonymous, a companionless twosome slipping in and out of each other's rooms, going out on the town, dining in restaurants, taking in plays, enjoying steamer trips to the islands in the bay, hiring a barouche to carry them out on day trips to Cambridge or Cape Cod. They behaved as if they were a newly married couple enjoying their honeymoon – a honeymoon that took place half a dozen times a year. Then they returned to the life of their farms, keeping temptation at bay, until another trip to Boston was mooted. Cashel found he could bear the solemn frustrations of his life with Bríd more easily knowing that the next trip to Boston was beckoning.

He unpacked his bag and went out into the city, deciding to walk to the North End where Ignatz had asked him to collect three pairs of pruning shears, ordered from Germany, from a cutler. Then he planned to visit a tailor to be measured for new shirts and a suit, and to pass by the bank to confirm his appointment for the next day. He left the broad elegant streets of mid-town, with their astonishing traffic of carriages and trams, and entered the cramped and winding lanes of Old Boston, keeping his eyes open for the cutler's shop. As he walked along he felt he could have been in Cork or Dublin, such was the variety of Irish accents he overheard from passers-by. Of course, he knew all too well that the famine was driving whole populations from Ireland to America – over a million souls, he had read in a newspaper. It made him think back, hearing the familiar lilt of their voices, and he felt strangely, bizarrely, at home – and when a barefoot child with a Sligo accent asked him for a penny he gave the boy a silver dollar.

It was growing dark by the time he returned to the Franklin House and he turned up the gaslight in his room. He lit a cigar and paced about, full of sensual anticipation. When would gas come to New Banbury, he wondered idly? He realized that the life they were living there, two dozen miles away, would be entirely familiar to the first colonists of the seventeenth century. Now in this new Bostonian world a candle was an irrelevance or prettily decorative. The room was perfectly warm – no need for a fire. He could read the small print of any newspaper in any corner of the room at midnight. There was carpet on the floor; thick drapes hung on—

The doorbell rang. The bellboy told him Mrs Broome was returned and was in her room, number 139.

Cashel went down the staircase one floor and found the room. He rang the bell.

'Count to ten and then come in,' he heard her call.

He waited, then opened the door.

Frannie Broome stood in the middle of the floor under the gas chandelier, brightly lit. She was wearing a dark charcoal day-dress with a velour jacket and had a fine woollen scarf covering her hair.

'You've gone and had it done,' he said, smiling. 'Let's have a look, then.'

'I certainly have. And I hope you like it, sir.'

'I'm sure I will.'

She untied the scarf and revealed her hair. It was tied up in a loose round bun at the back of her head and she reached behind her to pull out the pins, letting it fall over her shoulders.

Cashel felt the shock, at first, then tears nip at his eyes.

'It's perfect,' he managed to say. 'I like it.'

Her hair had started to grey prematurely and she had talked

287

about having it coloured, dyeing it black to cover the grey. Anything but black, Cashel had said. Don't have black hair, please. On their last trip to Boston they had found a coiffeur who promised them any shade from darkest ebony to fairest blonde. Frannie had said she would have a think and make her decision. The hair transformation had been the main reason for the Boston visit but she wouldn't tell Cashel what she had decided. And now he knew.

He stepped towards her and took her in his arms. He wound a hank of her hair – dark, rich, auburn hair – about his fingers and raised it to her pale cheek. Raphaella incarnate, he thought. She could never have known, never have guessed – it was the most miraculous of coincidences. He kissed her lips.

'I love your hair,' he said softly, hearing the catch in his voice. 'You're very beautiful.'

'Missed me, honey?' she whispered in his ear. 'I missed you.'

Cashel positioned the chair carefully so he had a good three-quarter view of the bed. Frannie lay in the tangled sheets, naked, flicking through a guidebook to the city that she had taken from her bag on the bedside table.

'Where shall we go tomorrow?' she said. 'Somewhere different.'

Cashel tightened the belt on his dressing gown and lit his cigar from the gas mantle. He sat down and looked at her.

'Arlington? Brookline?'

'Could you be so good as to throw the sheet off you, my darling one?' he said.

She looked up. He had her attention.

'Why?'

'I want to create something – an image – something I'll never forget.'

'You want to see me naked. Just spit it out.' She flung the sheet off herself.

Cashel felt an almost physical pain in his chest.

She smiled at him, curious. 'What's going on, Cash? What's the game?'

'Can you raise your right knee up?'

'Oh, you want to see everything, do you?' She laughed. 'Once this charade is over it's my turn. You've been warned.' She raised her right knee, however, staring at him.

'Just ease your hair back . . . Please.'

Frannie looked at him, intrigued, a small, curious smile on her lips.

'What's going on, Cash?' she repeated.

He was rigid with concentration. It was uncanny. It was as if the years between Ravenna and this evening in Boston had disappeared.

'Have you ever thought, Frannie,' he said softly, 'that we should get married?'

'Oh, sure,' she said. 'You have a wife, remember? And, besides, I'm not the marrying kind any more.' She turned in the bed, showing the shadowed furrow between her buttocks, and put the guidebook on the bedside table.

He groaned, closed his eyes and arched his back. It was like magic.

'Let's get our clothes back on and go out on the town,' she said.

The doorbell rang.

'Mr Ross? Reception clerk, here. I have a bottle of champagne for you, sir,' came a voice.

'Did you order champagne?' Frannie asked.

'No. But I'll take it.' Maybe the bank, he thought: a sweetener. A good sign.

He tightened the belt of his gown and crossed the room. Frannie flipped the sheets and coverlet over herself and sank down in the bed.

In the vestibule outside the room, Cashel checked that he was decent. Then he opened the door.

Shay Corcoran and his son Devin stood there.

They barged in, pushing him roughly aside, followed by a man in a brown suit vigorously chewing a plug of tobacco.

'What the fuck do you think you're doing?' Cashel raged at them.

The three of them were now in the room.

Corcoran pointed at Frannie.

'Do you see what you see, Mr Norbury? You are our witness!'

'Yes, sir,' said the tobacco-chewer loudly. 'Naked man, naked woman.'

Cashel grabbed Devin Corcoran and tried to manhandle him out but Devin pushed him back against the wall.

'You're dead, you English cunt,' he breathed in Cashel's face, plosive flecks of spittle hitting his cheeks. 'You're finished!'

Shay Corcoran was visibly trembling, standing there in the middle of the room, his gaze darting between Cashel and Frannie.

Frannie had squirmed over to one side of the bed, fumbling in her reticule.

She turned, a small vest-pocket pistol in her hand. She cocked it.

'Get out,' she said flatly, loudly. 'You disgusting pigs. You don't deserve to be called men. You pigs, you swine. Get out before I shoot your balls off.'

Shay Corcoran took a swing at Cashel, missed his face but punched him heavily in the shoulder.

'Get out!' Frannie yelled, levelling her gun.

The tobacco-chewer, seeing the pistol, was gone in a second. Cashel, emboldened, pushed Devin out of the door with both hands. He grabbed Corcoran by the collar and flung him into the corridor, seeing the old man fall to the ground with a cry. He slammed the door behind them and locked it. He was panting heavily, strangely exhilarated.

Frannie was laughing, with some harshness.

'There goes my reputation,' she said. 'Maybe it was gone, already.'

Cashel went to the bed and hugged her, kissed her neck, took the little pistol from her hand and put it on the bedside table.

'I knew that would come in useful one day,' she said. 'However, I wouldn't swear it would fire.' She laughed. 'My Daddy gave it to me. Always have it with you, he said, you never know.'

He saw her face harden, then, and a hint of tears coming.

Shame and upset taking over after the rush of feverish excitement, of high, outraged passion.

'What would I do without you?' Cashel said, almost in tears himself now, kissing her again, holding her close, but already feeling a black tide of foreboding building in him.

They both agreed that it was best not to linger in Boston. Cashel had to try to discover what the Corcorans were planning, what consequences awaited this discovery of their affair, and the mood of adventure, of indulgence, was inevitably gone. But how had Corcoran known? they asked themselves. How had they been tracked down to Franklin House? Was the man in the brown suit some sort of investigator or agent of some kind? Something had gone wrong, clearly. Obviously, Corcoran had become suspicious – and now his suspicions were confirmed.

Cashel knew, almost at the moment he turned the buggy into Willow Creek's lane, that Bríd and the girls would be gone. He wandered through their rooms, noting empty drawers and wardrobes all cleared of clothes. This departure was not short-term. Most telling was the empty space where Bríd's icon of the Virgin Mary had once hung, and the prie-dieu was gone as well.

Cashel sought out Ignatz. Yes, he said, they had left yesterday, everything loaded into a wagon with young Mr Murphy Corcoran. Mrs Ross had merely said they were going on a trip but had not specified any destination.

'Come with me, Ignatz, I know where they are.'

Cashel went back to the house, found his double-barrelled musket, loaded it, fitted the percussion caps and laid it carefully in the back of the buggy under some sacking. They headed off to Rockfell.

'What's happened, sir?' Ignatz asked apprehensively.

'They've been kidnapped. We have to get them back.'

Once at Rockfell, Cashel made sure to pull up the buggy some distance from the front door.

'Corcoran!' he shouted. 'Send out Bríd and the girls – or else I'll serve a writ on you!'

Corcoran and his two sons emerged from the front door. Cashel saw at once that Corcoran had a pistol in his hand, one of the new holster-pistols, with a revolving chamber for the bullets. As Cashel reached back for his fowling piece Corcoran thrust his revolver in Cashel's face.

'Get off my land, you disgusting degenerate, you whoreson English bastard. Bríd and the girls are here of their own free will. Bríd knows what you were up to in Boston with your harlots on all those trips you made. You think we're fools? They want no part of you, Ross. They're finished with you.'

'Let me talk to the girls. I insist—'

'Don't you get it, Ross? It's over for you, I'm telling you. Finished. You'll never see them again in your life. Bríd won't have you contaminate their minds with your filth and your godless sins.'

Cashel closed his eyes as Corcoran ranted on.

'You can't stop me from seeing my children,' he said, raising his voice.

'If you set foot on this property I'll shoot you down like a stray dog. You've been warned, Ross, and your man here is the witness. Now get out.' He smiled a weird smile. 'And I ain't done with you yet, you gobshite.'

Cashel flicked the reins and turned the buggy round and they headed off. Ignatz sat hunched beside him in evident misery, his hands clasped between his knees.

'My God, Mr Ross, what's happened?'

'I made a mistake. There are . . . problems. Problems between me and Mrs Ross. Passions are high. We'll let them cool down a bit before we sort everything out.'

Cashel went to see Frannie's attorney in Stow. The man suggested the name of a law firm in Boston. He was reluctant to take sides, Mr Corcoran being the First Selectman of New Banbury and a personage of high standing in the locality – Mr Ross would surely understand. Cashel thanked him for his time. Outside, he thought of going to Five Oaks to see Frannie – the need was almost overpowering – but he knew it would be unwise. The fact that Corcoran had never referred to her by name made him suspect that he hadn't recognized her, had taken her for a prostitute that Cashel had brought to his room. Maybe her hair being down and the new colour of it had been a form of disguise. Perhaps that was the single good consequence of this fiasco. The only piece of good fortune. In any event, this was a fight between him and Corcoran – Frannie had no part in it.

And it wasn't long before the next round began. A local by-law for the municipality of New Banbury was promptly issued by the Selectman Committee of the township. All breweries and alcoholic stills within the municipality had to apply to the Selectman Committee for a licence to brew beer or make alcohol, the fee for such a licence to be determined by the said committee. Furthermore, in the case of breweries there would be a new tax imposed on any beer brewed to be sold commercially – three dollars a gallon.

When Cashel read the printed document he felt a shout of wild laughter rise in his throat. A barrel of Rossbrau contained thirty-two gallons. A butt had one hundred and six. Even a nine-gallon firkin would attract a tax of twenty-seven dollars. 'Punitive' was ridiculously unsuitable as an adjective. This was a clear attempt to force bankruptcy or closure. He looked at the signatures at the bottom of the directive. S. Corcoran, D. Corcoran, T. Bennett. There would always be a guarantee of two votes to one in favour. He'd forgotten that Devin Corcoran was a Selectman as well. He felt the first inklings of Corcoran's impunity – and his own powerlessness. The bitter revenge of Shay Corcoran seemed complete.

He crumpled the ordinance up and threw it in the fire, thinking hard. He supposed he could have recourse to the law, bring a suit against the committee. How much would that cost? And, more importantly, what chance would he have of winning – a wealthy, interloping brewer challenging the right of New Banbury to administrate its own municipality, to confront the edicts of the township's elected officials? Cashel poured himself a glass of brandy – at least he could drink in his own house now, he reflected ruefully. It looked very much as if Shay Corcoran had won and Willow Creek Farm would not survive. Certainly, the brewing days were over. Rossbrau had come to the end of its short, successful life. Cashel sat down and brooded, sipping at his brandy – was there a way he could exact some retribution? His career as a brewer may have been terminated, as had his life as a husband. But he was still a father to his daughters. They would not be kept from him. He would not pay that price.

'What're you going to do?' Frannie asked. They were sitting in her parlour.

'I'm going to go back to England,' Cashel said. 'For a while. Then when I return I'll make sure I won't be living in New Banbury.'

'What about the farm?'

'That's where you come in.'

Two days earlier, Cashel had received a letter from Corcoran's attorney outlining a proposition. Mr Shay Corcoran was prepared to buy Willow Creek Farm and its 'accoutrements' for a fair market price. He wants me gone, Cashel reasoned. Bríd and the girls could live in the house, and the fields – and the brewing business – would become part of the Corcoran family's wider holdings. It made perfect sense; and that he wasn't trying to cheat Cashel was the implication of 'fair market price'. But that proposition had given Cashel an idea. He saw a course of action ahead, a way of thwarting Corcoran.

He took Frannie's hand.

'I'm going to sell you Willow Creek Farm for one dollar. We'll close down the brewery. You'll get a nice income from the ice on the pond – a hundred and fifty dollars – and the hay in the meadows.'

'But I don't want another farm.'

'You don't have to do anything. Every winter, this man Frederick Tudor sends his team – his horses and wagons and his ice-cutting plough. He cuts the ice in blocks, takes it away and pays you money. If it's really cold, he'll come twice in the winter and you double your money. You can rent out the farmhouse.'

She thought for a second or two, frowning.

'He pays you a hundred and fifty dollars for ice? Each year? Just ice – frozen water?'

'Yes. That's how I could afford to set up the brewery. It's what paid for the beer.'

'That's more than I make from my apples.'

'He pays that much because the ice from the pond is so clear, so transparent. It's worth more, he says.'

'All right. But I have one condition.'

'What? I don't want a "condition". I just want to frustrate Corcoran. Make him suffer.'

'I'll send you half the money I make from the ice. If you don't come back I'll keep it all.'

He took her in his arms and kissed her. Then they heard her son Whitaker call out as he came in the front door. They stepped apart a yard or two and smiled at each other.

It took Cashel and Ignatz most of a day to empty the stock of Rossbrau into the pond. Then they made a huge bonfire of the empty barrels and set it alight.

He and Ignatz drank the last of the beer as they watched the flames leap and crackle and the thick smoke rise in the still afternoon air. He hoped Corcoran could see the dark fuming column from Rockfell – a dire augury. It was not an exultant moment, far from it. The mood was one of stoic realism, he hoped – Cashel had explained everything to Ignatz by now and even he could see that it was impossible to continue.

'What about the hops?' Ignatz asked.

'Let them run wild, I don't care. Mrs Broome can cut the vines down or sell the hops to other brewers. I'm going back to England – I have affairs to settle. When I return I'll buy a property in Stow or Concord. I won't live in New Banbury again, that's for sure. Maybe Boston. Who knows?'

Ignatz looked thoughtful.

'I have money for you, Ignatz. I want you to be free to start up once more, in your own way, free to choose.'

'Perhaps I could come with you, Mr Ross?'

'What? With me?'

'To England. I could be in your service.'

Cashel thought suddenly of two previous offers from his past. That boy in Arles – what was his name? – yes, Jaufret. And then Timoteo in Ravenna.

'I can't pay you what you might earn here. Any brewer will hire you, Ignatz – you're a genius.'

'Some bread to eat and a dry corner to sleep in, Mr Ross. It's all I ask. I would prefer to work with you in England.'

Cashel had to admit that the thought, and the prospect, cheered him. Maybe that was what he needed in his new life – a loyal manservant. He looked at Ignatz. Stocky, bearded, melancholy Ignatz. How old must he be, now? Well into his thirties. He realized, again, that he would have achieved nothing at Willow Creek without the young man.

'I would be honoured, Ignatz. I'm delighted we can continue our association.'

They looked warmly at each other, each knowing that the instinctive embrace they should make at this decision was denied them: social rank, as ever, keeping them apart. Cashel raised his pewter pot instead.

'Here's to England.'

'To England,' Ignatz repeated and clinked his own pot dully against Cashel's.

'You know, I am looking forward, sir,' he said with a shy, rare smile. 'To the future of Mr Ross and Mr Vlac.'

The future, Cashel thought two months later, as he stood – mid-Atlantic – on the aft deck of the Cord Line's steamship *Heracles*, a week or so before they docked in Southampton. What was his future now . . .? It was very calm, the ocean, the slightest of breezes blowing, but the *Heracles* was forging on at a steady twelve knots, all her sails furled on her three masts, the twin screws turning at her stern, her two smokestacks leaving a dirty but diminishing trail of sooty steam behind her, an aerial wake.

Cashel looked at his fob. The immediate future was luncheon. He had his own cabin (Ignatz was in steerage, 'Tween Decks) and he would dine with the cabin-class passengers off white linen napery and fine china, with silver forks and knives. His fellow diners at the table consisted of an American novelist (whom he had never heard of) with his wife, a couple of Yorkshire merchants heading home and a distinguished Unitarian minister about to embark on a lecture tour in England.

He thought back to his voyage out to America, all those years ago – his hopes, his dreams of Libertania, his vast ignorance – and compared the young man he was then with the person he was now: almost fifty years old, good God. Cashel Greville Ross, solvent, with a servant, but with his wife and two daughters left behind, lost to him. No, he said to himself, vehemently – poor demented Bríd may be gone irretrievably but not sprightly, naughty Maeve and sweet, solemn Nessa – not in his lifetime, never. He would find a way of reuniting with them, he told himself, he would. And, as he articulated that determination, recognizing that this was perhaps a measure of how much he had changed, that he wasn't a young romantic fool any more, he saw at once that such a project would be made more feasible and easier with money. Money, yes, that was the key element, now. It would be money that would defeat Shay Corcoran and it would be money that would bring his daughters home . . .

He strolled across the deck to the other side of the steamship and looked out at the boundless ocean – the masterless, undrinkable sea – with its effortless propensity to symbolize anything that any spectator wished to infuse it with: loss, majesty, infinity, time, indifference, mutability, God's omnipotence, puny mankind's insignificance and so on. Everything had been going so well, Cashel thought, and then his heart had led him astray. But no, that was a harsh judgement, he rebuked himself. Bríd's sudden mental collapse after Nessa's birth had made normal life impossible. And what love she had felt for him became a kind of obsessive disdain, a hatred – expressed in her violent rages – as if in his being he represented everything she despised. In these circumstances – unhappy, troubled, lonely – he would naturally be drawn to any source of relief, of solace, of a kind of love. And, coming as it did in the shape of Frannie Broome, it had proved irresistible. He sighed. Get rich, Cashel Ross, he told himself. Then ruin Shay Corcoran utterly, rescue your daughters from his evil influence and marry Frannie Broome.

12

Mr Cashel Ross, Esq., was riding in a hansom cab along Oxford Street heading towards Hyde Park where Mr Theobald Rackham's ice house was located in Grand Junction Street by the reservoir. He was on a mission: Frannie Broome had written to him asking him to check on the supplies of Willow Creek ice in London. Tudor's American Ice Co. was trying to reduce the tariff they were paying, claiming that sales in England were dying out, and she suspected this was a lie.

Rackham's Ice House, purpose built, looked at street level like a small unremarkable warehouse. There were no windows in the simple brick facade, just a wide double door that provided ingress and egress for the wagons and drays on their ice deliveries. Theobald Rackham himself was a bald gloomy-looking man in his fifties with pronounced bags under his doleful eyes, like small flesh purses hanging there, Cashel thought. However, on learning who he was, Rackham's slumped face became more animated and Cashel was greeted with enthusiasm as the co-owner of the Willow Creek pond.

'It is far and away my bestseller, Mr Ross, but that ain't saying much.'

He led Cashel downstairs to the huge underground storage area, swinging open a thick door insulated with cork. He lit the gaslights and Cashel saw the gleaming blocks of ice stacked like giant bricks on beds of straw. Mr Rackham explained that most of his ice trade was with wholesale grocers, butchers and fishmongers.

'They take any old ice – dirty, opaque, dead fish, leaves, twigs – they don't care. But when it comes to Willow Creek – that's for hotels, gentlemen's clubs, the exclusive houses of the aristocracy.'

He showed Cashel where they stored the Willow Creek ice. It was cut in small cubes, about twelve inches square, that were stacked in an eight-foot pile. There was a steam engine in the yard that powered a conveyor belt to lift the blocks to a loading bay at street level.

Mr Rackham stood looking proudly at the wall of ice.

'No, my customers ask for it by name. "Has the Willow Creek come in from America?" Specifically. It's renowned, Mr Ross.'

'How much do you sell it for?'

'Tuppence a pound. That block there is worth five shillings. I could sell twice as much – if I could get my hands on it.'

Rackham took a sharp, pointed ice hammer out of his pocket and chipped off a corner the size of a walnut. He held it up to the gaslight.

'This is ice you put in your glass of champagne. Look at it. Like cut crystal – not a bubble, not an impurity.'

'If it's your bestseller why not order more?' Cashel asked.

'Because Mr Tudor keeps ninety per cent of it to sell in America. In New York he sells it at ten cents a pound. That's cheaper than here but Americans like ice. They love ice, love their cold drinks. We English don't care, one way or another, worse luck. He makes more money selling it for less in America than he does selling it to me.'

'If I could guarantee you the quantity you needed would you guarantee to buy it?'

'You bet I would, Mr Ross. Like a shot.'

'Could you write me an official letter to that effect? Then I will make sure it gets into Mr Tudor's hands.'

Cashel reasoned that such a letter would be enough to hold Tudor to his contract – he could hardly claim the English market was dying. It was important, also – his share of the money they made from the ice trade was his only income. It paid for the life he led in London.

Rackham took him back upstairs and wrote out the letter of guarantee on the firm's headed notepaper. He folded it up, slipped it in an envelope and handed it to Cashel.

'Much obliged, Mr Ross. I'll take as much Willow Creek ice as can be supplied.'

42 Long Acre
Covent Garden
London

16th September 1853

My Dearest Frannie,

Enclosed is the letter to show to the company. Rackham Ice Ltd will take all the Willow Creek it can get, so you can tell Tudor to 'go hang' in your own sweet way. In fact, you could take this letter to any of his rivals in the ice trade and maybe obtain a better price. I leave that up to you.

My own news is discouraging. After many months of searching it's clear that the hop farms in Kent are either too expensive or too small to provide the significant income I need. I'm still to receive the share of my inheritance from my dear departed mother but my younger brother, Hogan, has charge of it and it is proving devilish hard to prise it from his grasp, for some reason. Prevarications and excuses are all I receive. As soon as I retrieve it I will book passage to Boston. I long to see you, I long to hold you in my arms and I long to – you can imagine the rest. I do, constantly.

In anticipation of our impending reunion I remain

your loving friend (and lover),
Cashel

When he arrived back in England, Cashel had gone first to stay with his brother Buckley and his wife in their large and roomy rectory in Claverleigh, near Lewes, Sussex. Buckley and his wife, Emily, now had three young children, two boys and a girl, and after a boisterous, exhausting week, Cashel decided to move to Claverleigh's inn, the William IV, and took a bedroom and sitting room there. He had already installed Ignatz at the inn so it was practical – and quieter – for them both. Cashel rented a brougham and they set about systematically looking at properties in eastern Sussex and Kent that they might buy, aiming to replicate the success of Rossbrau in England.

However, it was quickly apparent that England was awash with beer and the big brewers would not easily admit interlopers. The larger hop farms they looked at were too expensive and the smaller ones that he could afford would barely pay their way. In the event, he was happy to leave his Rossbrau profits (some £1,400) in his London bank if it looked as though brewing beer in England was not going to provide him with the income he needed. The legacy he had inherited on Elspeth Ross's death was another £400.* If he returned to America with almost £2,000 he could establish himself in some style in Stow or Concord. And then he could contemplate how best to revenge himself on the Corcorans.

Cashel had written to Hogan in Oxford several times, asking him to transfer the legacy to his London bank. Hogan promised that he would – as soon as 'a minor problem' had been sorted out in his own financial affairs. There might even be more money, he promised, once he had resolved a dispute over some pastureland behind the cottage in Woodstock. Cashel was in no particular hurry and so left it to Hogan to make the transfer in his own time.

As the prospect of hop-farming and beer-brewing in Kent seemed more and more unlikely, if not impossible, Cashel decided to move back to London. He rented a furnished, narrow house on Long Acre, near Covent Garden. Ignatz lived in the basement. Cashel now occupied himself with lawyers trying to secure the ownership of his two books – now the property of Purvis Yelverton's printers who, on Yelverton's absconding and

---

* In 1841, for example, Anthony Trollope's annual salary as a senior civil servant at the Post Office was £140. In 1862, George Eliot was paid £7,000 for her novel *Romola*, a tremendous sum for the times. These figures give a sense of the comparative worth of the money Cashel had accumulated. The capital sum was substantial, though not a fortune.

subsequent bankruptcy, had acquired the publisher's list of authors in lieu of monies owed.

The printer, a dour, intransigent man by the name of Maxwell Bishopson, admitted that Cashel's books – the *Journal of a Tour* and *Nihil* – were still in print and selling in new cheap editions, though he refused to concede that he owed the author any money. Cashel showed him his contract with Yelverton – both books had been published on the 'share-of-profits' model. As both had also made a profit in several published editions, Cashel argued that Bishopson only had a claim on Yelverton's percentage of the revenue the books had generated, not the whole 100 per cent. Letters from lawyers went to and fro. There was not a lot of money owing – something close to £200, Bishopson reluctantly calculated, but for Cashel every contribution to his return to America was to be welcomed. He sensed that Bishopson was wary of the prospect of litigation – some sort of compromise could surely be reached.

One Monday morning, some two weeks after the visit to the Rackham ice house, Cashel took a cab to the City and went to his bank, Brookes & Co. He needed cash and he wanted to see if Hogan's transfer had arrived. The answer was no. Cashel was being served by a young clerk, new to the firm, called Joseph Summerbee. He seemed intelligent and alert.

He handed over Cashel's sovereigns and some printed cheque forms.

'Did you ever receive the bundle of letters we've been holding for you, Mr Ross?' Summerbee asked.

'No. What letters?'

The bundle was found and duly brought to him. There were about a dozen letters sent to his bank over the years he had been away in America and never forwarded. Cashel went through them at a chop house on the Strand where he stopped for lunch. Only two were interesting. One, almost eight years old, was from Mary Shelley, congratulating him on the success of *Nihil*.* Mrs

---

* Mary Shelley died in 1851. So this warm encomium was being read posthumously.

Davenport had finally let the secret slip, she said. The other was more recent, sent three months ago, from someone he had never expected to hear from again in his life – Deveron Gilchrist-Baird, last seen in the jungles of Kandy, in high fever, being transported in a litter to Trincomalee. It was very brief.

The Garrick Club
35 King Street,
London

Monday, 4th June 1854

Dear Ross,
   Will you remember this voice from your distant past? Last week at a friend's house I chanced across a book called Journal of a Tour through Italy and France by one Cashel Greville Ross. Could this author be my old comrade in arms? thought I. Of course, indeed it was. I take the liberty of writing to you care of your bank – as you once advised me – in the hope that you receive this missive and that we might meet. I have a lucrative proposition to put to you – and I need a writer! If the idea intrigues you then you may contact me through the good offices of the Garrick.
   In anticipation, I remain etc.
   Deveron Gilchrist-Baird
   (Hon. Sec. of the benighted survivors of the 5th Madras Light Infantry)

The Garrick Club was an easy stroll from Long Acre. Cashel handed his reply to Gilchrist-Baird to the porter at the club. He had written that he was indeed intrigued and gave him his address, 'just around the corner'. Gilchrist Baird replied within twenty-four hours. A rendezvous at the Garrick was proposed.

Deveron Gilchrist-Baird had not changed a great deal, Cashel saw, and politely told him so. He was stouter, more florid, but still with a good head of hair and that tired, slightly debauched look about him, as if he hadn't been sleeping well. He was very complimentary in turn about Cashel. 'As if I'd seen you yesterday, by God. What's your secret, Ross?'

They went to the club's coffee room, the walls clustered with portraits of actors, old and new, where Gilchrist-Baird ordered them a gin punch with iced soda water. Cashel looked at the small nuggets of ice floating in his glass and thought it would be an astonishing coincidence if their punch was cooled by frozen water from Willow Creek. Maybe that would be a good omen . . . He forced himself to concentrate on Gilchrist-Baird, who was filling him in on the missing years of their acquaintance.

'. . . No, my problem is that my father refuses to die. He's eighty-one, God not preserve him, so I'm still just an Honourable, I haven't inherited anything and I live off the old chap's fluctuating benevolence. It's not easy.'

'Are you married?'

'I was – but she died. Consumption. Very sad. No children, though. When I left the army about five years ago my father bought me a business – a dry-salting company. Unfortunately, I speculated – very unwisely, as it turned out – in indigo. My father paid my debts but he now keeps me on a very tight leash.' He sat back and smiled. 'I need to make money, Ross.'

'So do I, as it happens.'

'There you are. The stars are aligning in our favour. But I have a plan. Shall we go in?'

Over luncheon – a curry called 'Fried Fowl of Mohammed Khan' – Gilchrist-Baird outlined his scheme. A wealthy aristocrat, the Earl of Bassett, to whom he was distantly related, had offered a prize of 5,000 guineas to the first person who could discover the source of the Nile.

Cashel stopped him.

'Is this your "plan"? You're proposing that we discover the source of the Nile?'

'Yes. It's been baffling mankind for centuries. A thousand years. Where is the damn thing? Five thousand guineas is all very nice but, so I've been told, where you make your real money is the book you write about your adventure. You could make ten thousand pounds. Then there are the talks, the lectures, the foreign editions – it's a gold mine.'

'In theory.'

'A cove here at the Garrick told me that Dickens made twenty thousand from *Oliver Twist*.'*

'That's a novel.'

'I know. Of course I know that. But the point is that books that sell can make a fortune. *How I Found the Source of the Nile* by Cashel Ross. Imagine.'

'What if we don't discover it?'

'Then you write a fascinating, exciting account explaining why we didn't. We – you and I – become celebrated throughout the land, known through Europe, throughout civilized America. Explorers are the new . . .' He searched for a word. 'The new . . . knights errant, demigods, heroes. We would be heroes, Ross.'

Cashel said nothing, thinking hard.

'I've a friend,' Gilchrist-Baird went on, 'at the Geographical Society. He told me about this map, drawn by a German missionary called Erhardt. It shows a huge lake in the middle of Africa, eight hundred miles long, big as the Caspian Sea. That's got to be it – the source. We go to Africa, we travel inland – we can't miss it.'

'But we're not experienced.'

'We're soldiers. Ex-Indian army officers, Ross. We're as experienced as anyone. You were at Waterloo, for God's sake.' He broke off to order a bottle of claret.

'This friend at the Geographical Society,' he went on, 'can give us all the practical advice.'

'I still think—'

'Did you go to the exhibition, the Crystal Palace one, couple of years ago?'

'Yes.'

---

* Gilchrist-Baird was spreading Garrick Club gossip. However, for example, Dickens's share of the profits of *Bleak House* (1852) was £11,000.

'Didn't you think it was astonishing? The machines, the equipment, the sheer ingenuity? Our expedition will be equipped with every modern device and invention. Weapons, clothes, preserved foods, medicines, measuring implements . . .' He ran out of inventions.

'All this equipment will cost money,' Cashel said.

Gilchrist-Baird approved the wine and it was poured.

'True,' he said. 'We would have to invest. But we'd be investing in ourselves. No profit without investment.'

'How much?'

'Two thousand. A thousand each.'

'Jesus Christ, man. What makes you think I've got that sort of money just lying around?'

'You look like a man with a spare thousand. Just as I do. Maybe not a spare ten thousand but we only need one each. And think of the reward. What a return on our investment.'

Cashel began to feel, despite his natural caution, a mounting excitement.

'Everything we make will be split fifty-fifty,' Gilchrist-Baird went on. 'The prize, the publishing contracts, the lecture tours. We would be partners, equals.' He looked across the table into Cashel's eyes.

There was, Cashel felt, an irresistible, crazy logic to what Gilchrist-Baird was proposing. Explorers were the new heroes . . .

'Why me?' he asked bluntly. 'After all these years.'

'Because I came across your book. I admit, freely, I'm not much of a reader, but there I was, in a library. It was a wet weekend, pouring rain, no chance of hunting. I picked out a book at random, and it was yours. It was a sign, Ross. Fate. We're old friends, old-soldier friends. But you can write – I can't. And that's where the real money is – the book. The damned book.'

Cashel sipped at his wine, thinking hard. Even if they made half of what Gilchrist-Baird was projecting – even a quarter – it would be more money than he'd ever earned in his life. All problems solved – the Corcorans at his mercy – all potentials achievable.

42 Long Acre
Covent Garden
London

20ᵗʰ October 1855

My Dearest Frannie,

An amazing financial opportunity has presented itself – out of nowhere – in Africa. I genuinely believe this will be the answer to all our concerns and the great advantage is that the rewards arrive very swiftly. The disadvantage is that we must wait at least two years before I can return to America and you. But two years' absence should be seen as an investment in a long future together.

I'm embarking on this adventure with an old friend from my soldiering days in India. He has all the experience and the necessary contacts we need and we will both be equal partners in this endeavour. It won't be easy – but I quickly add we are not prospecting for gold and diamonds, it is an expedition of discovery. We need only our own energies and robust constitutions – but even a modest success will be overwhelming. Everything will change for you and me, for Maeve and Nessa, for Conway and Whitaker. I will write in more detail as our plans take verifiable shape. In the meantime, we have extensive preparations to make before the long voyage to East Africa.

Trust me, my darling. I had given up hope of achieving anything substantial here in England but this opportunity has arrived like a gift from the gods.

With all my love, dearest,
Your own
Cashel

Cashel looked out of the window as the train rattled steadily through the Oxfordshire countryside at forty miles an hour – it was almost inconceivable. Fields, copses, small farms, villages, church spires, children waving as the train sped past. Through the window, everything looked unchanged – England as she always was. Yet here he was, sitting in comfort, a book open in his lap, travelling from London to Oxford to have luncheon with his brother and he would be back in London before night fell. It still seemed extraordinary. He looked around at his fellow travellers – dozing, reading, conversing – it had all become 'normal' with astonishing speed.

As the train pulled in to Grandpont station he saw the bulky figure of Hogan standing on the platform waiting for him, in his long black coat and his stovepipe topper. Cashel felt a spontaneous, natural surge of affection for him. Hogan, his complicated brother, so different from Buckley, the parson, with his wife and sweet, noisy children. Cashel had seen Hogan once, briefly, since he'd returned from America but he was still taken aback by the changes wrought in his brother. He seemed the older sibling, his hair and whiskers prematurely greying, his face deeply lined, as if careworn by hard work and life's manifold problems. His voice was deeper and rougher also, and his life in the countryside had made his Oxfordshire accent more pronounced.

Hogan broke into a wide smile as he saw Cashel step down from the carriage, and the two of them shook hands warmly, Hogan spontaneously reaching out to clap and squeeze Cashel's shoulder with his left hand.

'First class, eh?' Hogan said. 'You must be doing well, you old bastard.'

They walked out of the station and past a row of hacks waiting there.

'Where're we off to?' Cashel asked as they crossed Folly Bridge and strolled up into the town, everything familiar, past Christ Church and on to St Aldate's.

'The Nag's Head. Remember it?'

'That dirty dram-shop?'

'Not any more, my son. Oh, no.'

The Nag's Head was off St Aldate's, just before it reached the junction with the High Street, and was, to Cashel's astonished eyes, unrecognizable. The modest storeroom drinking parlour, with a candle in the window, had been replaced by a pilastered door with an entablature. Wide plate-glass windows looked out onto the street and, inside, gaslight cast a brilliant glow on the pewter-topped bar of French-polished mahogany. Wooden settles with horsehair cushions lined the walls.

'My God,' Cashel said, amazed.

The place was busy – men, women and children standing on the deal floorboards in front of the bar with its ivory pulls of beer engines. Behind the bar were varnished casks of spirits with brass spigots. A splendid drinking emporium, Cashel thought.

'What'll it be?' Hogan asked. 'We can have a spot of lunch round the corner when our whistles are nicely wet.'

Cashel asked for a pot of porter and Hogan ordered a gin and water. Cashel could sense Hogan's slight nervousness, now that the affable meeting and greeting was over. They moved to a quieter corner of the bar with their drinks.

'I know why you're here, Cash,' Hogan said. 'I can only apologize.'

'You had care of my inheritance,' Cashel said. 'And that was all well and good while I was in America – but now I'm back and I need it.'

'I don't have it,' Hogan said brusquely. 'It's all spent.'

He told Cashel a story about his partner in the stud farm, Enoch Starkie, who had died suddenly in an accident. Hogan had bought his widow out with his legacy – and part of Cashel's. 'Otherwise I'd have been ruined,' he said. Then he had discovered the scale of Starkie's hidden debts and the rest of the money was gone. He had had no choice, Hogan said.

'But I need that money,' Cashel said, as reasonably as he could. 'I told you, I'm going to Africa.'

'I'll pay you back, don't worry. Problem is, the fucking railways are killing off the coaching trade. That's half our business going. Thank God the English army still has cavalry.'

Hogan drained his gin and signalled to the publican's wife for another one.

'We just need another war,' he said, 'and the horse trade will pick up. I've great hopes of something stirring in the Black Sea. Just you wait. The fleet's despatched. And the French too.'

310

'You're well informed.'

'I've a lot of friends amongst the military,' Hogan said. 'They get through a devil of a lot of horse flesh.'

'I know,' Cashel said. 'I've seen it, remember?'

'Of course, Mr Waterloo man. Here, have another. They do a fine joint of beef round the corner.'

Cashel gave up hope of securing his mother's inheritance in the immediate future. He and Hogan ate a substantial meal in a chop house on the High Street and reminisced about Elspeth Ross and their early life in Oxford. Cashel gave him a few more details about the disaster that had occurred in New Banbury and the need, therefore, to accumulate money so that wrongs could be righted.

'What about your wife, Bríd?' Hogan asked.

'My latest information is that she's been moved to an insane asylum outside Boston. The girls are being brought up by her brother – their uncle – and his wife.' He paused, thinking about the girls – his girls – and feeling the pang of their absence. He thought back to the letter from Frannie that had contained this news. The other very worrying information was that Maeve and Nessa had abandoned their Ross surnames and now were known as Corcorans. Slowly, incrementally, they seemed to be receding from him, the 'Ross' in them being erased and replaced by something alien.

'So you can see why I need to get back there and reclaim them,' Cashel said, suddenly bitter. 'Before they forget who I am.'

Hogan frowned and scratched his head, pushing his empty plate away.

'It sounds to me that main force would be your best strategy,' he said. 'In my experience when you find yourself in these situations you have to make a threat – a serious threat of serious harm so they know you're not joking, like. But a threat is no good if you don't follow it up.'

'He's a powerful man, Corcoran. A local dignitary – a kind of mayor.'

'You put a knife at his throat and his power is gone.'

Cashel gave a sceptical, dry laugh.

'You just can't do that sort of thing any more, Hogan.'

'It worked with Starkie.' Hogan laughed in his turn and poured himself more wine from the bottle.

'I thought you said he died in an accident.'

'Right enough, he did. I warned him and he paid no heed. Then he accidentally fell down a well. A deep well, as it happened. So deep that nobody heard him crying out. He hung on for a couple of days but when they finally came across him he was dead. Drowned.'

'Right . . .' Hogan's skewed, brutal logic was disturbing. Cashel changed the subject.

'You thinking about marriage, yourself, Hogan? You're not getting any younger.'

'I don't think I'm the marrying kind,' he said. 'I'm sort of wooing a widow in Thame. From time to time, like. When I'm in the mood for a bit of wooing, if you catch my drift.'   ·

Cashel had to admit that he was impressed by Gilchrist-Baird's energy and competence. He had spent far longer in the army than Cashel had and seemed more thoroughly a soldier, with a soldier's habits and methods – he had a quartermaster's diligence. They were standing in an empty stable in the mews behind Gilchrist-Baird's London residence. The loose boxes were crammed with supplies for their expedition. Gilchrist-Baird pointed out the bales of coloured cotton cloth, the many spindles of brass wire and sacks filled with various denominations of beads – from cheap white buttons to multicoloured glass – all for bartering, for securing safe passage. Plus, he added, two years' worth of ammunition.

'Ten thousand copper caps. Boxes of ball, grape and shot. Six fire-proof magazines, two barrels of fine powder, ten of coarse powder, a dozen pistols and a dozen muskets.'

'We're not going to war, for God's sake,' Cashel said. 'We're explorers.'

'We have to eat off the land,' Gilchrist-Baird explained. 'You and I have to shoot for our supper – and for our porters' supper every day. They won't march if they haven't eaten, so I'm told.'

He went on pointing out the tents, the cork mattresses, the chronometers and the sextants and other surveying equipment, cases of medication.

'We'll buy rice and grain once we reach Zanzibar. And mules and asses.' He smiled at Cashel. 'We're spending our money very wisely, I can assure you, Ross. This is going to be the best-equipped expedition ever to venture out into the interior.'

As the date for their departure drew nearer Cashel asked Ignatz if he wanted to accompany them to Africa or remain in London.

'Of course I will come with you, sir,' Ignatz said instantly. 'I think I can be very useful.'

'But it's not without its risks, its dangers, you know.'

'The same risks and dangers attend us throughout life, anyway,' Ignatz said with strange conviction. 'Even the voyage to Africa is risky. Even the journey to the port has its dangers. Step outside your front door, sir, and there are no assurances. And in the security of your own house there are stairways, open fires, boiling kettles—'

'Yes, yes. Point taken, Ignatz. Thank you. It'll be very reassuring to have you with us.'

It took them just under a month to sail to Cape Town, booking passage on a timber clipper heading for Burma and its virgin teak forests. Both he and Gilchrist-Baird grew beards on the voyage. They would not have the luxury of shaving on the expedition, and they both thought it a wise pre-emptive move and, curiously, a measure of their seriousness of intent.

However, a few days short of Cape Town, Ignatz developed a fever that went to his lungs. He began to cough sputum, flecked with blood. By the time they managed to have him admitted to a hospital in Cape Town he seemed alarmingly near death. He was shockingly pale and malnourished, unable to keep solid foods down, and drifted in and out of consciousness. Cashel visited him each day but there seemed no diagnosis forthcoming – and no cure.

In the meantime, Gilchrist-Baird had transferred all their stores, baggage and equipment to a vessel he described as a 'jack-ass frigate' that was heading to Zanzibar. The island would be their jumping-off point for the long journey into the interior, many hundreds of miles. Their final preparations on Zanzibar would be the hiring of porters and guides.

Gilchrist-Baird accompanied Cashel on his final visit to Ignatz before they left for Zanzibar. They stood by the bed, looking down at his wasted body, semi-visible beneath the thick gauze of the mosquito curtain.

'Is he breathing?' Gilchrist-Baird asked.

'Of course he is,' Cashel said and lifted the netting briefly. 'Look.'

'I wouldn't give him long odds on lasting twenty-four hours,' Gilchrist-Baird said.

'He's stronger than you think, I have every hope.'

'Have you left instructions?'

'Yes. And money for all eventualities. A funeral or a long convalescence.'

'We can't linger, Ross. The weather is our master.'

'I know, the rainy season,' Cashel said, feeling a profound gloom descend on him. He had come to think of Ignatz as part of his life, almost as a member of his family. To leave him seemed like a bad omen. He thought he could detect a malign pattern in his life – that he was always moving on, for some rea-son or other, and leaving someone precious behind. First his mother, then Raphaella, then Maeve and Nessa, then Frannie and now Ignatz. After all their talk of risk and danger, real peril had come so soon to visit Ignatz. This felt like a kind of mal-ediction on the journey before him. Another abandonment. But what could he do . . .?

'From the blue, shallow sea, Zanzibar looks enchanting, as one approaches,' Cashel wrote in his notebook.

Set against this refulgent blue surface are low-lying buildings of white coraline stone, interspersed with the vivid green of palm trees, tamarind and fig. Closer to shore, a mephitic stink becomes more evident – rotting fish and putrid mud, charcoal smoke and human filth, overlaid by the cloying perfume of cloves. The smell of Zanzibar. One hundred thousand people live on this small island, crammed into the noisome, narrow alleyways of the old town, and their effluvia is everywhere.

The British consulate in Zanzibar was a tall, three-storey building, recently enlarged, its white and gleaming walls still winning the battle against sea-salt tarnish. It was situated on the front by the harbour and benefited from whatever breeze emanated from the ocean. A large Union Jack flew from its flagpole on the roof and, next door, in a slightly smaller, less kempt edifice was the consulate of the United States of America. However, it did fly a larger flag in compensation; the Stars and Stripes was the size of a bed sheet.

The British consul, Lieutenant Colonel Atkins Hamerton, was a large, genial Irishman with white hair and whiskers. He was also the local agent for the Honourable East India Company and he was delighted to be of service to two former members of the HEIC's Madras army. Rooms in the consulate were provided immediately, free of charge. Hamerton was evidently in chronic ill-health – he had been in Zanzibar for well over a decade and was paying the price. 'Something to do with my liver, they tell me,' was his explanation and Cashel quickly confirmed that the diagnosis must be right: Hamerton's skin was a jaundiced yellow, his eyes a watery sepia. He only emerged from his quarters at dusk when the temperature dropped. Luckily, the consulate had a resident apothecary, a Mr Frost, and his careful prescription of various medicaments – mainly morphine-based – seemed to keep Colonel Hamerton functioning for at least a few hours of the day.

Hamerton – who spoke fluent Arabic and was a trusted confidant of the Sultan of Zanzibar – was a man of real influence on the island. He secured the employment of eight Baluchi mercenaries from the Sultan's own bodyguard as the expedition's armed escort. He also introduced Gilchrist-Baird and Cashel to an Arab-Swahili guide and interpreter called Sidi Muzembi who would be the so-called *kafila-bashi*, the captain, of the expedition. Sidi Muzembi was a disarmingly placid, enigmatic man with thin half-closed eyes that gave him an oddly drowsy appearance, Cashel thought. He spoke a rudimentary English and seemed happy to leave much of the hard work to his nephew, Sosha, a tall young lad of eighteen or so who, in contrast to his uncle, was eager and full of energy.

Cashel left all the Zanzibari administration to Gilchrist-Baird and spent his time writing up his notes for the eventual book he would write, conscious of its importance to the whole enterprise. He had decided that no detail was too insignificant to be registered and consequently took precision to new lengths, noting that along with the American cotton they had bought to barter ('Merikani cloth' as the natives termed it) there were several rolls of sprigged muslin for turban-making, and that the most valuable beads they had with them had actually been created in Venice. He pedantically listed their provisions ('*2 boxes cigars, 2 dozen brandy, 2 bottles curry stuff, 1 tin canteen with knives and forks, 3 portmanteaus for clothes and books, 1 mountain barometer, 2 dozen pencils, 9 hatchets, 12 augurs,*' etc., etc.) and, as the list grew, became more and more impressed with Gilchrist-Baird's organizational abilities.

The evening before their departure for the coast, Hamerton gave a dinner for them. The American consul was invited, a couple of Dutch merchants and Mr Frost, the apothecary. A fish course was served before the stew of goat and sweet potato and a great deal of whisky and water was provided. Towards the end of the meal, Cashel excused himself and stepped outside onto the terrace to smoke a cigar in peace.

He stood by the low balustrade looking out to sea, listening to the modest surf surge and plash softly on the beach below him. The air was warm and enfolding, but not uncomfortably so, and the metallic chirrup of the cicadas in the nearby bushes and trees filled his ears. It was strange being back in the tropics again, the heat, the smells and the noises reminding him of Ooty and Ceylon. Apart from poor Ignatz, everything, he had to admit, was going according to plan and, for some reason, he found that unsettling. Maybe that was because of Ignatz's life-threatening fever. The initial bad luck maybe prefiguring more to come. How was Ignatz? Cashel wondered, frustrated. Was he even still alive . . .?

He, Cashel Ross, was about to embark into the complete unknown for many months, for years, possibly, where all communication with the people he knew and loved would be cut entirely. For a second or two, as he stood there in the darkness, cigar in hand, he wondered if he had lost his mind – but he quickly banished these thoughts. This was not some fantasy, not some romantic dream of fame and fortune – there was a sound pragmatic reason behind it all. He thought of Frannie Broome – and Maeve and Nessa – and his eventual return to America, confident and powerful, ready to redeem himself and re-establish his place in his world, a world he had built, unchallenged and unchallengeable.

Yes, and he would write a wonderful book as well, he encouraged himself, and if it were half as successful as Gilchrist-Baird had promised he might never write another and never need to be a farmer – or a brewer – again. Thus encouraged, he found his mood remarkably cheered. He had bought a dozen fat notebooks in which he would record every step of their celebrated journey. He flicked his cigar butt out into the Indian Ocean – suddenly he was excited by the prospect of what lay ahead of them.

The jackass frigate landed the Gilchrist-Baird and Ross East African Expeditionary Party ashore in a small bay on the eastern mainland of Africa about twenty miles south of a village named Bagamoyo on 26th April 1856. Sidi Muzembi and Sosha, who had preceded them, had mustered some sixty porters and two dozen pack animals. What with the Baluchi mercenaries and their wives and concubines the straggling column, when fully loaded and under way, stretched almost half a mile. Gilchrist-Baird led, riding a fair-sized mule, beside a Baluchi soldier carrying the Sultan of Zanzibar's red standard. Cashel rode at the rear, also on a mule. He didn't particularly enjoy being the last man in the line, feeling somewhat exposed, but Hamerton had told him it was both standard practice and symbolic – the presence of a 'mzungu', a white man, armed, of course, would be a good deterrent to any porter who contemplated slipping away with his valuable load. Desertion on expedition – on safari – was a constant risk.

Once they left the thick forests that lined the coast they entered a dry area of savannah, the grasslands badged with baobab trees and huge conical anthills. They made good progress in the first fortnight's march. Two asses died of tsetse fly and three porters deserted. Sidi Muzembi said this attrition rate was normal, if not better than normal. They were progressing westwards on the main up–down caravan route into the interior and they could pick up additional porters from passing caravans that were heading back down to the coast.

The procession inland started early, at first light, and they tended to halt in the early afternoon as the heat built and became insupportable. If they weren't at a village then loads were dropped and stacked, camp was made, firewood gathered and fires were lit. In Zanzibar, Cashel and Gilchrist-Baird had hired a Goanese servant and cook, called Joao, and it was he who would pitch their tents, lay out their camp beds, wash their clothes and cook their meals, and then pack everything up the following day.

Before dusk, Cashel would go out with Sosha – whose English was improving dramatically, thanks to their close contact – armed with fowling pieces and shoot partridge and guinea fowl and an antelope or two. The carcases were delivered to Sidi Muzembi who supervised the butchering and the distribution of cuts of meat to the porters and the soldiers.

They quickly became accustomed to their routine. Both wore

flannel shirts and trousers tucked into jackboots, and so-called wideawake hats, the generous brims affording good protection from the sun. On their third evening out, having dined on guinea fowl and rice, and enjoying a cigar and a glass of brandy by the fire built between their tents, Cashel stopped Gilchrist-Baird's endless anecdotalizing and told him to listen.

They could see the many scattered fires where the porters were gathered and they could hear them singing, a rhythmic chanting, a pattern of declaration and response, overlaid by the whoops and shrieks of animals and birds beyond the light cast by the flames – and everywhere the constant *creek-creek* of the crickets calling.

'Amazing, isn't it?' Cashel said.

'God, yes,' Gilchrist-Baird admitted. 'This is the life, Ross. Just think, a few months ago we were lounging around London without a clue.'

'Well, it's all very well for us, with our mules, our servants and our food and our well-equipped tents. I wouldn't like to be tramping through Africa lugging sixty pounds of baggage on my back.'

'It's their way of life, Ross. And they'll be paid,' Gilchrist-Baird said impatiently, reaching for the brandy bottle. 'They're not doing it as a favour to us, you know.'

'I know. But without them, and Sidi—' He stopped himself, realizing it was pointless.

'Anyway, cheers,' Gilchrist-Baird said. 'I think I'll turn in.'

Cashel lay in his camp bed, under his mosquito net, the embers of the fire visible through the thin canvas of the tent, Gilchrist-Baird's snores carrying to him faintly. Even though he was tired, Cashel initially found it hard to sleep, everything being so new and strange – and the future so blank. He lay there thinking back over his life, marvelling that it had brought him to this camp in unmapped Africa. *Terra incognita*. He thought of his mother and his guileless, unknowing childhood in Ireland. He skipped over Waterloo and focused his memories on Raphaella and her insolent, beguiling beauty. Raphaella . . . God,

Raphaella, Raphaella . . . What would she say if she knew where he was? Did she ever wonder about him? What had become of Cashel Ross after the fool rejected her? What if he hadn't abandoned her in Ravenna? What if he'd stayed? He groaned out loud. He wouldn't be lying here in a tent in Africa, that was for sure.

He thought again of this pattern he had discerned in his personal history: always moving on, leaving people he loved behind. But he hadn't discarded them, he insisted to himself. He hadn't abandoned Maeve and Nessa and left them to their fates. Circumstance intervened – as it had with Ignatz – and courses of action were forced upon him. There was nothing heedless or selfish in his nature, he told himself defensively. One day he would return, he was convinced, and make everything right.

But then, he reasoned, when you came to think about it, nothing in your life was really sure or preordained. Wandering through Africa wasn't that much different, in a sense, from wandering through London, or Paris, or Boston. You thought the road ahead was obvious and well marked but more often than not the destination you had so clearly in mind would never be reached. Never. Things got in the way. There were diversions, problems, changes of mind, changes of heart . . .

Stop. Think about Frannie, he urged himself. Frannie Broome, strong and self-confident. She at least had some idea of what he was up to, and where he might be, highly sceptical though she was, expressing herself in no uncertain terms when he had told her of the expedition and what was at stake. He had written to her just before leaving Zanzibar, giving her a more detailed idea of what they were doing and how long they would be away. He sighed and rolled over. Calm yourself, brain, he admonished. Stop churning away. Don't examine the what-ifs and the maybes, the wrong turnings and the dead ends in your life. That way madness lies.

They plodded on under the sun, day after day, eventually entering a hillier and more forested region that gave cooler nights with heavy, soaking dews. There were no roads as such, just trodden paths, some as wide as a road, some as if made by sheep or goats or deer, no more than a meandering ribbon of pounded earth dividing the grass. But now there were also unpleasant and unsightly encounters with half-eaten corpses or perfect, picked-clean skeletons by the pathways. Smallpox victims, Sidi Muzembi told them. But Cashel could see that some of the bodies were bound with lianas or had crude metal collars round their necks. Ah, yes, slaves, Sidi Muzembi admitted with a shrug. When they get sick it's easier to kill them than continue with the burden they would become. The column passed by and soon the bodies by the road became the props and decor of some ghoulish fever-dream. They were 'off the map', now, deep into the empty central space beyond the surveyed and measured shoreline of the continent. *Terra incognita* had arrived.

The humidity began to be more intense and the mosquito numbers increased exponentially. At one village ten porters disappeared overnight and they had to wait until another caravan passed and pay for more porters with Merikani cloth to replace them. These new porters, it turned out, had a strong aversion to the Kiswahili from the coast and, suddenly, fights would break out in camp, almost every night. Instead of the atavistic and moving chants, came angry shouts and imprecations and screams. Sidi Muzembi walked menacingly amongst the quarrelling factions, his gleaming broadsword drawn, speaking quietly, silencing all arguments.

About two hundred miles from the coast they began to climb through a series of mountain ranges, cutting through passes, only to find there was another range facing them. One day, a month into their journey, Cashel urged his mule forward up the length of the column to ask Gilchrist-Baird a question. He spotted him, riding as usual alongside the man bearing the Sultan's standard, but he seemed to be swaying in his saddle, almost as if he was falling asleep. Then he fell with a thud onto the ground. Everybody halted.

Cashel turned Gilchrist-Baird over. His face was bloodlessly pale and limned with sweat. He seemed unconscious but smelling salts revived him. He said he thought his skull would split with the headache he had and he was soon shivering with fever. A primitive litter – a kind of hammock – was rigged up by Sosha and, suspended from two poles, Gilchrist-Baird was carried to the next village by six porters.

They waited two weeks as Gilchrist-Baird remained trapped in the prison of his fever. Eventually he began to come round and was able to sup a little broth before lapsing into a laudanum-induced sleep.

Cashel took the decision to press on but progress was slow with Gilchrist-Baird still requiring his portable hammock. Fording anything larger than a stream became hazardous. Cashel stopped their progress for another week so Gilchrist-Baird could rest properly (five porters deserted), Cashel dosing him with quinine and laudanum syrup. He deliberately upped the dose one day and Gilchrist-Baird slept uninterrupted for forty-eight hours. However, the ploy seemed to work. Soon he could walk with a stick and felt well enough to continue on his mule, though Sidi Muzembi took the precaution of lashing him to his saddle so he wouldn't fall off if he lost consciousness again.

Cashel also felt fever begin to brush him from time to time – copious sweating, his face hot and red, a strange bitter and earthy taste in his mouth – the fit would last an hour or two and then pass, as if he had managed to shrug it off somehow.

One evening as they camped, Cashel sawing away at an antelope steak, Gilchrist-Baird drinking brandy and water, Cashel heard him begin to weep softly. Abruptly, he pulled himself together, controlling his emotions.

'I'm damned sorry about this, Ross. After twenty years in the Indian army I thought I was made of stronger stuff. But look at me – a milksop.'

'It's normal, G-B. Every *mzungu* gets African fever at some stage. I've had a few shivers and flarings-up myself. Felt rotten.'

'But we're losing time because of me. The rainy season's coming. We're meant to be a hundred miles further on.'

'Look, we've given ourselves two years,' Cashel said. 'A few days lost is neither here nor there.'

But Gilchrist-Baird's mood worsened even as his health stabilized somewhat. At one stage he even suggested that they call the expedition off, turn around and head back to the coast.

Cashel tried to hide his shock.

'What? And lose everything?' he said. 'All the money we've put into this? No, a thousand times no. We have to have something to show for all our endeavours, man. Something. Even for our own self-esteem.'

'Sorry, Ross. Sorry. Ignore me, please. It's this black mood I'm in – I can't seem to shake it off.'

Cashel poured him a brandy. They had brought forty-eight bottles in four heavy wooden cases, screwed down to prevent pilfering. They were going through their supplies at speed.

'When we reach Kazeh we'll rest up. Take a few weeks to get our strength back, resupply ourselves. Then we can discover the source of the Nile.'

Gilchrist-Baird managed a weak smile.

'Absolutely, old chap. Ignore my whingeing.'

Kazeh was an established trading post at a crossroads of several caravan routes, frequently used by slavers searching for their human commodity and hunters bringing ivory and hides down to the coast. There were several mud-walled houses, *tembes*, windowless, but with courtyards inside. There was even a kind of store run by an Indian merchant where provisions could be bartered for with beads and wire. Palms and fruit trees grew in the small vegetable gardens by the main houses. It was entirely lawless, unregulated and unsupervised and yet, bizarrely, Kazeh gave the impression of a stable community – in the middle of nowhere.

Cashel and Gilchrist-Baird were allocated a cool whitewashed *tembe*. In the courtyard there were orange and lemon trees. While Gilchrist-Baird rested, Cashel and Sosha, as translator, went to visit and pay their respects, and offer presents of beads, cloth and a couple of muskets, to the Sheikh of Kazeh, Snay Bin Amir. Cashel knew, after this long journey, that they were at the threshold of the lake region and he wanted to see if Sheikh Snay could tell them anything about this massive inland sea.

Sheikh Snay looked puzzled at the question.

'The sheikh say that there are three lakes, not one,' Sosha translated. 'Nyasa, Ujiji – and the big one, the most big – Ukerere.'

Three lakes? Cashel thought – initially cast down. So, three potential sources of the Nile, not one. He realized at once it would be impossible to visit them all – they could spend the rest of their lives tramping around Central Africa. It had taken them one hundred and twenty-eight days to reach Kazeh from the coast – more than four months, effectively.

'Ask him which lake is closest to Kazeh,' Cashel said.

Sosha and the sheikh conferred.

'Ukerere,' Sosha said. 'But to get there may be danger. He say better to go to Ujiji.'

Cashel felt a form of chronic inertia descend on him. Ujiji or Ukerere? Maybe he should toss a coin – but what if they ended up at the wrong lake? He suddenly had a nightmare vision of spending the rest of his life at Kazeh debating this very question.

He wandered back to their quarters to discuss the matter with Gilchrist-Baird, and found him out of his bed, crawling across the floor. He was raving and, once again, sweating heavily. It looked as though the fever had returned. Cashel hauled him back to his bed, wet a cloth and laid it across his boiling brow.

'I can't feel my legs, Ross. I'm paralysed.'

'Just keep calm – you'll be fine. The fever's returned, that's all.'

Another two weeks passed before Gilchrist-Baird felt well enough to take a few tottering steps around their courtyard. But even with this improvement he seemed to have developed a new affliction – he was finding it difficult to swallow and painful to speak. Cashel asked him to open his mouth and with the aid of a lit candle and a magnifying glass he was able to discern a fresh ulcer on the back of his tongue, about the size of a shilling, and, so it seemed, very inflamed.

Gilchrist-Baird couldn't eat, of course, and had to wash his mouth out every hour with hot salted water which had the side effect of generating a near-intolerable thirst. The ulcer then sundered and Cashel dabbed tincture of iodine on the suppurating crater. By this time Gilchrist-Baird had grown emaciated as a result of his long experience of fever. The portly, robust figure who had sat opposite Cashel in the coffee room of the Garrick Club was now a starveling scarecrow who looked as if he were dressed in the borrowed clothes of a far larger man.

Another week went by and the ulcer seemed to be healing. Gilchrist-Baird managed to eat a cold maize porridge but, he now complained, he had lost all feeling in his feet. He could walk but experienced only acute pins and needles. Cashel ordered him back to bed. He had another horrible vision of his future life in Kazeh – nursing Gilchrist-Baird, year upon year, as one ailment succeeded another.

They had been in Kazeh for some two months now, and Cashel felt the same familiarity with the place as he had in New Banbury. In the evening he had developed the habit of going for a stroll around the settlement, cigar in hand, as the light faded and the first bats began to flit around the gardens and *tembes*. His thoughts flitted about also, like the bats, as if unwilling to determine any cogent direction, basically leaving him in a state of irritating uncertainty, constantly wondering what he should do next.

Then, turning round the corner of a house, he saw the astonishing sight of four camels. He drew closer and saw a number of men in flowing *thobes* and *kufiyas* arguing with Sheikh Snay. Beyond them, sitting silently on the ground, were a group of about thirty Africans, virtually naked, young men and young women, yoked to each other by ropes and thin lengths of wood, some with chains linked to metal collars round their necks. The air above them was dark with humming flies. Sheikh Snay spotted him and peremptorily waved him away. Cashel turned and walked back quickly to their house, very disturbed by what he had seen. He knew, of course, that the slave trade between Africa and the Arabian and Persian Gulfs was still in full active and profitable business. He had seen the corpses by the track on the way to Kazeh, and Zanzibar was full of slaves; they made up half its population. There had been a treaty banning the trade signed by the Sultan in 1845 – largely as a result of Consul Hamerton's energies and influence – but it was utterly ineffective. How did you curtail a centuries-long history of slavery in Central Africa from a small island off the coast with an eighteen-gun frigate?

But that sobering vision of the slavers and their captives gave Cashel new energy. He couldn't sit month after month in Kazeh waiting for Gilchrist-Baird either to die or to regain some form of reasonable health. There had already been some sharp, drenching thunderstorms in the last few days indicating the imminent arrival of the rainy season. Once the season was fully established, the journey back to the coast would be ten times more laborious and hazardous. No, he thought – he needed to do something. He would assemble a small party and go himself to the closer lake, Ukerere. At least something would be achieved; at least there would be something to write about.

He sought out Sidi Muzembi – who was quite happy being paid to idle at Kazeh – and told him his new plan. A small column would attract less attention and could move faster. He would need perhaps four Baluchi soldiers and maybe a dozen porters. Sosha could come as guide and interpreter. With a bit of luck, he could be there and back in a month or so. Time enough for Gilchrist-Baird to recuperate or at least have a proper litter constructed that would safely carry him back to the coast and Zanzibar.

It took Cashel and his reduced expedition three weeks to march from Kazeh to Lake Ukerere. The country they traversed, heading north, was quite widely populated and most nights they were able to bivouac in or close to a village. Sosha would approach the headman with the usual offerings of cloth, brass wire and beads and a welcome was almost always assured, as soon as it was perceived that the *mzungu* was not in the slavery business. At noon each day, Cashel measured their progress with sextant and chronometer. Their route led them northwards through scantily forested shrubland, following the paths that led from *kraal* to *kraal*. Then, nineteen days into their journey, Cashel noticed a change in the landscape: taller trees, more foliage and undergrowth. The lake must be close, he reasoned. And then he saw it.

He came over the rise of a low hill and in front of him saw what he could only describe as a sea – an ocean, even – stretching ahead of him to a distant horizon. There was no sign of a further shore. He stopped abruptly and consciously tried to analyse the emotions he was feeling at confronting this prospect, this unique panorama in front of him. He took out his notebook and, with a pencil, scribbled down his thoughts:

3rd December 1856

The first sighting of Nyanza Ukerere at 4.27 p.m. Before me lies a grey, endless expanse of water stretching to its own distant horizon on all sides, north, east and west. There are a few hilly wooded islands, offshore. Flocks of birds fly low over the wind-ruffled wavelets. A small village about a mile away on the shoreline. Canoes with fishermen. The body of water is so vast that no sense of its extension can be posited or imagined. I tell myself that I am the first European witness, the first white man to gaze upon this huge inland sea and to establish its position on the map of Africa and verify its height above sea level. I feel a strange humbling as I contemplate this phenomenon – which is not a phenomenon to the thousands of Africans who live on its shore, of course – just as the Serpentine is not a phenomenon to Londoners nor Willow Creek pond a phenomenon to me. However, the map of Africa will be altered for ever and I will be the man who has brought about this tremendous, unforgettable discovery.

He stopped writing, his heart reverberating. Calm down, calm down. Plenty of time for more philosophizing later, he thought. He led the column through the trees to the village below. Sosha talked to the headman, offered cloth, wire and beads and was given permission to make camp. Cashel immediately had a fire built, placed a tin can of water on the griddle above it and, when the water was bubbling, placed his thermometer in the can, then removed it a few seconds later. Water boiled at a lower temperature the higher you were above sea level – the lower air pressure affected the boiling point. It was a simple but precise way of measuring altitude. He looked at the calibrations on the thermometer and saw that the simmering water was at a temperature of 203 degrees Fahrenheit. At sea level water boiled at 212 degrees. A difference of 9 degrees meant that the lake was approximately 4,000 feet above sea level.

He closed his eyes and felt a lightness in his head as if he were about to faint. He knew the consequences of this measurement. The Nile had been navigated far south from Cairo – over 2,000 miles south – as far as Gondokoro (4.9 N, 31.6 E) where the river ceases to be navigable. Gondokoro had an elevation above sea level of 2,000 feet. If Lake Ukerere did indeed feed the White Nile then this significant difference of altitude was crucial evidence. No, he told himself, restraining his excitement, better than crucial – utterly compelling evidence.

He and Sosha went back to meet the headman of the village – which he now learned was called Mk'hali. The headman was elderly, with grey hair, many silver bangles on his thin wrists and very few teeth. He had two broad parallel scars on each cheek. Sosha asked him what was the size of the lake. The headman made a strange gesture, rolling his hand over and over, then clicking his fingers twice, then again rolling his hand over and over. He did this several times before speaking.

'He says there is no end to this sea,' Sosha translated. 'He has never seen an end to it in all his life. They do not go far out into the water. They stay by the land. They fear to be away from the land, too far.'

Over the next few days, Cashel and Sosha walked ten miles in each direction from the village and from no vantage point or promontory could any sign of a 'further shore' be discerned. Cashel made drawings and charted a rudimentary map of the lake

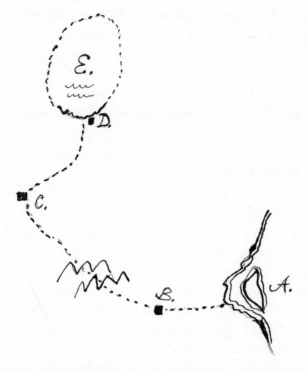

The Gilchrist-Baird/Ross Expedition to the Lake Regions of Central Africa,
1856–7. A. Zanzibar. B. Zungomero. C. Kazeh. D. Village of Mk'hali. E. Lake
Ukerere (dimensions unknown).

coast they had traversed. He realized that there was nothing more
they could realistically achieve here. In fact, the great and enduring discovery of the Gilchrist-Baird and Ross Expedition had now
been made.

The day before they planned to leave, a small party of Omani
slavers passed by, heading south in search of their human quarry.
Cashel invited their leader to eat with them and gave him some
coloured cloth. Sosha, who spoke passable Arabic, was instructed
to ask key questions. Yes, the man said, he had often journeyed
down the eastern side of the lake – it took him many weeks, but
he had no idea of its true size. He had never seen the further
shore – in fact, he doubted if there was one, so immense was the
expanse of water. Cashel showed him the map he had drawn and

extended the eastern shoreline by approximately two hundred miles.

'Ask him if he has seen a river flowing northward out of the lake.'

Sosha did so and the Omani nodded. He pointed to a place on the redrawn map. Cashel marked it with a cross.

'The Nasaniki river, they call it,' Sosha translated. 'Here there are . . .' He paused, not knowing the English word. 'Where the water is falling down.'

'Waterfalls.' Cashel wrote 'Falls' by the cross. 'Is he sure?'

'Yes. He has seen them many times.'

Cashel wrote – with a little surge of excited vainglory – 'Ross Falls' on his map. The family name would go down in history, after all.

The return journey to Kazeh took them longer than the outward one. Three porters absconded and heavy rain slowed their progress. On their last day they covered eighteen miles and arrived back at Kazeh in the late afternoon. They had been away for forty-three days in total. As they approached, the Baluchi guards fired their muskets to announce their return.

Sidi Muzembi walked out to greet them. Cashel was slightly alarmed not to see Gilchrist-Baird.

'Where is the *sahib mzungu*?' he asked. 'Is he still unwell?'

'He is dead, sir,' Sidi Muzembi said impassively. 'He is dead for twenty days.'

Gilchrist-Baird's body had been embalmed and was tightly wrapped in one of their waterproofed blankets secured with bands of brass wire. The thin bundle looked like the mummified remains of a child or a youth, about four feet long. Then Sidi Muzembi explained that the legs had been folded tightly back at the knee (cutting the tendons) to make the body easier to carry. Only two porters would be required, he said. It was also very light, being very wasted, anyway, and emptied of its innards and organs. Cashel could pick up the cloth package that used to be Deveron Gilchrist-Baird with one hand.

★

Cashel waited until late January – hoping the rains would abate – before setting out on the return journey to the coast. He was cast down by Gilchrist-Baird's death. He had come to like the man, appreciating his bluff, guileless personality, his easy enthusiasms. Pitiless Africa had done for him and the loss of his partner seemed to underscore Cashel's dark premonitions about the journey – its cursed nature. First Ignatz, now Gilchrist-Baird. But at the same time, underneath the gloom, he couldn't suppress the current of quiet exhilaration he was feeling – the expedition hadn't been entirely cursed, because the discovery of the huge lake changed everything. He wished that G-B, as he had come to think of him, could have survived long enough to learn that the expedition had achieved its objectives – and, perversely, he found himself annoyed that the man had gone and died before he could be informed of their good fortune. Perhaps such triumphant news would have stimulated recovery. In the event, the rains didn't abate, and he decided to initiate the journey anyway.

It was a much-reduced caravan but well supplied. They had some thirty porters plus the original Baluchi armed escort and their camp followers, with a dozen asses and a small herd of goats, roped together, as potential sustenance if the rains made it difficult to shoot game. Cashel now led the column with the standard-bearer. The small cloth and brass bundle that was Gilchrist-Baird's remains, looking like a giant cocoon, was suspended from a pole carried by two porters directly behind him.

They made good going despite the regular drenching thunderstorms and crossed through the serried ranges of the Usambara mountains without incident, even quickening their pace as they made their way through the foothills down to Zungomero. Here they were obliged to halt for some time as Cashel had a recurrent bout of malaria. After a few weeks he was still weak and feverish but decided he was well enough to press on for the coast, regardless.

It was on the sixty-seventh day of their journey to the coast that the disaster occurred.

The column arrived at a ford – a normally insubstantial one on an unnamed tributary of the Kisangani river along whose valley they were making their way. But the rains had sent the usually placid shallow river into spate and the body of water was turbulent and twice as wide as normal, some thirty yards or so across. Sidi Muzembi, clinging to a mule, had managed to make it to the far bank and soon a rope was stretched over the torrent for the porters to hold on to as they waded through the chest-high water. Sosha, in the meantime, had cut down timber to make a raft for Cashel who was too weak to get across on his own. The raft was solid – half a dozen substantial logs roped together and further secured by the remains of their brass wire. Cashel was placed on the raft with Gilchrist-Baird's body, and the portmanteaus containing their personal possessions. Four porters steadied the corners and they pushed off with due caution into the rushing brown water, Sosha following closely behind.

Halfway across, one of the porters screamed that he had seen a crocodile. He let go of his corner and the raft, thus partially released, tilted viciously up in the current, throwing Cashel, Gilchrist-Baird's remains and their leather cases into the water. As Cashel went under he felt his collar being grabbed and he was hauled to the surface by Sosha. The raft had bucked itself free of the other porters' grasp and could be seen surging down to the confluence with the Kisangani.

With Sosha's help, Cashel made it to the far bank. He recovered himself enough to order Sidi Muzembi to send an immediate search party down to the Kisangani, in case Gilchrist-Baird's body or any of their baggage could be retrieved.

The search party returned at dusk with two boxes and a small trunk. There had been no sign of the body. It was only then that Cashel realized that his personal attaché case with all his notebooks was also missing. Everything he had recorded and noted about the discovery of Nyanza Ukerere had gone.

Cashel arrived back in Zanzibar on 17th May 1857 on board a dhow chartered from Bagamoyo, having been away for just over a year. He had made a good recovery from his fever but his mood was low and growing darker as he thought about the consequences of the loss of his notes, maps and documents. He cared more about them than the disappearance of Gilchrist-Baird's embalmed and mummified body.

In truth, that was something of a blessing as he had not welcomed the prospect of transporting the body's husk back to England and delivering the parched remains to Gilchrist-Baird's grieving family. He knew that it was imperative that he try and recreate, as best he could, all the details of his journey from Kazeh to Ukerere and back. He was confident he could remember a great deal – his excitement had imprinted every detail on his memory; he wasn't going to forget names, dates, facts and figures – and he would not contemplate a return to England until everything was properly written up once more. This information was unique and his alone – only he, Cashel Ross, could confidently speak of the great lake lying at the centre of Africa.

However, Lieutenant Colonel Hamerton told him the unwelcome news that two other Englishmen, who had arrived some months before and were staying at the consulate, were also actively planning an expedition to the lake region, funded by the Geographical Society of London, no less. Cashel was instantly wary and alarmed – but still, they hadn't embarked on their journey yet and for a good while, surely, only he occupied the field, so to speak. He had at least a year to steal a march on his competitors.

Hamerton's health was manifestly worse, it was very apparent, his jaundiced skin and eyes making a stark contrast with his white hair and whiskers. Moribund or not, he always made an appearance at dinnertime and smoked, ate and drank as if there were nothing to be alarmed about.

Cashel settled into his former quarters in the consulate and the first thing he did was to shave his beard off. He felt, contra-Samson, a strange rejuvenation in the act. His face was gaunt from the privations of the long journey and the illnesses he'd suffered but seeing himself as he always used to be – beardless – was strangely comforting: it was as if he had discarded a disguise. He wrote to the hospital at Cape Town asking about Ignatz's fate, requesting that any reply be forwarded to his bank in London. He was in no hurry to receive bad news.

Cashel met the two Englishmen before dinner – both, coincidentally, were officers in the Indian army. There was a Captain Richard Burton of the Bombay army and a Captain John Speke of the Bengal. Burton was in his mid-thirties, Cashel estimated, and was the more impressive figure, swarthily charismatic and with a drooping brigand's moustache and deep scars on both cheeks. Speke, five or six years younger, was tall and fair, diffident, with a great bushy, corn-coloured beard, as if he wanted to hide his features behind it, in an attempt to conceal anything that made him individual and memorable. He was all beard, Cashel thought – a walking beard.

Over dinner, the two men were naturally full of questions and Cashel was as circumspect as possible, happy to describe their journey as a frustrating series of setbacks and disappointments, where nothing of any note was achieved owing to Gilchrist-Baird's almost constant ill-health.

It turned out that Burton and Speke had arrived in Zanzibar at the end of the previous year and had been unaware of the Ross and Gilchrist-Baird expedition that had preceded them. They could barely hide their satisfaction as Cashel listed their conspicuous lack of achievements. They had made it to Kazeh, that was about it. Gilchrist-Baird had then fallen ill and died and he, Ross, had struggled home. Nothing to show for a year's hardship and endeavour.

'What about the lake?' Burton asked. 'The huge one – eight hundred miles long. You must have seen the Erhardt map. Any sign? Any talk of it?'

'There is actually no single big lake, so it seems,' Cashel said carefully, thinking fast, and realizing that Burton and Speke would swiftly find out the reality for themselves. 'There are in fact three, we were told.'

'*Three?*' Speke's voice was shrill with surprise. 'Are you sure?'

'I can only recount what we were told,' Cashel said. 'I wish I had more detail.'

'You had damned bad luck, Ross,' Burton said. 'Perhaps we can solve the mystery.'

Cashel smiled ruefully and said nothing.

'Do you know of a man called Cooley?' Burton asked.

'No.'

'He wrote a terrible book, but he was very adamant about the "single sea" theory.'

'And the sheikh at Kazeh was very adamant that there were three lakes,' Cashel said.

'Can you believe an Omani slaver?' Burton pointed a finger at Cashel as if he were on trial.

'Well, he does actually live in the region,' Cashel said. 'None of us does. Neither does Mr Cooley.'

'True, true,' Burton conceded. 'You see, I think the whole thing arises out of a corruption of African vocabulary.' Burton now seemed to be flushed with new enthusiasm. 'The word "Nyanza" simply means water. And this giant lake was called "N'yassi" by Erhardt. Nyanza-N'yassi. Same word. You're basically saying "Water-water" – hence this notion of a vast single lake.'

'Yes, I see,' Cashel said vaguely.

Burton continued his monologue, adjoining the names of other German missionaries – Krapf, Iseiler, Müleizen – then various ancients – Pliny, Ptolemy, Strabo – and Cashel suddenly began to tire under his onslaught of words. The force of Burton's manic personality was very wearing and he wondered how the silent Speke would cope with him over the months and years an expedition demanded. Burton, Cashel realized, was an example of pure, unalloyed self-regard – now he was talking of Daniel Defoe and Marinus of Tyre – someone for whom other people really didn't exist, or were just shadows on the fringe of his own blazing luminescence. This kind of solipsism, this raging indifference to others, was almost fascinating. But Cashel had to stop the flow somehow, so he interrupted.

'What do you think of all this, Captain Speke?'

'What? Well, I'm hoping to bag some decent specimens of local wildlife,' Speke said.

Burton laughed, a little wildly.

'Jack Speke, here, is never happier than when he is killing defenceless creatures.'

'That's unfair, Burton.'

Burton grinned unpleasantly and turned to Hamerton.

'May I request some more of your excellent port?'

Hamerton pushed the decanter over in Burton's direction and asked to be excused. Burton talked and talked, exhausting everyone. After Hamerton's departure, Speke went to bed and then Cashel slipped away. He imagined Burton haranguing the salt-cellar and the empty decanter of port, perfectly happy to have them as an audience. He was clearly an intelligent man, fiercely intelligent – but to be confined in a room with him . . .

Cashel spent his mornings in the so-called 'library' of the consulate. There were some tables and chairs set out and a few dozen heat-swollen volumes looking lonely on empty shelves, gifts of previous visitors. But the room was cool, the wide windows opened onto the sea and breezes circulated before noon. Cashel was writing almost as an automaton, forcing himself to recall everything about the expedition and his personal journey to Nyanza Ukerere. He remembered the name of the village where they made camp and he was able to draw an accurate map of the twenty miles of shoreline they had surveyed. The evidence of the boiling-point thermometer was absolutely crucial – and unanswerable, he would claim.

He stretched and stood up, feeling a sharp pressure in his bowels, and went downstairs to the inner courtyard where there were two privies and emptied himself, holding his nose against the vile stench. He worried that he might have a form of mild dysentery – he felt a near-irresistible urge to shit every two hours or so. He sat there for a moment on the rough wooden seat, recovering himself from the spasm, his breeches round his

Map of Lake Ukerere (observed by Speke). A. Kazeh. B. Mk'hali village.
C. Supposed position of Ross Falls, source of the White Nile. D. Lake Ukerere
(approximate dimensions).

ankles. He touched his forehead with his fingertips – hot,
sweaty – but that was normal in Zanzibar. He didn't feel feverish, which was the main thing. Perhaps the food they were
served at the consulate didn't agree with him – Hamerton liked
everything very heavily peppered, claiming that pepper killed
noxious germs.

Instead of returning to the library he went to see Mr Frost, the
apothecary, and told him what was wrong. Frost suggested a
patent powder to be dissolved in water and drunk before retiring –
guaranteed to slow the movements. He went into his dispensary
to measure the dose and wrap it in a spill of paper. While he
waited Cashel sat looking at Frost's pet monkey that was sitting
on top of the oil lamp on the desk. It was a young male Vervet
monkey, Frost had told him. It perched on the lamp, eating a date,

its long tail twitching. Cashel looked into its small black face, and its round eyes, somewhat fascinated by the tiny fingers, with their tinier fingernails, clutching the date. Bizarrely, Vervet monkeys had turquoise testicles and a bright scarlet penis – and everything was on show, naturally. Why would you want a pet with these lurid genitalia? Cashel wondered. The monkey had a greenish hue to its otherwise grey fur. It was a sweet, docile thing, he supposed – always interesting to look at. Then it urinated on Frost's desk.

Frost came back with his powder and Cashel thanked him and climbed the stairs back to the library.

Captain Speke was standing at Cashel's work table, bent over, looking at his notes. He turned when he heard Cashel enter.

'Ah, Ross. How do? Good morning. I was looking for some reading matter – couldn't help noticing the map you'd drawn. Fascinating.'

'Just trying to illustrate the wilder speculations we heard.'

'Right.'

Cashel moved a notebook so it covered the map.

'What were these speculations, as a matter of interest?' Speke asked casually, moving away.

'They came thick and fast. All very weird and wonderful.' Cashel tapped his notebook. 'I'm thinking of writing a book, you see.'

'Excellent idea. Wish I could write. That's Burton's forte.'

They looked at each other, smiling.

'Well, I'll leave you to it,' Speke said and wandered out. He seemed less diffident when Burton wasn't around, Cashel thought.

That evening Cashel and Hamerton dined alone as Speke and Burton were at the docks supervising the loading of their stores and equipment on board the Sultan's corvette.

'I think I'd better see them safely ashore,' Hamerton said, 'given your mishaps.'

'Is the Geographical Society paying for everything?'

'I fancy Captain Speke is making a sizeable contribution.'

Hamerton told Cashel of Burton and Speke's previous

explorations in Africa. Both men were lucky to be alive after being attacked by Somali tribesmen. Speke was stabbed over a dozen times before he made his escape.

'Burton got a spear right through his face. In one cheek and out the other, missing the tongue, luckily. Hence the scars.'

'My God,' Cashel said, trying to imagine what that must have been like. 'Does that explain his peculiar nature? I've never known a man talk so much and so aggressively.'

'Funny that, isn't it?' Hamerton said. 'You can be damned intelligent – he speaks twenty languages, you know – and the world's biggest bore at the same time.'

They laughed. Hamerton winced and reached for more port.

'What about Speke?' Cashel asked.

'I just can't make him out. Can't fathom him. He's no match for Burton, that's for sure. Strange fellow.'

The next morning, while Cashel was working at his notes in the library, a consulate servant came and told him there was a person at the front door who wished to speak with him. Cashel went down to see who it was, wondering if it might be Sosha, whom he had left behind in Bagamoyo. But at the door there was nobody there. He stepped out into the courtyard and called Sosha's name but there was no reply. Strange. The guard at the gate told him no one had entered the compound. How very odd, Cashel thought and went back into the consulate and up to the library.

When he arrived at the library door Speke was leaving. Cashel stood to one side and Speke strode past him with a brisk good morning, a book in his hand. Cashel quickly looked at his papers – they were slightly rearranged, not as he had left them. The map which had been securely concealed by his notebook was now half-visible. Speke, he realized, had been responsible for the little subterfuge of the person at the front door – giving him enough time to have a proper look at what Cashel had written. And the map, of course. Cashel felt a dark surge of anger as he looked at his map of Lake Ukerere. Distances had been noted, the boiling point of water, coordinates listed. Dull Jack Speke was not so stupid, it seemed.

Cashel stood on the main terrace of the consulate, some twenty feet above the small breakers furling onto the beach below, and watched the Sultan's corvette, the *Artémise* – with Burton and Speke on board – sailing slowly out of the harbour towards the mainland. Good riddance, he thought, wishing them ill-fortune. Then, as if in rebuke for his mean spirits, he felt a sharp spasm run through his bowels. He thought he should visit Mr Frost and ask him for more of his magic powder – it had seemed to calm his mild dysentery, if that was what he was suffering from.

He wandered along the wide terrace to the end where Frost had his consulting room and dispensary. The little Vervet monkey was capering about, a fine chain around its neck secured to one of the balusters. It came scampering up to him as if looking for food, Cashel thought, and he shooed it away.

He knocked on Frost's door but there was no answer. He'd come back later, Cashel thought, and anyway the intestinal crisis seemed over. Wandering back to the terrace edge he rested his hands on the balustrade – the *Artémise* had made open sea and its mainsails were being unfurled. Perhaps he should wish Burton and Speke *bon voyage*, he thought – fellow explorers, after all, who would be exposed to the same dangers and privations . . . But he was still resentful of Speke's petty act of espionage. Let them get on with it as best they could, he decided – he'd save his good wishes for someone more deserving.

He turned away and accidentally stood on the monkey's tail. It gave a screech of pain and bit his ankle, its sharp teeth penetrating his flannel trousers. Cashel aimed a kick at it but missed and it scuttled away. He pulled down his stocking and saw the blood-beads on his left Achilles tendon where the teeth had broken the skin. No real damage. He licked his fingers and rubbed spittle on the puncture marks. Little bastard.

That evening at dinner – just him and Frost, Hamerton having gone with Burton and Speke on the *Artémise* to see them safely off – Cashel could feel his ankle throbbing painfully. In the morning he could see that the wound was inflamed and somewhat swollen. He went to see Frost, who was unsympathetic, very much on his monkey's side, but gave him a poultice to bring the swelling down. The next day his foot was a dark purply-black and he felt nauseous and dizzy.

Frost told him to go back to bed and elevate his foot on some pillows in a position higher than his heart. He took a small bottle out of his doctor's bag and tipped a few drops of dark liquid into a glass of water.

'Take a swig of this from time to time – it'll ease any pain,' he said.

'What is it?'

'It's called Kendal Black Drop. The best – a type of laudanum, you know.'

Cashel drank the decoction and it quickly made him drowsy; he slept or dozed most of the day. In the evening he was awakened by dull but unignorable pains in his stomach and down his left side. Frost gave him more Black Drop and that allowed him to sleep through the night. But the next morning the stomach cramps were worse and his bitten foot was breaking out in small crusty ulcers, gleaming with pus. Frost bandaged his foot and increased the dose of Black Drop.

'It's a miracle worker, Ross. You'll sweat it out in a few days, mark my words.'

'Your filthy pet ape has poisoned me.'

'Nonsense – I've been bitten by the little fellow a dozen times.'

But now Cashel developed a fever, far worse than the malarial ones that he'd experienced on the expedition. He felt raging heat flaring up, in and around his body, and his bed was soon soaked in sweat. Then he began to lose track of time, not knowing whether one day or three had past, or which night he awoke, doubled up with agonizing, contorting cramps in his abdomen. His whole left leg was now discoloured, the skin hard with a dark brown crust that cracked and oozed blood when he put any weight on it. Only Kendal Black Drop provided any release or oblivion.

However, in that state of unconsciousness he began to see visions. He saw Raphaella, posing naked, promiscuously, and

Burton, of all people, drawing her on a sketchpad – the artist and his model. Then Ignatz came to him, weeping, pointing out the dead, pale bodies of Bríd, Maeve and Nessa, lying on the grass by Willow Creek pond. He saw Frannie, also, sitting on a bollard at the end of the Long Wharf in Boston harbour waving goodbye and calling his name – yet all the time he was standing one pace behind her. When he woke, the memory of these delusions began to trouble him more than the pain he was feeling. He was convinced they were an augury of his impending death. At one stage he grabbed Frost by his lapels and shouted at him, demanding to know if in fact he was dying. Frost, of course, declined to answer – and just fed him more Black Drop.

Cashel became convinced that his death was imminent. He was in constant pain. His navel had become a suppurating ulcer as if the venom and corruption within him was seeking an exit. He felt he was lying on hot coals, every movement provoking new agonies, as if his bones were on fire. Faces hovered over him – Frost, Speke, Bríd, Frannie, Ignatz, Raphaella, always Raphaella, come to say goodbye, he was convinced. Perhaps, he thought in his delirium, Africa was claiming him in the way it had claimed Gilchrist-Baird. Had they crossed some invisible border in their explorations, innocently violated some taboo, and that's why they were subject to this strange and deadly malediction? He felt so weak he couldn't raise a hand – and then spearing pain flashed through his gut as if he was being stabbed by red-hot daggers.

Gasping for breath, crying out for more Black Drop, he opened his eyes and saw Frost walking away from his bed to speak to someone standing at the door of the room.

'He's finished,' Cashel clearly heard him say. 'He won't last the night.'

FROM THE *LONDON TIMES*

IN MEMORIAM. As reported from the latest despatch from H.M. Consul in Zanzibar, East Africa. The recent expedition into the Lake Regions

of the African interior, in search of the source of the River Nile, undertaken in 1856 by Captain Deveron Gilchrist-Baird and Lieutenant
Cashel Ross (both officers of the 5th Madras (European) Light Infantry),
has sadly resulted in the demise of both men. Mr Gilchrist-Baird's body
was lost somewhere near the native township of Zungomero. Lt. Ross
departed this earth at the British consulate, Zanzibar on 22nd June 1857.

13

Ignatz Vlac hammered the carpet tacks into the corner of the poster and stepped back to examine his handiwork. The poster was in bold black type on bright yellow paper – ideally eye-catching, Cashel thought.

> 'HOW I DISCOVERED THE SOURCE OF THE NILE'
> *A Public Lecture*
> *by*
> *Lt. Cashel Ross (ex-5th Madras Light Infantry)*
> *Honoree of the WATERLOO MEDAL*
> *Shadwell Hall, High Holborn*
> *15th December 1863*
> *At 6 o'clock promptly*
> *Admission 1/-*

Cashel helped position the sandwich board on Ignatz's broad shoulders, then circled him, checking on the impression made, fore and aft.

'It looks very good,' Cashel said. 'You're right, Ignatz – the yellow is very striking.'

They were standing in the small courtyard of Shadwell Hall (converted from a Methodist church). It could seat a hundred easily, though Cashel's audiences for his public lecture were rarely higher than thirty or so. But there was, at least, always an audience, and maybe this sandwich-board idea of Ignatz's would bring a larger one. The public enthusiasm for tales of African exploration was very marked – it was keeping him in funds.

'Do a couple of hours up and down Oxford Street,' Cashel said. 'I've got to go and collect those photographs.'

Cashel watched Ignatz set off and looked at his fob. He had

three hours before the talk was due to begin. Plenty of time for his errands.

He sauntered down to the photographer's studio on the Strand. He had had the image taken the week before, because he wanted to send a photograph of himself to Frannie and, while he was at it, to Maeve and Nessa. Ignatz had suggested they could pin a photograph on the poster or even sell reproductions of the visiting-card version to those people who attended the lecture. Sixpence a time – all things to be considered.

He climbed the stairs to the studio on the first floor. The photographer was called Norman Prendergast, a thin, enthusiastic man who had precise ideas about portrait-photography, always insisting on natural light – there was a large skylight in the studio – absolutely no re-touching and no props, no potted plants or faithful dogs, with the sitter posed in front of the plainest backdrop, grey or black tarpaulins. Cashel was curious to see the result – surprisingly, it was the first time he had been photographed, and he was intrigued to see if the picture matched the image of himself that a mirror provided. Everyone seemed to have a photograph of themselves nowadays, it was all the fashion.

Prendergast's assistant, his daughter, Miss Prendergast – a slight, diffident presence – asked him to take a seat. Everything would be ready in ten minutes, she said, apologizing profusely. They were rather overwhelmed with business. Cashel was happy to wait. Might he smoke a cigar? Please do, sir.

Cashel sat down on a creaking cane chair and lit his cigar with a lucifer. He wasn't at all nervous about the upcoming lecture – he had given dozens in London and the South of England since his return from Zanzibar – yet he felt a kind of heartburn in his chest. The lecture notion had been one of his brighter ideas, he now thought, and it provided him with a steady income. His slight unease, he recognized, came from the prospect of reuniting himself with his daughters through this new medium of photography. For the girls an image of their father would be better than twenty heartfelt letters, he reasoned. A letter including a photograph would perhaps change everything; they would see their father plain; remember the man they had known during the happy days at Willow Creek, albeit somewhat trans-figured by the years and the recent privations he had undergone in Africa. He was a gaunter, leaner figure since then, that was true. Still, he had to try – they were his children, after all, and he didn't want to lose them, or lose their remembrance of him.

But this acid burn in his chest now seemed to prompt his old pains, somehow. He felt a tightening in his gut and, with that, the particular ache – dull but insistent – that he referred to as his 'Zanzibar' pain. He placed his palm on his stomach and massaged himself gently through his waistcoat.

He removed his wallet from his coat pocket to count how many pound notes he had on him and as he did so the yellowed cutting from *The Times* about the news of his death fluttered to the floor.* He picked it up and read it for the thousandth time. 'Lt. Ross departed this earth . . .' It was not given to many to read the announcement of their death, which was why he always car-ried the cutting with him – a perverse good-luck charm, he thought.

Frost, the apothecary, was to blame. In Hamerton's absence he was perforce the acting consul and, knowing there was a boat home leaving that night for Aden – and that any news from Zan-zibar would otherwise take months to reach England – he decided to pre-empt mortal confirmation and, confidently assuming Cashel would be dead by the morning, wrote his swift obituary, placing it in the official consulate mailbag that would in due course be delivered to the Foreign Office.

In fact, Cashel was still alive the next morning but the boat had sailed. However, Frost seemed confident that his prognosis would be verified within a day or two and Cashel noticed that, when he still hadn't died a week later, the apothecary started exhibiting a cool irritation towards him. It was as if Cashel's

* This cutting has survived.

survival was a form of personal rebuke and made him look foolish and unprofessional.

A month later when Cashel began to take his first steps on the
consulate terrace, Frost was compelled to send another message
to the Foreign Office admitting his mistake. Lieutenant Ross was
in fact very much alive, H.M. Consul in Zanzibar apologized for
any distress incurred, deeply regretted the confusion etc., etc.

Yes, he was alive but the poison in his body, in his blood –
whatever it was – lingered on, if not so virulently. From time to
time he was incapacitated for some hours by violent stomach
cramps that almost made him cry out. There was blood in his
urine and faeces, also – Frost couldn't explain why this should be
the case – and the only palliative that worked was Kendal Black
Drop.

During his illness Cashel had lost almost fifty pounds of his
body weight. He was very easily fatigued and knew his convalescence would be a long one, but made gradual progress, slowly
regaining his strength and starting to put on some weight. He
was able to spend a few hours each day in the consulate's library
writing up his account of the Ross and Gilchrist-Baird Expedition. He also sent many letters – to Frannie, to his brothers, to
Gilchrist-Baird's parents, and to the Geographical Society of London hinting pointedly at his discovery of the great lake – but
deliberately not specifying – and implying that he had conclusive
proof of where the source of the Nile was to be found. He would
be more than happy, he suggested, to present his more detailed
findings to the Society when he returned to London. He received
no reply.

In fact he spent almost a full year in Zanzibar regaining his
strength before feeling confident enough to survive the long
journey home. He took a ship to Aden where he hoped to pick up
a P & O liner en route from Bombay to London via the Suez isth-
mus. Once in Aden he had to wait another frustrating two months
before he was provided with a medical certificate confirming he
was fit to travel. The so-called 'overland' route from Suez to Alex-
andria was now far easier, what with the new railway line, but he

didn't arrive back in London until January 1859. Somewhat to his astonishment he realized he had been away from home for more than three years.

The best news he had on his return was in a letter from Buckley which was waiting for him at his bank and invited him to stay at the rectory at Claverleigh 'for as long as you wish'. Buckley added cryptically in a postscript that, 'You will find an old friend here, keen to reunite with you.' Ben Smart? Cashel thought. Someone from America? Frannie? Surely not . . .

Very curious, he telegraphed Buckley with the date and time of his arrival and when he stepped down from the train at Lewes station he was astounded to be met by none other than Ignatz Vlac. Cashel threw convention aside and embraced him warmly, both of them unashamedly tearful.

Ignatz had also made a slow recovery in Cape Town and, once well – and realizing there was no possibility of rejoining Cashel and Gilchrist-Baird (now disappeared into the *terra incognita* of Central Africa) – he had spent some time investigating the possibility of growing hops in South Africa. He was not convinced he could make a go of it and so returned to England, thanks to the funds that Cashel had left him, and sought out Buckley, whom he knew, reasoning that when Cashel returned from Africa the first person he'd seek out would be his brother. And he was correct, though it had been a longer wait than he'd anticipated, during which time he worked for Buckley as a gardener and part-time churchwarden. He had become a popular figure in the parish.

Cashel was happy to continue his convalescence at Claverleigh and Ignatz resumed his duties as manservant. Cashel persevered with his book but with waning confidence, realizing that without the convincing proof of the discovery of Lake Ukerere his narrative amounted to a long string of failures and setbacks and an account of Gilchrist-Baird's progressive ill-health – followed by his own. Keen as the reading public was for books of African exploration they wanted more than a long lamentation. He set the book aside on the eve of his sixtieth birthday and was not sure if he would ever take it up again.

The decision was encouraged by the alarming news that a new expedition to confirm the source of the Nile was being mounted – led by Speke and one James Grant. Cashel knew by now that Speke had claimed to be the first European to see the great Nyanza Ukerere – which he had swiftly renamed Lake Victoria – but his claims were refuted by Burton and met with scepticism elsewhere. Notwithstanding those doubts, however, Speke was embarking on another journey to the Lake Regions – funded by the Royal Geographical Society, as it had now become – to try to establish once and for all whether the headwaters of the White Nile were to be found at the northern edge of Ukerere.

As Cashel read about all this in the newspapers he felt the bite and weight of injustice. He knew – it wasn't just suspicion – that Speke had seen and noted the map he had made in Zanzibar and had effectively 'stolen' his own discovery. He went up to London to the Geographical Society and learned that the new expedition was due to leave for Zanzibar in 1860. Speke would be away for approximately two years, maybe longer. And it was at this stage that the idea of giving his lectures came to him. While Speke was away and out of reach of all contact he, Cashel, could reclaim the territory that was rightfully his. Whatever happened it would be on public record that Cashel Ross had been the first European to see the great Nyanza Ukerere.

He slipped his wallet back in his pocket as Miss Prendergast appeared with the photographs. There were several copies of a full-length portrait set against a dark backcloth. He had made an effort to dress as well as he could, wearing a cut-away morning coat with tapered peg-topped trousers. He looked closely at the photograph. To his eyes he was still somewhat underweight but, as a result, his features appeared sharper – his hollowed cheeks and clean-cut jawline made him look more brooding and intense, he thought, rather pleased with the atmosphere and the person- ality displayed in the monochrome image. He ordered a hundred small visiting-card reproductions to be printed immediately. Miss Prendergast informed him that, should he need more, a week's notice was all that was required.

Cashel walked down the Strand, his stomach cramps unusually still bothering him. Foolishly, he had left his supply of Kendal Black Drop back at the house he was renting in Southwark. He hadn't time to make it there and back before the start of his lecture so he searched for a druggist on the Strand and was eventually directed to a shop not far from St Clement's church.

It was a small shop, its shelves crammed with multicoloured bottles with mysterious Latin code names – *S. DE QVIN, Q.RAD, S.JUJUBIN, PULM.VULP.* The druggist wore a leather apron – more like a boot maker or a carpenter, Cashel thought – and informed him that they had no Kendal Black Drop. Cashel felt a small flicker of panic. The idea of lecturing with stomach cramps was unsettling.

'Have you anything similar to the Kendal?' Cashel asked. 'I need something strong.'

'You could try this,' the man said and reached for a bottle on a shelf behind him. It was blue and the label read, *'MRS DASH-WOOD'S INFANT QUIETENER'*.

'This is for crying babies.'

'In principle, yes,' the druggist said. 'Funny thing is, I sell ninety-nine per cent of my stock to young gentlemen.'

'Right,' Cashel said. 'What's the dose?'

'A teaspoon for a mewling child but . . .' He looked Cashel up and down. 'For a man like you I'd say a third of a bottle.'

'I'll take four,' Cashel said, and handed the man half a crown.

There were forty-odd people seated in Shadwell Hall waiting for his lecture. Very pleasing – the sandwich board had more than proved its efficacy, and it would be a fixture now. Five shillings for the rent of the hall for the evening – a profit of almost two pounds. And what if another twenty wanted a photograph for sixpence? More to the point, the two large swigs he had swallowed of Mrs Dashwood's Infant Quietener had calmed his cramps instantly and set him up in a mood of energetic confidence. Good old Ignatz, he thought, seeing him unrolling the large map of Africa, eight feet by six, that Cashel used to illustrate his lecture. He had it hanging on the wall behind him when he spoke, using an old billiard cue as a pointing-rod that allowed him to animate the talk, showing his journeys, indicating the presence of the lake and the cataracts that became the White Nile. A few places were named on the map – Bagamoyo, Kazeh, Zanzibar – but it was the white void at the centre that was the most telling, that dramatized by its very emptiness and nullity what he had achieved and what poor Gilchrist-Baird had died for.

He was standing in a small anteroom at the rear of the hall, waiting for the last members of the audience to arrive and settle down. Through the half-open door he could see the lectern on its dais. He turned away, pulled the cork from the bottle of Mrs Dashwood's Infant Quietener and took another quick mouthful. It wasn't as bitter as the Black Drop and had an underlying sweetness that made it easy to drink – honey? – behind which was a distinct kick of alcohol, a crude brandy perhaps. No wonder babes in arms stopped crying when they had a teaspoonful. He checked – he had drunk half a bottle and felt the warm glow of the alcohol in his chest and stomach. You could go happily into battle with stuff like this, he thought, corking the bottle tightly and dropping it in his coat pocket. He was glad to have a good supply in reserve.

Ignatz slipped into the room and handed him a leather pouch heavy with shillings.

'Forty-three tonight, sir.'

'Pop out and buy us a fowl for supper, Ignatz – and a bottle of something. Gin or brandy.'

'We have brandy at home, sir.'

'Well, buy us a good red wine then. I think our fortunes are on the turn, thanks to your famous sandwich boards.'

Cashel smiled, feeling a form of euphoria slowly creep through him, warming him internally somehow, as if he were standing with his back to a blazing fire, gently heating his entire body and at the same time miraculously clearing his head. He felt absurdly sure of what he was going to say, how he would astound the audience with his eloquence and conviction. He took a deep breath and strode out into the auditorium, picking up his pointing-rod with a flourish as he took his place behind the lectern, nodding and smiling at the applause.

'A very good evening to you all, ladies and gentlemen,' his voice boomed out confidently. 'As you can see, I lived to tell the tale!'

Cashel and Ignatz took a hack home to Southwark. There had been spontaneous cries of 'Bravo!' when he told the story of seeing the great lake for the first time, and two minutes of adulatory applause after his talk. Several people asked if he had written a book and encouraged him to do so. Cashel felt powerfully elated and took another covert swig of Mrs Dashwood's to prolong the sensation.

He had rented a terraced house, furnished, in Baalzephon Street on the Southwark–Bermondsey borders. He was deliberately making economies, nurturing his small reserves of capital after the £1,000 loss occasioned by the failure of the Lake Regions expedition. Hogan had repaid their mother's legacy which had been very opportune. Indeed, Hogan seemed to be prospering; the war in Crimea had been 'very good' for him, he confided. Just in time.

There was nothing fashionable about this part of East London, which was why he could afford a whole house. The immediate neighbours at his end of the terrace were a wheelwright, a carter, a hatter and a soap maker – small artisanal professionals and their families. The houses in Baalzephon Street had been constructed in the 1840s and, although there was no gaslight, there were outdoor privies in the small back gardens and many rooms were fitted with fireplaces. From his bedroom window on the top floor, Cashel could see the market gardens and pastureland that spread beyond the southern edge of the great smoky city. Depending on the direction of the wind, he could smell the peculiar, pungent odours from the huge tanning yards on Long Lane and hear the whistles from the steam trains at the Dover Railway depot. There was always a steady traffic of pure-finders down the street, heading for the tanneries with their closed buckets of dog turds. They made good money selling dog shit but the neighbours and their children shunned them.

As it turned out, Ignatz had been unable to find either a roast fowl or a good bottle of red wine in the environs of Shadwell Hall so Cashel sent him to the public house at the end of the street, the Lord Wellington, from where he brought back two slices of pork and ham pie and a jug of porter for supper. Before retiring to bed, Cashel showed Ignatz the empty bottle of Mrs Dashwood's and told him to buy as many more as he could find. He drank another long draught before falling into a tremendous dream-filled sleep and woke in the morning feeling entirely refreshed and full of unaccustomed energy. He was both astonished and grateful – he had stumbled across the perfect elixir for his Zanzibar cramps, and hadn't felt so healthy and alive in months. His new vigour had the further beneficial effect of making him feel more optimistic; everything was possible, he now thought. He would see off Speke; he would write his book and set the record straight; he would return to America and be reunited with his daughters.

Cashel stood outside the bookseller in Piccadilly and weighed the volume in his hand. It was a substantial, thick book, just published. He put on his spectacles and turned to the title page. *Journal of the Discovery of the Source of the Nile* by John Hanning Speke. He made his way down St James's to his club, Brydges', where he was going to treat himself to a generous luncheon and then, in the afternoon, read Captain Speke's book from cover to cover.

There were several abrupt consequences of Cashel's reading of this *Journal*. The first was that he changed the title of his lecture to 'The Calumnies of Captain Speke Regarding the Discovery of the Source of the Nile'. Over the Christmas period when the lecture round ceased (he spent the holiday with Buckley, Emily and the children at Claverleigh) Cashel revisited his own journals and edited them down to a concise thirty pages dealing exclusively with the 1856–7 expedition from Kazeh to Lake Ukerere (he refused to call it Lake Victoria) and back, pointing out the uncanny coincidences that existed between his journey and that of Captain Speke a year later.

He further adumbrated these 'Grotesque Similarities' by writing a new postscript of how on two occasions he had discovered Captain Speke covertly going through his notes and journals in the library of the British consulate at Zanzibar. He asked his readers to note the precise echoes of Speke's later journey with his own and to draw their own conclusions. He pointed out that he himself had positioned and named the cataracts at the northern shore of the lake as 'Ross Falls' – the very same cataracts that Speke had now re-dubbed 'Ripon Falls'. He cited as evidence letters he had written to the Geographical Society from Zanzibar and from Aden in January 1859 and rested his claims and his accusations on 'the good common sense of my readers', and invited them to examine closely the astonishing replication of his discoveries of 1856–7 with Captain Speke's of 1857–9.

He wrote with great vigour and purpose, fuelled by regular recourse to Mrs Dashwood's Infant Quietener. He sent Ignatz to druggists all over London to secure extra supplies. He was beginning to have a horror of running out and wanted there always to be a reserve of four to six bottles at any one time.

What he relished most about Mrs Dashwood's was that not only were his stomach cramps eradicated, seemingly permanently, but he had gained a clarity of vision and resolve that was both bracing and unfamiliar. His dream-life was also changed in remarkable ways. His dreams had become panoramic – as if he were standing on some high mountain with a prospect of cities and limitless landscapes: deserts, glaciers, distant ranges, forests and savannahs, peopled by vast multitudes. There was nothing modest about his new dreams, nothing domestic – no small rooms or cramped corners, no household objects, no cloistered conversations and encounters. These were like epic cycloramas – imperial, dominating, containing whole geographies – and they gave him enormous confidence. He felt a faith in his own natural abilities that was inspiring. Captain John Speke – the craven, mendacious thief – would escape neither his wrath nor his vengeance.

Consequently, in the New Year of 1864, Cashel initiated the

revised series of lectures, pointedly retitled. He booked larger meeting rooms and church halls throughout London and the counties surrounding the capital. The aim was to deliver a steady cannonade of counter-opinion and challenge at least two or three times a week. He visited his old printer from the Yelverton years, Maxwell Bishopson, and paid for a private edition of one thousand copies of his pamphlet to be printed up with the same title as the new lecture series. It was thirty-seven pages long and priced at one shilling. A postcard portrait of the author was also offered for an extra sixpence.

Considerable capital outlay was required but, gratifyingly, Cashel found his revenues significantly increased. Whether they were in Guildford, Brighton, Worthing or Hastings – or, in London, in the boroughs of Hampstead, Mayfair, Kensington or Chelsea – the process soon established its particular routine. The lectures were always at six o'clock in the evening. In the afternoon before, Ignatz and his team of sandwich-board men (locally hired) would parade in the high streets of these provincial towns or in the busiest London streets around the lecture hall.

Following the success of the sandwich boards, Cashel began to take out small black-bordered advertisements in newspapers:

Mr Cashel Ross will deliver his acclaimed lecture, 'The Calumnies of Captain Speke regarding the Discovery of the Source of the Nile' at six o'clock sharp in——Meeting House/Lecture Hall/Assembly Room.

And it worked. His audiences were now always well over a hundred. By March he began looking for even larger venues – theatres, churches, music halls.

There would be a backlash, he knew, but it would be covert, discreet. Speke would not want public controversy, as his claims were already being challenged and discounted by Burton and Dr Livingston amongst others. Any notorious debate or lawsuit with Cashel would further weaken his position. Sure enough, in April Cashel became convinced he was being followed. The house in Baalzephon Street was being watched, he was certain. At railway stations when he left the train, or when he stepped down from a cab, he frequently saw, in the corner of his eye, a figure slipping away furtively out of sight.

Annoyingly, Ignatz, who was posted to keep a watch – and who now followed Cashel's cab in another one – could find no evidence of this surveillance.

'Please, sir, forgive me, but I think Mrs Dashwood's is making you have these ideas.'

'Wrong, Ignatz – and how dare you, by the way! I take this syrup for the pains in my belly. Would you have me in agony?'

'It is a very strong syrup, sir.'

'Precisely. So much the better. That's why I need it.'

In fact, Cashel was now consuming three bottles of Mrs Dashwood's a day. The profit he was making from his lectures was significantly diminished by what he was spending on the Infant Quietener. Ignatz, having read the list of ingredients on the label, offered to make his own version. Cashel agreed and supervised the process. Two ounces of brown opium were macerated and dissolved in a pint of brandy that was then heated and steeped for three days. Cloves, cinnamon and honey were added and another three days of maceration ensued. The liquid was then filtered through a muslin sieve and bottled and corked. Cashel tasted the new syrup and declared himself satisfied though he thought the mixture might benefit from a dash of orange cordial. The taste was almost identical to Mrs Dashwood's concoction and, more importantly, the effect was the same, if anything more potent; the brown opium was the best quality, the brandy he used was better than the raw alcohol in Mrs Dashwood's syrup. Cashel drank deep and experienced the same clear vision and steady determination; the same energy and the same remorseless conviction that everything he was doing was right.

Of course, Ignatz was a brewer and making this syrup was child's play to him. Cashel ordered larger quantities to be made and stored in demijohns. All he needed to do was fill his hip-flask of a morning and replenish it whenever necessary. Moreover, the costs of Ignatz's home-made version were a quarter of what he had been paying over the counter. All these druggists were thieves, he decided, but he had outsmarted them and felt pleasingly smug.

Cashel sought out his old friend Ben Smart, now the editor of the *London Star*. He happily agreed to give Cashel a reduced rate for his advertisements and ran an account of one of his lectures in the newspaper.

Mr Ross's expedition to the Lake Regions of Central Africa in 1856–7 most dramatically prefigured that of Captain Speke's and Captain Burton's in 1857–9. Mr Ross made a solitary journey from Kazeh to the great lake discovered in the north and made scientific measurements to determine the lake's altitude above sea level, also establishing that there were cataracts that evacuated the lake on its northern shore. So too did Captain Speke, a year later, returning with the very same observations. The coincidence is very noticeable, not to say astonishing. Mr Ross, in his stimulating lectures, claims that on two occasions in Zanzibar he discovered Captain Speke examining his personal notes and maps just days before Speke and Burton embarked on their own expedition. In the unmapped, savage wilderness of the Lake Regions, is it not remarkable that one explorer should so conspicuously emulate the results of his predecessor? Can this be accepted as happenstance? So far, Captain Speke has declined to make any rebuttal. We leave it to the intelligence of our readers to make up their own minds. Perhaps if Mr Ross had named the lake he discovered after the Monarch we would be talking about him rather than Captain Speke.

Cashel stood outside the Masonic Hall on Drury Lane looking at the long queue of people waiting patiently to gain entry to his lecture. A very big crowd. Three hundred? Four hundred? His pamphlet had been reprinted five times and, to his amazement, the revenue he now made from his lectures far exceeded what he had earned from the trade in frozen water. He supposed there was nothing like a sprightly controversy to stimulate business.

'Mr Cashel Ross?' he heard a voice enquire.

He turned. A man stood there, vaguely familiar. He removed his top hat, smiled and made a gesture with his fingers – as if he held a brush in his hand and was painting.

'My God!' Cashel said. 'Is it really you?'

'It certainly is,' replied Brooke Mason, his smile widening. He gave a little bow and then they shook hands.

'Mason. In the flesh. I can't believe it.'

Cashel stared at him in astonishment. Mason's hair was grey and he had a double chin, but no beard, so the man Cashel had known in Arles – his lodger – was still recognizable here in London decades later.

'Have you been following me?' Cashel asked, suddenly suspicious.

'What? No. No need. You're a very easy man to find, Ross. I can't open a newspaper these days without finding one of your advertisements. I know that man, I says to myself. We had notable adventures together in France. I should pop along and say hello.'

'You've not sought me out at my house, have you?'

'I've no idea where you live, my dear fellow, believe me. I find myself in London – your lectures are widely advertised and here I am. Well met, sir.'

Cashel wasn't entirely sure if he believed Mason – he was always a damned shifty character.

'However, now we're reunited, can we meet in more comfortable circumstances?' Mason smiled his wily smile. 'I've a proposition that might interest you. Financially rewarding, needless to say.'

Cashel thought for a second or two – then agreed, remembering his strange affection for the man. He suggested that they meet at his club, Brydges', the next day for luncheon.

'Capital,' Mason said, clapping him familiarly on the shoulder. 'How good it is to see you again, Ross. I can't tell you! I'll leave you to your public. À demain!'

Cashel watched him saunter away. Brooke Mason, he thought.

Who would have believed it? Back in his life again. What might that portend?

Brooke Mason outlined his proposal in the smoking room of Brydges', after lunch. Mason sat down with his cigar and Cashel withdrew for a moment to the water closets and took two large gulps of his home-made Mrs Dashwood's, the better to clear his mind. Mason and he had filled in some of the enormous gaps in their respective lives over slices of roast mutton and cheese souf-flé. Now they sat in the corner of the smoking room, well fed and wined. Cashel lit his cigar as Mason began to go into details.

'No, as I told you,' Mason said, leaning forward, 'despite the disaster in Venezuela, I realized I'd developed a liking for the trop-ics and the opportunities they offered. I moved to Bogotá, first of all, but that didn't work out – so I travelled on to Nicaragua where, as luck would have it, I turned out to be very useful to the then President, an American man called Walker. William Walker.'

Mason explained further. Walker was an adventurer, a so-called 'filibuster' who, amazingly, had managed to become President of Nicaragua for a year.*

'I became, you could say, a kind of Cardinal Richelieu to him. Very much in the shadowy background but with a finger in every pie, so to speak.'

'This is all very fascinating, Mason, but what's it got to do with me?'

'I'm currently what you might call a "Minister without Port-folio" for the Nicaraguan government.'

'Congratulations.'

'And I'm therefore able to confer certain official appointments – abroad, or here in England, or in Europe – that will benefit my adopted country.'

---

* William Walker, an American adventurer and mercenary, became President of Nicaragua in 1856 by taking advantage of a civil war. He was deposed a year later and returned to the United States. Unwisely revisiting the region a year later, he was captured, tried, and on 12 September 1860 executed by firing squad.

'I repeat. What's it got to do—'

'How would you like to be the Nicaraguan consul in Trieste?'

'Trieste, in Austria?'

'The very same.'

'No, thank you. I have a score to settle here that's taking up all my time.'

'Do think about it, Ross. Settle your score, then ponder Trieste. By the way, the salary is five thousand dollars a year.'

Cashel did a quick calculation. Five thousand dollars was close to a thousand pounds.

'Plus expenses,' Mason added. 'Accommodation, travel. Within reason.'

'What would I have to do?'

'The usual duties of a consul. You are a kind of commissariat. Concentrate on trading matters. Represent the interests of Nicaraguan citizens and merchants.'

'Why me?'

'Because I can trust you, Ross. You came to my aid in my hour of need and I've never forgotten. It creates a bond between us.'

'That's very white of you, Mason, but – to be frank – it's not for me. It's not how I see my future.'

'Don't say no. I'm in no particular hurry. Think it over and we'll meet again.' Mason smiled and took a visiting card from a case that was in his pocket and handed it over. Cashel glanced at it: there was a crest and underneath it in English it read, 'Brooke M. Mason, Minister without Portfolio, Government of Nicaragua'. And then the same rubric in Spanish. There was an address, also. 34 Albany, Piccadilly.

'Is this fellow Walker still President?'

'Alas, no. He's dead. Shot by firing squad in 1860. But I am, if you like, still benefiting from the patronage he bestowed on me, during his time in office.' He shrugged modestly. 'I still have considerable influence with the current government.'

Cashel politely said no, thank you, once again, with extra emphasis, but he was, he had to admit, intrigued. One thousand pounds a year was not to be casually rejected. He looked up

Trieste in an encyclopaedia in the club library and discovered its reputation as a significant port on the Adriatic, the 'Hamburg of the Mediterranean', a vital trading post for the Austrian Empire even though the largest part of the city's polyglot population was Italian, amongst whom irredentist tendencies were hotly simmering. However, there was something alluring about Mason's offer – to be a recognized diplomat with all the privileges that went with the role and, more importantly, not to have to worry about money any more . . . But, no, he told himself – he mustn't be diverted from his purpose.

By the summer of 1864 it was clear that Cashel's public lectures were, if anything, oversubscribed. He could book a hall that sat three hundred and fill it with ease. And, almost as if in response to Cashel's claims, Speke published another book, provocatively entitled *What Led to the Discovery of the Source of the Nile*. As far as Cashel was concerned it was a clear indication that the message of his lectures and his pamphlet was beginning to hit home and cause some disturbance. He knew Speke would have to confront him, sooner or later.

And the day duly arrived. He was in Guildford, in a school hall. Two hundred and seventeen people had attended and the applause had been sustained. Ignatz was busy taking down the map when Cashel was interrupted by a knock at his makeshift dressing room. He slipped his flask of home-made Mrs Dashwood's in his pocket and opened the door.

A man stood there who bore an astonishing resemblance to the late Prince Albert, Cashel thought, taken aback for an instant. The same weakish chin, whiskers down to the jawbone, a poor moustache, thin dark hair combed over to disguise a bald pate.

'Mr Ross?'

'Yes.'

The man handed him a visiting card. '*Montague Sansom, solicitor, Lincoln's Inn.*'

'I represent Captain John Speke.'

'What bad luck,' Cashel said, emboldened by Mrs Dashwood's.

'Captain Speke proposes a meeting. I suggest at my chambers.'
'I've absolutely no desire to see Captain Speke ever again.'
'I advise it would be in your best interests, sir. Shall we say next Monday morning? Ten o'clock?'

Mrs Dursley's School for Girls
Cambridge
Massachusetts

13th June 1864

My dear Father,

How strange it is to write these words! My heart is beating with unusual passion as I do so. Mrs Broome forwarded on your letter to me, including your recent photograph. It was a shock to see your image, a pleasant shock, I should add. And to see you as you are today, so grave and mature. It stirred memories of our former happy life at Willow Creek, hence this letter after all these years.

My own news is that I am a teacher at the above institution. I moved here to be closer to Mama. She is well but not well. Calm, but in a world of her own – a world of near constant prayer and devotion. She dresses in a nun's wimple and carries a heavy wooden cross with her wherever she goes. She seems entirely happy at the hospital. It is possible to converse with her about inconsequential matters – the weather, her health, the view from her window. She is not interested in the world beyond the confines of her room – her 'chapel' as she calls it. She is entirely ignorant of this terrible war we are currently engaged in, for example.

Maeve is married and lives in Providence, RI. Her husband, Bowman Lewis, is a pharmacist. She has a son, Elliott, aged three – your grandchild, of course.

Mr Corcoran, the elder, died two years ago. The farm, Rockwell, is now Devin's. He has four children, all boys. Murphy, who was for a time my sweetheart, has joined the Union Army and is somewhere on the banks of the Mississippi, so I am informed.

I will not list the deep regrets I feel over the way our family was divided and will not apportion blame. The emotions I experienced on

receiving your letter were sufficient to remind me that, whatever
wrongs were committed on whatever side,

   I remain your dutiful and loving daughter,
   Nessa Ross Corcoran

Cashel wept when he received this letter and replied immediately, asking Nessa to send photographs of herself, Maeve and little Elliott – and his son-in-law, Bowman, he added diplomatically. He saw this reconciliation as the best of omens, even a kind of vindication of the justice of his fight against Speke and his lies. He wrote to Maeve, care of Nessa, urging that contact between them be renewed, though he was aware that Frannie would have forwarded the photograph and his letter to Maeve, also. She had clearly chosen not to reply, but he still felt there was a chance that both his daughters might once again be part of his life. He would go to the meeting at Lincoln's Inn with adamantine resolve.

Montague Sansom's chambers were dimly lit, even for a summer's Monday morning, as if the gaslight was not turned up enough or the mantles were dirty. The windowpanes were grimy, also, and the walls were papered with a heavy, predominantly brown pattern. It felt as if dust motes were hanging everywhere. While he waited, Cashel asked for a glass of water that Sansom's clerk duly provided. He wanted the taint of Mrs Dashwood's off his breath. Suddenly feeling nervous in the hack that brought him to Lincoln's Inn he had found a quiet corner and drained half his flask. He was calmer now, ready to take on Sansom and Speke – let them do their worst.

Cashel was shown into Sansom's office, as dull and dreary as the anteroom. The solicitor waved him to a chair across his desk. After the usual insincere pleasantries about the journey, the weather, and the apparent bloodbath that was the American Civil War, Sansom wasted no time in making his point.

'The thing is, Mr Ross, we wish you to cease your lecturing and to withdraw your slanderous pamphlet against Captain Speke.'

'I refuse.'

'Please reconsider. We have refrained from taking legal action against you, but—'

'I look forward to my day in court, Mr Sansom, with genuine enthusiasm.'

Cashel turned around in his chair and noticed that the door to the adjoining room was ajar.

'Why don't you come in, Speke, instead of lurking outside like an eavesdropper?'

There was a pause before the door swung open and Speke appeared. He was wearing striped trousers under his short black coat which had the effect of making his already long legs seem unnaturally so. His russet beard sat on his chest like a hirsute bib, obscuring his cravat. He looked very uncomfortable as Sansom drew up a chair for him.

'Good day to you, Speke.'

'Good morning, Ross.'

Cashel stood up, the better to make his point, giving thanks to Mrs Dashwood's for all this bottled confidence.

'Here's my proposition – no, my conditions. I will not cease my programme of lectures until you, Captain Speke, publicly acknowledge my role in the discovery of Lake Ukerere.'

'That's impossible. I cannot.'

'Then there is no more to say. Thank you for your time, gentlemen.' Cashel strode to the door.

Speke appeared to lose his temper at this and his voice became shrill.

'You and Burton are trying to destroy me! Trying to erase everything that I've—'

'What has Burton to do with this?' Cashel paused at the door. 'I've nothing against him. I haven't seen him since Zanzibar in 1857. Captain Burton did not steal *my* discoveries.'

Speke then went into a long rambling account of Burton's own counter-theories about a different lake – Lake Tanganyika – that he was convinced fed the White Nile. Cashel regained his seat while the peroration continued. What made everything worse was that Burton had enlisted the support of Dr Livingstone, Speke went on. Both of them discounted Ukerere – Victoria.

'Nonsense,' Cashel said. 'Lake Tanganyika is two thousand feet lower than Ukerere. Is water meant to flow uphill to feed the Nile?'

'I wish you would shout that in Burton's face!' Speke squeaked passionately. 'And the lake is named Victoria, damn your eyes!'

'Named by you. Not by the people who live by it! Damn *your* eyes!'

'Gentlemen, please,' Sansom interrupted.

They calmed down, Cashel feeling an urgent need for some Mrs Dashwood's. He had to get out of these dingy brown rooms with their occluded, powdery light. Or was there something going wrong with his eyes? he wondered.

'Acknowledge my role, that's all I ask, Speke. I want no money, no honours, no decorations. Just make it clear to all and sundry who happen to be interested in the matter that the first European to see that great lake was me. Me – not you. Then you can receive all the prizes and the plaudits.' He stood up again. 'It's as simple as that. Otherwise the lectures will continue. Good day to you, gentlemen.'

Cashel walked briskly out through Lincoln's Inn to his waiting hack on Portugal Street. Ignatz was sitting inside and Cashel sensed concern coming off him in waves.

'How did it go, sir?'

'Well, they know what they have to do. They must make a decision.' Cashel took out his flask but realized that it was empty. 'We must go at once to a druggist, Ignatz. Full speed.'

'Let's go home and rest, sir. No more Mrs Dashwood's today.'

'I'm in severe pain, man! Intense pain! For the love of God!'

They went to the druggist on the Strand.

Some days later Cashel dined with Ben Smart. They had taken up their regular Friday-night dinners again, old friends that they were. Ben was now quite bald with a trimmed grey beard – stouter, also, with a prominent belly straining at his waistcoat.

'Are you well, Cashel? You're still abominably skinny.'

'Never been better. Nor so full of energy.'

'Have a look at this.'

Ben pushed a folded copy of the *London Star* across the table and topped up their wine glasses. Cashel put on his spectacles and read the advertisement that Ben had circled. It was for a so-called 'vacational' or summer meeting of the Royal Geographical Society in Bath. Captain John Hanning Speke and Captain Richard Burton would debate their opposing speculations about the origin of the Nile. The President of the RGA, Sir Roderick Murchison, would be in the chair.

'Bless you, Ben. This is what I've been waiting for. Everything will be out in the open now – recorded, printed, disseminated. This is my moment.'

'I hope you know what you're doing.'

'If I did nothing I could never forgive myself.'

Ben laughed.

'You are a prodigy, Cashel. Most men our age are nodding in front of the fire wondering what's for supper.'

'Well, I have new fuel for my fortitude – injustice. Grotesque injustice. No force more powerful.'

Cashel wrote to Speke, care of Montague Sansom.

17 Baalzephon Street
Southwark

21ˢᵗ July 1864

Dear Speke,

I will be brief and to the point. I am fully aware of the impending debate on 16ᵗʰ September, in Bath, between you and Captain Burton. Here is your – and our – opportunity. If, during the debate, you acknowledge the fact that I 'discovered' Lake Ukerere a full year before your claim I will cease my lecturing and withdraw my pamphlet from sale.

The further advantage for you would be that you would now benefit from my support. It has always been obvious to me that Lake Ukerere feeds the White Nile. You and I with our separate measurements, our

witnesses (and I include Mr Grant, of course, from your second
expedition) would trounce Burton and Livingstone with their
preposterous insistence that the source is Lake Tanganyika or the
Mountains of the Moon or wherever else. We would be triumphant on
the field, all logic and science backing our observations.

My sole condition remains the same, namely that I, Cashel Ross,
preceded you to Lake Ukerere in 1856, long before you. However, I am
happy to concede that your second expedition with Mr Grant of
1860–63 bore out what was in fact deduction on my part. I will not
insist that you reveal how you profited from my notes that you covertly
read in Zanzibar before you and Captain Burton set out.

Alas, if you decide not to comply with my simple and justified
wishes during the debate then I am obliged to tell you that my
campaign to ensure that the truth will out is going to continue with
renewed and unforgiving vigour.

I remain, sir,

sincerely yours,
Cashel Ross

Cashel received no reply, not even an acknowledgement from
Sansom, and he found that troubling. Why would Speke not realize he had nothing to lose and everything to gain by simply telling
the truth? To his alarm, Cashel found that his Zanzibar stomach
cramps began to return with their old ferocity and he was obliged
to increase his consumption of Mrs Dashwood's to ameliorate
them. He instructed Ignatz to make a new batch of the syrup
with three ounces of opium in the pint of brandy, not two. It
seemed to work.

As the date for the debate approached, Cashel decided he
needed an ally, if only another strong shoulder to the wheel of his
individual endeavour, and he wrote to Hogan asking if he could
spend the night in Oxford before moving on to Bath for the debate.
If Hogan had no pressing business, Cashel hoped he would be so
good as to accompany him, to be his 'second', as it were. Hogan
replied at once – sending a telegraph to say he would be delighted

and that they 'would give them hell' – whatever that meant, Cashel thought. Still, it cheered him. It would be good to have Hogan by his side. Dark, potent Hogan, his strong lieutenant.

In fact, he discovered that there was to be a preliminary meeting announced for the day before the debate, the 15th, at which the participants would meet informally with Sir Roderick Murchison to decide the order of speaking, the length of speeches, the process of rebuttal, how many interventions would be allowed from the floor, and so forth. Cashel wanted to be present – it might provide him with a better chance of a conversation with Speke and it would certainly let him know that he'd be present at the debate itself.

The night before he left for Oxford he bathed. He had a copper footbath placed on the kitchen floor, Ignatz heated kettles on the range and he washed himself – with soap provided by his soap-making neighbour – almost, he thought, as a kind of ritual, like a warrior about to go into battle, washing himself clean. He stood naked, up to his shins in the basin as Ignatz dipped a long-handled pot in the sudsy water and poured it over his head and shoulders.

'Let me come with you, sir,' Ignatz said, his voice sounding unusually anxious.

'I'll be with my brother. There's no need.'

Cashel stepped out of the bath and Ignatz handed him the big linen towel. Cashel wrapped himself in it, luxuriating. It was a warm night anyway, and the hot water on his body had calmed him.

'Just make sure I have plenty of Mrs Dashwood's,' Cashel said. 'Two pints.'

'Yes, sir.'

Hogan met him at Oxford station on the 14th and they rode out in his curricle to Starkie's Farm. There was a solid, functional-looking main house surrounded by an assortment of outbuildings, byres and sheds and a paddock filled with restless horses. A pungent smell of horse shit hung in the air.

'You should shift that paddock further away,' Cashel said as he looked about the place. 'How can you live with that stench all day and night?'

'You don't notice it after a couple of days, I can assure you,' his brother said with a laugh.

Hogan kept a slovenly, ramshackle house. Two young girls worked in the kitchen and cooked for him and served at table with winsome, knowing smiles. They ate beefsteaks and drank too much, breaking into a second bottle of port as Cashel told the whole detailed story of the Zanzibar experience and how Speke had stolen his glory from him.

'But you say Speke is right about the Nile,' Hogan said. 'So why the debate?'

'I know he's right – I do, absolutely – but nobody else seems convinced. Burton and Livingstone want to prove their case. Speke is a weak man – he doesn't debate well. Burton will eat him alive, I reckon.'

'And you offered to support him.'

'But he never replied,' Cashel said. 'Thinks he doesn't need me, I suppose. Pride comes before a fall.'

Hogan sat there thinking, puffing at his fat cigar.

'I remember I told you once, Cash, that there comes a moment in any dispute, argument, negotiation – what you will – when main force is the only way to make people see sense. See what the truth is.' Hogan gestured, shoving both hands forward. 'They just need a push, like. A physical push to set them off in the right direction.' He poured Cashel another glass of port. 'Sounds to me like your Captain Speke needs a talking-to.'

'Well, let's see how he behaves tomorrow. I'll be standing right in front of him – and so will Burton. He'll have to choose.'

Cashel woke the next morning with a murderous hangover that two gulps from his hip-flask miraculously cleared. He and Hogan caught an early train to Bath. They booked rooms in the Arlington Hotel and then made their way to the lecture theatre at the Mineral Water Hospital where the debate would take place. Cashel felt his nerves beginning to return and wondered if he could find a quiet corner where he could swig some Mrs

Dashwood's but the room was already filling up with people. Hogan took a seat at the back while Cashel wandered down to be closer to the stage. Roderick Murchison was already sitting there on his throne-like adjudicator's chair. Cashel saw Speke and Burton sitting as far apart as possible in the front row, neither of them looking at the other. There was a woman beside Burton – his wife, he supposed – who kept glancing pointedly over in Speke's direction. Cashel beckoned Hogan forward.

'That's Speke with the big beard,' he whispered in his brother's ear. 'And that one there on the right is Burton.'

'Right.' Hogan went back to his seat.

Then Cashel crossed the room, moving along an aisle between the ranked chairs. Hundreds had been set out – they were obviously expecting a big crowd. He saw Dr Livingstone in quiet conversation with Burton, who was also bearded like some magus or shaman, with two sharp points of whiskers sticking out of his chin. Burton saw him, recognized him, stood up and came over.

'Ross, my God. I never thought to see you here.'

They shook hands.

'I do have a significant interest in the matter,' Cashel said, suddenly feeling his anxiety building again.

'But you're of Speke's party. Damn you,' Burton added with a grin. 'Do you want to meet Livingstone? See what he thinks of your theory?'

'Some other time, perhaps. It's Speke I need to talk to.' Cashel turned to see that Hogan had come down to join them.

'This is my brother, Hogan Ross.'

'How do,' Hogan said and shook Burton's hand.

'Perhaps we might have a chat tomorrow, after the debate,' Burton said.

'Of course, glad to.'

Burton returned to his wife and Cashel walked on down to the front row, his brother at his side. Speke turned his head and on seeing Cashel approaching, looked away and began to fidget with his fingers, ignoring him.

'Captain Speke?' Cashel said, raising his voice slightly. 'Did you receive my letter?'

Speke stood up abruptly.

'I cannot stand this any longer!' he exclaimed, almost as if shouting at Murchison on the stage, and marched out of the hall, past Cashel and Hogan, without even looking at them.

Everyone stared as Speke left the lecture room. Hogan watched him go, hands on his hips.

'There's your answer, Cash. Looks like a no to me.' Hogan made a curious circular gesturing motion with his hand. 'I'll see you at the hotel later,' he said. 'I need a drink.'

Cashel spoke again to Burton and his wife, introduced as Isabel. She was full of contempt for Speke's behaviour. Cashel said he'd see them both the next day and went back to the Arlington, calmed himself with some draughts of Mrs Dashwood's, and dozed off for an hour or two. Then he went for a stroll through Bath and, suddenly feeling hungry, stopped in a tavern for a pie and a pot of stout. When he returned to his room at around five thirty, Hogan was there, sitting on his bed, waiting for him. He grinned at Cashel – a strange, leery, knowing grin.

'What's going on, Hogan?' Cashel said, wondering if his brother was drunk.

'There'll be no debate tomorrow.'

'What are you talking about? Why not?'

'Because I've done for him, your Captain Speke.'

'What do you mean, "done for"?'

'He's dead. Dead as that stuffed curlew on your mantel, there.' Hogan pointed.

Cashel looked over at the scrawny bird in its glass display case and felt sick. He poured himself a glass of Mrs Dashwood's, sat down opposite Hogan and – keeping his voice level – asked him to tell him everything that had happened.

Hogan said he had been angered for Cashel by Speke's behaviour. 'That fucking popinjay,' he called him. Very angered indeed to see him stalk out of the debating hall without even a glance at Cashel. Speke was clearly a coward, Hogan said, and cowards only understood one language. Power, brute force, domination. So he had followed him out.

He saw Speke climb into a carriage and then, signalling for one of the hacks waiting outside, he jumped in and followed Speke back to a place called Neston Hall not far out of Bath, a grand house in an estate, he said. Hogan paid the cabby to wait nearby and then shinned over the boundary wall and prowled around, making sure he was unobserved, hoping to find Speke alone and 'have a quiet word with him'. There was no sign. And then, around four o'clock in the afternoon, he saw Speke and another man, and a gamekeeper, stroll out into the park with guns – obviously intending to walk-up some partridges or pheasants before dinner.

Hogan then circled round through some young woodland of ash and elm. The men would spread out with their guns and Hogan reckoned that this would be his best chance of confronting Speke.

'But he was armed with a double-barrelled shotgun, mind you,' Hogan said. 'I wasn't going to take any chances, oh, no.'

Through the trees he saw Speke and the other man take up shooting positions behind a stone wall facing a big copse of mature woodland. They were about a hundred yards apart from each other while they waited for the gamekeeper to head into the wood and mark-up the birds.

Hogan crept as close as he could to Speke's position.

'He was about twenty yards away from me on the other side of the stone wall. I could see his big stupid beard – and he had his gun closed, ready to fire. So I gave him a whistle and he looked round. "Speke!" says I. "I have news from Mr Cashel Ross."'

Then, Hogan went on, Speke climbed over the wall and came towards him and, as he approached, Hogan saw him cock one hammer of his shotgun.

'Then suddenly we were face to face. He seemed to recognize me. He raised his gun on me and said, "I will converse no more with that liar, Ross" – and that's when I lost my mind, Cash.'

'What happened?'

'I grabbed the barrel of his gun to point it away from me. I was swearing at him, something foul. He fought to get the gun back from me and as we struggled it got caught in his jacket and the barrels stuck under his armpit – left armpit. I knew there was a barrel cocked and I must have given the gun a kick or something because "Bang!" it went off.'

'My God . . .'

'He would have shot me, Cash. He had his gun on me, cocked. I was damn lucky.'

'Sweet Jesus. What happened?'

'He went down. He wasn't quite dead. Bloody big hole under his left arm. Whimpering and groaning. So I dragged him back to the lee of the wall and left him there with his gun. I could hear the other fellow shouting, "John! John!" so I skedaddled.'

'Is he dead?'

'Most like, I'd say. He took a cartridge of shot in the left armpit, range of one inch. He looked done to me . . .' Hogan looked at Cashel's glass of Mrs Dashwood's. 'I'll take a drop of that, if I may.'

Cashel poured him a measure.

'Nobody saw you?' he said carefully. 'You're sure.'

'Only Speke. The other fellow was out of sight, a hundred yards off.'

'You'd better get home.'

'Right. Yes. Good idea. What about you?'

'I should wait – as if I'm going to the debate. It would look a bit odd if I suddenly disappeared. I'll say you left right after the meeting this morning.'

'Smart thinking,' Hogan said and stood up and drained his glass. 'That's good stuff, whatever it is. Makes you feel good.'

'It was an accident, wasn't it, Hogan?'

'Exactly as I described it to you, Cash. If I hadn't grabbed that gun off him, I'd be lying there dead, now. It was him or me.'

Hogan left for the station. Cashel didn't sleep that night, going over and over Hogan's narrative of the fatal encounter in his

373

head. He had doubts – he knew his brother, knew what he was capable of. He remembered his letter about Yelverton lying on the ground in the Place Royale as Hogan broke his knees by stamping on them and left him crippled. When a man lived with death all the time – even the death of animals – as Hogan did, then it didn't seem exceptional; it seemed commonplace, rather, a constant part of life's daily round. 'I've done for him,' he had said – what exactly did that mean?

The next morning, Cashel, duly fortified and made lively, took his place in the lecture hall as it slowly filled with the excited audience ready for the 'Debate of the Century', as some of the more excitable newspapers had dubbed it. Burton was already up on stage behind his desk going through his notes. Speke's desk, on the other side of Murchison's administrator's throne, was empty. There was a delay, ten minutes, twenty minutes. Burton left the stage, then returned. Mutterings filled the hall as people began chatting. Ladies fanned themselves with their programmes (it was a sunny day). Some gentlemen stepped outside to smoke. Then, after half an hour, a small group of men stepped onto the stage – Sir Roderick Murchison, the members of the RGA council and a few honoured guests, including Dr Livingstone. It was obvious from their sombre expressions that something was very, very wrong. The large room grew instantly quiet as Murchison stepped forward to the front of the stage and announced, with great regret, that Captain Speke had died yesterday, 'in a tragic shooting accident'.

There were some stifled screams. Gasps of incredulity. A sobbing woman had to be helped from the hall. Cashel felt an immense, bowel-shifting relief. An accident! Then he heard the whispers around him: 'Suicide, suicide.' But the main thing, he realized, his head reeling, was that there was no suspicion of foul play, no malign third party. He stood up, left the hall, went back to the hotel and had a porter carry his case to the station.

On the train back to London, Cashel began to sift through other more worrying probabilities. What about the driver of the hack that had taken Hogan to Neston Hall? Had Hogan been spotted prowling around the grounds? Even more damning, he worried, was his own letter to Montague Sansom threatening a vigorous and unrelenting pursuit of personal vindication. Who had motive to end Speke's life? It seemed to him – and he was trembling slightly now – that if these new facts emerged then it might suggest a conspiracy between two brothers, an act of revenge by an embittered explorer who had spent the last few years loudly proclaiming his bitterness . . . He reached into his coat for his flask of Mrs Dashwood's and had a quick, soothing sip, ignoring the disapproving glance of an elderly woman sitting opposite. What should he do? he wondered, panic rising again. What if circumstantial evidence emerged that might suggest a murder? How could he be sure he would be safe?

17 Baalzephon Street
Southwark

17th September 1864

My dear Mason,
    I have been thinking long and hard about your kind offer. Life in England suddenly seems so boring and uninspiring and I am tempted anew by the prospect of adventure. If the position is still unfilled, I would be very happy indeed to undertake the duties of consul in Trieste for the Republic of Nicaragua. Let us meet, quam cellerime, to discuss the details.
    I remain, dear Mason,

    your ami fidèle,
    Cashel Ross

14

Cashel Ross saw Raphaella Rozzo, for the first time in over forty years, at the junction of Via Solferino and Via Pontaccio in Central Milan.

He had been living in Milan for many weeks, waiting for Brooke Mason to authorize him to take up his appointment as consul in Trieste. In fact, the delay had suited him, not least because he remembered and enjoyed the city, thinking back to his first sojourn in the winter of 1821–2, but also because he could more easily be informed of any troubling developments in the Speke affair.

He had gone to the central post office to collect his mail. There was a reassuring letter from Ben Smart with all the latest information. In fact, Speke had been buried fairly swiftly after his death – listed by the magistrate as a 'shooting accident' – but according to Ben's letter public consensus was that it had been a suicide. The thinking was that Speke knew he was incapable of besting Burton in any debate and the humiliation that would ensue from such a defeat would gravely undermine his claims that Lake Victoria was the source of the Nile. Therefore – suicide. Further circumstantial evidence was advanced in that Speke was a very accomplished shot. The supposed 'accident' that killed him – tripping over his gun as he crossed a wall – might have applied to an amateur but hardly to the first-rate hunter that Speke was. Cashel read the arguments laid out by Ben, feeling his relief grow.

He was genuinely relieved, but he had another image in his mind of Hogan confronting Speke that refused to go away. Hogan wresting the shotgun from Speke's hands, thrusting it into his armpit and pulling the trigger. He also fretted about his own possible complicity in Speke's death. He looked back at his life since Zanzibar and began to wonder if his obsession with the Nile and the strange energies that possessed him were all generated by the infernal syrup that he had become addicted to . . . The more he thought about it the more he saw its malign influence everywhere. That fool of an apothecary in Zanzibar, Frost, had fed him Kendal Black Drop whenever he called for it. And then the fortuitous discovery of Mrs Dashwood's Infant Quietener had compounded the craving and led him down another dark road.

He had confessed as much to Ignatz when he returned to London from Bath, and Ignatz, ever the diplomat, had said merely that if he, Cashel, was in pain then he needed to take medicine. But it had to be the right medicine, he added, his only reproach. Before they left Baalzephon Street, Cashel had taken his demijohns of Mrs Dashwood's out to the privy in the back garden and had symbolically emptied them there. No more laudanum for him, ever again – though the craving would hit him from time to time – unless he had a toothache.

But his mood changed, now that the shadow of Speke's death had been removed and his guilt was receding. And in this improved mood his thoughts turned to Raphaella. Raphaella, who of course had come to live in Milan after Ravenna. Was she still in the city? he wondered. What was the name of the man she had married? He tried, but he couldn't remember. A rich man, with a palazzo named after him, he recalled Timoteo saying to him at their last meeting. But so long ago. As he urged his memory to function the letter M came to mind. Count M-something. Yes, Raphaella's second husband's name began with an M. He looked up in a guidebook all the palazzos in Milan that also began with an M. There were quite a few: Marino, Melzi, Mogliano, Menoni. He started to visit all the M-palazzos, as he called them, wondering if a visual image might trigger the crucial recognition.

One evening he was at his fifth M-palazzo, the Palazzo Mazzolino. That did sound familiar, somehow. Outside, waiting, was a line of three carriages, led by black horses with thick ribbons of black crêpe wound around the harness. The coachmen were in black, the shades in the carriages were black, also, and half-lowered. Figures in dark clothes emerged from the palazzo's main door and boarded. Someone important had died, clearly. The carriages set off at walking pace and Cashel followed, curious. They made one turn, then another and stopped outside a large church – Santa Maria della Povere. There was a substantial crowd of mourners waiting inside. No coffin, however – odd. Cashel took up a position from where he could see the passengers emerging before they entered the church.

A young man descended from the first carriage and held out a hand to help an older woman down. She was all in black silk but her veil was up, pinned to her bonnet. Manoeuvring the wide crinoline skirts of her dress was complicated by the narrowness of the carriage door but eventually she was standing safely on the paving in front of the church door and Cashel instantly experienced that shock, the body-shudder of recognition.

Raphaella . . .

She looked around at the gathered crowd before lowering her veil and for a few seconds Cashel saw her beautiful face. Older, her long face fuller, her jawline softened, lines bracketing the corners of her lips – but Raphaella, in the flesh. And, apparently, a widow.

She went into the church and Cashel waited, filing in himself behind the last of the mourning crowd. He crossed himself on entering – he knew what to do – and found a place at the rear where he could stand and observe. It wasn't a burial, it was a Requiem Mass. He didn't linger. On his way out, he asked a priest who the Mass was being said for. *Il Conte Mazzolino. Un uomo sacro buono.* It was the first anniversary of his death, apparently.

Cashel went back to his hotel – he was staying at the Hotel Moderne, near the station – in a roiling ferment of emotions. It was as if he had seen her yesterday, all the months of their Ravenna love affair detonating in a moment outside a church. But what to do next? The question was redundant – everything in his being, everything in the person that was Cashel Ross, made him utterly determined to see her again.

He told himself to be steady, to compose himself, to take his time. He couldn't just blunder up to her and embrace her, saying, 'It's me, Cashel. I'm back.' No, this had to be done delicately, with proper decorum. Normally he'd have soothed himself with a glass of Mrs Dashwood's but those days were behind him, permanently, however much he found himself yearning for the potent syrup from time to time.

He could still have a calming drink instead, however, so he went to a café, ordered a brandy and water and smoked a cigar. Maybe the Requiem Mass was the symbolic end to a year of mourning, he thought. Possibly she might now be able to take some tentative steps back into Milanese society. If so, then that was where any first encounter should occur – in a public place with other people present. The shock she would experience would be diluted as a result, or so he hoped, making it seem like a coincidence, fate – not something meticulously engineered.

And it was fate, he supposed, that he was in Milan – Brooke Mason's idea, not his. Mason had said to use Milan as a staging post while he went on to Trieste to ensure the consulate was ready for business and that everything was in good working order. He had telegraphed the other day to say that Cashel's letters patent had been cleared with the governor of the Austrian Littoral, as the so-called Crownland of the Austrian Empire that contained Trieste was named, and his exequatur as consul had been granted. Trieste was the main imperial port and, profiting mightily during the Emperor Franz Joseph's reign, it was now a rich and important asset. Mason had said there was a slight problem with the consulate's annexes – whatever they were – and as soon as all was approved he would send for Cashel. But now that Cashel had seen Raphaella he was in no hurry to be a consul in Trieste: life in Milan was suddenly far more interesting and seductive.

The Hotel Moderne was ideally comfortable. He had a bedroom, a sitting room and a water closet. Ignatz – who was to be his vice consul – was staying at an *albergo* round the corner. And he was enjoying being in the new, united Italy, in bustling prosperous Milan. He thought he could measure a palpable change in the civic atmosphere, quite different from the quarrelling and competitive kingdoms and principalities he had known in the 1820s. He also realized something else about himself – he was instinctively accustomed to being 'abroad'. Very little of his life, he calculated, had actually been spent settled in England. But England was always there – as consul, he had annual leave which he could take anywhere he fancied. He could go back to England and visit his brothers and their families. Now that the Speke disaster seemed resolved he had been quite looking forward to his new incarnation as a diplomat – but then the Raphaella revelation had intervened and he was very aware that everything might once again change.

Ignatz was shaving him. There were ten barbers within a hundred yards of the hotel but Ignatz's touch was sure and familiar. He took great care.

'How good is your knowledge of Italian?' Cashel asked him.

'Good but not very good, sir. Not like my English or my German.'

'Never mind. I want you to go to a palazzo – I'll tell you which one – and get in conversation with the servants, the coachmen, the doormen. Get to know them if you can.'

'May I ask why, sir?'

'I want to know, if possible, the movements of the contessa who lives there, the Contessa Mazzolino. I used to know her many years ago. I'd like to renew the acquaintance.'

'It's very easy, sir. I could take your visiting card. You write a note saying you are in Milan staying at this hotel.'

'No. I want to do it more naturally, more casually. I'm not entirely sure she'll remember me.'

'Oh, she will remember you, sir. I guarantee.'

'Thank you, Ignatz, for your faith in me.'

They both laughed.

Two days later Ignatz returned with some information. Often, on a Sunday, he had been told, the contessa would meet her daughter and grandchildren at a café for cake and ice cream. It was called the Caffè Gonzaga. There was a terrace and a small garden – if the weather was clement she liked to sit outside. Spring was a long way off, Cashel thought, but there were still sunny days in wintry Milan. The next bright Sunday he'd be there.

He had to wait two weeks but, that second Sunday morning, seeing the cloudless blue sky above and feeling the warmth of sun on stone, he felt confident that today might just be the day. He was at the Caffè Gonzaga at noon. He found a table in the corner of the terrace, ordered a coffee and a pastry and settled down to read the newspaper. For luncheon he ordered veal *scallopini* and a carafe of cold white wine. He ate an ice cream and smoked a cigar. He had gone through the entire newspaper and so took a book out of his coat pocket, *The Ordeal of Richard Feverel* by George Meredith, and pretended to read.

At around three o'clock he was back on brandy and water. The terrace was fully in the unseasonal sunshine, the light clear and glaring and surprisingly warm. He became aware of a mild commotion at the terrace's entrance – waiters scurrying around, a lot of bowing and greeting – and a party entered.

It was Raphaella, still veiled and in mourning and wearing a black fur coat, accompanied by a younger woman and a governess or nursemaid (he assumed) who had the care of three young children, all under six or seven, he thought. They were taken to a table at the other end of the terrace from Cashel but he had a good view. He was amazed that his heartbeat wasn't audible, ringing out like timpani being bashed – *ba-boom, ba-boom, ba-boom!*

He watched as cakes and ices were brought to the table for the party and coffee was poured. Raphaella was obliged to raise her veil. He couldn't see her hair under her hat but her face was wonderfully familiar to him. The eyes still sleepily hooded; the sweet asymmetry of her lips. He looked at the daughter and saw that she had inherited very little from her mother. The three grand-children were gratifyingly well behaved. When he had calmed down somewhat, and realized that he must stop staring, he wondered what he should do next. He was prepared to be both recognized and not recognized. That was only natural. Of course, she could always *pretend* not to recognize him, also. He decided to act spontaneously – absolutely unprefigured – depending on her reaction when she saw him. He hoped he could hold himself together.

He paid his bill and gathered himself. He took a deep breath. Then, abruptly, he decided to call the whole thing off: this was absurd – it had been far too long. He sat back in his seat, suddenly light-headed. What if he passed out? And yet – everything he remembered about their love for each other urged him on. He wanted to be with her again. To hold her hand, to kiss her, to tell her that he had always loved her. He felt he was back in his twenties again.

He ran his hands over his hair, oiled flat, though these days well shot with grey. He was glad he wore no fashionable beard. His suit was light charcoal, his cravat pale yellow, his overcoat navy blue with a fur collar. He was still very slim, thanks to his African illness, and therefore, he hoped, still recognizably the man he had been forty years previously.

He stood up and walked slowly between the tables – customers around him chatting, eating, drinking – and, as he moved towards her, he took off his hat and paused close to her table, taking his fob from his waistcoat pocket as if to check the time. He was right opposite her, a few feet away. He turned his head and stared at her, willing the force of his gaze to make her look up.

And she did. There was a momentary, unmistakable stiffening of her body as she recognized him. Then, to his astonishment, she smiled and lowered her veil.

'Excuse me, do I know you, sir?' she said in Italian.

Cashel managed to take a few steps forward, his feet obeying his brain's instructions.

'No, Contessa,' he said, also in Italian. 'I was acquainted with

your late husband. I wish only to offer my sincere condolences.'
He gave a little bow and took a visiting card from his pocket. He
had had them made up in London:

Cashel Greville Ross
Konsul der Republik Nicaragua, Trieste, Österreich

On the back he had written the name of his Milan hotel.
She took his card and read it.
'Your name is familiar, sir,' she said, then introduced him to
her daughter, the governess and the children.
My God, she is good, Cashel thought, bowing and smiling
hello, wordless. World class.
'*Grazie.*' She glanced at the card. 'Mr Cashel Greville Ross,' she
said in English.
'I'll trouble you no further, Contessa, ladies. Good day.' He
raised his hand in salutation and left the café.
He drank too much that night – champagne, wine, port –
running repeatedly through those few seconds, that minute or
two, when he had been in her presence again, trying to analyse
their import – or decide if they had any import. Every time
he thought of her face he felt salt tears in his eyes. Was he just
the world's biggest fool? Yes. What kind of man loves a woman
he hasn't seen for forty years? The world's biggest fool. The
world's biggest preposterous romantic fool. Or, a man who knows
what true love really is. All he could do now was wait.
The next day a telegraph was delivered to his room. Already?
My God, so soon! He ripped the envelope open. It was from
Brooke Mason:

CONSULATE PREPARED. EXPECT YOU SOONEST.
ADVISE ARRIVAL DATE AND TIME. MASON

He went at once to the telegraph office and sent his reply:

VERY UNWELL. ARRIVAL DELAYED. ROSS

Mason replied later that day:

MUST LEAVE TRIESTE 21ST. PLENTY OF DOCTORS
HERE. MASON

Cashel checked the calendar. There was a week to go until the 21st. It would take him a day by train to travel from Milan to Trieste. He noted Mason's lack of sympathy – perhaps he was bluffing? Still, he was being paid by Mason on behalf of the Republic of Nicaragua, quarterly, in travellers' cheques, and he had already cashed his first quarter's stipend. He bought a train ticket to Trieste. He would wait until the last possible moment. Please, he begged the gods of love and lovers, let Raphaella come to me.

The gods responded. A simple unsigned note was delivered to his room: '*Noon. Hotel. 18th. A rivederci.*'

On the 18th he rose early, bathed, shaved, had the room cleaned and the bed made up with fresh linen. He bought flowers. He had sweet biscuits, Madeira and a bottle of champagne sent to his room. He sat waiting from the middle of the morning onwards in a kind of stupor, trying to anticipate nothing, keeping all speculation to an absolute minimum. At ten to twelve he allowed himself a small glass of Madeira. At five past twelve there was a knock on the door and he opened it.

Raphaella stepped into the room.

He closed the door and turned to her. She was still in her rustling, shining black silks.

'Cashel Ross,' she said. 'Here you are.'

'Raphaella . . .'

He sank weakly to his knees on the rug, as if in supplication, and covered his face with his hands. No tears, he told himself, no tears.

'What are you doing, sir?'

He climbed back to his feet.

'I'm sorry. I'm just a bit overcome, after all this time.'

He showed her to a chair. She didn't want anything to eat or drink. He sat opposite her, staring at her. She had changed, of course – he had changed too – but nothing about her seemed really different to his eyes. She was a beautiful woman in her late fifties. Her face was pale and smooth, her eyes searching, flicking over him. He felt weak again, as if his body were all jelly, boneless.

'May I kiss you?' he asked.

'You may.'

He knelt in front of her and kissed her gently on the lips, then pressing slightly so that her lips yielded. His eyes were closed, concentrating on the physical sensation. He heard her exhale, a kind of gasp.

He sat down again.

'You know I still love you,' he said matter-of-factly, as if he was talking about the weather outside. 'I've never loved anyone in the way I love you. Never, all these years.'

She pursed her lips, still scrutinizing him, and frowned slightly, like a sceptical judge in a courtroom hearing a dubious plea, he thought.

'I can only stay half an hour,' she said flatly.

She explained. She had a chaperone with her – Mademoiselle Duhamel, whom he had met the other day, her grandchildren's governess, as it turned out; she had come to know her as a friend, not just an employee. She was downstairs in the lobby reading a novel by George Sand while she waited for her. Raphaella had told everyone she was visiting a sick friend.

'Does Mademoiselle Duhamel know the truth?'

'She's French, she's intelligent – I'm sure she can spot a clever subterfuge.' She suddenly smiled. 'Cashel – look at you. You're very thin and still very tall. Tell me about the life you've lived since we last saw each other.'

Cashel gave her a swift résumé with many gaps. He told her he had written a successful novel. He didn't tell her about the Marshalsea. He skimmed over his years in America. He supplied more detail about the great African adventure.

'My God!' she exclaimed several times. 'What a life.'

When it was her turn she prefaced her account with the fact

that she had lived an entirely orthodox and rather boring existence. She had married Count Mazzolino, 'a kind man, a good man', and she had borne him five children – two of whom had died very young, one stillborn, one at six months. She had two surviving sons and a daughter. Her oldest son, Rodolpho, the new count, was a serious man and involved in the governance of the recently unified Italy.

'Apart from that,' she said, with a rueful shrug, 'I did what women of my station do. I had my children. I took up painting. I read books. I travelled in the summer. My children grew up. One son married, my daughter married. I have seven grandchildren. Rodolpho is not yet married. All very boring, compared to you.'

Cashel wondered if this were true, if like him there were gaps in the narrative, secret adventures along the way. He had made no mention of Frannie Broome. He knew Raphaella – she was anything but boring but could easily become bored.

'And it hasn't stopped,' she said. 'You nearly die in Africa and now you go to Trieste to be a consul. Why Nicaragua?' She clearly found the idea amusing.

'It's convenient for me. But I don't have to go immediately.'

'Good,' she said. 'I'll come back tomorrow to check on my sick friend. For one hour.'

'Thank you.'

'You didn't tell me. Did you marry? Do you have children?'

He'd forgotten to tell her he was married. Bríd Corcoran.

'No . . . I mean, yes. I have two daughters. But my wife is mad – insane. She's in an institution – an asylum in Boston, in America.'

'You see, Cashel, everything you do has excitement, is dramatic. Has a story. Nothing is normal.'

'You're my story, Raphaella. My only story.'

She laughed.

'And now I'm a widow. And you're married to a madwoman.'

'I can change that. My marriage is a farce. A nightmare.'

At the door he asked if he could kiss her again and she let him. This time he held her close and felt her body through her stiff skirts and whalebone bodice. Their tongues touched and he was glad to see when they broke apart that she was a little breathless.

'Now I'm part of your story again, Cashel.'

'And that makes me very happy.'

'I'll see you tomorrow.'

After she'd gone Cashel sat thinking for ten minutes and drank three glasses of Madeira. It was no dream – he had held her in his arms, they had kissed. And she was coming back tomorrow.

He went to the telegraph office and sent another message to Mason:

STILL VERY UNWELL. WILL ADVISE ARRIVAL. ROSS

Nicaraguan affairs would have to wait.

The next day when she came at noon they dispensed with polite conversation. She went into his bedroom and called for him when she had undressed. She lay waiting in the bed in a filmy shift and Cashel stripped off quickly, leaving his shirt on. It was wonderful to make love to her, he recognized – though not so wonderful in that he ejaculated after what seemed like three seconds.

They lay in each other's arms and reminisced, re-living their months in Ravenna and the episodes of their love affair. Cashel slipped his hand under her shift and re-familiarized himself with her body, softer, plumper but still the same.

She threw the sheet back and made him roll onto his front so she could see the puckered Waterloo scar on the back of his thigh.

'Yes, it's definitely you,' she said.

Cashel was aroused again but she had to go, she said, adamant, shooing him out of the room so she could carefully dress herself. Mademoiselle Duhamel was waiting downstairs with her novel. She had to rearrange her hair, perfectly. One hour was all she could give him.

'I'll come back tomorrow,' she said. 'Same time.'

The next day was altogether more satisfactory, Cashel thought. All reserve abandoned, in a state of total nakedness. Afterwards she allowed herself to drink some wine. Cashel poured himself a glass as well and sat down on a chair. She lay on the bed, her head propped on pillows, sipping, unselfconscious. Like the old days, Cashel thought, staring at her body. Like it used to be.

'Don't look at me like that. I'm an old lady, a grandmother.'

'A grandfather can look at a grandmother. There's nothing wrong with that. And you're very beautiful.'

'Thank you, kind sir. You are *un gentiluomo galante, grazie.*'

'Will I see you tomorrow?'

'I'm going away tomorrow. To Germany. My son Rodolpho is on a mission to the Prussians. Like you, a sort of diplomat.'

'Why're you going with him?'

'Because he's not married he needs me by his side, he says. As a hostess.'

'That's absurd. Tell him you can't go. You have a sick friend.'

'I can't.'

'Why not?'

'Because he is the new count and he has all the money, the palazzo, the estates, everything.'

'You must have some money of your own, surely?'

She laughed at him.

'What is this world you live in, Cashel?'

She sent him out of the room so she could dress herself. Before she left they made a plan to write to each other – Cashel should write care of the Palazzo Mazzolino – until they could arrange to meet again, but Raphaella insisted on a type of code. Anything he wanted to express about himself had to be done through the medium of a fictitious woman, as if he were reporting the doings and observations of a mutual friend. And he must only sign his name with initials. She explained that her son Rodolpho was a serious person, a man who revered the memory of his father. That was why when she left the palazzo each day she took Mademoiselle Duhamel as a chaperone. Not the slightest suspicion must be raised.

'Rodolpho is – what's the English expression? – a very "properly" person.'

'Proper.'

'Yes, my son is very "proper". He would not be happy to know about his mother's love affair with Il Signor Ross, oh, no.'

'All right, I can write in this code, just to be safe,' he said, wondering again at the swiftness and assuredness of the clever proposal, as if she had done this before.

'What name shall we use?' he asked.

'I know. How about Francesca?'

Now it was his turn to laugh and he took her in his arms more powerfully, kissing her neck and face until she pushed him away.

'Don't ruin my hair,' she said. 'We don't want to do anything to confirm Mademoiselle Duhamel's suspicions.'

They made their farewells, Cashel insisting she tell him the minute she returned from Germany. Trieste wasn't far away. He could come to Milan at very short notice.

'I'll write promptly to Francesca, don't worry,' she said with a smile and closed the door on him.

That evening Cashel telegraphed Mason in Trieste:

ARRIVING TOMORROW. 6 P.M. MUCH BETTER. ROSS

Cashel caught a brief glimpse of Trieste through the windows of the railway carriage as the train took a curve on the coastal track and, for a few moments, the glinting Adriatic and a small white castle on a cliff edge were served up for him like a diorama, perfectly lit by the setting sun, and then came the view of the city. He was travelling alone, deliberately – Ignatz would follow in a couple of days with the bulk of his luggage – as he had thought it best to encounter Mason on his own, given that he was arriving somewhat late to take up his appointment.

In his snatched look through the carriage window, Cashel saw a busy port – many large steamers and a mass of smaller boats – with the usual vertical and horizontal fritter of masts and yards. The city seemed smaller than he had imagined, ringed with wooded hills, with an old castle at the centre and a great expanse of what looked like newly constructed docks and warehousing and even a shipyard. And then the train entered a long tunnel that emerged almost in the heart of the city at the central railway station.

Cashel felt strangely elated on arriving, though he knew it wasn't Trieste that was responsible for his quiet exhilaration. Raphaella and their entrancing, moving, passionate reunion was responsible for everything. On the journey from Milan to Trieste he had been pondering his options, what he saw as the way ahead for the two of them. She was a widow – perfect. He was married – this was a massive obstacle. But his marriage was a sham, something that existed in name only. He had been estranged from Bríd for years and years, and he hadn't seen her in two decades, or thereabouts. She wasn't even *compos mentis*. There had to be some method for the Roman Catholic Church to annul this preposterous figment of a marriage, this monstrosity, this non-union – surely. And then everything would become possible. Everything.

Thinking ahead in this way, contemplating a different life, made him realize that happiness, hope – even sheer excitement – were not emotions reserved solely for young lives. Here he was in his mid-sixties, in a strange new city, embarking on a wholly unfamiliar profession but doing so with a heart that was full – not wearied or jaded. He felt, strange though it may have seemed, that now, at this stage of his life, he had everything to live for.

Even the sight of Brooke Mason's surly face didn't give him pause.

'You've made me late, Ross. It's damned inconvenient.'

'I had a raging toothache, infection, I could hardly think. What was I to do? You know what it's like, Mason, remember?'

Mason could hardly maintain his frostiness and his usual wry amiability returned as they clip-clopped in a fiacre through the streets of the city – solid and impressive, very Austrian, Cashel thought – towards the new consulate. The building – an entire house, in fact – was on Via Vecker* in the eastern precincts of

---

* By strange coincidence, during the years 1907–9 James Joyce regularly visited an apartment in this very house (it was converted from a single building in 1891), to teach English to a young Triestine journalist.

Trieste, not far from the narrow chock-a-block streets of the Old Town that circled around the foot of the small hill on which the castle stood.

Mason unlocked the main door and gave Cashel the keys. The consular offices were to be on the ground floor. Cashel's private apartments were on the two floors above and Ignatz could reside in some attic rooms below the red-tiled roof. The place was unfurnished and, as there was no gas, it was back to the old days of candles and kerosene lamps. Cashel declared himself very pleased.

'We'll pay for you to furnish the place, of course – and for a horse and carriage,' Mason said. 'We've rented you a stable in the next street.'

'That's very generous, thank you.'

'Trieste is an important posting for us, Ross,' Mason said seriously. 'You won't be over-busy but what you'll do will be very significant. Count on that. We'll count on you.'

Cashel wondered what precisely this meant but decided not to enquire further. He and Mason returned to the latter's hotel – the Europa – where Cashel would spend the next few nights until the consulate had basic furnishings. They dined together and Mason drank too much, reminiscing about the time they had spent together at Vache Noire. As he became drunker, Mason grew more indiscreet, hinting that, on his last fraught night at the farm, he might have killed a man who was pursuing him, using the gun that Cashel had lent him. Cashel wondered if this was drink talking, fabricating some fantasy of memory; he remembered that Mason had returned the gun to him, and then stolen it back. That was the odd aspect about Mason, he thought – he seemed on one level a feckless, good-natured *boulevardier* type, always getting into 'scrapes' of one sort or another. Then there was another, more submerged aspect of the man that was altogether more venal and ruthless. Cashel listened to him talk on, not really caring – his heart was full, after all; love had re-illumined his life and he could plan a future for himself and Raphaella. Being a consul in Trieste was ideal at the current moment. He was only a day's train journey away from Milan – he'd hand in his resignation as soon as Raphaella returned from Germany and everything became feasible once more between the two of them. It was an interlude, nothing more significant, and, in the meantime, he would happily and responsibly do his consular duty for the Republic of Nicaragua.

The next morning, Mason took him down to Trieste's 'Porta Nuova'. As they wandered through the streets and then along the seafront promenade Cashel gained a more immediate sense of the city's wealth and busy prosperity. The harbour was very crowded with shipping being unloaded and loaded. International lines were visible and all the commerce of the Eastern Mediterranean seemed congregated, also. Cashel heard Turkish spoken, Greek, Italian, Yiddish, Slovenian, French and English voices. Here and there people were wearing Oriental clothes – turbans, fezzes, leather shoes like slippers that pointed up at the ends. The buildings on the seafront were substantial and confidently decorated. The great jutting stone pier, the Molo San Carlos, was as wide as a city boulevard, thrusting almost a kilometre out into the harbour, a veritable thoroughfare of commerce, lined with ships of all nations.

Mason took him to a warehouse in the new port area, the door to which was locked with a chain and padlock. This belonged to the consulate, he said, pointing to an enamelled oval containing an image of the Nicaraguan flag and the usual rubric in German, Italian and Spanish. Cashel was struck by how small this official insignia was, smaller than a small saucer. You had to peer to read the lettering.

Mason found the correct keys and unlocked the door, sliding it to one side. They stepped into a cool empty space. Dusty sunbeams speared in from high, square windows.

'This is a bonded warehouse,' Mason said, handing Cashel the keys. 'It belongs to us. Goods will come in under a customs seal. When they arrive – you'll be alerted, of course – then I'll tell you where they're to be forwarded on to.'

'What sort of "goods"?'

'I've no idea. A variety, that's all I know. As consul, your funda-
mental, essential role is to expedite their onward transportation.'

'Right. Is that all?'

'It's not complicated – but there's a certain amount of paperwork required by the Austrian authorities.'

Ignatz can deal with that, Cashel thought – German was his
first language, after all.

'All seems very clear to me, Mason.'

Back in the hotel Mason gave him his official certification as
Consul for the Republic of Nicaragua – a parchment hung with
ribbons and seals and several illegible, highly cursive signatures –
along with his diplomatic passport. He also handed him several
files full of other useful documentation – empty passports and
visas, in the main – should they be required by any citizens of the
republic to further the economic, commercial and trading duties
that the consulate was there to promote. Mason provided a telegraph address in London for all regular communication.

'If there's anything confidential or delicate then it's best to
contact me directly through my bank.' He handed Cashel a card.

'What do you mean by "confidential"?'

'All these questions, Ross! I don't *know*. It's a question of judgement, of unusual eventualities, I suppose. You're an intelligent
man, and as consul you can make the decision yourself. Let's say
any matter you'd prefer not to consign to a telegraph.'

'Understood.'

Cashel offered to accompany Mason to the station to see him
off but Mason said there was no need.

'Oh, yes,' he added. 'I'll be back one day soon with the Minister for Foreign Affairs. He's coming to visit Europe – soon. I'll
give you due warning. He's a very agreeable fellow, by the way.
One of us.'

With Ignatz's help the consulate on Via Vecker was swiftly and
comfortably furnished. The nearby stables had been rented for
him and contained a newish phaeton and two horses and a lad to

look after them. Cashel settled down to lead the life of a consul. And it turned out to be an easy one. His salary went a long way in Trieste: as well as a cook and a housemaid, he was able to employ an interpreter (who spoke German and Slovenian), an elderly Triestine named Giorgio Zaule who had worked for Monsieur Henri Beyle, he claimed with pride, very briefly French consul in Trieste in 1830. Cashel said the name was unfamiliar to him. It was only later that he realized this Henri Beyle was in fact Stendhal, the French novelist. He saw it as a good omen that another novelist had been a consul there.

Months went by. Summer proved very agreeable on the Adriatic. He went sailing. He went riding in the nearby hills. He visited Ljubljana and Vienna. In the winter the powerful wind from the mountains – the 'bora' – blew strongly, confining him indoors, but the consulate was comfortable and the fires efficient. In 1866 the war between Italy and Austria quickened irredentist fervour in the city but as the conflict had no bearing on the Republic of Nicaragua nothing ruffled the calm waters of self-indulgent inertia at the consulate on Via Vecker.

Cashel wrote to Raphaella once a month, care of the Palazzo in Milan.

14 Via Vecker
Trieste
Austrian-Littoral

10th March 1866

My Dear Friend,

I've really come to relish and enjoy this strange city. Imagine, if you can, a sizeable Austrian provincial town with its solid civic buildings – a stock exchange, a theatre, mercantile offices, streets full of fine shops – and a substantial and efficient bureaucracy (that naturally conducts all its business in German). Then move it to a beautiful corner of the Adriatic coast and fit it out with a harbour and shipyard as busy as Lisbon or Hamburg. Then populate it with a majority of Italians, middle class and resentful, who speak a

Venetian dialect and who long to be part of Italy, not Austria, and a sizeable peasantry of Slovenians. Add a seasoning of Turks, Greeks, Armenians and any other foreigners from the Eastern Mediterranean and you will have some sense of this unique metropolis. Its vast and busy port brings seamen and sailors from around the world – Sweden, Japan, Egypt, to name but three. It is a rich city in a rich crown-land of a rich empire. Daily life pullulates around me. I visit the opera to hear Bellini or Mozart. I can go to working-class taverns and expensive restaurants. I can buy coffee from Brazil and cigars from Cuba. It all seems somewhat unreal but it suits my state of mind and – maybe – my personality.

Social life is limited. I occasionally dine at other consulates (British, American and French) and return the invitation. I attend the odd official function on independence days. It is not a 'giddy round', I assure you.

My news of our mutual friend Francesca is interesting. As you know her husband is seriously ill and is restrained at an insane asylum in the United States. Francesca thinks there is a distinct possibility that her marriage to him may be annulled. She has written to a Roman Catholic priest to see how the process may be instigated and she has promised to keep me _au courant_ – it is a complicated matter, by all accounts. However, she wishes me to tell you that you are constantly in her thoughts and, indeed, that it is simply thinking of you that makes her life worth living.

My job here is dull but I am happy to be thus dully under-employed. I paint, I ride, I read, I write, I sail, I swim. I'm thinking of taking up fencing. I'm paid well to live in this way – I have no right to complain.

I remain, my dear friend,

your dear friend,
C.R.

It was over a year after taking up his appointment in Trieste that Cashel received the first telegraph notifying him of the date of a shipment (just two crates) arriving on a French ship, the *Aurore*. He and Ignatz went down to the docks and supervised the crates – which were very heavy – being winched out of the hold and deposited on their waiting wagon. The paperwork was conducted by the Austrian customs, the stamped lead seals were checked, new seals attached and the two crates transported to the warehouse where the seals were inspected again. Cashel read the bill of lading. The crates had come from France, from Marseilles. Their contents were listed as 'Marble for paving only'.

Cashel telegraphed Mason:

GOODS ARRIVED. AWAIT INSTRUCTIONS. ROSS

Twenty-four hours later he received those instructions. The crates were to be shipped to the United States, to Charleston, South Carolina, to a Mr A. B. Smith (Builder). Cashel duly supervised the delivery of the two crates (customs being satisfied that the seals were intact) and they were craned aboard a Blue Star steamer heading for London and then the United States.

Everything went smoothly. Cashel was pleased to be at last fulfilling his duties as consul – though why inferior marble was being sent to South Carolina by the Nicaraguan Republic was beyond him. He had done his job. Good. He had more important matters on his mind – he was trying to get his marriage annulled.

23 Mortimer Street
Philadelphia
USA

September 3rd 1867

My Dear Cashel,
  You will be surprised to receive a letter from me at this address. My broken heart has delayed my writing to you. My son Clayton was a victim in the last skirmish of our terrible war. He was wounded at the so-called Battle of Palmito Ranch in May 1865. He had miraculously survived many battles during the war – Antietam, Shiloh, Cold Harbor – and, as a veteran, he had been transferred with other veterans to a unit called the 54th Indiana Regiment. With the 54th he had been

sent to Texas to supervise the arrangements that the end of the war
had brought about. The war was over, Cashel. But there was a
short-lived battle fought between the Union and Confederate forces for
reasons that no one can determine and Clayton was grievously
wounded in the leg. His leg was amputated to the hip. He was sent
home and I nursed him but to no avail. I watched him slip slowly away
over several months.

He died in early '66. At his funeral he was described as the last
casualty of our civil war but the wounded and maimed soldiers can be
seen everywhere. There will be many more 'last' casualties. Once he
was gone, I could not continue. I have left the farms to Whitaker and
returned to my parents' home in Philadelphia. You would not recognize
me as your Frannie Broome. I am an old, bitter, grieving woman and
all that is writ upon my face.

Whitaker will continue to send you whatever revenue there is from
the frozen water trade but it is much diminished as the new industrial
machines seem to make ice better all year round than our winters can.

Don't forget me, Cashel. I'll never forget you. I send you my fondest
love, as always.

Your own
Frannie Broome

Cashel found this letter most upsetting. It seemed that not
only was Clayton Broome an absurd victim of the American war
but so was Frannie's familiar indomitability. He wrote back to
her, sending love and sympathy, telling her of his new incarnation as consul and urging her to promise to keep writing to him.
He felt guilt also, in the way he had knowingly made Frannie
some sort of substitute for Raphaella. And now Raphaella was
back in his life – after a fashion – and Frannie Broome had become
an episode in a life he used to lead . . .

This letter seemed to provoke a flow of communication from
the United States. Father O'Malley replied, pleased to hear from
Cashel, but declaring that it would be very difficult, almost
impossible, to have his marriage to Bríd unilaterally annulled.

The marriage had been consummated and his two daughters were the living proof. Perhaps if Mrs Ross were inclined to agree that there had been a separation of many years then possibly some sort of conclusion could be reached, though he warned Cashel that they might also need the intercession of the Bishop of Boston. Would Mrs Ross be prepared to meet the bishop?

That prospect was dashed with another letter from Nessa (Maeve still didn't reply to any letter or present he sent her). Nessa said that she had gone to visit Bríd on 'one of her more lucid days' and had put Cashel's proposal to her that their marriage should be formally ended by an annulment:

I'm sorry to say, dear father, that her response was a violent one. Never! Never! Never! was all she cried.

Cashel felt equally violent at this news, cursing himself for the choices he'd made in his life. Why had he converted to Roman Catholicism? Because that was the only way he could marry Bríd. But the transformed Bríd after the birth of Nessa, the religious votary, the maniac, was not the vibrant young girl he'd proposed to. And yet, here he was, with the woman he loved miraculously free to join him, trapped and confined by a code of behaviour and religious doctrine that he no longer recognized. Now he was older he could look back down the years and see how blithe or headstrong decisions could resonate disastrously, years, decades later, casting an unforeseen curse on your life, shaping your present circumstances in a way you could never imagine.

One night, he sat up late drinking brandy with Ignatz, feeling bitter and sorry for himself. He told Ignatz of his woes. About his amazing reunification with Raphaella, of the renewal of their love for each other. And now the frustration of Bríd's crazed, adamant refusal. Of course, Ignatz had also known her – the Bríd before and the Bríd after. Their conversation was gravid with their shared history.

'So it seems,' Cashel said, 'that I'm condemned to be married to her for ever – or until I die or she dies. If I marry again I'll be a bigamist.'

'Why bother about marriage, sir? Why not simply be with this person, La Contessa Raphaella? Why do you have to be married?'

'Look, personally I don't care about marriage vows but I'm not sure she'd agree. Or she wouldn't be allowed to agree. Her son is very . . . very protective of his mother's reputation – and of his own reputation, and of his dead father's. And she relies upon this son for money to fund her way of life. It's complicated. It's impossible for her to run away to Trieste and simply be together with me.'

Ignatz shrugged and nodded sadly. Cashel poured them both another drink, looking at him. Ignatz's sharp little beard was grey, his hair was grey, yet he seemed as strong and solid as the day they had met.

'Talking of marriage – why have you never married, Ignatz? Where is your sweetheart? Don't you want to have a wife? To have children?'

'No,' he said, simply. 'I'm very happy with the life I've had, thanks to you, sir. The day I met you, the day I came to Willow Creek. That was the great miracle in my life.'

'You're allowed to have other miracles. Little Ignatzes running around.'

Ignatz looked awkward.

'To tell the truth, Mr Ross, I've always felt that, in a way, I *was* married.'

'What d'you mean?'

'I'm married to you, Mr Ross. I feel my life is joined to yours. Almost as if I was your wife – or your husband. I'm explaining badly. I only wish for nothing more than to continue as we are.'

Cashel smiled vaguely at this surprise confession, a little perturbed, in fact, and decided it was best to say nothing. Yet there was something true about what he'd said – he and Ignatz had suffered many good times and many vicissitudes together. They had been separated and had met again, joyously. And he realized that, throughout the years they'd been together, he'd relied on Ignatz, unreflectingly, utterly. And he imagined the same was true of Ignatz. It made him think of the old saying: 'No man is a hero to his valet.' Perhaps it could be rephrased: 'No man is a hero to his wife . . .' Ignatz saw their relationship as a form of marriage. Who was he, Cashel Ross, to gainsay it?

He looked across the table at Ignatz and topped up his glass. Ignatz smiled his thanks; his eyes were drowsy with the many glasses of brandy they had shared and he had a dreamy half-smile on his lips. Perhaps it had been the liquor talking – there was no need to take the analysis any further.

The life of the Nicaraguan consul started to become busier. Heavy crates from French ports were arriving every month, now, and their handling and onward despatch – always to port cities in the United States – became a matter of routine, so Cashel happily left the administration up to Ignatz. By now Cashel felt established in Trieste as one of its minor diplomats, and had had an embroidered pseudo-military uniform made for his attendance at official events. He had become a proficient amateur watercolourist, he thought, roving around the Triestine countryside looking for picturesque views. He was indulging in a chaste flirtation with the wife of the French consul, the aptly named Madame Crèvecoeur. He knew he could have taken matters further, had he wished, but he had no desire to betray Raphaella – now ensconced in Berlin with her son. Annoyingly, there seemed to be no date set for her return to Milan.

He took two months' leave in late 1869 to celebrate his seventieth birthday with Buckley and Hogan, leaving Ignatz in charge of the consulate. He extended his stay by a further month sorting out his literary and financial affairs. There was still a trickle of revenue from the cheap editions of his two books; and despite the invention of industrial refrigeration, monies continued to accrue, via honest Whitaker Broome, from the pure quality of Willow Creek ice, which was still in demand in the great cities of the eastern United States. He found himself, not a rich man, but a reasonably well-off one. He informed Raphaella of Francesca's relative solvency but she never referred to it in her replies. Once a countess, always a countess, he supposed. Something in their lives would have to change radically, he realized.

He was a reasonably well-off man, true, but one with no property, it struck him, and so, during his time in England, he looked for houses and cottages with some land, starting near Buckley's parish, but quickly decided provincial life in the southern counties around London wasn't for him. He wondered if his time in Trieste had changed him, somehow – as if this peculiar, polyglot, many-cultured city with its unique anomalies and absurdities was, in fact, the perfect home-from-home he had been looking for all his life.

He returned there with surprising enthusiasm – only to discover that not all had gone well with the last shipment to have arrived at the consulate's bonded warehouse.

Cashel and Ignatz contemplated the damaged crate. It had fallen a few feet from an ineptly operated davit and a couple of planks had splintered open, but though the crate remained more or less entire it was possible to see something of the contents. Ignatz had refrained from touching it, waiting for Cashel's return. Cashel pulled away one of the splintered planks.

'I could see that it was not "marble for paving only", sir. I wasn't sure what to do.'

Cashel heaved away another plank and took out some handfuls of straw packing to reveal the side of a large decorated terracotta amphora.

'Let's get everything out.'

They levered off the top and removed three heavy layers of slabs of a coarse grey marble veined with a distinctive rusty-orange. Beneath these top layers there was a dense packing of straw concealing six other decorated pots, a small white marble sculpture of a centaur and three stone plaques with carved inscriptions in ancient Greek.

'Where's this crate meant to be going?' Cashel asked.

'New Orleans, sir.'

Cashel nodded – all was suddenly becoming clear. He felt his complacency, his easily assumed indifference, fall from him like a

discarded cloak slipping from his shoulders. He had always realized that the consulship in Trieste was too good, too easy, to be
true, and now he had the evidence of his lackadaisical complicity.
He was obviously involved in an elaborate scheme to smuggle
Greek antiquities to the United States. He felt suddenly sick as the
retrospective logic of his thinking made itself apparent. Brooke
Mason. Brooke Mason had known the perfect man for the job.
$5,000 a year, plus consular expenses. Free accommodation; stab-
ling for complimentary carriage and horses, no questions asked . . .
He stopped himself and picked up a small terracotta vase. It was
beautiful and delicate, still with some crusts of dried earth adher-
ing to it. He brushed that away to reveal a lightly clad nymph
gambolling with a naked warrior with a shield and an impressive
erection. How much would an American magnate pay for this? he
wondered.

Now he felt anger building. He had to make sure that he could
protect himself. How could the bitten bite back?

'Can you re-do this crate, put all this together again, Ignatz? So
it looks untouched, secure?'

'Of course.'

'Right. We'll make a note of the contents and send it on as if
nothing has happened. But from now on we open every crate and
take an inventory.'

Shortly after this discovery, Brooke Mason announced his
return to Trieste, in the company of an American called Waldo
Gunning. Cashel met them at the station, disguising his wariness.
Gunning was young, in his thirties, and plump in a dissipated
way, fat-cheeked and double-chinned, sporting a pale blonde
moustache with the ends waxed vertical. He was all smiles and
politesse.

Mason was full of congratulations. The expediting of the
crates was going very smoothly. Everyone was very happy. Cashel
was blandness personified – eager to help in any way.

They went for dinner in the restaurant of the Europa Hotel.
Gunning ate everything like a man with a tremendous appetite,
as if he'd been starved for days.

'We're expecting the traffic to increase,' Mason explained. 'Maybe double the usual amount. There's great demand for this marble. Gratifyingly.'

'That won't worry us,' Cashel said. 'It runs like clockwork here.'

'Exactly. Hence Trieste,' Mason said. 'The great entrepôt of the Mediterranean.'

'Is that why you chose Trieste?'

'Well, it's just easy here, I mean,' Mason said. 'A huge port like this – procedures set in stone. Austrian rigour, all that.'

'It's efficient, that's for sure,' Cashel said. He turned to Gunning. 'Are you in the marble trade, Mr Gunning?'

'Ah. Yes, you could say so,' Gunning admitted, then quickly changed the subject. 'Have you ever been to the United States, Ross?'

Cashel gave a short account of his years there. Gunning listened, nodding.

'But you were in rural Massachusetts,' he said. 'You need to go to the cities. The amount of wealth – the amount of wealthy people – these days is prodigious,' Gunning went on, tearing up a bread roll and stuffing it in his mouth. He chewed for a while before he could speak again. 'And the wealthy people're building their great palaces throughout the land. Marble palaces. They just can't get enough marble.'

Or Greek antiquities, Cashel thought, smiling.

'Anything more I can do, just let me know,' he said.

'You're doing a splendid job, Ross,' Mason said, lighting a cigar. 'We're very grateful. The government is grateful.'

'Thank you. How are things in Nicaragua?'

'What?'

'I've yet to encounter a single Nicaraguan in Trieste.'

'Well, ah, yes, that's why Gunning is here. He's Minister for Foreign Affairs.'

'Yes, we're thinking of opening other consulates – thanks to the success of yours here. Copenhagen. Marseilles. Istanbul. You've set the bar high, Mr Ross, and we're very grateful.'

Cashel inclined his head modestly, thinking, Do they really think I'm that stupid?

'What would you recommend for dessert, Ross?' Gunning asked. '*Île flottante* or *gâteau Forêt-Noire*?'

As Mason had forewarned, the flow of marble crates increased to three or sometimes four shipments a month. Cashel was instructed to send them on to Charleston, Savannah, Houston, New Orleans – one or two to Havana, Cuba. There seemed no obvious pattern yet all the crates arrived from French ports – Marseilles, Toulon, Nice. There was no indication on the manifest where in Greece or the Aegean islands the crates originated from.

He and Ignatz routinely emptied, inventoried, repacked and resealed each crate before its onward despatch to the United States. Ignatz claimed the customs seals he fabricated were identical to the real thing, impossible to challenge. The antiquities were astounding – even Cashel, not the remotest expert, could sense their quality and rare beauty. Bronzes, marble statues, a whole mosaic floor, once, countless pots and amphorae. He could have filled a sizeable museum with the artefacts that passed through the Nicaraguan warehouse in Trieste harbour, he realized. What he couldn't calculate, however, was the amount of money Mason and Gunning must be making as they sold them on to the new plutocrats of the United States. Then one vast crate arrived and, when it was opened and unpacked, revealed a giant marble lion, one paw raised, twice life-size, in immaculate condition despite a few patches of moss on its back. It was spectacular, Cashel could see, the ultimate collector's trophy. The Venus de Milo of the animal world. He decided he had to act.

He took a slab of the grey, orange-veined marble that accompanied each delivery – the notional contents of each crate – and showed it to various stonemasons in Trieste. It was low-grade marble, he was told, not of the highest quality or density, hard to work or shape, hence its usefulness as paving. Ideal for hallways, stairways, courtyards, that sort of utility. However, one stonemason, a Turk from Smyrna, recognized it immediately.

'Oh, yes,' he said, 'this is probably marble from Latmos.'

'Latmos?'

'In Ródos.'

Ah, Ródos, Cashel thought, wherever that might be. The first clue.

'It's the orange veining, and that grey colour. It can only come from one place. Ródos.' He smiled. 'Rhodes, that's the English name.' He looked askance at Cashel's baffled face. 'It's a big island. Off the coast of Turkey.'

Cashel now had a destination. Perhaps a source. And a plan. He created a new passport for himself in the name of Greville Soutar – a little nod of recognition to his mother, Elspeth Soutar. It was a wise precaution to travel under a pseudonym, he realized, because whoever was sending the antiquities to Trieste would know the name of the Nicaraguan consul who was facilitating their onward journey. He left Ignatz in charge of the consulate once again and took an Austrian Lloyd steamer to Athens, a four-day journey, as it turned out.

In Athens, Cashel had to wait two days for a French steamer that would take him directly to Rhodes. He noted that there were more, and more efficient, French steamer routes to the Levantine islands and the Dodecanese. Perhaps that explained the complicated itinerary of the antiquities, he thought: from one empire, the Ottoman, to France – in transit, as it were – before heading to a small, insignificant consulate in another empire, the Austro-Hungarian (as it had recently become). And then to the United States. Hard to trace slabs of 'marble for paving only', far from their original quarries, criss-crossing the Mediterranean. It had all been very cleverly worked out.

In Athens he stayed at the Hôtel des Étrangers on Place de la Constitution, 'fitted up in the style of the better Italian hotels', his guidebook informed him. He was rather amazed that most of the principal streets in Athens had French names. As he went for a stroll he found the modern city handsome and expansively laid out. He ate tolerably well at the Brasserie et Restaurant d'Europe and, after his lunch, went to an antique shop off the Rue d'Hermes to see if he could gain any information about the trade in antiquities from this part of the world. There he was told by the owner himself that, categorically, with no exceptions, the export of antiquities from Greece was entirely forbidden. Everything in his shop, however, was for sale, cleared for export. 'What about antiquities from Rhodes?' Cashel asked disingenuously. Ah, well, he was told, Rhodes is part of the Ottoman Empire, the 'Sublime Porte'. Rhodes was not part of Greece – and, anyway, the Turks didn't care about Greek antiquities. Cashel began to see the subtleties of Mason's trade and how it could operate, unchecked.

That night, Cashel lay in his bed, the gaslight extinguished, the clatter of carriage wheels echoing faintly from the paved streets around the square, wondering what exactly he thought he was doing. Here he was, a man over seventy, halfway through a half-thought-out adventure in the Eastern Mediterranean. What would Raphaella think of him now, lying in bed in the Hôtel des Étrangers? He was the appointed consul in Trieste of the Republic of Nicaragua. True, he responded in dialogue with himself, but he was also a consul who was very caught up in what was clearly a substantial and complex operation involving the smuggling of Greek antiquities to the United States. Shouldn't he just live his life and turn a famous blind eye? He was very comfortable and well recompensed in his role as ignorant expeditor of stolen antiquities. Why make everything more difficult and possibly dangerous?

He turned over and punched a dent in his hard pillow. The answer he gave himself was always the same: he did what he did because it was what he felt he had to do – right or wrong – however lame that reasoning appeared. That simple motivation had determined almost every action of his life. He was being gulled and exploited by Brooke Mason and Waldo Gunning – that was incontrovertible, now. If he was going to thwart them in their endeavours then he needed more information. That was why he was lying sleepless in a bed in a hotel in Athens, planning a trip to Rhodes. It was as simple as that – and sufficient reason, he thought – except he was feeling his old stomach cramps returning as the tension and pressures of his journey mounted. Mrs Dashwood's would have helped abate them. That monkey bite in Zanzibar would not let him alone.

A Messageries Maritimes steamer carried him safely to Rhodes. His first impression of the old, walled town around the port, with its almost theatrical castle, was that it was semi-ruined – the piled buildings in bad repair, crumbling away as if their walls were made of cake or damp toast. He saw a large tower, half-fallen, standing in its own pile of weed-sprouting rubble, as if it had been bombarded by cannons.

He disembarked and paid a porter – a thin, ancient man – to carry his baggage to the 'best' taverna in town. It turned out to be a dark, noxious place, busy with hundreds of flies. In his room he found a bed with a straw mattress and walls speckled with tiny bloodbursts from flattened mosquitoes. And yet, out of the window, the sea was a searing refulgent blue and the sky above even bluer, if that were possible. He decided to pay a visit to the British consul, one Alexander Bonson.

He received directions to the consulate that turned out to be a mile out of town. He walked up the dusty road in the autumn sunshine, feeling the heat on his shoulders and wishing he'd worn a straw hat. The orchestra of cicadas sawed away, delivering their creaking monotone, and there was a scent of pine resin in the air. Some ragged barefoot children followed him for a while and then lost interest. A pale brown dog, covered in sores, was more persistent, plodding along at his heels as if Cashel had been unilaterally selected as his new master. It sat patiently waiting for him at the gate of the consulate's courtyard, suddenly loyal.

Alexander Bonson was a small, bustling man in his thirties with luxuriant waves of chestnut hair. He greeted Cashel – 'Mr Greville Soutar' – very affably. He refused to let him stay in the filthy taverna and sent his dragoman to retrieve Cashel's luggage. Dinner would be served at sunset, Cashel was told.

Bonson was obviously short on company and keen to hold forth about the dissatisfactions of his job. His low remuneration – £200 a year – the steady impoverishment of the island and the

Dodecanese in general as the 'Sublime Porte' deliberately taxed the population into ever more egregious poverty.

'Did you see that tower at the harbour?' Bonson asked. 'Fell down in an earthquake in 1851. Good God, 1851! No one can afford to rebuild it. That's Rhodes for you, in a nutshell.'

Cashel commiserated, watching in some amazement as Bonson took a comb from his pocket and – unembarrassed and unselfconscious – combed his luxuriant hair. He did this three times during the course of their dinner. As the dusk thickened and the bats began to fly, Cashel felt the air cool and his mood change to a kind of quietistic inertia as he drank the pungent cold wine Bonson served. Was he wasting his time? Was this the ultimate fool's errand? Somehow, he couldn't be bothered to rebuke himself for his impulsiveness.

He offered Bonson one of his cigars and they both lit up.

'I have to confess, Soutar,' Bonson said. 'I'm no Philhellene. I get on much better with the Turks. The vizier in Smyrna is a fine fellow. Very hospitable. No – I'm no Lord Byron, I'm afraid.'

'I knew Lord Byron,' Cashel said, without thinking.

'Good God! Really? How astonishing. What was he like?'

'A very complicated man, let's say.'

'Do you mind if I ask your age, Soutar?'

'I'm in my seventies. I met Byron in 1822.'

'How extraordinary. 1822, my goodness.'

As he made this spontaneous admission, Cashel felt he was talking about another world, another era in history entirely. It did seem extraordinary that he had lived through it.

Bonson ran his comb through his hair again and set it down beside his fork.

'Well, old Byron's love of the Greeks didn't do him much good, did it.'

They talked on, Cashel explaining that he was touring the Dodecanese, working as an agent for a large building firm – he was not specific – that was looking for a cheap and reliable source of marble.

'There's no white marble on Rhodes, unfortunately,' Bonson

said. 'There are marble quarries here and there – though it's not the best quality.'

'Could I visit any of them?'

'There's one about a couple of hours' ride from here. I'll get my dragoman to take you. This is what this island needs, Soutar – commerce. Pure and simple. There's no silk made any more, the wine and the olive oil are very substandard. The only trade that flourishes is sponge-fishing, and the bloody French buy everything.'

He puffed at his cigar, thinking.

'If your firm could order a few tons of marble on a regular basis then I could argue that British steamers should call here directly. Which they don't, most inconveniently. Otherwise you'd have to ship your marble to Smyrna – and then onwards. All adds to the cost.'

Bonson seemed quite excited by the prospect. Cashel nodded and smiled, saying guardedly that there might be something in the idea.

'Actually, you might like Smyrna,' Bonson said. 'I could introduce you to the vizier. I try to pop over once a month or so – and there's a very decent brothel there. Clean.'

'I might pay a visit on my return journey.'

'Small glass of brandy, Soutar? I can't tell you how pleased I am you've arrived. Let's move back inside.'

They wandered into Bonson's high-ceilinged, white-painted drawing room, Cashel a little reluctant to leave the terrace. There was a cool, seductive softness about the night and the trilling of the crickets reminded him of Africa. Memories were stirring.

He sat down and Bonson handed him a brandy.

'Soutar . . . Is that a Scottish lilt I detect?'

'I was born in Scotland – grew up in Ireland.'

'You never get rid of a Scotch accent, I was told. Never. However hard you try.'

Cashel, feeling comfortable, enjoying his cigar and brandy, told Bonson of his row with Byron about the poet's Scottish accent.

'Byron was born in Aberdeen? Are you sure? Well, I never. You should write all this stuff down, Soutar. Fascinating.'

Bonson's dragoman was a young Smyrniote in his twenties, with big brown eyes and a wispy chin-beard. His name was Ferkan. He spoke fluent Turkish and Greek, good English with some French and Italian, and could make himself understood in Ladino. The perfect dragoman for Bonson.

Cashel and Ferkan set out in the morning for an easy two-hour ride from Rhodes Town to the marble quarry at Glymphonos. The day seemed to reverberate with blue whenever they came in sight of the sea, almost painful to the eyes. When they moved inland the perfect white of the tall, rising clouds had the effect of making the sky's blue even more intense. The landscape became more ruggedly hilly, with the track they were following winding round deep ravines, the air pungent with pine. As well as pines, the hills were covered with cypresses, myrtle and wild figs. Along the way they would pass ancient orchards of olive trees with the harvest heaped in great piles on the ground.

'Is it good to leave olives like that?' Cashel asked.

'No. Is bad,' Ferkan said. 'Is not good for making oil. Too much dirt.'

'Why don't they press them?'

'There is no market, sir. Nobody wants this oil.'

At midday they stopped in the shade of an umbrella pine and ate some bread and hard cheese, drinking a sour white wine from a wineskin. The autumnal sun was ideally warm; swallows and swifts were flying low, dipping and diving over the scrub. From somewhere came the dry monotone tinkle of a bell – a goatherd traversing the valley below them.

'Do you only wish to see the marble?' Ferkan asked.

'Why? What else should I see?'

'Now you come this way – at Glymphonos, there is the acropolis.'

'Really? An acropolis?'

'Is big. This is where Mr Bonson is digging.'

'I'd love to see that.'

At the quarry, Cashel saw the grey marble with the orange vein-ing. He was told this was very similar to the marble from Lentos – but better. He went through the motions with the quarry-master, Ferkan translating. Taking down details in a notebook. How much marble could he provide? Was there enough in the quarry to supply orders over several years? He received the usual confidently optimistic affirmations. And the price? He should ask the manager at the warehouse in the harbour, he was told.

The acropolis at Glymphonos was more impressive. On a flat-topped hill near the remains of a substantial palace there were several rows of tall columns set on massive plinths. Ruined build-ings lay all around, overgrown with ivy and columbine, and here and there he saw the neat-edged deep trenches of excavations.

Cashel stood on the edge of a trench about four feet wide by twenty long. Cut stones had been piled carefully beside it.

'This is where Mr Bonson digs, yes?'

'He sends some men here to dig.'

'Do they find anything?'

'Oh, yes. They find many things.'

Ferkan led him down a gentle hill to a small arena with ranked, curved rows of seats. They entered the amphitheatre through a triumphal arch upon which stood a single marble lion, twice life-sized, one paw raised. As Cashel stood and looked up at it he experienced a strange emotion of recognition. A magnificent sculpture, indisputably, and its pair was sitting in a crate in the Nicaraguan consulate's bonded warehouse in Trieste.

He felt that his journey was vindicated – but he was also angered now he knew the part he had inadvertently played in the separ-ation of the twin lions of the Glymphonos acropolis, and – in a kind of revelation – understood almost instantly how the whole itinerary was put together. Bonson unearthed the antiquities. Because Rhodes was in the Ottoman Empire there was no control over their clandestine export. So, Rhodes to France. France to Tri-este. Trieste to the United States. No doubt the twin lions of the Glymphonos acropolis would be reunited soon enough. This was

411

all the evidence he needed, he realized. Bonson, Gunning and Brooke Mason. Not to forget the consul in Trieste – the unwitting, crucial hub in the journey. A very tidy, significant operation in antiquity robbing and smuggling – all tracks covered and no questions asked. No doubt, after Glymphonos had been emptied of its booty, there were many other sites to move on to.

They were back in Rhodes Town by dusk and Cashel asked Ferkan to show him where the marble warehouse was. It was closed but they would return in the morning to enquire about prices. Back at the consulate Bonson was absent – gone by boat to Symi for a couple of days – so Cashel dined alone on a spicy stew of goat and olives. He went to bed early, exhausted by his long day in the sun.

The next morning Ferkan and he went to the warehouse at the port. He was shown tons of grey Glymphonos marble and also other types of stone, should he require them – red limestone, breccia and what looked like a kind of slate. Cashel dutifully took notes and was given a list of prices depending on the size of the order.

He noticed some large wooden doors at the far end of the warehouse, from behind which he could hear a sound of banging – hammers on nails.

'What's in there?' he asked Ferkan.

'This is Mr Bonson's store,' Ferkan said and got the warehouse manager to unlock it. The room was large and windowless. Sun beamed in through a skylight. The place was filled with rows of pots and statuary – all produced from the diggings at the acropolis, he assumed. He saw an altar screen and piles of stacked capitals of Corinthian columns, a complete staircase with balustrades and various inscribed tombstones. There were terracotta statuettes, dozens of oil lamps, bangles, diadems, coins, helmets and figurines. He felt he might be standing in a wing of the British Museum. Large, empty, wooden crates stood here and there, freshly constructed, curls of wood-shavings on the floor. Two carpenters were making another. They stopped when they saw Cashel and stood back, smiling politely.

'What does Mr Bonson do with all this?' he asked Ferkan innocently, gesturing at the artefacts all around them.

'He is helping to make a museum in London, I think,' Ferkan
said, with an indifferent shrug. Cashel walked up and down the
rows of plunder from Glymphonos, marvelling at it. He picked
up a terracotta fragment from a broken pot – he could see the
beak of some creature with a fish in its mouth – and having
checked that Ferkan wasn't looking he slipped it in his pocket.
Everything had fallen into place. Time to get back to Trieste. He
would make sure he left well before Bonson returned from his
trip.

Cashel was back in Trieste by early December. The winter wind
from the mountains – the 'Bora' – was blowing fiercely through
the streets of the town and along the esplanade when Cashel
stepped down from the gangway onto the Molo San Carlos. The
Bora snatched powerfully at his coat tails, buffeting him, almost
like an embrace, the city pleased to welcome him back. Ignatz
was there to meet him, a hand firmly placed on the crown of his
hat. Cashel's luggage was packed swiftly into a fiacre and they
returned to the Via Vecker.

The next morning, he and Ignatz went down to the warehouse, Cashel almost superstitiously wanting to see the giant
lion that had been removed from the arch of the arena at Glymphonos. There it stood – all the evidence he needed. He was his
own best witness.

'We need it properly recorded, Ignatz, as evidence. It must be
photographed.'

The photographer duly arrived in the afternoon – a young
man, in a tight suit, somewhat humourless – and took a photograph of the lion and then one of the crate. Cashel asked for ten
prints of each image – he wasn't sure why: one photograph was
all that was needed to prove the desecration of the site – but he
wanted to feel covered for any eventuality. He could give copies
to Ignatz; he could deposit others at his bank.

'What're you going to do with the photographs?' Ignatz asked.

'I'm not sure. It's a form of protection, I suppose. Evidence. We have to protect ourselves, Ignatz.'

He suspected that the second lion would be arriving before too long. A perfect pair, flanking the entryway to some grand mansion in Maine or Connecticut. But what to do with this evidence? Who would most appreciate it? Not the 'Sublime Porte' or its emissaries. They didn't care about Greek antiquities – they had enough of their own. Bonson's friend, the vizier at Smyrna, was probably reaping his own dividend from the trade. The new government of independent Greece, perhaps? The British government? The United States Customs Service? Who would Mason and Gunning fear the most? He was in a quandary: he felt like a prosecutor of a crime, with perpetrators identified, the telling evidence in hand, but without a court of law to try them in.

Then, just before the year turned, Cashel received an official invitation, printed on stiff card:

Her Majesty's Consul in Trieste and the Austrian Littoral, Captain Richard Burton, requests the pleasure of your company to mark the initiation of his office. At the Hôtel de la Ville, Riva della Posta, Trieste, on Wednesday, 18th December 1872, at 6 p.m.

Burton in Trieste. How utterly astonishing . . . Cashel accepted immediately.

Burton and his wife, Isabel, had taken over the smaller of the two ballrooms in the hotel. A string quartet played in one corner. There was a buffet laid out with an assortment of canapés. Waiters circulated with trays of champagne. All the consuls of Trieste were present as well as most of the staff from the governor's office.

Cashel was able to enter unnoticed and circle around before properly greeting the couple. Burton and Mrs Burton stood surrounded by various diplomats and dignitaries. It had been a long time since Bath and Speke's death, Cashel thought. Burton hadn't changed much – the shaman's beard had gone, however, leaving only the shaggy circumflex of his drooping moustachios. Swarthy, broad-shouldered, he still gave off his particular atmosphere of self-regard and wounded belliger- ence. Cashel waited until Mrs Burton had moved away before making his approach.

'Good evening, Burton. I wonder if you remember me. Cashel Ross.'

'Good God, Ross!' Burton was genuinely surprised, rocked back, almost, as if Cashel were some kind of apparition. Then he gathered himself.

'Ross – by all that's holy – you of all people. What're you doing in Trieste? I can't tell you how pleased I am to see you.'

Cashel explained his new role of consul for Nicaragua. Burton seemed familiar with the country – he had been consul in Santos, in Brazil, he said, and had travelled widely in South America.

'Which rather begs the question: why does a small country in Central America need a consul in Trieste, of all places?'

'Fair point, though – as it happens – I do know the precise rea- son,' Cashel said. 'Perhaps we could have a talk about it when you're properly settled in.'

'Of course. We're staying in this hotel. Very nice suite of rooms – we've no intention of moving.'

Early in the new year Cashel met Burton in the Caffè degli Specchi in the Piazza Grande. They talked initially about Speke and his death.

'Obvious suicide,' Burton said adamantly.

'But Speke was an excellent shot, at ease with any kind of arm – rifle and shotgun.' Cashel rather wished he hadn't started a counter-argument as he saw that there was no possibility of Burton letting it go unanswered.

'Which makes suicide the obvious candidate. He couldn't face me in debate – and lose – so he shot himself.' Burton stood up and illustrated, using his cane as a prop. 'This is Speke's shotgun. Cock one barrel. Click. Just so. Tuck the gun under your armpit and knock the butt sharply against a stone or a root. "Bang!" Looks like an accident but it ain't.'

'I see what you mean,' Cashel said carefully. Burton's version was plausible, and that was gratifying – though he felt it was not the true story of what had happened that afternoon.

'Speke was wrong,' Burton went on, sitting down again. 'And he knew it. That's another reason why he killed himself.'

'Wrong about what?'

'The source of the Nile.'

Cashel said nothing and changed the subject.*

'I need your advice, Burton,' he said and showed him a photograph of the lion sculpture. 'I and my consulate are being used – illegally – to traffic ancient Greek antiquities to the United States.' He explained the provenance of the lion. 'The British Consul in Rhodes, one Alexander Bonson, is part of the criminal group.' He used the word deliberately. 'He provides the antiquities, another Englishman and an American are involved in their transportation and sale. I am the feckless, unknowing middleman. Everything comes through Trieste and is then shipped on by me under customs seal with all the official documentation as "marble for paving only". Very clever, I admit.'

Burton was shocked.

'The British Consul in Rhodes? Are you sure?'

'I went to Rhodes myself. Met the man. Saw his excavations at Glymphonos. I saw the arch where this lion –' he tapped the photograph – 'used to stand. Now it's in our warehouse a few hundred yards from here. There's another one on the triumphal arch, they make a pair. It'll be coming my way soon, I wager.'

'Jesus Christ.' Burton looked serious. 'You're a part of the larger conspiracy, Ross, that's your problem.'

'Unwittingly part of it. When I discovered what was happening

---

* In fact, Speke wasn't wrong, but Burton was. Speke's claim that Lake Victoria and the Ripon Falls were the source of the White Nile was proved conclusively right by Henry Morgan Stanley in 1876. The same claim, incidentally, that was made by Cashel for his Lake Ukerere and Ross Falls – preceding Speke's. Yet Speke has the glory and the place in history.

I started to take an inventory of everything that passed through my hands. Every single artefact. I wish I'd had more photographs taken.'

Burton smoothed his moustache with thumb and forefinger, making little popping noises with his lips.

'There's only one recourse,' he said. 'You write the whole thing up and you send your dossier plus this photograph to the Secretary of State for Foreign Affairs in London. George Gower – I know him – and Edward Hammond, his under-secretary. It's cut and dried. This fellow will be recalled – what's his name?'

'Bonson.'

'Bonson'll be called back to London and carpeted. His career's over – he'll probably go to prison. But that stops the trade, you see. Stops it dead. Bonson is the weak link in the masterplan. He provides the goods, the antiquities. The other two are just mountebanks. You'll never catch them once they know the game is up. They might try to set it up somewhere else, of course – but it won't be so easy to find a corrupt consul once the whole affair goes public.' He looked at Cashel with overt admiration. 'Excellent sleuthing, Ross. You're wasted in the Nicaraguan Foreign Service.'

He called for a carafe of wine and the two of them sat on for an hour, drafting out Cashel's devastating accusatory letter.

Cashel polished his account of the antiquities smuggling, giving as much detail as possible, adding his inventory and the photograph. He made no mention of his own role in the operation, merely saying that Bonson was the source.

He and Burton decided that it was wise not to send on the lion even though its non-arrival might alert suspicion. And it was noticeable that no new shipments arrived in February or March.

Cashel could hardly write to Mason and ask what was going on. Burton made discreet enquiries and discovered that Bonson was still in post in Rhodes. They just had to wait it out. The wheels of Foreign Office justice turned slowly.

They met up from time to time – Burton was stimulating

company whose astonishing life made Cashel's own adventures seem like something that had taken place in a school playground. Time and again the same questions arose: the source of the Nile; Livingstone's bizarre theories about the Mountains of the Moon; the precise chronology of Speke's actions on the day of his death. Cashel kept his counsel – he wanted Burton to ask his friend George Gower directly what was going on, as he was coming to think that the whole affair was being swept under a Foreign Office carpet, but Burton was unwilling, saying he was in enough official disfavour without provoking accusations of professional jealousy.

Now that the shipments had ceased, however, there was no work to be done in Trieste; yet, alarmingly, Cashel's quarterly stipend arrived as normal – the usual travellers' cheques drawn on the London Exchange Banking Company. It seemed a proper professional institution. However, as a precaution, he decided that he and Ignatz had to make economies. The stables, the carriage and the horses were dispensed with. Just one visit to the theatre per week. Dining in restaurants was only permitted in cheaper establishments in the Old Town.

However, he did entertain at home from time to time. Isabel Burton, a devout Catholic, discovering that Cashel was a convert to Roman Catholicism, suddenly warmed to him and, having seemingly been unaware of or indifferent to his previous connection with her husband, began to treat him as something of a confidant. She told him of Burton's bitterness at his professional disappointments – colleagues that turned against him (notably that rat in human form, Speke), postings that were beneath his dignity, the jealousies he seemed to provoke – and alarming health problems about which Cashel had never heard Burton complain: of tumours that grew in his groin and on his back and had to be removed without chloroform.

Cashel sympathized.

They were all having dinner at Via Vecker one evening when a loud banging could be heard at the main door of the downstairs office. Cashel sent Ignatz to investigate and to tell whoever it was to come back in office hours. Ignatz returned in a minute, his face full of warnings.

'It's Mr Mason, sir. He says it's urgent.'

Cashel asked to be excused and went downstairs to the office. He lit a kerosene lamp and opened the door. Brooke Mason stood there, just about managing a thin smile. He looked harassed, edgy.

'Ah, Ross. Thank God you're in. Got a bit of a problem.'

He stepped into the office, leaving the door open, and looked around.

'Map of Nicaragua,' he said, pointing at the large map that took up most of one wall. 'Like that. Nice touch.'

'I've got guests upstairs for dinner, Mason, if you don't mind.'

'Sorry, sorry. I just need you to put someone up here for a few days. Incognito. He's in a spot of bother – it's very urgent.'

He gestured outside and Cashel saw a fiacre waiting, blinds down at the windows.

'He's a good friend but he needs to lie low for a few days. Spot of bother,' Mason repeated. 'Then he'll be on his way once I've done a bit of investigating.'

Cashel could see that despite the air of bravado Mason was on the edge of panic.

'All right. We've plenty of spare rooms on the top floor. Nobody'll know he's here.'

Mason stepped out of the door, put two fingers in his mouth and gave a surprisingly loud, shrill whistle, like a shepherd directing a sheepdog. Cashel saw a figure step out of the cab and hurry up the path to the consular office.

'What kind of "spot of bother" is this fellow in, if I may ask?' Cashel said quietly.

Then Alexander Bonson came through the door.

'Ah, Bonson,' Mason said. 'Here's your Good Samaritan. Meet Consul Cashel Ross.'

Mason clearly felt the shock-ripples reverberate through the room as Cashel and Bonson stared at each other in frank amazement. Bonson's luxuriant hair was greasy and uncombed. He had stubble on his jaw and looked exhausted.

'This man's name is Greville Soutar,' he said.

'Nonsense. This man is—'

'This man is the Scottish cunt who gave me up! He's the bastard who came to Rhodes!'

'You'd both better leave at once,' Cashel said and pointed at Bonson. 'This man is a thief and a criminal. I'll have nothing to do with him.'

Brooke Mason stood there for a second or two, head bowed, then turned and advanced on Cashel.

'What've you done, Ross?' he said quietly. 'Was it you? Have you any idea what this'll cost us?'

'Everything all right, Ross?' Burton said, coming through the door from the inner hall and the stairway. Ignatz was behind him. Cashel could see that he had a poker in his hand.

'These fellows bothering you?' Burton asked with a strange, wide smile.

'Let's get out of here, Mason,' Bonson said. 'This is a disaster.'

Mason turned again to Cashel and pointed a finger at him. 'We'll have our day of reckoning, Ross. There will be a heavy price to pay, I assure you.'

They both walked through the door and back into the night. Cashel closed and locked the door behind them. He heard the sound of the fiacre turn in the street and clip-clop away.

'Those your esteemed colleagues in the antiquity trade?' Burton asked.

'Yes. The little chap was Bonson. Not happy colleagues at all, however.' Cashel smiled, actually feeling quite pleased with himself. Clearly, his letter to George Gower had worked. Everything was in total disarray. Excellent result.

'Shall we continue our dinner? Mrs Burton will be wondering what's happened to us.'

Within two days Cashel closed the consulate and terminated the lease on Via Vecker. His final act as Consul to the Republic of Nicaragua was to authorize two new diplomatic passports in the names of Michael Finnegan and Sextius Perce. He and

Ignatz booked rooms in the Hôtel de la Ville under their new aliases.*

Subsequently, Cashel and Burton met on a daily basis, Burton clearly excited by the adventure and all the *Sturm und Drang*, which he said added vital spice to his boring day. It was Burton, through his Foreign Office connections, who was able to unearth the news that Bonson had indeed been recalled to London, had not appeared and, therefore, was formally relieved of his post as British Consul at Rhodes. Bonson had simply disappeared, and no one knew where he might be.

Cashel took Burton down to the warehouse and showed him the magnificent sculpture of the lion. It was their key bit of evidence. Burton even found, in his library, an eighteenth-century etching of the Triumphal Arch at the Glymphonos arena with its two giant lions.

'He's done for, Ross,' Burton said in one of their morning conferences at the hotel. 'But Bonson will go and hide for the rest of his sad life in Belgium or Scandinavia under a false name. He's not your problem – the other two are. You've probably cost them a lifetime's fortune – and, just as significantly, you know too much. Everything in my blood tells me they'll come after you, looking for revenge. If I were you I'd get out of Trieste immediately. Go to Damascus – I've good friends there. You can live like a lord on a pound a week.'

Cashel was strangely reluctant to run and hide. In fact, he didn't think Mason and Gunning would come after him. The whole of the Dodecanese chain was ripe for further plundering and exploitation while it remained part of the Ottoman Empire. Sure, Bonson on Rhodes had been exceptionally useful but there would be other middlemen on other islands. And it wasn't hard to find a bonded warehouse in a Mediterranean port.

Burton issued another warning, however. He had managed

---

* 'Michael Finnegan' is the name of an accident-prone character in a popular Irish folksong that Cashel would have sung at school in Castlemountallen. Sextius Perce is a Latinized version of Sancho Panza.

to look at Cashel's 'Letters of Authority' from the Nicaraguan Republic.

'You do realize they were issued posthumously by a president who had been shot by firing squad in 1860.'

'I do know about William Walker, yes. But Mason said they were still entirely valid.'

'I don't know how they got through the governor's office. Probably because no one there knew where Nicaragua was. Anyway, it makes you look like part of the conspiracy. You, Mason, Bonson and this other fellow – the Yankee—'

'Gunning. Waldo Gunning.'

'I wouldn't linger, Ross. Those two know you're probably still in Trieste. They'll come and find you. Or else tip the wink to the Austrians that you're a bogus diplomat. Then *they*'ll arrest you.'

This warning did disturb him. Cashel told Ignatz to pack their trunks and be ready to leave at the shortest notice.* He began to think, also, of returning to the United States. But then Gunning was an American . . . Perhaps England was safer. London or Oxford, then.

He went cautiously back to the consulate one night, as a message had been sent there saying that the landlord's representative wanted to repay the cash deposit left when the lease had been signed. But strangely, there was no one there. With his pocket knife he unscrewed the small enamel plaque next to the door – '*Konsulat der Republik Nicaragua*' – as a little souvenir of his diplomatic life. Another chapter closed, he thought. Where would he and his trusty Sancho Panza end up next?

He walked back to the hotel, taking a deliberately roundabout route. Why hadn't the landlord or his man shown up when they had requested the meeting? And what about the money that was owed? Annoying. It was late and the shops were closed – but in

---

* Cashel gave Burton the keys to the bonded warehouse and told him to do whatever he saw fit with the sculpture. Burton shipped it to the British Museum as an 'anonymous donation'. The 'Lion of Glymphonos' can still be seen today in Room 13 of the Department of Greece and Rome.

the Old Town the taverns were busy and raucous with drinkers spilling out on to the street.

He crossed the road away from the glare of the gaslight, suddenly conscious of a set of footsteps following him. He stepped into a doorway and looked round. Nothing. Some drunken man staggered out of a tavern into the roadway, singing. Another Triestine Friday, Cashel thought.

'Ross!'

He heard his name called and didn't respond, striding off rapidly for a dark alleyway.

Then there came the flat clap of an explosion and a chunk of plaster was blasted out of the wall by his shoulder. Now he sped up, veering across the road, heading for a crowd outside another tavern. Numbers – safety, he was thinking. Another shot was fired. Cashel crouched. Shouts erupted from the taverns – the gunshots had been heard. Such incidents were not unusual in Trieste. Italian irridentists were enthusiasts of assassination and revenge.

Cashel stood up and ran, hearing another retort from the gun. Someone screamed, hit by the stray bullet. Cashel reached his alleyway and peered out.

The drinkers from the taverns had spread across the street, righteous and angry – looking for the gunman. Cashel saw a man in a black greatcoat running away, fingers pointed at him by the irate drinkers. Bottles and pewter pots were thrown as the injured man was helped inside.

The running man had looked stout and ungainly. Gunning, not Mason, Cashel thought. But Mason, he suddenly realized, would have set up the false meeting at the consulate. Gunning would have followed him from there.

Cashel slipped away in the general confusion. Burton had been right – they were indeed going to come after him. And now shots had been fired and an innocent bystander wounded. Investigations would follow. It was time to leave.

That night, Cashel and Ignatz left Trieste by train. The consulship was well and truly over.

15

The gondola slipped easily and powerfully under the Rialto Bridge and headed down the Canal Grande. Cashel sat back in his comfortable leather seat and reflected that to be in Venice in a gondola on an early summer's day was probably one of the most intense and sophisticated pleasures that the world could offer. How many times during his years in Venice had he said that to himself? How many millions of visitors had expressed the same sentiments over the centuries? All the truer for its spontaneous, regular repetition, he thought to himself, and no doubt he would say it again the next time he was on the canal.

He re-lit his cigar and watched the facades of the palazzos gliding by, experiencing the momentary illusion that they were moving and he was static. At the same time he remembered the phrase 'City of empty palaces . . .' Who had said that? It was also certainly true. There was something minatory about the visual pleasure of the place, something decadent in the pure sense of the word. On either side of the canal, it wasn't hard to gain the impression that the city was rotting – buildings were black with damp and mould, sprigs of greenery grew from the cracks in the masonry. He had noted the same effect in Rhodes, he recalled, a feeling that the buildings were constructed from something soft and malleable, like marzipan or pastry, so fragile did the edifices seem – so fragile and dangerously porous, as if the water that lapped at their pilings was drawing them down into the silty lagoon.

He stroked his beard and tugged at its point – and immediately rebuked himself. It was a habit he was trying to cure himself of, this form of self-caressing. He had grown a beard for only the second time in his life when he'd come to hide in Venice, all those years ago. It had seemed a sensible precaution – a near-instant disguise – rather than something pragmatic as it had been on his explorations in Africa. Now his beard was dense and white, like his hair, and he'd become used to the grizzled patriarch he saw in the mirror each morning.

He glanced at the newspapers in his lap – *The Times*, the *New York Herald*, *L'Intransigéant*. He went to the railway station every Monday morning and slipped a few coins to a porter he knew, Alessandro, who collected the foreign newspapers that were left aboard the trains when the passengers disembarked and, after refolding them neatly and ironing them flat, sold them on. They were always a few days late, of course, sometimes a week, but through them he managed a contact with the world beyond Venice that was important to him. He very rarely left the island – once, two years had gone by before he'd set foot on the mainland at Mestre – and it was all too easy, in Venice, to forget about the world and its noisy business beyond the lagoon.

He put on his spectacles and opened *The Times* – he managed to read a few lines about the continued reverberations of the Phoenix Park murders in Dublin. Lord Cavendish and what's-his-name – Burke. Stabbed to death by Nationalists. Phoenix Park, Dublin. Made him think of Ireland and Stillwell Court. Who lived there now . . .? These fuses that fired your memories. Good sign – brain working, active. He glanced at some other headlines, but the breeze had increased and the paper snapped and flapped in his hands so he folded it up again and put it away.

The gondola deposited him at the wooden jetty at the end of the Riva del Carbone. He tipped the gondolier, who helped him out; he knew him, as he did so many now.

'Grazie, Signor Finnegan.'

'Prego, Federico.'

He limped down to find the narrow *fondamenta* alongside the Rio San Salvatore* that would lead him to his own crumbling Venetian home, the Casa Alberoni, where he lived in a large furnished apartment on the first floor, well positioned but half the usual price because there was no view of the Grand Canal.

---

* The Rio San Salvatore no longer exists. It was filled in and diverted in 1963.

He pushed himself through the heavy wooden doors on the ground floor, grunting with the effort and suddenly for a few seconds feeling like a weak and feeble old man. Absurdly heavy doors, he thought, catching his breath, before climbing the marble stairs to the *piano nobile* where the Finnegan apartments were situated. His knee – his left knee – was aching today for some reason, and his onset of shortness of breath whenever he did anything remotely physical was a little worrying.

Yet he had felt well throughout his seventies – very well, considering. He always sensed that his old man's relative robustness was his body's recompense for the miseries he had endured in Zanzibar. But since he'd turned eighty he had become more and more conscious of his corporeal decline, slow but unmistakable. He wasn't fat – his legs were skinny shanks – though he did have an old man's belly and had been obliged to have his waistcoats let out. He paused on the landing, letting his breathing steady. In every natural way, he thought, being eighty was already too old, let alone being eighty-two. But although he could sense his body flagging even at the modest efforts he demanded of it, there was nothing you could do about it, of course – short of ending your own life. The cost of living a long time. Getting tired. Maybe this was the human consolation, he thought, that when you reach such a state of increasing physical incapacity or difficulty you begin to welcome death – the end of the daily struggle, the embrace of oblivion.

He banished these morbid thoughts as he opened the tall door into the apartment and walked into the hall, hanging his hat and coat on the stand. High ceilings, marble floors, always a bit cold even in high summer, always that dampness seeping upwards, however many fires and stoves you had burning. Yet these were the most splendid rooms he had ever lived in, built on a grand scale. On the floor above was a tailor and his family and, above them, a stoneworker and his young wife with a mewling baby whose sex Cashel had yet to discover.

He looked into the grand salon. Nessa sat by the fire, darning one of his shirts. She glanced up and smiled.

'I'm back,' he said redundantly.

'Any interesting news?' She still had a strong Boston accent and that triggered something he'd read, a headline he remembered.

'They've just hanged the man who shot President Garfield.'

'Good.'

'Thought that would make your day.' He looked around. 'Where's Ignatz?'

'Gone to the Rialto market.'

He raised his hand in acknowledgement and wandered through to his room, the thought coming to him once again – spontaneously, instinctively – that Ignatz and Nessa were having an affair. A sexual affair. He didn't know why this possibility came to mind as he had not the slightest evidence but the notion kept nagging at him. Maybe they were – and so what? Maybe it was a good experience at this stage of their lives. And, yet, in his presence, their relations were completely formal. She called him 'Ignatz'; he called her 'Madame Corcoran' or a simple 'madame'. But he sensed some different undercurrent between them, he felt sure. What happened when he left the apartment?

In his vast room there was his high bed, two sofas and a wide desk by the window. There were many bookshelves. He wandered behind a folding screen, dropped his trousers and urinated into his commode. He checked: all seemed well – the blood he had passed last month seemed not to have reappeared. There was a bathroom with a water closet between Nessa's room and Ignatz's but he felt stupidly self-conscious using it. Either Ignatz – or their maid, Solferina – saw discreetly to his pot. He was familiar with the old ways, after all.

He sat at his desk and put on his spectacles, noticing how he strained to focus. He needed new spectacles. He spread out *The Times* with its tapestry of small advertisements on the front page, picked up his magnifying glass and scanned the columns. Yes, there it was. Every random issue of *The Times* that he picked up from Alessandro at the railway station contained the same advertisement. It had been running for years and must be paid for on a recurring daily basis.

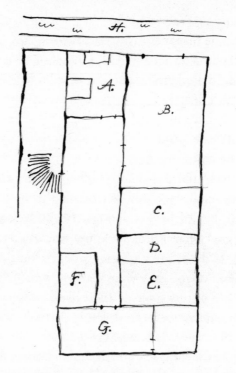

The apartment at Casa Alberoni. A. Cashel's room. B. The grand salon. C. Nessa's room. D. Bathroom and water closet. E. Ignatz's room. F. Maid's room. G. Kitchen/ scullery. H. Rio San Salvatore and fondamenta.

SEEKING THE WHEREABOUTS OF OUR DEARLY BELOVED BROTHER,
CASHEL GREVILLE ROSS, LATELY CONSUL AT TRIESTE, AUSTRIA.
SIGNIFICANT REMUNERATION OFFERED FOR ANY INFORMATION.

That was it, with a box number for communication. Of course, it was placed by Mason and Gunning, still looking for him after all this time, not prepared to give him up. In a way he was glad to see it as it meant they had no idea where he was. The day the advertisement didn't appear would be the signal to quit Venice and find somewhere else to hide.

When he and Ignatz had left Trieste, he had thought at first of going as far away as possible – even taking up Burton's offer of Damascus. He himself had thought of Cape Town for a while, or Australia but, as their train had approached Venice, Cashel had a sudden inspiration: Mason and Gunning will be expecting me to go far and wide, he reasoned. So why not stay close, instead. Venice was an island, crowded with dwellings of all sorts, a good place to get lost in. Perhaps it was not quite 'hiding in plain sight' but it was the next best thing. He was confident that in moving to Venice he would have thrown his pursuers off the scent an hour after leaving Trieste. And, so far, several years later, that had proved to be the case.

He folded away the paper and turned to the clutter on his desk – his notes and his notebooks, all the material that was going to go into the story of his life. The night before he had written some guidance on a sheet of paper. He found it.

AUTOBIOGRAPHY

How have I become the person I am today?
Will I always be haunted by my origins and past?
What kind of futures did I successively imagine for myself at the crucial junctures of my life?

Reasonable questions, he thought, especially if you were planning to write the honest story of your own life – or anyone else's, come to that – but they were surprisingly hard to answer.

First of all, he had tried to write a simple chronology of his life consisting of all those dates he could recall and confirm accurately – such as his date of birth, the Battle of Waterloo, or the day he left Zanzibar – imagining that these fingerposts would act as a memory-catalyst and he'd be able to fill in the gaps between them, the roads he'd travelled. But it didn't quite work out that way. He was an old man and a lot of time had passed.

With a little effort he could remember some incidents and places with absolute clarity but great tracts of his life, and what he'd done, month by month, even year by year, were a kind of blur. Ignatz was sometimes helpful – he had every detail absolutely right about the Rossbrau years – but of course it was the Ignatz Vlac perspective that interested him, not the Cashel Ross perspective. Sometimes, when he quizzed Ignatz, a version of himself, Cashel Ross, emerged that was at odds with the reality as he thought he had experienced it. Ignatz would say Cashel had reacted to a fraught situation 'with great calm', whereas Cashel recalled feeling a just-controllable panic. Was Ignatz 'remembering' things mistakenly . . . ? But if so, what applied to Ignatz applied to him, also.

More and more he came to see memory as elusive and tricky – like imagination – and it was surprisingly malleable and transforming, as if it wanted to be pleasing rather than accurate, like a fawning courtier to its master the autobiographer; desirous of giving a version of the past that conformed with what Cashel *wanted* the past to be, rather than what it had actually been. He found that he was beginning to mistrust his memory – not a helpful state of affairs for a man writing his autobiography.

He was also interested to note that he found nothing depressing or gloomy looking back over his past in this analytical frame of mind, nothing macabre or ghoulish about writing his way towards his natural termination, when all autobiography would cease.

It was perhaps curious that he rarely thought about dying – his death – these days. Another one of the consolations of great age, he supposed. When you were, by simple definition, near death as he was now, into his ninth decade, the fact that you might die tomorrow or next week, or next month or in five years' time, appeared all the same to him. It was when you were younger that you 'feared' death – then the awful prospect of your demise underpinned your every waking moment as you realized that it would prevent you from doing so many things you'd dreamt of doing. Death – then – would have been a terrific disappointment; but death now, at his great age, was a matter of indifference to him. Except . . . He smiled ruefully to himself. Except for Raphaella. Perhaps it was Raphaella who was keeping him alive.

He heard a noise in the hall and, thinking it was Ignatz returning, peered out of his room. In fact it was Giovanna, the robust young girl who brought the drinking water to the house, carried on buckets slung from a kind of wooden yoke that rested on her broad shoulders. She went into the kitchen and poured the water into the big earthenware jars set beside the soapstone sink. She would bring fresh milk, if asked, the bottles nestled in baskets lined with straw. He gave her a wave as she greeted him. Such were some of the many pleasures of living in Venice, he recognized.

He was and had been happy here – watchfully happy – although life had been simple and a little austere until Nessa had arrived some two years ago. The apartment became very much a home under her supervision. Floors were regularly washed, soft furniture bought, new curtains hung. They started to eat very well.

He had always written dutifully to his daughters, once or twice a year – Maeve never replied, but Nessa did and their correspondence flourished. In one letter, quite spontaneously, she said she wanted to come to Europe and meet her English family. She sailed to England and stayed with Buckley and Hogan and then joined Cashel in Venice and, after a month, asked if she might stay. Cashel remembered that she knew Ignatz well from the early Willow Creek days so, in a sense, living with the two of them in Venice was as close to a homecoming as she could imagine.

He had told her a little about the scandal of Trieste and the need for a pseudonym and constant discretion. She seemed untroubled by the subterfuge. In fact she wanted to be known as Mrs Corcoran, not Miss, and Ignatz and Cashel were happy to be complicit in the story she would tell anyone who was curious about a husband who had died in the Civil War. Such reinventions seemed unexceptionable in Venice – every day a modest *ballo in maschera*.

Nessa told him about Bríd, still in her Cambridge asylum, for ever locked in her mania. Maeve had moved away, had four children now as well as a husband. In coming to Europe, Nessa acquired real uncles and aunts and cousins – as well as an errant father and his manservant. That she chose to stay with him in Venice made Cashel happy, and his guilt over the destruction of his family receded somewhat.

How would he incorporate that into his life story with any

candour? Frannie Broome and the harsh feud with the Corcorans? The stark loneliness of the farmhouse at Willow Creek and what it signified when he returned from Boston that day was still vivid to him – his wife and daughters gone, the house empty of their possessions. It was a shock that refused to diminish. His memory for once would simply not be servile and conforming. Should he even write about that episode in his life? Maybe pass over the separation, and the enduring rift and hostility, with a few bland homilies . . . Perhaps he should concentrate on those aspects of his life for which there was better documentation – such as Africa. He realized he was backsliding, already playing himself false, creating in retrospect a version of the life he wished he'd had, 'remembering' only what he wanted his memories to be. It was a form of cowardice, he supposed.

All this recollection was making him feel uncomfortable. He took his fob watch out of its pocket and looked at the time. Maybe he should stroll down to the post office on the Piazza San Marco after lunch and see if there were any letters for him. Buckley and Hogan knew where he was – and so did Burton, who was still consul in Trieste, much to his disappointment and Isabel's bitterness.* But no one else knew who 'Michael Finnegan' really was. Or where. Anyway, he had discovered as a result of living in Venice all year round that if you had an empty morning, or were bored, or simply needed some kind of change in your daily routine, there was a simple cure available – go to the Piazza San Marco. He followed this urge several times a week and was also a committed Florianista. He knew all the waiters at Caffè Florian and, winter and summer, spring and autumn, would make himself at home there with a book, a cigar and a glass or two of wine. There was no acceptable alternative.

Consequently, after lunch – Ignatz having returned from the market with its ingredients, a sea bream and new potatoes – he

---

* Burton remained as British Consul in Trieste until 1890. He had been successively British Consul in Fernando Po, Santos, Brazil and Damascus. He died in Trieste, in post, from a heart attack at the age of sixty-nine.

decided to head off. He would walk, he thought, not take a gondola, get that left knee working again, but he took his cane and, in no hurry, made his leisurely way to the post office. There was in fact some mail – a letter from Buckley for him and one for Nessa. He opened Buckley's in the post office to find it dealt with various unimportant banking matters. After the flight from Trieste, Cashel had closed his account at Brookes & Co. and transferred his savings to Buckley's bank in Eastbourne. All mail also went via Buckley as a precaution. He slipped Nessa's letter in his pocket and sauntered back into the piazza, heading for Florian's.

Something was afoot. He saw a crowd of people making for the Riva degli Schiavoni with almost a carnival aspect to their excitement. He asked a passer-by what was going on and was told that a balloon ascent was taking place in the Giardini Pubblici. He had never seen a balloon setting off and was tempted by the novelty, and so, spontaneously, joined the stream of people heading for the park.

Hundreds had assembled, he saw as he arrived, and on the small hill with the café he could see the balloon, a huge brown ball like a giant pig's bladder, already inflated. A bystander told him, uninvited, that it was filled with coal-gas. Whatever that was, it was certainly buoyant. Two men were sitting in the balloon's basket that was tightly tethered with ropes tied to iron pegs hammered into the ground; a third was making some kind of announcement through a megaphone about future balloon ascents, but he was only semi-audible to Cashel from where he was standing.

Suddenly, the balloon was released and rose up into the air with surprising speed, high into the clear blue sky. The crowd cheered and applauded, while the men in the basket above them flung down sheets of paper. Some sort of advertisement? Cashel wondered. A manifesto? In any event, soon the breeze steadily carried the balloon away northwards towards Murano and the crowd slowly dispersed.

Cashel stood there a while, watching the balloon disappear on its airy journey, entranced by its incredible gravity-defying lightness. So silent, he thought, so unlike a locomotive – immediately recognizing the comparison as both stupid and absurd the moment it entered his head. But then he thought that this would be how to escape from Venice should Mason and Gunning ever track him down – simply jump into his balloon filled with coal-gas and soar away out of sight.

He picked up a steam ferry at the Giardini Pubblici landing and it chugged him back up the Grand Canal to the Riva del Carbone. He hadn't made it to Florian's but felt the day had been unusually rewarding – unforgettable. Perhaps the ascent of the balloon could be the ideal way to end the final chapter of his autobiography . . .

He handed Nessa her letter and went into his study to make a note of the idea. About two minutes later there was a knock at his door and Nessa came in, her cheeks glossy with tears.

'Nessa? Darling, what is it—?'

'She's gone. She's dead.'

'Who?'

'Mother. Your wife. Bríd Corcoran.'

Cashel felt a tremor run through him as he took this news in. Then he was suffused with a curious elation – like a drug, as if he'd swallowed half a bottle of Mrs Dashwood's Infant Quietener. Bríd was dead. He was a widower. More importantly, he was free. He stood up, keeping his face solemn, and took Nessa in his arms, gently patting her back as she sobbed, thinking only that he must go to Raphaella. Urgently. Finally, after all these years, he could be with the one woman he had truly loved.

Cashel wrote to Raphaella, guardedly as always, care of the Palazzo Mazzolino in Milan:

Our mutual friend, Francesca, has some very interesting news that she would like to share with you face to face as soon as possible.

A week later he received a brief reply:

I'd be delighted to meet Francesca after all this time. Tell her I'm staying in Baden-Baden, at the Hôtel Stéphanie-les-Bains until the end of July.

He confided in Ignatz, telling him he was going to Baden-Baden as soon as possible and why, but that Ignatz was not to reveal his destination to Nessa. Cashel would tell her that he was going to Paris to sort out some financial issues with Buckley. Ignatz only had to confirm that.

But he was troubled. 'Is this wise, sir?'

'It has nothing to do with wisdom,' Cashel said forcefully. 'It's to do with love and, therefore, is doubtless the very opposite of wise.'

He began to make his plans. He telegraphed the hotel in Baden-Baden where Raphaella was staying; it was fully booked but he found a room free in another one close by, the Grand Hôtel du Parc. *'Every modern convenience'*, it advertised. *'Closets approved on the English principle'* – whatever that meant.

He packed a small suitcase, including his evening dress as he knew something of the formalities of the Baden-Baden summer season. He had his beard trimmed and his hair cut; and he bought a new cotton-drill summer suit, the colour of milky tea, with the jacket cut in the fashionable 'lounge' style, and several bright neckties. He had no idea what the future might hold, only that he had to see Raphaella again and let her know that at last he was a free man. Nessa entirely believed his story about meeting Buckley in Paris and gave him a letter for Buckley to pass on to Mildred, one of his children, a cousin she'd become close to. Cashel maintained the pretence with aplomb. He felt the years fall away from him, a new vigour in his body, a surge of enthusiasm that he hadn't experienced in ages.

Ignatz accompanied him to the station, frowning, nervous.

'What if I come with you, Mr Ross? Wouldn't that make more sense?'

'Absolutely not, Ignatz. I must go alone – it's essential. I'll be sure to telegraph you when I'm returning home.'

If I come home, he thought, now allowing his fantasies total freedom. He was old, Raphaella too, but there was still precious time that could be spent together, that could be shared. Time postponed, he told himself, even for decades, is better than time cancelled for ever.

He caught the train from Venice to Geneva where he spent the night before travelling on to Strasbourg the next day and changing trains for Baden-Baden. A fiacre took him from the station to his hotel – a new building, he saw as he arrived, well positioned just off the Lichtentaler Allee.

'Herr Finnegan, welcome to Baden-Baden,' the reception clerk said, handing him his keys. 'Manfred here will show you to your room.'

Cashel followed the bellboy through the foyer to a small door. They stepped inside a box. Two other people joined them. The bellboy, Manfred, turned a handle on the side of the box and Cashel felt himself surging upwards. So this was the fabled 'elevator', he thought. An excellent invention for old men with bad knees who didn't like climbing stairs.

They emerged on the fourth floor and Cashel was shown to his room, number 412. Manfred opened the door and turned a switch set in the wall. Suddenly the room was filled with light – electric light. His suitcase was placed on a wooden rack, then Manfred showed him how to open the windows that gave on to a view of the park and pointed out the complimentary bottle of mineral water by his bedside. He showed Cashel the bathroom with its bath and bidet and a toilet that cleaned itself when you pulled on a chain attached to a cistern.

Cashel looked on, bemused and interested, as Manfred talked him through the complexities of the new appliances available to him. He thought, This is good, this is apt – here he was entering a new world, a new phase of his life. He was glad he had lived long enough to have use of elevators and telegraphs and hot-water heating and toilets that flushed your shit into distant sewers. He would not have missed it. Maybe it was a sign that his final years on earth would be similarly novel. Married to Raphaella. Was that the coda that his life was waiting for?

Manfred left him and Cashel sat on his bed, suddenly wearied by his two days of travel, the longest journey he'd undertaken since his trip to Rhodes and back all those years ago. He had become used to living in a small, flat city and the wonderful practicality of gondolas. He thought he might have a snooze for a couple of hours, then a bite of light supper and early to bed. He didn't want to rush anything, happy to wait another day to encounter Raphaella, to be properly rested. He didn't want to appear before her as an exhausted old man.

The next morning, well slept, he breakfasted in the hotel dining room wearing his new suit and a light blue cravat that complemented his eyes, he thought, indulging in a little personal vanity. He was feeling strangely nervous, however, and rebuked himself for reverting to adolescent insecurities. Pull yourself together, man, he said, calling for more coffee.

He went for a stroll to compose himself, looking about him at the small, pretty, tree-filled town that was Baden-Baden, noting the prosperous and well-dressed people toing and froing, patronizing the many expensive shops and elegant cafés. The 'Summer Capital of Europe' was what they called this little town on the edge of the Black Forest. The maître d' at the hotel told him excitedly that the Prince of Wales was expected any day now.

Then he began to notice something strange as he wandered about the busy streets. Passers-by seemed to stare at him, or do a double-take when they saw him – then smile and nod a welcome, as if they recognized him somehow. He smiled and nodded back. Maybe it was a Baden-Baden custom, he thought, a way of collectively acknowledging their part in this European elite, as if they were members of an exclusive club, even though the casino had been ordered closed – too much of an unwelcome French influence on the municipality, so the new Germany had decided.

Cashel wandered on, unconcerned, vaguely amused. Then an elderly man came up to him, gave a small bow and spoke a few excited words in Russian.

'Batiushk, ne mozhet byt!'

Cashel paused, perplexed, but said nothing, gave a little bow, tipped his hat and moved brusquely on at more speed. Yes, clearly, all these smiles were directed at him as a doppelgänger of some Russian notable. How bizarre! Yet not everyone in Baden-Baden was Russian, and they all seemed to recognize him.

He put the matter out of his mind as he approached Raphaella's hotel, Baden-Baden's grandest, the Stéphanie-les-Bains. It was almost noon, perhaps an ideal moment to announce himself to her. He felt his guts quiver and tighten and, strangely, sensed unwelcome tears in his eyes. Maybe all his life, he thought, all his struggles, voyages, sojourns, successes and disappointments, betrayals and vindications, had been leading to this moment . . .

No, stop! he told himself abruptly. Don't overburden this encounter with too much freight of emotional significance. Just see Raphaella again – let the meeting occur, that was all he needed to do. Everything that happened subsequently would be obvious, logical, almost preordained. He should just wait and see.

Still, he couldn't entirely suppress his nervousness as he walked into the plush lobby of the Stéphanie. It was busy with guests planning excursions, meeting friends and new acquaintances; there was laughter and conversation in half a dozen languages. He could hear waltz music coming from a palm-court orchestra in some nearby salon. He waited for a few moments until the crush by the reception desk had diminished and approached the reception clerk.

'Do you speak English?' Cashel asked.

'I do, sir. How can I help you?'

'I'm here to meet one of your guests, the Contessa di Mazzolino. I wonder if you could let her know I've arrived. I'm Mr Cashel Ross.'

The clerk looked briefly puzzled. He consulted the ledger containing the names of the resident hotel guests, turned a few pages and looked up.

'We have no Contessa di Mazzolino staying here, sir. Perhaps you have the wrong hotel.'

Cashel felt suddenly weak. He almost laughed.

'She said she was staying in this hotel until the end of July.'

'We have no record of that name, sir. I apologize.'

Cashel looked helplessly around him. Beyond the foyer was a large, airy room with tall French windows, filled with little congregations of armchairs and sofas that gave on to a wide terrace set out with tables and canvas umbrellas, overlooking the park and the River Oos. The terrace tables were filled with people drinking coffee and pre-prandial aperitifs. Men in linen suits, smoking. Women wandering by with dainty parasols and bright summer dresses.

He saw Raphaella cross the terrace, appearing miraculously in window after window in front of him like a series of images moving magically from frame to frame.

'There she is, man!' he said to the clerk, a little angry, pointing Raphaella out. 'What d'you mean she's not staying in this hotel?'

'Excuse me, sir. You gave me the wrong name. That lady is the Gräfin Henningen zu Altenhausen.'

'The what?'

The clerk repeated the absurd name.

Gräfin? Cashel wondered. Why was she now Gräfin something zu something-or-other?

He walked as quickly as he could through the salon and on to the terrace. He paused and looked at her, unobserved, for a moment. She had her back to him as she talked to some people sitting at a table on the terrace edge. She was tall and slim, in a powder-blue dress with a complicated bustle behind, all swags and rosettes; her hair was a dark grey, held in a woven bun of braids at the back of her head, visible under the brim of the small straw hat she wore, showing her long neck with a pearl choker.

Then, as if she could sense the intensity of his scrutiny, she broke off her conversation and turned to see him, just as she had done that day in Milan. He stood, rigid, a boiling crucible of emotions. She crossed the terrace towards him, smiling. He felt weak, suddenly, as though the rush of joy engulfing him might make him fall over. She still had this effect on him. How wonderful.

'You must be Francesca,' she said.

'Come to meet you face to face.'

'You're most distinguished in your elegant suit and your walking cane, Francesca. Very Baden. And you look good with a beard.'

'Thank you,' he said lamely. 'I'm very pleased to see you.'

'*Moi aussi, mon chéri.*'

'At reception they said you were called Gräfin something-or-other.'

'Yes, that's right, of course.'

'What does that mean? "Of course"?'

'I wrote and told you.'

'No, you didn't.'

'I wrote to you in Trieste about it. I told you.'

Cashel thought hard. His intermittent correspondence with Raphaella had always been very one-sided. It took four or five letters from him to procure one from her. She was still worried about being discovered, she had claimed.

'When did you tell me?' Cashel asked.

'When it happened. Three, no, four years ago.'

'But I wasn't in Trieste, then. I moved to Venice, long before . . .'

'Ah.'

She pouted her lips, frowning. They stood there for a moment, incomprehensibility separating them like a wall. He looked at her as she thought what to say. She had aged, he realized, but that facial gesture, her eyebrows raised sharply at the ends as she frowned, made her look younger all of a sudden. It brought back old memories. They could have been in Ravenna, in a coach, fucking. Timoteo lurking outside.

She looked up, not frowning.

'Come to my suite – number 233 – this afternoon at three o'clock.'

'Number 223, yes.'

'No. It's 233.'

'Sorry. 233.'

Now she smiled at him again.

'Don't forget,' she said. 'Cashel Ross. Don't forget.'

She strolled back to her friends and Cashel turned away. He left the hotel and wandered back into town, trying to switch off his brain. He found a small tavern and ordered a glass of schnapps and some food, pointing randomly at items on the menu. A plate of fried eggs arrived with some kind of dumpling. He ate everything.

'So – you're married,' Cashel said, feeling an immense self-pity and hopelessness fill him, even though he was expecting the answer.

'Yes. To the Graf Henningen zu Altenhausen. You would like him. He's kind and clever.'

'Who is he?'

'A politician. My son introduced us. He – the *graf*, Tobias – is very close to the chancellor.'

'Where is he?'

'In Berlin. He comes here next week on holiday.'

'I thought you were a widow. That's why I came. I wouldn't have come if I'd known.'

'I can't help that, Cashel. You must understand. I have no money of my own. A woman like me, in my level of society, can't live "alone" if she has no money.'

'I can understand that.'

'Please sit down.'

He sat in an armchair in the pretty green-and-yellow sitting room of her suite. He closed his eyes and inhaled deeply. Raphaella went to a bureau, opened it to reveal an array of cut-crystal decanters, and poured them each a small glass of Madeira. They toasted each other.

'Here's to you, Cashel. *Die Liebe meines Lebens.*'

'Don't torment me. I know what that means. You're the love of *my* life. As simple as that.'

'Well, it's true for us both, then. That's something to celebrate, no?'

'Have you any idea what it's like to berate yourself for one foolish mistake for sixty years?' He emptied his little glass. 'I feel like weeping. Ravenna, 1823, to Baden-Baden, 1882. Jesus Christ.'

'It wasn't your fault. The count lied to you. Deliberately.'

Cashel remembered.

'He lied because he knew the effect it would have, the old bastard.' Cashel said slowly, then paused. 'He knew what reaction he'd get from me. He knew what kind of a person I was.' He gave a throaty half-chuckle. 'I should have it carved onto my headstone. "The fool buried here ruined his life in Ravenna, September 1823." Quite simple.'

'You can't, you shouldn't do this to yourself. No one can tell what the future will bring. Not the next minute, not the next hour. As for a year or more, it's impossible. You were . . .' She smiled at him fondly. He wished she wouldn't. 'You always listened to your heart, Cashel, that was your nature. How could you have done anything different?'

'By thinking. By taking stock. By listening to reason. By making a plan. But that's not what fools do. I was so headstrong, so convinced.'

She shrugged and spread her hands.

'It's just life, you know. That is you. The way it goes. There could have been a thousand different outcomes.'

'But I hate myself for what I did.'

'Stop it, Cashel!' She wagged a warning finger at him. 'Here we are in a hotel in Baden-Baden. Two old people with our happy memories. That's not given to everyone.'

He sighed and heaved himself out of his armchair, going to the bureau where the decanters were, polished and winking with spangled light. He found the one with brandy, took a bigger glass, poured himself a dram and drank it down. Then he walked over to her chair and slowly, with difficulty, knelt by her side.

'Was that wise?' she said. 'Will I have to help you up?'

'Wisdom doesn't apply in our case,' he said. 'I would like to kiss you.'

'I remember this game,' she said and offered her face to him.

Their lips touched – dry, cool. He inhaled the scent that came from her – lavender? Yes, that was it. Lavender. The scent of the woman that was Raphaella. He broke away.

'Thank you,' she said. 'What're you going to do?'

'I'll go back to Venice and write to you from time to time. Send you news of our friend Francesca.'

'Perhaps I'll come to Venice myself, and visit her.'

'That would be wonderful.'

'We'll always be part of each other's lives, Cashel. What we experienced. No one can deny that. It's the secret between us. Our secret bond. Look at what you've done, how you've lived. And look at me. Three husbands, some children. Maybe, if you had stayed in Ravenna, your life wouldn't have been as full, as rich.'

'What do you mean?'

'I mean, we have to accept the lives we've lived. Not imagine lives we might have lived.'

'I don't care.'

'Think about it.'

'Maybe you have a point. Something to think about.' He touched her cheek with his knuckles. 'Will you be all right without me?'

'Yes. And I'll think about you every day.'

Cashel managed to struggle back to his feet, his left knee throbbing.

'I should go, now,' he said. 'Come to Venice – soon.'

'I will, my darling.'

'If the Graf dies, you have to promise to marry me.'

'I promise.'

'I'll be waiting.'

'I promise.'

After he left her, Cashel wandered the weedless gravel pathways of the park beyond the hotel. He looked at the turbid brown flow of water in the shallow river, feeling an immense melancholy, but also – oddly – a sense of vindication. He loved Raphaella, and he knew the proof of that love was because he was more concerned about her well-being than he was about his own. She was better off being the Gräfin Henningen zu Altenhausen than being Mrs Cashel Ross, let alone Mrs 'Michael Finnegan'.

Now he thought about it, that was a fair definition of 'love' – to care more about the person you loved than you did about yourself.

He kicked a pebble into the stream, hearing its quiet splash.

A middle-aged couple wandered by, staring at him and smiling warmly. The man doffed his hat and spoke to him in Russian.

'*Neuzheli, Ivan Sergeevitch? Chto pishete? Ili prosto razvlekaetes?*'

Cashel smiled, nodded, gave a vague wave of his hand. What was it about these Russians? So friendly.

He returned to his hotel and packed his bag.

His journey back to Venice was more complicated than the trip to see Raphaella had been because it was spontaneous. He had expected to spend more time in Baden-Baden, after all. He caught a train in the afternoon from Baden-Baden to Strasbourg and from there made a connection to Vienna. The quickest route would then be to go from Vienna to Trieste, from where he could catch a ferry to Venice or a train. But he felt uneasy – superstitious – about returning to Trieste, as if it would somehow expose him anew to the Mason–Gunning menace, so he opted to leave the Vienna–Trieste train at Graz and then travel on to Milan and home. How easy it was to move around these days, he thought, though he was glad he wasn't over-encumbered with luggage.

It was late, after ten o'clock, when he stepped off the train at Graz and he found the station almost empty. The gaslights were burning brightly in the dark blue summer evening. He had a two-hour wait until his connection and, feeling hungry, was lucky to be able to buy a jam-filled sugary bun and a coffee in the station restaurant before it closed.

He sat munching on his bun and drinking his coffee as the woman who ran the place bustled around, wiping tables and shoving chairs under them with an annoying scrape. As she had hoped, she drove him out and locked up, so he went to the waiting room. It was a cool night and he was glad someone had had the foresight to light a stove. He had his cigars and his flask of brandy so he went into the smoking room, thankfully empty, dumped his case and lit his cigar.

He thought back to his encounter with Raphaella. Maybe his journey to Baden-Baden and their meeting might make the ideal coda to his autobiography. Everything they had said to each other had a powerful resonance, stretching back through his life. The woman he had truly loved, cruel fate intervening and, finally, a strange kind of catharsis at their last meeting . . . Yes.

He thought about what she had said. 'You always listened to your heart, Cashel.' Was that a great strength in a person – or a terrible weakness? He thought about the love he had for Raphaella and the idea came to him that maybe, for someone like him, someone with his nature, love for someone who was unavailable was more powerful than love for someone available. He, himself, had made Raphaella unavailable by his act of folly in Ravenna. But maybe that was what caused his feelings for her to be so intense and enduring over more than half a century. Would it have been the same, he wondered, if she had always been there, if they had been free to be together? He smiled sadly. Who could say? Was it the fact that they couldn't requite their love, however hard they tried, that made it so compelling for him? Like Paolo and Francesca in Dante's poem, he thought. They had been passionate lovers but, condemned, they were compelled never to be lovers again, whirled around for eternity by the infernal winds, close but never united, trapped in their circle of romantic hell . . .

He drew deeply on his cigar, pleased with the conceit, the conception, the symbolism. That was the perfect coda. Maybe, if his book were ever published, people might see that it was a kind of lesson for those who so intemperately—

It was as if a red-hot sword had split his heart in two. He gaped and blinked at the paroxysm as it seemed to bloom in his chest

445

like a mordant red flower. He tried to breathe. Everything in his body was suddenly incredibly wrong. He closed his eyes and felt himself keel over on the bench. No, no, no! Was this it – was this what it was like?

He saw a man in black, a tall man with a black hat, leading a black horse, who came up to him and said, 'What's your name, little boy?'

Epilogue

It was Ignatz Vlac who tracked Cashel down. Before quitting Baden-Baden, Cashel had telegraphed, as promised, to say he was leaving and hoped to be in Venice within the next twenty-four hours or so. He gave no details about which route he would take. There was no need to be met at the station, he instructed.

The next day arrived and there was no Cashel Ross. Another day went by. A week. Ignatz telegraphed the Grand Hôtel du Parc and they informed him that Herr Finnegan had left after staying only one night. Nessa became very worried and Ignatz confessed. Cashel had gone to Baden-Baden, not Paris. Baden-Baden? It was the resolution of an old love affair, Ignatz said, hence the secrecy. He would go himself to Baden-Baden and find out where Cashel was, or what had become of him. He kissed Nessa goodbye and told her not to worry.

Ignatz journeyed to Baden-Baden. At the Grand Hôtel du Parc the reception staff remembered Herr Finnegan very well. All the Russian guests thought he was Ivan Turgenev, returned to Baden – where he had had a house once – after an absence of many years. Everyone was pleased to see that the great writer was back. When the resemblance was explained people found it very amusing. This Englishman mistaken for Turgenev! Can you imagine? Who exactly is this Turgenev? Ignatz asked. He was duly enlightened.

Ignatz diligently visited all the other hotels in Baden-Baden asking for the Contessa Mazzolino, the name Cashel had given to him. He had no luck – no one knew the person he was asking about. All he could discover was that Cashel had arrived, spent one night, been mistaken for Ivan Turgenev, and decided to return to Venice. Ignatz checked the railway timetables on the day Cashel had decided to leave, based on the time he had sent his telegraph. At Baden-Baden station, he was told that there were only two options available for someone who wished to travel to Venice leaving at this particular time of day. Either Strasbourg to Vienna, or Strasbourg to Geneva. Ignatz saw at once that the Strasbourg–Geneva train had left half an hour before Cashel sent his telegraph – so he must have gone Strasbourg–Vienna.

Then Ignatz had an idea. He went back to the Hôtel Stéphanie-les-Bains and asked if there were any photographic reproductions of this Ivan Turgenev. Of course, he was told – every bookseller in town had postcards of the celebrated people who visited in the past or had residences in Baden-Baden. Pauline Viardot, the Prince of Wales, Hector Berlioz, Gogol, Gérard de Nerval, Queen Victoria, Wilhelm I and numberless German aristocrats and princelings. Ignatz went to a bookseller and purchased a photograph of Ivan Turgenev. It was true – there was a similarity: white beard, neatly parted white hair, tall, solemn-looking. Turgenev, he was told, was a very tall man – so was Cashel Ross. Armed with this photograph Ignatz travelled to Vienna on the same train that Cashel must have taken. On arrival he noted the hour and then calculated what trains were available that might take him to Venice or some convenient nearby city. There was one obvious train – Vienna–Trieste – and Ignatz assumed this was the one Mr Ross would have taken. At Vienna station he showed the railway staff and workers his photograph of Ivan Turgenev. Nobody recognized him. No, sorry, never seen a man like that.

It was a simple matter of elimination, he decided. Assuming that, a week or so previously, Cashel Ross had travelled on the Vienna–Trieste train, then, at every stop that the Vienna–Trieste train made, he, Ignatz, would disembark and show his postcard. He would then take the next train to the next station and do the same. Somebody, surely, would have some memory of this tall, white-haired, white-bearded man? Perhaps he might find Cashel himself, hiding in some provincial hotel, having lost his mind.

So he made his way slowly down the line – Neustadt, Semmering, Bruck. Everyone peered closely at the photograph, searched their memories and gave a negative response.

But then, in Graz, a thin, nervy woman who served behind the counter of the small station restaurant said, Oh, yes, she remembered that tall old gentleman – exactly like the photograph – who had bought a bun and a cup of coffee and spoke bad German with a strong, strange accent. He was waiting for the connection to Milan, she said. Ignatz felt a surge of elation after days of disappointment.

'Can you tell me anything more?' he asked.

'Yes. I remember him because he was found dead in the smoking section of the waiting room the next morning. I was the last person to see him alive.'

Ignatz felt the acute blow – confirming his mounting pessimism. He felt a sudden nausea but managed to thank the woman and then went and sat down on a bench for ten minutes coming to terms with this disaster. He blamed himself – he should *never* have let Mr Ross travel alone. Never. He knuckled away the tears in his eyes and went to investigate.

The stationmaster, once he had looked at the photograph of Turgenev, had all the necessary information.

Yes, that old man had been found dead in the waiting room. He couldn't be identified because he had been robbed. No luggage, no documents. Cufflinks stolen, no watch and chain, no boots on his feet, even. He was identified as an 'elderly Italian male' as the suit of clothes he was wearing had the label of a tailoring establishment in Verona.

'What happened to the body?' Ignatz asked, gratified that his fluent German should be so useful again after all these years.

Either in a police morgue, he was told, or buried in a common grave with other dead, unidentified indigents.

A day later, after a visit to the Graz police headquarters, Ignatz paid to have the body of the recently buried 'elderly Italian male' exhumed from the common grave in the municipal cemetery near the police station and transported back to Venice.

Cashel Greville Ross was buried on 27th July 1882 in the Roman Catholic cemetery on the Isola di San Michele in the Venetian lagoon. The headstone was simple:

It made everything easier with the authorities, Nessa said, adding discreetly that she would have it changed as soon as possible.*

It was a small gathering of mourners. Buckley and Hogan had arrived from England. Richard Burton and Mrs Burton had come from Trieste. Ignatz and Nessa made up the numbers. A priest from the church of San Michele was paid to recite the usual prayers for the departed.

It was a cool and overcast day with a blustery wind and their journey to the island had been uncomfortably choppy. San Michele, under the grey skies, with its solid encircling terracotta walls and palisades of sharply pointed cypresses, looked even more like a fortress than usual.

Cashel's coffin was placed into the grave and the priest began to intone the funeral rites. Everyone was aware that the men who had carefully lowered the coffin were also the gravediggers and they now stood only a few yards away – impassively, leaning on their spades – waiting to shovel the hump of damp earth back into the neat narrow rectangle of the grave they had dug. And, as if unnerved by their presence, two of the mourners – Nessa and Isabel Burton – cast their bouquets of flowers into the grave before the priest had finished. Then, to the quiet astonishment of those present, Ignatz stepped forward and threw in a book that landed with a loud dull thud on the coffin lid. A book? What book?† Who threw a book into a grave?

Everyone looked away in embarrassment, only then to notice

---

* The headstone was quietly replaced later that year. The new stone read, *Cashel Greville Ross, 1799–1882, Dearly Beloved*. Cashel's remains were transferred to an ossuary in 1902 as the graveyard on the island was filling up and old graves were having to give way to new. His plaque can be found today on the wall lining the north-west corner of the Catholic cemetery.
† It was Dante's *La Divina Commedia*, the copy Raphaella had given to Cashel in Ravenna.

the increasingly threatening sky – a dense, buckled mass of purple and slate-grey clouds sweeping rapidly towards the city from the south – and, thus noticed, the dark clouds prompted a hurry to return to the landing area where the small steamer that had brought them all to San Michele was waiting.

As they made their way to the steps and the jetty, the first fat drops began to freckle the wide dry flagstones of the landing area and, flustered by the suddenness of the potential downpour, and keen to get back to the familiarity of the city, some of them quickly began to put up their umbrellas as flimsy protection against the cold, oncoming rain.

However, as suddenly as it had started, the rain stopped and a watery, honeyed sunshine lit the waters of the lagoon. Umbrellas were closed; people laughed at the fuss they had made over a few drops of rain; even the choppy wavelets seemed to subside somewhat.

Then, to everyone's astonishment, came the noise of fireworks – the fizz and crack – and all eyes turned to the city as, offset against the dark clouds, the explosions of light, the spangled flower-bursts of golden sparks, were quite visible, even given the time of day. How marvellous, someone said, how wonderful.

And then, from the point of the island across the lagoon, from the public gardens, they saw the beginning of a balloon ascent – the perfect sepia ball rising incredibly swiftly above the city below, buoyantly seeking higher altitudes above La Serenissima. The mourners' eyes were held as the balloon effortlessly rode up into the air, the men in its little hanging basket gesticulating and waving; and then some brisk breeze from the east took it hurriedly away, whisking it off, and the balloon became no more than a diminishing dot against the gathering cloud banks, as it was almost lost to sight over Giudecca, and then slowly disappeared.